KU-532-606

D. H. LAWRENCE: THE THINKER AS POET

D. H. Lawrence
The Thinker as Poet

Fiona Becket
Lecturer in Literature, Staffordshire University

First published in Great Britain 1997 by
MACMILLAN PRESS LTD
Houndmills, Basingstoke, Hampshire RG21 6XS and London
Companies and representatives throughout the world

A catalogue record for this book is available from the British Library.

ISBN 0–333–65027–1

First published in the United States of America 1997 by
ST. MARTIN'S PRESS, INC.,
Scholarly and Reference Division,
175 Fifth Avenue, New York, N.Y. 10010

ISBN 0–312–17503–5

Library of Congress Cataloging-in-Publication Data
Becket, Fiona, 1962–
D. H. Lawrence : the thinker as poet / Fiona Becket.
    p.   cm.
Includes bibliographical references and index.
ISBN 0–312–17503–5
1. Lawrence, D. H. (David Herbert), 1885–1930—Knowledge–
–Psychology.   2. Psychoanalysis and literature—England–
–History—20th century.   3. Lawrence, D. H. (David Herbert),
1885–1930—Aesthetics.   4. Subconsciousness in literature.   5. Body,
Human, in literature.   6. Metaphor.   I. Title.
PR6023.A93Z5665 1997
823'.912—dc21   97–5826
                                                              CIP

This book is printed on paper suitable for recycling and made from fully managed and sustained forest sources.

10   9   8   7   6   5   4   3   2
06   05   04   03   02   01   00   99   98

Printed and bound in Great Britain by
Antony Rowe Ltd, Chippenham, Wiltshire

For Deirdre Becket and Jon Salway

Contents

Acknowledgements

The author gratefully acknowledges Laurence Pollinger Ltd and the Estate of Frieda Lawrence Ravagli for permission to quote from the Penguin editions of *Psychoanalysis and the Unconscious* and *Fantasia of the Unconscious*, and the Cambridge University Press editions of *The Rainbow* and *Women in Love*, as well as the poem, 'The Rainbow', from *D.H. Lawrence: The Complete Poems* (Penguin). I am also grateful to Ginette Katz-Roy for permission to draw on material first published in my '"Star-equilibrium" and the Language of Love in *Women in Love*', in *Etudes Lawrenciennes*, no. 11 (1995).

Many people were involved in the debates that have led to this book. In particular I would like to thank Michael Bell, whose suggestions helped the study to take shape in its earliest stages, and Michael Black, who very generously read drafts of the book, and whose comments were invaluable. My thanks must also extend to Howard Booth, Gerry Carlin, Athena Economides, Graham Rees and Frank Wilson for their help in many different ways, and to Charmian Hearne at Macmillan for her support of this project, and for seeing it through to book form. Special thanks are overdue to Deirdre Becket, as they are to Jon Salway for his time and much else.

*The poetic character of thinking is
still veiled over.*

Martin Heidegger

1

Introduction: Thinking Metaphorically

The title of this book, *D.H. Lawrence: The Thinker as Poet*, is drawn from Martin Heidegger's essay, *Aus der Erfahrung des Denkens*.[1] The main premise is partly articulated by Heidegger's dictum, the epigraph of this book, that,

> The poetic character of thinking is
>   still veiled over[2]

and in particular Lawrence's awareness of the validity of this observation (or rather, Lawrence's own acute sense of it, without any prompting from Heidegger).[3] This book does not deal with the poetry of D.H. Lawrence or with 'local' instances of metaphor, which have attracted critical attention, but examines Lawrence's deeply metaphorical idiom in prose, initially and particularly in nominally 'discursive' contexts. Special attention is paid to the metaphorical articulation of central aspects of Lawrence's thought in contexts where metaphor might not be expected to dominate; in the Foreword to *Sons and Lovers*, in 'Study of Thomas Hardy', 'The Crown' and related essays and forewords. The longest discussion of the 'discursive' writing is reserved for the startling metaphoricity of Lawrence's books on the unconscious, *Psychoanalysis and the Unconscious* and *Fantasia of the Unconscious*, at the centre of this study. This is prior to an examination of the principal metaphorical modes of the major novels, *The Rainbow* and *Women in Love*. These novels are often the foci of debates on Lawrence's relation to language, and in this instance on the intimacy of his language and thought.[4]

Whatever his faults, as his earliest champions supposed, Lawrence was a creative thinker, famously bemoaning the moment when, in his view, philosophy and fiction became distinct and separate modes of knowledge:

1

It seems to me it was the greatest pity in the world, when philosophy and fiction got split. They used to be one, right from the days of myth. Then they went and parted, like a nagging married couple, with Aristotle and Thomas Aquinas and that beastly Kant. So the novel went sloppy, and philosophy went abstract-dry. The two should come together again, in the novel. And we get modern kind of gospels, and modern myths, and a new way of understanding.

('The Future of the Novel', in *Study of Thomas Hardy and Other Essays*, p. 154)[5]

This reference to a 'new way of understanding' is pertinent. Such figurative works as Foreword to *Sons and Lovers*, 'Study of Thomas Hardy', 'The Crown', *Psychoanalysis and the Unconscious* and *Fantasia of the Unconscious* communicate volumes about the need in Lawrence to think metaphorically. Indeed, it is metaphor which becomes a new mode of understanding in Lawrence, distinct from other modes of enquiry, like psychoanalysis for instance, which belong to a rational and positivist tradition disliked by Lawrence because, from his viewpoint, they limit the adventure of thought. His profoundly metaphorical style is a mode with which Lawrence challenges the culture of ratiocinative thought. He has nowhere to go but into the domain of the Poetic.

Lawrence does not *talk about* language but he gives it free play, giving his champions the space to say, as they have, that in him the language *is* the thought. I do not share the common view of Lawrence as a writer who experiences problems with language, although clearly at times his narrative control fails. My emphasis does not fall on Lawrence as struggling with problems of expression, therefore, but on an understanding in his work of the limitations, as well as the potentialities, of language. He sees it as his business after all to put the wordless into words; indeed, this is the paradox which, as an artist, he explores. The focus is, then, on the different levels of attention to language in Lawrence's work, and on his responsiveness to the levels of metaphor within language.

Where the reader might expect Lawrence's prose to be barely metaphorical, for instance in the 'discursive' essays, he is in fact most extremely and radically metaphorical. It is this paradox (and Lawrence enjoys paradoxes) which I pursue with special reference to his essays. I do not analyse singular events of metaphor in Lawrence (which would lead to a purely stylistic analysis), but attempt to address a particular body of language and thought within Lawrence's *oeuvre* where the metaphorical, the poetic and the philosophical are intricately enmeshed. Lawrence emerges as one who pulls metaphor away from its merely rhetorical moorings: his distinctive style is the hallmark of one who thinks not analytically but poetically; hence 'the thinker as poet'.

The discussion begins with a chapter on the language of the Foreword to *Sons and Lovers*, written in 1913 and never intended by Lawrence for publication. It is an extremely metaphorical piece of writing in which Lawrence deploys quasi-Biblical poetry and his own brand of plant imagery to articulate the birth of the self out of a background of non-specific forms. As such, it is the first *poetic* articulation, outside the fiction and the poetry, of Lawrence's 'metaphysic' or personal philosophy, what he sometimes called his *Weltanschauung*. The self, in Lawrence's lexicon, has a specific value: it is not to be confused with identity, but merges with individuality. He was as clear about this in 1913 as he was in 1921, writing *Fantasia of the Unconscious*:

> The quality of individuality cannot be derived. The new individual, in his singleness of self, is a perfectly new whole. He is not a permutation and combination of old elements, transferred through the parents. No, he is something underived and utterly unprecedented, unique, a new soul.
>
> (*Fantasia of the Unconscious*, F&P, pp. 30–1)

In the Foreword to *Sons and Lovers* the self is articulated as 'the Word', a description derived from the poetry of John's Gospel, a text to which Lawrence was drawn partly because of its intensely figurative language. The Word is derived from 'the Flesh', argues Lawrence, inverting the usual Biblical order which has the Word as the beginning. Flesh becomes Lawrence's metaphor for undifferentiated life, the matrix out of which individual living forms develop. As the quotation from *Fantasia of the Unconscious* shows, Lawrence's objection was to a *genetic* explanation of the origin of the individual. Such determinism reductively denies the possibility of growth and transformation in the person, and it is transformation which, not least in the essays, attracts Lawrence's attention (*metaphor* bears the weight of resemblance and change, it brings something forth). His proceeding in the language of the Word and the Flesh in the Foreword establishes the tendency in his discursive writing to think in terms of dual structures (Word/Flesh, Man/Woman, Father/Son, Law/Love, and so on), but other terms are continually introduced as his first terms proliferate, terms which are themselves modified, to disclose the intimacy of these 'dual' forms as well as their opposition. In this, paradoxically as it might seem, Lawrence is engaged in dismantling the Cartesian duality mind/body.

The preoccupations of the Foreword to *Sons and Lovers* – the birth of the self, Lawrence's discourse on individuality, relations between men and women (articulated as an abstract family in the Foreword) – are present in 'Study of Thomas Hardy', written in 1914, a work which was never completed or indeed presented for publication, and in the event published posthumously. Precisely because of its war-time context, it establishes the first terms of Lawrence's critique of his own culture which is written into, not least, *The Rainbow* and *Women in Love*. Rather than having a single focus, 'Study of Thomas Hardy' acts as a series of sketches outlining a number of Lawrence's preoccupations. The first two chapters take up the threads of the debate in the Foreword to *Sons and Lovers* on individuality, against a background of what Lawrence regarded as futile self-preservation, the Great War, where self is the social self that resonates so negatively for him. While he does not speak in riddles, he temporarily closes the debate on individuality in an oxymoronic mode:

He who would *save* his life must *lose* it. But why should he go on and waste it? Certainly let him cast it upon the waters. Whence and how and whither it will return is no matter, in terms of values. But like a poppy that has come to bud, when he reaches the shore, when he has traversed his known and come to the beach to meet the unknown, he must strip himself naked and plunge in, and pass out: if he dare. And the rest of his life he will be a stirring at the unknown, cast out upon the waters. But if he dare not plunge in, if he dare not take off his clothes and give himself naked to the flood, then let him prowl in rotten safety weeping for pity of those he imagines worse off than himself.

('Study of Thomas Hardy', in *Hardy*, p. 19, my italics)

'The unknown' is a felt quality in Lawrence's 'metaphysic' which is quite unavailable to analysis: 'Analysis presupposes a corpse'.[6]

His resistance to psychoanalysis, implicit in much of the discursive writing and explicit in his writings on the unconscious, was principally a resistance to 'the Freudians' whose desire, as he saw it, to make conscious the unconscious, was wrong-headed. Any mode of enquiry which threatened to drive a wedge between the mind and the body would incur a negative response from Lawrence. The terms 'conscious' and 'unconscious' have a distinct place in Lawrence's lexicon, as the early discursive writing demonstrates, but by 1919, as he wrote the essays which were to become *Psychoanalysis and the Unconscious*, he was aware of the need to repossess them from the Freudians.[7] Lawrence's task in the books on the unconscious was in part to establish his own meanings, so that the word 'unconscious' would make sense in his terms. It is transformed (carried over), resulting in the uniquely Lawrentian metaphor of 'blood-consciousness'. The metaphors which articulate an irrepressible and unconscious living force in Lawrence, like the blood, and like the poppy in 'Study of Thomas Hardy', draw the reader's attention to 'the sensual, instinctive and intuitive body', which is where Lawrence sought to rehouse it.[8] The poppy reinforces the idea of growth, and is brilliantly alive. Like the famous phoenix, it is then a usefully *non-human* image, for Lawrence is after 'that which is physic – non-human in humanity', as he famously wrote to his editor, Edward Garnett, in June 1914 (*Letters*, II, p. 182). The poppy is a singular metaphor. As this study unfolds, the emphasis will be less on such instances as on an accumulative and pervasively metaphorical language which constitutes Lawrence's thought. It is Lawrence's language, profoundly metaphorical, dwelling on and in paradoxes, that will destabilize the values he rails against, not least from the perspective of the 'Study of Thomas Hardy'.

'The Crown', begun in 1915 and revised ten years later, is as figurative in its language as the Foreword to *Sons and Lovers*. In Lawrence there are ideas and phrases which recur across the works because they bear the 'metaphysic', or at the least the fundamental principles of that 'metaphysic'. One of these ideas is the necessity of a 'tension of opposites',[9] a principle of opposition which makes life possible: a conception, then, which is the basis of Lawrence's own creation-myths, and explains his fondness for expressing his philosophy, in the first instance, by means of dualistic notions. At the beginning of 'The Crown' he starts with a very simple text, a nursery rhyme, describing a conflict between the lion and the unicorn. He turns this into a metaphor which underpins his philosophy of productive conflict:

> But think, if the lion really destroyed, killed the unicorn; not
> merely drove him out of town, but annihilated him! Would
> not the lion at once expire, as if he had created a vacuum
> around himself? Is not the unicorn necessary to the very exist-
> ence of the lion, is not each opposite kept in stable equilib-
> rium by the opposition of the other.
>
> ('The Crown', in *Reflections on the Death of a Porcupine*,
> p. 253)

Crucially, 'the crown' itself, over which they fight, is a third
term, and it is the third term that disrupts the coherence of the
dual structure. The phrase and the idea surrounding 'stable equilibrium' in this passage occurs at a very deep level in *Women in
Love*, perhaps a more surprising context, in the articulation of
the central relationship between Rupert Birkin and Ursula Brangwen as, through them, Lawrence explores 'love', dismantling
romantic love and asserting a 'metaphysics' of the self. This tiny
instance, in the language of 'The Crown', of a nominally discursive work foregrounding the language and therefore the 'metaphysic' of a work of fiction, speaks to the logic of the structure
of the present book: that a productive critical distance from the
language of the fiction is gained by first examining the extremely
metaphorical language of the 'discursive' texts.

In Chapter 3 I shift from an emphasis on the self in Lawrence's
early discursive writing, to the body as the *locus* of the unconscious, constituted as such within Lawrence's 'metaphysic'. Lawrence is not writing at this time in the glare, or the shadow, of
Freud. As he wrote these early essays he was not under any
obligation to adhere to the binary structure 'conscious/uncon-
scious' which organizes psychoanalysis. Only by 1919 did he feel
the need to offer a critique of what he was to characterize later
as 'the vague Freudian Unconscious' (*Letters*, IV, p. 40), which
became the principal statement of his relocation of unconscious
functioning to the body, rather than the 'head'. In 'The Crown'
of 1915 he refers to 'the *flesh* conscious and unconscious' (my
italics), the flesh which has 'its own consciousness' (in *Reflections on the Death of a Porcupine*, p. 470). However, it is in the
books on the unconscious that we have Lawrence consolidating
his position against the supremely conscious modernist subject.

American publishers brought out *Psychoanalysis and the Unconscious* in 1921 and *Fantasia of the Unconscious* in 1922. Both were published in Britain in 1923. They provide the basis, in Chapters 4 and 5 of this study, of an examination of extreme levels of metaphoricity in the non-fiction, where Lawrence's critical stance is ostensibly provoked by psychoanalysis. On the face of it the essays which comprise the books on the unconscious are discursive, a forum where Lawrence can rehearse a number of his immediate preoccupations away from the discipline of the fictional narratives. Yet the extensive metaphoricity of *Psychoanalysis and the Unconscious* and *Fantasia of the Unconscious*, alongside the figurative tenor of the earlier essays, alerts us further to the distinctive relation between the poetic and thought in Lawrence. In the Foreword to *Fantasia of the Unconscious* we discover that Lawrence is writing down his 'metaphysic' 'in terms of belief and of knowledge'. 'Men', he suggests, 'live and see according to some gradually developing and gradually withering vision', but this vision is no longer sufficient. Then comes a statement of the artist's iconoclastic function, articulated in a way that adumbrates Heidegger's insight: 'Rip the veil of the old vision across, and walk through the rent. And if I try to do this – well why not?' (*Fantasia of the Unconscious*, F&P, p. 17). So it is that much of *Fantasia of the Unconscious* is written in a spirit of repudiation, and ushered in with a clear statement of artistic and intellectual intent. As a body of writing it is perhaps too conscious, but it allows the reader to focus on Lawrence's extensive metaphoricity away from the fiction, as the 'metaphysic' gets unpacked. More unexpectedly, in the shorter book, *Psychoanalysis and the Unconscious*, the reader encounters the few overt statements from Lawrence on metaphor, in contexts which draw attention to its relation in his work to knowledge, so that in his writing there is an implicit understanding of metaphor as a kind of knowledge.

We see in both Lawrence's early philosophical writing and the writing of the 1920s a highly idiosyncratic attempt to describe metaphorically (how else?) an unconscious or non-deliberate way of human being. The basis for his meditation is often a description of some modest activity, like writing (which he 'observes' at first hand). For Lawrence, the only authentic mode of experiencing anything (authenticity having something to do with a quality of response) is to be 'unconscious' (the travel-writing continually underlines this). Evidently what he means by this is a far cry from Freud's 'territory', and Freud's allegories of the unconscious caught between the twin poles of repression and resurgence.

The current study, which does not seek to provide a chrono-logical survey, begins with an examination of Lawrence's early philosophical writing, followed by an extended discussion of his books on the unconscious, in order to step back deliberately from the fiction. As I have suggested, this is because critics writing about Lawrence's language, in first addressing the fiction as they normally do, run the risk of being drawn into the narrative is-sues, thereby losing grip on the question of language. I do not ignore the content, the argument, of the early philosophical pieces or the books of the twenties, of course, but I do consciously privi-lege their language.

In Chapters 6 and 7 I turn my attention to, respectively, *The Rainbow* and *Women in Love*, underlining their different linguis-tic and, therefore, different metaphysical modes. The more con-scious uses of metaphor in the discursive writing tend to throw the unconscious modality of both *The Rainbow* and *Women in Love* into relief, different though these novels are, stylistically, from each other. The discussion of *The Rainbow* opens with a concen-tration on a certain kind of language within the novel as repre-sentative of a major body of metaphor and thought within the work. The chapter fixes on the question of how an instance of metaphor within the narrative can also come to be seen as the language of the whole novel. I examine the deployment (implicit and explicit) in *The Rainbow* of a kind of metaphorical language which erupts into, and sustains thought in, other contexts, but which achieves a distinct and independent importance in the novel. Once again the focus is on transformation, both as a theme and as something which happens to, or within (indeed, which con-stitutes), the proliferating field of metaphor: the (positive) ten-sion is between metaphors which singularly bear the thought and a profoundly and unconsciously metaphorical style. In the philosophical prose Lawrence has begun to define his terms, and one consequence of this is the subtle putting of metaphor to both a structural and philosophical use in the mature fiction.

The Rainbow's medium is under scrutiny as quite different from the medium of its sister novel, *Women in Love*, traditionally the focus for the debate on Lawrence and language, often with an eye to his problems in this domain. In both novels, I suggest, Lawrence challenges the merely rhetorical function of metaphor and opens us up to 'metaphoricity' as a non-analytical mode of thinking about language itself, because language is one of Lawrence's central and most enduring themes, quite as much as human relations, human being, the relation of experience and knowledge, and cultural analysis. In *Women in Love* Lawrence is trying to get a range of complex notions *into* language. In the course of this, his aesthetic is shown to be based on an oxymoronic dynamic which operates at the deepest levels of his language and thought. In his writing the simple oxymoron finds a philosophical appropriateness which is radical because of the ways in which it is iconoclastic and intuitive.

Having concentrated very closely on the operations of metaphor in the early discursive work and in these four key texts by Lawrence, *Psychoanalysis and the Unconscious, Fantasia of the Unconscious, The Rainbow* and *Women in Love,* I conclude with a chapter on '"Forbidden Metaphors": Lawrence and Language'. It is Lawrence's dedication to the Poetic, and his sense of metaphor as the proper medium of thought, which aligns him most immediately with those other highly individual stylists Nietzsche and Heidegger. They have in common a recourse to the Poetic as the most fertile ground of dissent. In Nietzschean terms, Lawrence as a modernist artist is engaged in 'shattering and mocking the old conceptual barriers', speaking perhaps in 'forbidden metaphors'.[10] There is a proximity between poetry and thought that Lawrence's language attests and asserts. Lawrence is not in possession of a theory of language, or of metaphor. He is not interested, or does not articulate an interest, in the nature of language, which would be a philosopher's stance, but he is profoundly sensitive to language as *his* medium. He has himself struggled into 'verbal-consciousness' ('This struggle for verbal consciousness should not be left out in art', Foreword, *Women in Love,* p. 486); is in possession of a language-*sense*, among his other senses. It is true that language is not merely decorative or expressive for Lawrence, who would agree with Heidegger, who *is* interested in the nature of language, that '[a]s expression, language can decay into a mere medium for the printed word' (*Poetry, Language, Thought,* p. 215). More interestingly, Lawrence's writing asks questions of language (questions also asked by Nietzsche and Heidegger, and examined by more recent theorizers of metaphor, notably Paul Ricoeur). This takes us to Lawrence's radical practice but not, in the first place, to his fiction.

2

Thinking Poetically in the Early Discursive Writing: The Birth of the Self

The Foreword to *Sons and Lovers* was never intended for publication. After the publisher had received the text of the novel Lawrence sent it to his editor Edward Garnett as an afterthought, for his attention and not, as Lawrence clearly stated, for the public gaze: 'I wanted to *write* a foreword, not to have one printed' (*Letters*, I, p. 510). This is just one sign that, for Lawrence, writing was thinking. The Foreword to *Sons and Lovers*, printed posthumously by Aldous Huxley in 1932 with Lawrence's letters, has only recently been published with the novel.[1] The Foreword, which seems incomprehensible to many readers, commences the series of discursive, or philosophical, writings, which preoccupied Lawrence all his life, not separable from the fictions and the poetry. Of the discursive works these, primarily, are 'Study of Thomas Hardy' ('Le Gai Savaire', 1914); 'The Crown' (1915; revised 1925); 'Goats and Compasses' (1916, destroyed); 'The Reality of Peace' (1917); 'At the Gates' (1917, lost); the essays on American literature, where he also developed a 'psychology' (begun in 1917); 'Democracy' (1919); *Psychoanalysis and the Unconscious* (1919); *Fantasia of the Unconscious* (1921); *Etruscan Places* (*Sketches of Etruscan Places*) (1927); *Apocalypse* (1930). The dates given in parentheses are the dates of composition, not publication.[2]

As a Foreword it is badly named. It is not practical as an introductory statement to *Sons and Lovers*, which is only its nominal function. Perhaps only the final paragraph speaks clearly to the reader of the novel's content:

But the man who is the go-between from Woman to Production is the lover of that woman. And if that woman be his

out Lawrence's writing. This central metaphor has a parable quality:

> It is as if a bit of apple-blossom stood for God in his Wonder, the apple was the Son, as being something more gross but still wonderful, while the pip that comes out of the apple, like Adam's rib, is the mere secondary product, that is spat out, and which, if it falls to the ground, just happens to start the process of apple-trees going again. But the little pip that one spits out has in it all the blossom and apples, as well as all the tree, the leaves, the perfume, the drops of gum, and heaven knows what else that we never see, contained by miracle in its bit of white flesh: and the tree, the leaves, the flowers themselves, and the apple are only amplifications of this little seed, spent: which never has amplified itself enough, but can go on to other than just five-petalled flowers and little brown apples, if we did but know.
>
> (p. 470)

The amplification of the seed is the amplification of the self, out of a background of less specialized forms. Lawrence is usually represented as anti-Darwinian, but there is room within his 'metaphysic' for an evolutionary model, as here in the pip with its potential for development. The real contrast is less with Darwin than with a more modern determinism which gives rise to an understanding of an individual's development predicated on the language of the genetic 'code'.

Underpinning the descriptions of achieved selfhood in the Foreword is a continual return to marriage as the principal relationship. This is still couched in the Biblical language of the whole as Lawrence shifts from 'The Flesh was made Word' to 'Flesh of my Flesh'. 'Woman' is associated with the larger life principle, 'Flesh', out of which comes the individual. A statement of the woman's primacy in the abstract family directly precedes the 'apple-pip' passage. Lawrence:

> the whole chronology is upside-down: the Word created Man, and Man lay down and gave birth to Woman. Whereas we know the Woman lay in travail, and gave birth to Man, who in his hour uttered his word.
>
> (ibid.)

A shift then takes place where the Mother is substituted for the Father as the origin of life. Modern biology suggests that un-differentiated life is female, so there is a real logic in transforming the Father into the Mother, which is a shift Lawrence engineers a paragraph later: 'Protoplasm, the eternal . . . the Flesh, the Father – which were more properly, the Mother' (p. 470). In the third part of the Foreword the focus is the family (in the abstract). Marriage, we can see, is the nourishing medium which makes the birth of the individual possible:

> Now every woman, according to her kind, demands that a man shall come home to her with joy and weariness of the work he has done during the day: that he shall then while he is with her, be re-born of her; that in the morning he shall go forth with his new strength.
>
> But if the man does not come home to a woman, leaving her to take account of him, but is a stranger to her; if when he enters her house, he does not become simply her man of flesh, entered into her house as if it were her greater body, to be warmed, and restored, and nourished, from the store the day has given her, then she shall expel him from her house, as a drone. It is as inevitable as the working of the bees, as that a stick shall go down stream.
>
> For in the flesh of the woman does God enact Himself. And out of the flesh of the woman does He demand: 'Carry this of Me forth to utterance.' And if the man deny, or be too weak, then shall the woman find another man, of greater strength.
>
> (p. 472)

At this point the Foreword begins to refer more evidently to *Sons and Lovers*, and does, retrospectively, contribute to our under-standing of the 'metaphysic' underpinning that novel, apart from the more localized autobiographical context. It is interesting that Frieda Weekley said of the composition of the Foreword, 'We fought over it' (*Letters*, I, p. 510): this articulates an element of resistance that also got expressed at quite subtle levels in Law-rence's later novels. In the Foreword, man yet needs woman at his back (Lawrence's description in 1913 of *his* principal need)[5] in order to produce the word, which is the self, or the object (art and artefacts; philosophy and thought).

For Lawrence-the-gospeller the celebration of marriage results

in clear statements about affirmative and productive sexuality;
an affirmative Dionysian sexuality that Christianity is seen to
despise. This is the force of much of the emphasis and play, in
Lawrence, on birth, rebirth and resurrection, with the focus on
the birth of oneself, rather than the birth of children. '[T]he Word
is finite . . . But the Flesh is infinite, and has no end.' (p. 467):
the Flesh, that is to say, is the process of 'becoming' whereas
the Word is fixed as if on tablets of stone so that the process of
'becoming' is arrested ('So is The Word a rigid image', p. 469).
The birth of the self, oneself as an individual, is a momentary,
transient creation. It is different from, and distinct from, 'eternal
continuance', the permanent, infinite, generation of life. Consequently, the Foreword continually throws up images of that infinite unspecialized generation. 'For in the flesh of the woman
does God enact Himself' (p. 472) claims Lawrence in a statement that runs parallel to the Nietzschean 'Yes to life beyond
death and change; *true* life as collective continuation of life through
procreation, through the mysteries of sexuality' (*Twilight of the
Idols*, p. 109). The 'mysteries of sexuality' are brought to bear on
the birth of the self, in Lawrence. This gives rise to complex
metaphorical statements with abstractions like the Flesh and the
Word, given new meanings by Lawrence, interacting with his
own myth of marriage: sexual feeling is shown to have a transforming effect in Lawrence's work, out of which the individual
self is born, 'through' the woman. The references to the man in
the last paragraphs of the Foreword, 'that he shall then while he
is with her, be re-born of her', refer to the *constant* rebirth of the
(masculine) self, in that relationship. This prefigures other occasions of 'rebirth' of men and women, notably Ursula Brangwen
at the end of *The Rainbow*, and including Mabel Pervin in 'The
Horse-Dealer's Daughter', Lou Witt in 'St. Mawr' and Constance
Chatterley.

Lawrence's highly idiosyncratic exploration of the 'sensual,
instinctive and intuitive body' side-steps the category of the
human, indeed of the subject, in that other most effective image
of 'becoming' in the Foreword, the image of the apple-pip already touched on: 'But the little pip that one spits out has in it
all the blossom and apples, as well as all the tree, the leaves, the
perfume, the drops of gum, and heaven knows what else that
we never see, contained by miracle in its bit of white flesh'
(p. 470). It is a description that anticipates the 'white quick of

nascent creation' ('Poetry of the Present', in *Complete Poems*, p. 182), and, as Michael Black has observed, the metaphor here does the work of interpretation (*The Early Philosophical Works*, p. 136). In it is contained the aspect of Lawrence's philosophy of 'quivering momentaneity' (*Complete Poems*, p. 183) that the rest of the Foreword attempts to make perhaps too self-consciously. The apple-pip metaphor draws attention to an impersonal energy that for Lawrence transcends the much more banal category of human will. In the Foreword, then, Lawrence has also dismantled and reconstructed, in his own terms, the apple of knowledge. In a Foreword to a different and much later work, he provides a gloss on the evident friction in his work between discursive writing and poetic forms: 'it has always seemed to me that a real thought, a single thought, not an argument, can only exist easily in verse, or in some poetic form. There is a didactic element about prose thoughts which makes them repellent, slightly bullying' (Foreword to *Pansies*, in *Complete Poems*, p. 423). This reference to 'some poetic form' speaks volumes about the significance of metaphor in Lawrence's writing, not least in the metaphorically challenging Foreword to *Sons and Lovers*. For the poet in Lawrence, the individual who poetically thinks, this is the issue which comes out in a discussion of artistic production: so it is that ontological questions dovetail into the category of the aesthetic.

The unconscious, or as Lawrence has it, 'dark', aspect of production is articulated in ways which recall the artist Paul Morel's words to Miriam as he explains the specific quality of his sketches to her:

'as if I'd painted the shimmering protoplasm in the leaves and everywhere, and not the stiffness of the shape. That seems dead to me. Only this shimmeriness is the real living. The shape is a dead crust.'

(*Sons and Lovers*, p. 183)

In the Foreword it is stated that:

But what is really 'Rose' is only in that quivering, shimmering flesh of flesh, which is the same, unchanged forever, a constant stream, called if you like Protoplasm, the eternal, the unquestioned, the infinite of the 'Rose', the Flesh, the Father – which were more properly, the Mother.

(Foreword, *Sons and Lovers*, p. 470)

This is that moment in the Foreword where a cr
fade, of terms takes place as 'the Father', notion;
of creative acts, becomes 'the Mother'. The produ(
vidual creative moment is also codified in the Foreworu ս
Word', and here, as 'the Rose'. In 'The Reality of Peace' (1917)
Lawrence would use the rose to stand for a perfected state of
selfhood:

> For there are ultimately only two desires, the desire of life
> and the desire of death. Beyond these is pure being, where I
> am absolved from desire and made perfect. This is when I am
> like a rose, when I balance for a space in pure adjustment and
> pure understanding. The timeless quality of *being* is under-
> standing; when I understand fully, flesh and blood and bone,
> and mind and soul and spirit one rose of unison, then I *am*.
>
> ('The Reality of Peace', in *Reflections on the Death of a
> Porcupine*, p. 38)

In the third part of the Foreword Lawrence takes his cue positively from Whitman: 'And the Flowers of the World are Words,
are Utterance – "Uttering glad leaves," Whitman said' (p. 471).
To utter is to produce – a work, progeny, the self – and this is
consistent with the principal themes of the Foreword. The production of art, meanwhile, is codified in these terms: 'the Father
through the Son wasting himself in a moment of consciousness'
(pp. 470–1). For a moment the focus is on the process and not
on the object, 'that which falls shed'. Having the capacity to give
rise to something is where the richness of experience lies. Having given rise to something means having dwelt in 'a moment
of consciousness'. If 'the Flowers of the World are Words', Lawrence refers in the Foreword to 'God rippling through the Son
till He breaks in a laugh, called a blossom, that shines and is
gone' (p. 470). The metaphors of 'light' and 'shining' are certainly suggested to Lawrence by John's Gospel. The blossom itself is unconscious. This is a word introduced in the third part
of the Foreword:

> And God the Father, the Inscrutable, the Unknowable, we know
> in the Flesh, in Woman. She is the door for our in-going and
> our out-coming. In her we go back to the Father: but like the
> witnesses of the Transfiguration, blind and unconscious.
>
> (Foreword, *Sons and Lovers*, pp. 470–1)

The sexual is here to be seen as the means of access *to* something through the woman. The witnesses of the Transfiguration[6] are neither blind nor unconscious but they are, crucially, open to the experience, and it is precisely this openness that is meant by Lawrence's use, in the section from which this is taken, of both 'consciousness' and 'unconscious'. These are terms he is not compelled to use as binary oppositions: he subtilizes their differences as he writes. His emphasis here is on 'consciousness' but not 'mind-consciousness'; 'a moment of consciousness' not a moment of 'self-consciousness'. Blindness is an important trope in Lawrence's writing for a kind of non-analytical knowing. The blind man knows through touch, a central theme in Lawrence: to touch is both to establish contact with the other, and to make a claim, as in 'Hadrian' ('You Touched Me').[7]

In 'The Blind Man', written in 1918, Lawrence exploits the story of the Biblical Thomas, a narrative which implicates touch with knowledge (John xx. 24–9).[8] In Lawrence's text the protagonist who learns through his physical blindness to eschew the desire for (analytical) 'visual consciousness' is 'carried on the flood in a sort of blood-prescience.' ... 'Life seemed to move in him like a tide lapping, lapping, and advancing, enveloping all things darkly.... The new way of consciousness substituted itself in him' ('The Blind Man', in *England, My England and Other Stories*, p. 54). This description develops out of a description of the blind man's confident knowledge of his immediate surroundings through touch, the sense that Lawrence most celebrated. In a letter to Blanche Jennings in December 1908 Lawrence had written, 'Somehow, I think we come into knowledge (unconscious) of the most vital parts of the cosmos through touching things', a statement that underlines Lawrence's insistence on non-mental and non-verbal modes of knowledge as providing a route to genuine responsiveness, where 'feeling' and 'knowledge' intersect. Already in 1908 'knowledge (unconscious)' describes the mode of 'authentic' feeling that would consistently interest Lawrence, underpinning his later concentration on ancient ontologies. As a formula it resonates with an oxymoronic charge motivated by the word kept coyly in parentheses. The letter, never intended for publication, anticipates an aspect of the 'metaphysic' which the early discursive writing ironically attempts to make quite conscious. The context of the statement about the primacy of touch in Lawrence's sensual world concerns first the lovers' kiss and, just as significantly, the physical intimacy of mother and infant:

> it is exceedingly rare that two people participate in entirely
> the same sensation and emotion; but they do when they kiss
> as lovers, I am sure. Then a certain life-current passes through
> them which changes them forever; another such effect is pro-
> duced in a mother by the continual soft touchings of her baby.
> (*Letters*, I, p. 99)

Conscious of the inadequacy of his language in articulating
non-verbal experience (which is, after all, his aim) he writes, 'I
know my phraseology is vague and impossible' (p. 99). This early
exasperation with language grows out of the general relevance
of the recognition. Driven to *articulate* non-verbal modes of consciousness ('I, joining hands with the artists, declare that also
and supremely the sympathy with and submission to the great
impulses comes through *feeling* – indescribable – and, I think
unknowable', p. 99) he 'listens' to the 'speaking of language' in
metaphor, as metaphor increasingly becomes the fundamental
mode of understanding in Lawrence.[9] The body of language in
Lawrence must speak to, and about, 'knowledge (unconscious)'.

Consequently, in the course of his career, Lawrence's writing
provides a critique of the modernity that views itself as underpinned and nourished by rational forms. His concentration on
Freud, particularly in *Psychoanalysis and the Unconscious* and *Fantasia of the Unconscious*, is part of that critique, part of the vitalist
philosophy in which Lawrence privileges spontaneity and the
sensual body, over 'knowledge' and the 'head'. In the early discursive writing, as in the books on the unconscious, Lawrence is
shifting the concentration away from the psyche, located, increasingly he felt, in the head, to the body.

As a writer, Lawrence's principal problem is that his medium
is so conscious. Grieg and Wagner, he argues, in the same letter
to Blanche Jennings 'will run a knowledge of music into your
blood better than any criticisms', an observation which invites
us to read Lawrence's corpus non-analytically. Knowledge that
runs into your *blood* is borne in the subtle inoculation of understanding from various levels within the text. And in Lawrence,
language itself moves, like the sensitive hands of the blind man,
over the surfaces of a dark world, richly present. Metaphor is
very much at Lawrence's finger-tips.

To return briefly to the rhetoric of the Foreword to *Sons and Lovers*. Artistic production, or generation, which is discussed in the Foreword, is also discussed six years later in the Foreword to *Women in Love*. The polarities of the early writing are nowhere to be seen in this shorter piece. The optimistic tone which articulated the birth, and rebirth, of the self in 1913, has altered, but the belief in a transformative experience, and the potential in the individual for that experience, is still there:

> Man struggles with his unborn needs and fulfilment. New unfoldings struggle up in torment in him, as buds struggle forth the midst of a plant. Any man of real individuality tries to know and to understand what is happening, even in himself, as he goes along. This struggle for verbal consciousness should not be left out in art. It is a very great part of life. It is not superimposition of a theory. *It is the passionate struggle into conscious being.*
>
> (Foreword, Women in Love, pp. 485–6)

The emphasis on 'The Woman' of the Foreword to *Sons and Lovers*, through whom selfhood is achieved, has altered here to the 'creative, spontaneous soul' which 'sends forth its promptings of desire and aspiration in us' (p. 485). Fulfilling these promptings is the 'fate' of the artist (also 'Any man of real individuality'); the poetic language and the plant imagery of the Foreword to *Sons and Lovers* have given way to a more direct statement of artistic responsibility. The point, for Lawrence, is that these 'promptings' now come from within the self (in the language of his earlier piece they came from 'the Flesh'), are not 'dictated from outside, from theory or from circumstances' (Foreword, *Women in Love*, pp. 485–6). Between the two meditations represented by these forewords, Lawrence had thought the issues through, poetically, in other discursive contexts.

Of these, 'Study of Thomas Hardy' is important. Published posthumously, it is an unpolished set of chapters in draft form, and not a finalized text, but it succeeds in communicating many of Lawrence's major preoccupations, building on the Foreword to *Sons and Lovers*. Like all the early essays it represents Lawrence's tendency to begin his thought processes by recourse to the kinds of dualistic structures which his later writing, certainly his fiction, subtilizes. 'Study of Thomas Hardy' builds on the attempt in the Foreword to *Sons and Lovers* to describe personal and 'human' experience in impersonal and non-human terms (human relationships, and the birth of the self, articulated through the poetic language of Word/Flesh, Man/Woman, and in 'Study of Thomas Hardy', Love/Law). Plant or flower metaphors similar to those in the Foreword dominate the first six essays. Thereafter the Biblical terms deployed in the Foreword to *Sons and Lovers* return. In 'Study of Thomas Hardy' it is the statements on the artist's 'metaphysic' which endure as Lawrence's most useful proposition, coming to fruition as they do in the creative-critical injunctions of *Studies in Classic American Literature* and the earlier versions of these writings, some of which were collected posthumously as *The Symbolic Meaning*.[10] Aside from this, there is a meditation on the body in the 'Study' which relates to, and is yet different from, the functioning of the (instinctive) body in the later books on the unconscious. At one point in his meditation Lawrence refers to a mode of 'sentient non-knowledge' (*Hardy*, p. 35): this formula, which is not repeated again, describes the 'unconscious' state achieved by individuals most capable of loss of self (self-consciousness) within Lawrence's *oeuvre*. At this point in his development both as cultural critic and as artist Lawrence is largely untroubled by Freudian overtones adhering to his use of 'consciousness' and 'unconscious'. *The* unconscious is seldom of interest to Lawrence, at least not until the discursive books of 1921 and 1923 when it becomes *Lawrentian* unconsciousness.

His uses of the words 'conscious' and 'unconscious' from the outset of his writing career, reveal their centrality to his 'metaphysic'. The woman who spins in 'The Spinner and the Monks' section of *Twilight in Italy*, published in 1916 and a part of the general meditations represented in the Foreword to *Sons and Lovers*, 'The Crown' and 'Study of Thomas Hardy', is representative of the unselfconscious individual that figures so much in Lawrence's thought. He encounters the 'actual' woman on the Lago di Garda, appropriately enough after his visit to the church San Tommaso. Her lack of self-consciousness while she works the thread is thrown into relief by the 'conscious' northern European writer observing her:

She saw merely a man's figure, a stranger, standing near. I was a bit of the outside, negligible. She remained as she was,

clear and sustained like an old stone upon the hill-side. She
stood short and sturdy, looking for the most part straight in
front, unseeing, but glancing from time to time, with a little,
unconscious attention, at the thread.

(Twilight in Italy, p. 106)

The key words are repeated, becoming a major motif in the
whole design: the woman's eyes are 'unthinking, or like two
flowers that are open in pure clear unconsciousness'; 'Her world
was clear and absolute, without consciousness of self. She was
not self-conscious, because she was not aware that there was
anything in the universe except *her* universe'; 'It was this which
gave the wonderful clear unconsciousness to her eyes. How could
she be conscious of herself when all was herself?'; 'Her eyes remained candid and open and unconscious as the skies'; she 'went
on talking, in her half-intimate, half-unconscious fashion, as if
she were talking to her own world in me'; and finally, she leaves,
'She had cut off her consciousness from me. So I turned and ran
away' (pp. 107–9). These sentences describe a kind of 'unconsciousness' in Lawrence that needs to be asserted against any
conception that might be derived from Freud (that kind of unconscious response which does not require the attention of a cli-
nician). It is the kind of 'unconscious' from which Lawrence traces
an evolution (to achieved individuation) in *The Rainbow*. The actual
spinning woman is transformed by Lawrence's creative imagination into a character, a figure, who 'exhibits' a crucial aspect of
his own aesthetic: the substitution of non-analytical modes of
understanding for more 'rational' forms or modes. The spinning
woman, like the early generations of Brangwens in *The Rainbow*,
represents to Lawrence a mode of *belonging*: there is nothing in
her universe which is not continuous with herself and her way
of life.[11] Caught in the gaze of the artist, she is not conceived as
capable of self-consciousness in the available, and to Lawrence
negative, sense. In 'The Crown', for instance, a series of essays
which Lawrence intended to be revolutionary, self-consciousness
means 'the triumph of the ego' (*Reflections*, p. 278).[12] Instead of
an integral, vitalistic, relationship with the universe, the individual 'conceives itself as the whole universe' but 'does not know
that it is in prison' (p. 279). Here the metaphor of the birth of
the self is familiar from the Foreword to *Sons and Lovers*. The
negatively self-conscious subject is imaged as a 'sick foetus, shut

up in the walls of an unrelaxed womb'; 'the unborn' . . . 'conceives itself as the whole universe, surrounded by dark nullity' (*Reflections*, p. 279). These few examples indicate how Lawrence cannot be accused of playing on Freud's homeground: subjectivity is not his theme. However, by the time of writing the books on the unconscious he was certainly vulnerable to this accusation.

Most of Lawrence's efforts in the 'Study of Thomas Hardy' go into representing the unconscious life, the life of feeling, as impersonal. Michael Bell ensures that this recognition underpins his examination of Lawrence's 'metaphysic' and his comments have a synoptic value:

> At a time when the very idea of an integral self was being dissolved in almost every area of modern thought, scientific, social and psychological, Lawrence sought to keep faith with it. But he did so in a spirit that radically accommodated these opposing conceptions. And so he dissolved the 'old stable ego' of character to recognise the impersonal dimension within the personal. The personality became a dynamic and evolutionary matrix of competing forces rather than an autonomous ethical entity.
>
> (*D.H. Lawrence: Language and Being*, p. 5)

Michael Black has shown how these 'competing forces' are articulated as chains and systems of metaphor in the literary and cultural criticism embodied by the early philosophical writing. Most of the time, in this writing, Lawrence is showing the reader how he, Lawrence, needs to be read. Hence, the density of his metaphorical chains which insist on the complicity of female and male elements in the flower, root and stem, wheel and axle, sun, moon and stars imagery that fill the pages of, not least, 'Study of Thomas Hardy'. And while Lawrence explores the impersonal unconscious histories of Hardy's characters (fast being transformed into Lawrence's) he subsumes these individual histories to a broader background of 'proven experience' (*Hardy*, p. 34). This background is a version of (but not identical to) the impersonal life of human kind that figures in *The Rainbow*. (It is a question whether, in Lawrence, the impersonal is commensurate with the unconscious).

In *The Rainbow*, Lawrence was able to be less hierarchical than in 'Study of Thomas Hardy', allowing for the co-existence of a collective past and an individuated present, each modulating against the other. In 'Study of Thomas Hardy' to become a 'wonderfully distinct individual' is to be born again, but not into knowledge: 'Man's consciousness, that is, his mind, his knowing, is his grosser manifestation of individuality' (*Hardy*, p. 42). The novels of his mature period show Lawrence exploiting the subtle differences between 'singleness' and 'individuality'. Singleness belongs to the impersonal world into which Lawrence's main characters walk. Subjectivity is perhaps the notion that Lawrence is writing against, the more so inasmuch as it approaches the psychoanalytic categories that he resists. In Lawrence, individuation is about singleness, a singleness of spirit rather than of mind:

> In his fullest living [man] does not know what he does, his mind, his consciousness, unacquaint, hovers behind, full of extraneous gleams and glances, and altogether devoid of knowledge. Altogether devoid of knowledge and conscious motive is he when he is heaving into uncreated space, when he is actually living, becoming himself.
>
> And yet, that he may go on, may proceed with his living, it is necessary that his mind, his consciousness, should extend behind him. The mind itself is one of life's later developed habits.
>
> ('Study of Thomas Hardy', in *Hardy*, p. 41)

This is as close to a *definition* of *being* 'unconscious' as Lawrence at that time, revising *The Rainbow*, came. His later books on the unconscious returned to the materialism of 'naked jelly' and the 'germ' as constituting the origin of 'unconscious life'.

The concentration on birth in those books speaks to the passages in 'Study of Thomas Hardy' which underline the need to be 'born again'. The discourse in Chapter V of the 'Study' on this need constitutes a critique of the common need for an existing system of belief where it results only in a social, collective identity: 'Give us a religion, give us something to believe in . . .' (*Hardy*, p. 44). Lawrence's creed of singleness requires that such a need is arrested because the need itself leaves the individual precisely 'unformed, unbegotten, unborn' (p. 45). Predicating one's rebirth on a prior philosophy, creed or metaphysic is the problem. The figures of the phoenix and the poppy at the outset of the 'Study', for instance, are figures of rebirth proper, both utterly singular:

The phoenix grows up to maturity and fulness of wisdom, it attains to fatness and wealth and all things desirable, only to burst into flame and expire in ash. And the flame and the ash are the be-all and the end-all, and the fatness and wisdom and wealth are but the fuel spent. It is a wasteful ordering of things, indeed, to be sure: – but so it is, and what must be must be.

('Study of Thomas Hardy', in *Hardy*, p. 10)

And I know that the common wild poppy has achieved so far its complete poppy-self, unquestionable. It has uncovered its red. Its light, its self, has risen and shone out, has run on the winds for a moment. It is splendid. The world is a world because of the poppy's red. Otherwise it would be a lump of clay.

(p. 13)

The blossoming of the poppy is without a history and yet blossoming is a kind of recurrence, in the language of the Foreword to *Sons and Lovers*, an 'eternal continuance'. It speaks only to the present, about rich and full presence. The old man's grandson in the first chapter of the 'Study' whose deterministic explanation of the poppy's red the old man eschews, is a type of the rational, limited understanding that Lawrence despises: 'When his educated grandson told him that the red was there to bring the bees and the flies, he knew well enough that more bees and flies and wasps would come to a sticky smear round his grandson's mouth, than to yards of poppy red' (*Hardy*, pp. 8–9). The point about the poppy is that it does not know it is a poppy. Lawrence's fascination with the instinctive, we could say unconscious, life is that it shows us how to be and yet 'how not to know': 'The supreme lesson of human consciousness is to learn how *not to know*' (*Fantasia of the Unconscious*, in F&P, p. 76). The flowering of the poppy in the parable which begins 'Study of Thomas Hardy' stands for positive unconscious being. It was this sense of unconscious living that Lawrence wished to reinscribe over the space of the Freudian unconscious. Yet, maddeningly for Lawrence, in his time Freudian terminology and Freud's reductive view of human destiny was gaining the important ground.

These early philosophical writings are, then, hymns to the unconscious, but not to Freud's concept of it, the ambiguity of which Lawrence himself never addressed, although of course Freud did. The early essays are characterized by an order of extended metaphor that signals different degrees of conscious being. In the final chapter of *Psychoanalysis and the Unconscious*, called 'Human Relations and the Unconscious', Lawrence offers a definition which his next discursive book, *Fantasia of the Unconscious*, inherits:

> At last we form some sort of notion what the unconscious actually is. It is that active spontaneity which rouses in each individual organism at the moment of fusion of the parent nuclei, and which, in polarized connection with the external universe, gradually evolves or elaborates its own individual psyche and corpus, bringing both mind and body forth from itself. Thus it would seem that the term *unconscious* is only another word for life. But life is a general force, whereas the unconscious is essentially single and unique in each individual organism; it is the active, self-evolving soul bringing forth its own incarnation and self-manifestation.
>
> (*Psychoanalysis and the Unconscious*, F&P, p. 242)

Rudiments of the Foreword to *Sons and Lovers* are present in the distinction made between life as a 'general force' and 'the unconscious' as the specialized form, producing itself out of that general force. Lawrence would always draw attention to the unique, individual self, for which the phoenix is often shorthand in his work. In this later writing another echo from the past is heard in the unconscious, defined in *Psychoanalysis and the Unconscious* as material, a seed like the apple-seed, a cell which gives rise to mind and body. Lawrence's sense of a 'dark', unconscious, non-mindful state of being did not alter as his *oeuvre* emerged. These early writings, in their own linguistic excess, constitute a non-analytical mode of enquiry into philosophical (rather than psychological) questions relating to the self (in doing so turning the emphasis onto language). In them Lawrence poetically thinks his way through and around questions of consciousness using figures like the lighted circle and the darkness beyond it; the flame; the poppy; the phoenix. Rather than bearing fixed meanings, these figures, so often repeated in Lawrence, bear the weight of his thought about the general issue: consciousness; individuation; being. In the poetry, animals are supremely 'unconscious', acting from non-deliberate impulse untainted by self-consciousness: the animal has no self as such. In the discursive writing, the philosophical writing, Lawrence finds himself again setting about the business of giving expression (in a poetic idiom) to the unconscious life. So between 1913 and 1923 Lawrence's language changes, and yet some continuity in beating out the ideas, the 'metaphysic', exists. The feeling individual in Lawrence's thought is post-Cartesian, in 1913 as in 1923. Yet how does Lawrence deal with the spectre of Freud's 'unconscious' in his mature writing?

3

The Sensual Body in Lawrence's Early Discursive Writing

So it is: we all have our roots in earth. And it is our roots that now need a little attention, need the hard soil eased away from them, and softened so that a little fresh air can come to them, and they can breathe. For by pretending to have no roots, we have trodden the earth so hard over them that they are starving and stifling below the soil. We have roots, and our roots are in the sensual, instinctive and intuitive body, and it is here we need fresh air of open consciousness.

(*Complete Poems*, p. 418)

Primarily because of his reception in Britain, exemplified by the response of the establishment to *The Rainbow*, Lawrence articulated his desire to establish his reputation in America first. Of Lawrence's two books on the unconscious *Psychoanalysis and the Unconscious* was first published by Thomas Seltzer in New York on 10 May 1921. Martin Secker published it in Britain in July 1923. Its sequel, *Fantasia of the Unconscious*, was published in America by Seltzer in October 1922, and in Britain by Secker in September 1923. They are commonly published in one volume in Britain, in reverse order of composition. To New York publisher Benjamin Huebsch, Lawrence described *Psychoanalysis and the Unconscious* as 'six little essays on Freudian Unconscious' (*Letters*, III, p. 466); *Fantasia of the Unconscious* was first considered under various titles, including 'Psychoanalysis and the Incest Motive' (*Letters*, III, p. 730), and later, 'The Child and the Unconscious', 'Child Consciousness' and 'Harlequinade of the Unconscious' (*Letters*, IV, p. 93, p. 82, p. 97). The early versions of the essays which became *Studies in Classic American Literature*, usually represented as a work of psychoanalytic criticism, initially included descriptions of 'the biological psyche' as Lawrence calls it in *Fantasia of the Unconscious* (F&P, p. 104), incorporating the infamous theories of dual consciousness which were largely removed as Lawrence revised his literary material into book form. Together these texts comprise an important body within Lawrence's *oeuvre*.

The very earliest versions of the essays on American literature, begun in 1917, represent from time to time expressions of Lawrence's philosophy which are largely absent from the final versions of the American criticism published as the *Studies*. This is due sometimes to a change of direction in the thought of Lawrence as he developed his views, and sometimes for more tangible reasons of official censorship as he modified them.[1] We are not yet able to view all the extant versions of the essays in one volume. Of the early versions which are available in *The Symbolic Meaning* one essay in particular, 'The Two Principles', absent from *Studies in Classic American Literature*, departs significantly from the project of literary criticism, and demonstrates the extent to which Lawrence was at that time preoccupied with the ideas that surface later, slightly transformed, in, not least, the books on the unconscious. These are the notions of the 'dual psyche', 'sensual and spiritual', (*The Symbolic Meaning*, p. 184), which give rise to the 'biological psyche' and, of course, 'blood-consciousness' which locates knowing and feeling in 'the lower body': 'For we assert that the blood has a perfect but untranslatable consciousness of its own, a consciousness of weight, of rich, down-pouring motion, of powerful self-positivity. In the blood we have our strongest self-knowledge, our most powerful dark consicence [sic]' (p. 187).

In the course of these essays, Lawrence confirms the inseparability of the aesthetic and the ontological ('Art communicates a state of being', p. 19), and introduces 'art-speech' as the knowing medium which will play fruitfully across the centres and plexuses of the body of the reader:

Art-speech is also a language of pure symbols. But whereas the authorized symbol stands always for a thought or an idea, some mental *concept*, the art-symbol or art-term stands for a pure experience, emotional and passional, spiritual and perceptual, all at once. The intellectual idea remains implicit, latent and nascent. Art communicates a state of being – whereas the symbol at best only communicates a whole thought, an emotional idea. Art-speech is a use of symbols which are pulsations on the blood and seizures upon the nerves, and at the same time pure percepts of the mind and pure terms of spiritual aspiration.

(*The Symbolic Meaning*, p. 19)[2]

This is Lawrence writing about '*untranslatable* consciousness' (p. 187 my italics). The artist works from his head – his 'moral consciousness' – and from his 'unconscious or subconscious soul', working in 'a state of creation' (p. 19) to which the reader is attuned via the Poetic.

'THE CHARM OF A NEW PHRASE'

At the end of *Psychoanalysis and the Unconscious* Lawrence looks ahead to his next volume of discursive writing:

So, the few things we have to say about the *unconscious* end for the moment. There is almost nothing said. Yet it is a beginning. Still remain to be revealed the other great centres of the *unconscious*. We know four: two pairs. In all there are seven planes. That is, there are six dual centres of spontaneous polarity, and then the final one. That is, the great upper and lower *consciousness* is only just broached – the further heights and depths are not even hinted at. Nay, in public it would hardly be allowed us to hint at them. There is so much to know, and every step of the progress in knowledge is a death to the human idealism which governs us now so ruthlessly and vilely.

(*Psychoanalysis and the Unconscious*, F&P, pp. 249–50, italics mine)

It is typical of Lawrence, in the articulation of his own 'metaphysic', to blur what is to us (after Freud) the expected distinction between 'the unconscious' and 'consciousness' as he does here. Of course, that distinction was not at the forefront of Lawrence's mind. Much of his discursive writing, in fact, as in the passage quoted above, labours both to demonstrate and to explore the equivalence or correspondence of these terms within his own lexicon and, therefore, philosophy. One of Lawrence's principal preoccupations, certainly in his books on the unconscious, is to appropriate the word 'unconscious' from Freud and the Freudians, not simply to disagree with Freud but, as I have suggested, to communicate his own thought. His resistance to Freud's idea is ostensibly resistance to the creation of a model with a certain legislative function; a model, furthermore, which turns on assumptions about sexuality, and assumptions about mind/body distinctions, that Lawrence found difficult to accept. Lawrence, after all, would view Freud as a type of unreconstructed Cartesian. He called Freud's conception 'the unconscious which is the inverted reflection of our ideal consciousness' and, more poetically, 'a shadow cast from the mind' (*Psychoanalysis*, F&P, p. 212), which last speaks of Freud's Cartesian inheritance. His own notion of the 'true unconscious' he represents in terms of origins: 'where life begins the unconscious also begins.' The moment of biological conception, 'when a procreative male nucleus fuses with the nucleus of the female germ' also, for Lawrence, gives rise to another order of conception, of knowing; this he sets out calling 'unconscious', but as he becomes more expansive this new order of knowing is designated, apparently oxymoronically,' consciousness': 'at that moment does a new unit of life, of consciousness, arise in the universe. Is it not obvious? The unconscious has no other source than this, this first fused nucleus of the ovule' (p. 213). This is relatively consistent with Lawrence's remark that the unconscious is 'self-evolving' and 'brings forth not only consciousness, but tissue and organs also' (p. 242).

The sixth chapter of *Psychoanalysis and the Unconscious*, 'Human Relations and the Unconscious', is rich with definitions of the unconscious, and a distinction: 'And consciousness is like a web woven finally in the mind from the various silken strands spun forth from the primal centre of the unconscious' (p. 242).[3] This is a clear statement of the primacy of the 'unconscious' life in the development of the individual, but how well examined is the term? In the first place Lawrence insists on the materiality of the unconscious: '[The unconscious] is always concrete . . . it is the glinting nucleus of the ovule' (p. 242); 'We can quite tangibly deal with the human unconscious. We trace its source and centres in the great ganglia and nodes of the nervous system. We establish the nature of the spontaneous consciousness at each of these centres' (p. 243). These statements show the extent to which Lawrence wanted the unconscious to be located in the body; and this desire is a sign of his post-Cartesian credentials. Blood, heart, plexuses, ganglia, body: the *locus* of the unconscious, distinct from Freud's metaphorized 'domain'. 'Psyche and functions', Lawrence argues, 'are so nearly identified that only by holding our breath can we realize their *duality* in identification – a polarized duality once more.... The two are two in one, a polarized quality. They are unthinkably different' (p. 243). This is a familiar model in Lawrence's thought, the model of nearly identified differences.

References to the 'ganglia' in his books on the unconscious, as centres of spontaneous or unconscious functioning, often result in readers dismissing Lawrence on the grounds that such references are esoteric, or simply bad biology. For instance:

> Consciousness develops on successive planes. On each plane there is the dual polarity, positive and negative, of the sympathetic and voluntary nerve centres. The first plane is established between the poles of the sympathetic solar plexus and the voluntary lumbar ganglion. This is the active first plane of the subjective unconscious, from which the whole of consciousness arises.
>
> Immediately succeeding the first plane of subjective dynamic consciousness arises the corresponding first plane of objective consciousness, the objective unconscious, polarized in the cardiac plexus and the thoracic ganglion, in the breast. There is a perfect correspondence in difference between the first abdominal and the first thoracic planes. These two planes polarize each other in a fourfold polarity, which makes the first field of individual, self-dependent consciousness.
>
> (*Psychoanalysis and the Unconscious*, F&P, p. 233)

Such references need to be treated as metaphor except in one important respect, that they return the focus to the body.

In contexts where Lawrence is not shy of offering his own definitions of the unconscious, his instinct is to attack Freud's language: 'It is time the white garb of the therapeutic *cant* was stripped off the psychoanalyst' (*Psychoanalysis*, F&P, p. 202, my emphasis); 'Such is the charm of a new phrase that we accepted this sublimation process without further question. If our complexes were going to sublimate once they were surgically exposed to full mental consciousness, why, best perform the operation' (p. 204). The psychoanalytic mode of enquiry is for Lawrence symptomatic of modernity about which he writes so much, witness this statement from the 1925 text of 'The Crown':

And again, the supreme little ego in man hates an unconquered universe. We shall never rest till we have heaped tin cans on the North Pole and the South Pole, and put up barb-wire fences on the moon. Barb-wire fences are our sign of conquest. We have wreathed the world with them. The back of creation is broken. We have killed the mysteries and devoured the secrets. It all lies now within our skin, within the ego of humanity.
('The Crown', in *Reflections on the Death of a Porcupine*, p. 281)

This description exploits the 'pioneering' metaphor that he borrowed from Freud and developed ironically in *Psychoanalysis and the Unconscious*. Freud's 'work of culture' becomes in Lawrence the defining act of vandalism that distinguishes the path of the colonial master: he writes of Freud's trespass 'into the hinterland of human consciousness' (*Psychoanalysis and the Unconscious*, F&P, p. 202). Lawrence's response to this 'trespass' is to reinvent himself as a decolonizer (and, certainly in relation to Freud, a demythologizer), and as Frantz Fanon has observed:

Decolonization never takes place unnoticed, for it influences individuals and modifies them fundamentally. It transforms spectators crushed with their inessentiality into privileged actors, with the grandiose glare of history's floodlights upon them. It brings a natural rhythm into existence, introduced by new men, and with it a new language and a new humanity. Decolonization is the veritable creation of new men. But this creation owes nothing of its legitimacy to any supernatural power; the 'thing' which has been colonized becomes man during the same process by which it frees itself.
(*The Wretched of the Earth*, p. 28)

Compare this to Lawrence's decolonizing statement in the Foreword to *Women in Love* (1919) that,

We are now in a period of crisis. Every man who is acutely alive is acutely wrestling with his own soul. The people that can bring forth the new passion, the new idea, this people will endure. Those others, that fix themselves in the old idea, will perish with the new life strangled unborn within them. Men must speak out to one another.

(Foreword, Women in Love, p. 486)

Presumably they must do so in 'a new language', the new language(s) of the decolonized. It is highly appropriate that *Women in Love*, which makes conscious certain ideas about language, is the context for this statement.

Comparison of the 1915 and the 1925 texts of 'The Crown' shows Lawrence afterwards inserting psychoanalytic vocabulary into his text while repudiating the Freudian meanings. The later version of 'The Crown' is laced with negative references to ego-ism and the 'self-conscious ego'.[4] As at the conclusion to the (untitled) second section of 'The Crown', poetic and deeply am-biguous passages are substituted by slightly more direct state-ments against the development in the individual of a 'triumphant' ego which would always be, to Lawrence, circumscribed and lim-ited. The wrongness of the assertion of an 'absolute' which can be a self-conscious and self-interested identity (social, historical) standing apart from the greater wave or tide of undifferentiated experience, seems to be Lawrence's central point. 'Egotism' which Lawrence sees as working against his more dialogic understanding gives rise to 'nullity' and 'falsehood'. Many references to the ego in 'The Crown' were added in 1925 sometimes in place of 'soul' or the more overtly poetic 'waves'.[5] Lawrence's problems lie with the implications of asserting the first person. When he comes to examine the theme of singleness in his fictional works, he is far from asserting what he calls in the 1925 text of 'The Crown' 'the triumph of the ego' (in *Reflections*, p. 279).

Early in *Psychoanalysis and the Unconscious* Lawrence consoli-dates the action we have seen all along, the substitution of his own terms. Freud's scientism, his 'unconscious', is challenged by Lawrence's introduction of the 'pristine unconscious':

One thing, however, psychoanalysis all along the line fails to determine, and that is the nature of the pristine unconscious in man. The incest-craving is or is not inherent in the pristine psyche. When Adam and Eve became aware of sex in them-selves, they became aware of that which was pristine in them,

and which preceded all knowing. But when the analyst dis-
covers the incest motive in the unconscious, surely he is only
discovering a term of humanity's repressed *idea* of sex. It is
not even *suppressed* sex-consciousness, but *repressed*. That is, it
is nothing pristine and anterior to mentality. It is in itself the
mind's ulterior motive. That is, the incest-craving is propa-
gated in the pristine unconscious by the mind itself, even though
unconsciously. The mind acts as incubus and procreator of its
own horrors, *deliberately unconsciously*. And the incest motive
is in its origin not a pristine impulse, but a logical extension
of the existent idea of sex and love. The mind, that is, transfers the idea of incest into the affective-passional psyche, and
keeps it there as a repressed motive.

    This is as yet a mere assertion. It cannot be made good until
we determine the nature of the true, pristine unconscious, in
which all our genuine impulse arises – a very different affair
from that sack of horrors which psychoanalysts would have
us believe is source of motivity.

                    (*Psychoanalysis and the Unconscious*, F&P, p. 207)

This gives a certain literalness to Lawrence's famous formulation of 'sex in the head', with the mind acting as a malevolent
agency of sex-consciousness.[6] A respect in Lawrence for origins,
for first things, is here writ large. Freud and his followers have
gained access merely to a repressed by-product of 'mental-
consciousness' (p. 208), a second term, the 'foam' or 'spume' of
self-consciousness. It is the anti-Freud, anti-Cartesian chorus in
Lawrence: 'And every time you "conquer" the body with the
mind (you can say "heal" it, if you like) you cause a deeper,
more dangerous complex or tension somewhere else' (*Studies in
Classic American Literature*, p. 92). The '-consciousness' constructions are part of Lawrence's signature. In 'sex-consciousness' being
conscious or knowing is reductive, in Lawrence's lexicon, 'false'.
Elsewhere, in the books on the unconscious and in the fiction,
consciousness mediated through the heart, for instance, or more
usually through the blood ('blood-consciousness, the most elemental form of consciousness', *Fantasia*, F&P, p. 173) is entirely ac-
ceptable: the negative construction 'sex-consciousness' gives way
in this instance to the entirely positive 'blood-consciousness'.
'Mind', in the passage just quoted, equates with (negative) 'mental-
consciousness'. So it is that a number of often opposing meanings

modulate in the one word. The 'pristine unconscious' is a quality of being human that Lawrence habitually dramatizes in his fiction: the Lawrentian subject is most fulfilled when most 'unconscious'. So it is that Lawrence is happy to get rid of the definite article in the Freudian model.

IN THE FORESTS OF THE NIGHT

Such 'unconsciousness' is given a special status in the so-called digression of the fourth chapter of *Fantasia of the Unconscious*, 'Trees and Babies and Papas and Mamas'. Writing the book, Lawrence gives us his geographical location: 'One of the few places that my soul will haunt, when I am dead, will be this. Among the trees here near Ebersteinburg, where I have been alone and written this book. I can't leave these trees. They have taken some of my soul' (*Fantasia*, F&P, p. 46). The Black Forest becomes for Lawrence an important *topos*, the dark forest which figures the pristine unconscious; a bizarre pastoral that is other to Freud's breaking through the wall of darkness into the cave of unspeakable horrors, in Lawrence's earlier account (*Psychoanalysis and the Unconscious*, F&P, pp. 202–3). The sensual body of the dark forest is gendered masculine, yet in the light of Lawrence's previous discoursing on the mother, there is room for ambivalence in those moments when the trees (only the day before 'like a harem of wonderful silent wives', p. 42) seem to nurture the self-infantilizing writer. In the chapters preceding 'Trees and Babies and Papas and Mamas' his critical focus has been on the baby, and principally the child's word-less relation to the mother. This relation is momentarily echoed as Lawrence situates himself at the 'breast' and 'foot' of the 'preconscious' tree: 'Suppose you want to look a tree in the face? You can't. It hasn't got a face. You look at the strong body of a trunk; you look above you into the matted body-hair of twigs and boughs; you see the soft green tips. . . . The only thing is to sit among the roots and nestle against its strong trunk, and not bother' (p. 43). The foetal Lawrence, nestling, ceases to look and instead privileges touch; '*stroked* into forgetfulness' (p. 43, my italics), he 'dwells', as Heidegger would have it, unconscious, within the unconscious forest. His description of the trees in phallic terms speaks to his fictional descriptions of men who retire from the critical light into the darkness, to become unconscious:

The looming trees, so straight. And I listen for their silence –
big, tall-bodied trees, with a certain magnificent cruelty about
them – or barbarity – I don't know why I should say cruelty.
Their magnificent, strong, round bodies! It almost seems I can
hear the slow, powerful sap drumming in their trunks. Great
full-blooded trees, with strange tree-blood in them, soundlessly
drumming.
Trees that have no hands and faces, no eyes; yet the powerful sap-scented blood roaring up the great columns. A vast
individual life, and an overshadowing will – the will of a tree;
something that frightens you.

(Fantasia of the Unconscious, F&P, p. 43)

Here I am between his toes like a pea-bug, and him noiselessly
over-reaching me, and I feel his great blood-jet surging. . . .
Plunging himself down into the black humus, with a root's
gushing zest, where we can only rot dead; and his tips in high
air, where we can only look up to. So vast and powerful and
exultant in his two directions. And all the time he has no face,
no thought: only a huge, savage, thoughtless soul. . . .
A huge, plunging, tremendous soul. I would like to be a
tree for a while. The great lust of roots. Root-lust. And no
mind at all. He towers, and I sit and feel safe. I like to feel him
towering around me. I used to be afraid. I used to fear their
lust, their rushing black lust. But now I like it, I worship it.

(p. 44)[7]

There are resonances, but faint resonances, of Birkin in the vegetation after Hermione's attack; although in 'Breadalby' (*Women
in Love*, Chapter VIII) Birkin is not yet 'unconscious' in the positive Lawrentian sense. In 'Excurse' (*Women in Love*, Chapter XXIII)
the dark forest is Sherwood, where the terms of Lawrence's anti-
visual, anti-objectivist, 'metaphysic' are once more confirmed,
Ursula and Birkin entering into a sightless and '*unspeakable* communication' (p. 320 my italics) where the tactile is privileged. In
the presumably autobiographical episode from which I have
quoted above, Lawrence writes of 'losing himself among the trees'
which represent to him 'a vast array of non-human life, darkly
self-sufficient, and bristling with indomitable energy' (p. 45). This
is a potent metaphor in Lawrence's thought. In 'Life', an essay
written in 1917 and published in the February 1918 issue of the
English Review, he writes,

I am like a small house on the edge of the forest. Out of the unknown darkness of the forest, in the eternal night of the beginning, comes the spirit of creation towards me. But I must keep the light shining in the window, or how will the spirit see my house? If my house is in darkness of sleep or fear, the angel will pass it by. Above all, I must have no fear. I must watch and wait. Like a blind man looking for the sun, I must lift my face to the unknown darkness of space and wait until the sun lights on me. It is a question of creative courage.

('Life', in *Reflections on the Death of a Porcupine*, p. 18)

Gradually in Lawrence the individual moves into the forest, ceasing to inhabit the conscious margins. The reference to blindness is familiar, and retinal seeing is developed in his writing as an undesirable too-conscious mode of understanding, as in his story *The Blind Man* (1918).[8] In Ebersteinburg, the trees alter the man: they 'stroke' him into unconsciousness. They also *are* the man. The digression into the dark forest, then, touches on some of Lawrence's central preoccupations. Cutting the tree open will not reveal its darkness; that darkness is a matter of positive and unconscious presence.

In 'Study of Thomas Hardy' the forest is given a related meaning. There it represents the mysterious female body as the territory of the 'unknown'. The explorer/pioneer metaphors once more come into play. 'A man' gives himself up to 'losing himself' by daring 'to venture within the unknown of the female' like 'a man who enters a primeval, virgin forest' (*Hardy*, p. 104). 'The female' in this description is an abstraction: the sense of fear, fear of female sexuality, is strong. The man in this adventure returns 'rich with addition to his soul', oxymoronically 'rich with the knowledge ... of the unknown' (p. 104). As the description develops 'unknown' must resonate ontologically: 'all the magnificence that *is*, and yet which is unknown to any of us' (p. 104). The gap between the ego and the experience is closed. Writing to a male audience Lawrence explains 'And as we are dazed with the unknown in her, so is she dazed with the unknown in us' (p. 105). And, having arrived at his own terms, Lawrence then implicitly genders himself feminine in the rhetorical questioning to follow: 'Is it not a gratification for me when a stranger shall land on my shores and enjoy what he finds there. Shall I not also enjoy it? Shall I not enjoy the strange motion of the stranger, like a pleasant sensation of silk and warmth against me, stirring unknown fibres?' (p. 105). It is a description of sexual pleasure, which depends on the cliché of sexual discovery. Yet we are left in no doubt that this experience counts as 'authentic' within the life of feeling (the life of 'genuine impulse') that Lawrence is plotting, where a deep-seated impersonality loosens the conscious 'mental' hold which the ego has on the self. This is quite apart from 'the full-veined gratification of self-pleasure' (p. 105) of sex-in-the-head.

Returning to *Fantasia of the Unconscious*, there is in the tree 'a dark pre-mind' that Lawrence has, only a few pages before, situated in the child. The 'subtle interplay' described between the child and parents *develops* the child, as the writer is developed between the roots of the firs in the dark forest. Child and tree are also both pre- or non-verbal. Lawrence continually reminds us that the trees are faceless, headless, mindless: they lack the all-too-human *sense* organs, and just as Lawrence concentrates on the solar plexus in the human being, in the tree his principal focus is on the trunk. Communication, but wordless communication, underpins the descriptions of reciprocality throughout *Fantasia of the Unconscious*. With his concentration back on the family Lawrence writes:

> From the solar plexus first of all pass the great vitalistic communications between child and parents, the first interplay of primal, pre-mental knowledge and sympathy. It is a great subtle interplay, and from this interplay the child is built up, body and psyche. Impelled from the primal conscious centre in the abdomen, the child seeks the mother, seeks the breast, opens a blind mouth and gropes for the nipple. Not mentally directed and yet certainly directed. Directed from the dark pre-mind centre of the solar plexus.
>
> (*Fantasia of the Unconscious*, F&P, p. 32)

The attraction of the child as a subject for Lawrence rests in its pre-verbal condition. Why should Lawrence infantilize himself in relation to the silent nurturing trees of the forest unless it is to become, in a profoundly creative way, without language? Critics are usually exercised by Lawrence's relation to language: a recent commentator on Lawrence's radical practice underlines his attack on logocentrism;[9] a commentator on the politics of the

gaze in Lawrence's writing has asked 'what is [Lawrence] doing
championing *in writing* a pre-linguistic realm which by its very
nature is cut off from the writer himself?'[10] The point is that
Lawrence accepts this paradox: his function as a writer is to put
the non-verbal into words. His suggestion is that the only way
to do this is poetically: through the radical proliferation of metaphor, oxymoron, paradox. The problematics of language are something Lawrence has to think through *in* language, his principal,
if limited, medium. By thinking poetically, as he demonstrably
is in the passages quoted so far, he manages to think about, and
through, the various modes of enquiry and expression available
to him. Yet always, in Lawrence, being *too* verbal is the same as
being *too* conscious. In Lawrence's writing, being unconscious is
the most creative way of being conscious. The two terms 'unconscious' and 'conscious', then, run parallel in Lawrence, and
on the 'horizon', so to speak, like all parallel lines, they intersect.[11] For many readers Lawrence is 'too verbal' in his discursive essays and books. That metaphor becomes *his* mode of enquiry
is, however, essential.

'THE FLESH CONSCIOUS AND UNCONSCIOUS'[12]

Lawrence's representation of the body, or more specifically his
psycho- (or pseudo-)biology, certainly in the discursive writing
of his early to middle career, underpins a level of dissatisfaction
with the identity politics of his day, even while he apparently
colludes with it ('Men learn their feelings from women, women
learn their mental consciousness from men', *Fantasia*, F&P, p. 102).
We know that for Lawrence, not least in his discursive writing,
the first term is usually masculine.[13] We can see also that his
insistence on a (newly examined) recognition of deep-seated differences between the sexes is partially based on an idea of mutual respect for otherness which, he suggests, should result in
moments of 'accomplished marriage': 'The whole mode, the whole
everything is really different in man and woman. . . . the vital
sex polarity . . . the magic and the dynamism rests on *otherness*'
(p. 103). In fact, Lawrence examines otherness most effectively
when he departs from the space of personal relations, as in the
discursive writing where cultural difference is addressed as part
of his critique of European modes of knowledge, and in much

of the poetry where an examination of otherness is conducted through notions of animality.

In some ways in the discursive writing Lawrence writes against himself as he anatomizes feeling. At its worst his psycho-biology of plexuses and ganglia is, in his own terms, equivalent to peeling the bark off the tree in order to try to gaze at the darkness within. Most of the time, in the discursive books, Lawrence seems blind to the irony of this, and blindest, perhaps, when he attempts to deal with gender; or when he attempts to relate his perceptions about consciousness to gender. When he writes about consciousness/unconsciousness in relation to the child, he prefers to put gender in parentheses. When he does so, the metaphors which organize his thought are those of 'flow' and 'vibration', metaphors which have a curiously postmodern resonance as Lawrence describes the interplay of non-verbal 'information' from individual to individual; and the organization of feeling within the individual him/herself. The child *in utero*, argues Lawrence, has no 'idea' of the mother but is 'dynamically conscious' of her; otherwise, he asks, how could each relate as mother and child later:

> This consciousness, however, is utterly non-ideal, non-mental, purely dynamic, a matter of dynamic polarized intercourse of vital vibrations, as an exchange of wireless messages which are never translated from the pulse-rhythm into speech, because they have no need to be. It is a dynamic polarized intercourse between the great primary nuclei in the foetus and the corresponding nuclei in the dynamic maternal psyche.
> (*Fantasia of the Unconscious*, F&P, p. 70)

As Lawrence's project is intended to be heuristic so, too, is the process he describes. The interpersonal relation is later in the book adapted to explain an 'accomplished' relation of self and world, and Lawrence keeps up the level of metaphors of 'force' and 'flow' to describe a process which is, he protests, far from mechanical:

> The argument is that, between an individual and any external object with which he has an affective connection, there exists a definite vital flow, as definite and concrete as the electric current whose polarized circuit sets our tram-cars running and

our lamps shining, or our Marconi wires vibrating. Whether this object be human, or animal, or plant, or quite inanimate, there is still a circuit. My dog, my canary has a polarized connecton with me. Nay, the very cells in the ash tree I loved as a child had a dynamic vibratory connection with the nuclei in my own centres of primary consciousness. And further still, the boots I have worn are so saturated with my own magnetism, my own vital activity, that if anyone else wears them I feel it is a trespass, almost as if another man used my hand to knock away a fly.

(*Fantasia of the Unconscious*, F&P, pp. 131–2)[14]

The Marconi metaphor operates in Lawrence's alternative to the Freudian family:

A family, if you like, is a group of wireless stations, all adjusted to the same, or very much the same vibration. All the time they quiver with the interchange, there is one long endless flow of vitalistic communication between members of one family, a long, strange *rapport*, a sort of life-unison. It is a ripple of life through many bodies as through one body.

(*Fantasia of the Unconscious*, F&P, p. 32)

This is an example of Lawrence's 'decolonizing' language. The metaphoric representation of sympathetic understanding dismantles the Oedipal trinity by refusing it validity: it simply denies the categories of the Oedipal and pre-Oedipal, for instance, by instituting descriptions of community that operate only in the present. As Gilles Deleuze and Félix Guattari suggest, there is no body of desire awaiting organisation; no place in Lawrence's thought for the psychosexual explanations derived from Freud's restricted familial configurations.[15] It is nevertheless central for Lawrence's *frictional* 'metaphysic' ('frictional' is a word that gains currency in relation to Lawrence's style after the Foreword to *Women in Love*), that this mutual harmony breaks down. When he brings gendered relations back into the picture he also foregrounds the problem of understanding:

Even in the mind, where we seem to meet, we are really utter strangers. We may speak the same verbal language, men and women: as the Turk and German might both speak Latin. But *whatever* a man says, his meaning is something quite different and changed when it passes through a woman's ears. And though you reverse the sexual polarity, the flow between the sexes, still the difference is the same. The *apparent* mutual understanding, in companionship between a man and a woman, is always an illusion, and always breaks down in the end.

(*Fantasia of the Unconscious*, F&P, p. 188)

He singles out 'verbal language' as one option available to the human being, quite apart from the body language with which he is elsewhere preoccupied. In these examples Lawrence's interest is in modes of communication, and it is this interest that characterizes his discourses on consciousness and unconsciousness. The Marconi metaphors are about 'information' and exchange. Information is organized, or so Lawrence suggests, across the fields of the body: its organization into planes, plexuses and ganglia preoccupies the narratives of the two books on the *un*conscious. Information, he suggests, 'flows' and 'vibrates' from field to field: there is a commerce and exchange of non-verbal information which is 'felt', becomes conscious, in the sensual, intuitive body.

Inasmuch as these statements come from *Fantasia of the Unconscious* it is evident that Lawrence is consolidating his position against the conscious, indeed modernist, subject of psychoanalysis. This need not obscure his earlier attempts to bring to language a mute domain of feeling, within which the human being is defined. The non-verbal has an integrity for Lawrence which can only be approximated, paradoxically, by art-speech. Part of his objective in these books and, crucially, in the earlier discursive texts, is to dismantle the hegemony of a theorized world view – physics; natural sciences; biology; psychoanalysis. This theorized world view is principally rational and positivist, an extension of the Cartesian model for which Lawrence has no time. Most interestingly, he debunks theory by appropriating its language: 'relativity', or 'unconscious', for example.[16] His own sense-language, characterized by the highly metaphorical prose of his discursive essays and books, came to challenge, in its very metaphoricity, the rational *modus* of psychoanalysis, as Lawrence himself claimed. In doing so his language sets about dismantling the versions of knowledge represented by this and other master discourses. Lawrence's targets are more often than not modes of understanding or enquiry, such as psychoanalysis, which have developed out of, and which sustain, the broadly Cartesian model.

His distaste is with modes of conscious control and epistemological modes that hygienically reduce the human to a set of readily available and universally applicable criteria. His problem is with the reader who will do the same to the work of art, the 'sniffing mongrel bitch of a reader' with a 'carrion-smelling psycho-analysing nose' looking for explanations when 'there *is* no why and wherefore' (*Mr. Noon*, p. 205). *Mr. Noon* was begun during the writing of the books on the unconscious, so there is some 'local' context for the overt hostility towards psychoanalysis articulated here. The 'mongrel bitch' is the type of a consciousness which is no longer pristine; a hybrid of mentalized desire reading doggedly for confirmation of ideas. 'She' is historically the reader of novels; 'she' is also identified more closely than that, reminding us of the difficulties of reception faced by Lawrence:

An anonymous lady – she may even be yourself, gentle reader – once wrote to me thus: 'You, who can write so beautifully of stars and flowers, why will you grovel in the ditch?' I might answer her – or you, gentle reader – thus: 'You, who wear such nice suede shoes, why do you blow your nose?'

(*Mr. Noon*, p. 185)

The reference to nose-blowing contributes to Lawrence's efforts to return the focus to the operations of the body in order to challenge contemporary squeamishness. 'Nose-blowing' is a metaphor for those functions, principally excretion, which are taboo because 'shameful'. *Mr. Noon* has its mildly scatological moments.[17] In part, by disrupting the usually harmonious relationship between the narrating consciousness and the reader, Lawrence develops the gulf opening up between his novel and the *genre* by his iconoclasm with certain stock conventions. It has to be remembered that by this time he was disenchanted with his readers, particularly in Britain. The Foreword to *Women in Love* articulates this dissatisfaction, and underlines his willingness to prefer an American audience, ('In England, I would never try to justify myself against any accusation. But to the Americans, perhaps I may speak for myself', Foreword, *Women in Love*, p. 485). In *Mr. Noon,* as in the roughly contemporaneous *Aaron's Rod,* and *Fantasia of the Unconscious,* where the reader is also addressed, the sense is of a self-confident although increasingly defensive writer. That Lawrence feminizes his reader in *Mr. Noon* is also meaningful in the debates on attitudes to women which his works provoke. The immediate danger from Lawrence's point of view, however, is the reader who comes to the text in possession of a theory, for whom pleasure resides in having 'her' theoretical position confirmed. Other references in *Mr. Noon* suggest that the reader's position is reactionary, and the reader's responses derivative. His statement that '*I* am writing this book' (*Mr. Noon,* p. 137), and his other interventions, may be suggestively metafictional, but in Lawrence's terms they warn against 'the superimposition of a theory' (Foreword, *Women in Love,* p. 486) which might threaten to obliterate what he identifies in 'Study of Thomas Hardy' as the artist's 'sensuous understanding' (*Hardy,* p. 93).

4

Language and the Unconscious: The Radical Metaphoricity of *Psychoanalysis and the Unconscious* and *Fantasia of the Unconscious* I

> *We profess no scientific* exactitude, *particularly in terminology. We merely wish intelligibly to open a way.*
> (*Psychoanalysis and the Unconscious*, F&P, pp. 234–5)

Language is not identified explicitly as one of Lawrence's themes in *Psychoanalysis and the Unconscious* and *Fantasia of the Unconscious*, even though metaphor is so evidently the starting point for saying anything. The focus in this chapter is chiefly on the relation in his work between metaphor and 'metaphysic', a word that acquires a Lawrentian specificity. It does so as Lawrence repudiates, in the course of his career, Lascelles Abercrombie's view that fiction must be in possession of a controlling 'metaphysic'. Lawrence took an alternative view: '[I]f I don't "subdue my art to a metaphysic", as somebody very beautifully said of Hardy, I do write because I want folk – English folk – to alter, and have more sense' (*Letters*, I, p. 544).[1]

In the course of this examination I shall concentrate attention on some of the key areas of Lawrence's 'metaphysic' as they are mediated by his books on the unconscious: these areas include his approach to the body/psyche polarity which Lawrence perceives to lie at the centre of modern thought, and which he attempts to dismantle; vision and its relation to knowing; the metaphoricity of dream. In examining these preoccupations of Lawrence the discussion consistently returns to language: much of what is important in Lawrence has its own metaphoricity, or is articulated metaphorically, and for this reason, even, or perhaps especially, where the critical focus apparently lies elsewhere, the real subject of this chapter, and the next, is language and principally metaphor as an unavoidable mode of thought.

Lawrence's books on the unconscious are not marginal although they are typically relegated to that status. Critical approaches to them tend to concentrate on the 'literal' status of Lawrence's 'metapsychology'.[2] As these books are nominally about the unconscious, the reader first encounters Freud, or at any rate Lawrence's Freud: of *Psychoanalysis and the Unconscious* Lawrence said, 'It is not about psychoanalysis particularly – but a first attempt at establishing something definite in place of the vague Freudian Unconscious' (*Letters*, IV, p. 40). The distinction is useful and interesting from one whose friends included a number of pioneering psychoanalysts in Britain. Lawrence 'reads' Freud by interacting with certain levels of his thought and bypassing others, but with his own 'metaphysic' clearly in view. Given the temptation to read Lawrence 'reading' Freud, I suggest that, in assessing the significance of Freud in Lawrence's thought, the emphasis should be less on doctrinal questions and more on discourse. Lawrence's sensitivity to Freud was in the first place a sensitivity to Freud's metaphors, particularly as they, in Lawrence's view, constituted an unacceptably rigid model of the psyche. It is largely the fixed term, the dominant discourse, which Lawrence finds inadmissible.

Evidently Freud's ideas do not consistently determine the direction of Lawrence's books on the unconscious. My emphasis is on Lawrence responding to a certain kind of language in Freud, but I do not see these books of the early 1920s as *merely* a response, a repudiation or a commentary. Freud's metaphors, his conceptions, might have given rise to Lawrence's essays but by the same token these essays also give rise to (Lawrence's) Freud. This figure appears through the medium, as it were, of Lawrence who is creatively working in part with Freud's terminology, his discourse.

These preliminary remarks attempt to reveal a particular appropriation of Freud in relation to Lawrence. There is no attempt here to provide yet another psychoanalytical reading of Lawrence's texts: such an approach would be far from the point in this context. The focus is more especially on how Freud articulates his science and on the use of metaphorical structures like Oedipus (from which we can stand back), in contrast to Lawrence's radically metaphorical language (in which we are immersed), and which itself constitutes the deepest levels of creativity in Lawrence. I propose to refer to the fiction only when critical awareness of Lawrence's metaphoricity begins to deepen, which it must do through a reading of these texts.

FIGURING FREUD

The Interpretation of Dreams was available in various English translations from 1913. David Eder's translation of *On Dreams* was published by Heinemann in London in 1914, the same year as A. A. Brill's edition of *Psychopathology of Everyday Life*. *Beyond the Pleasure Principle, Group psychology and the analysis of the ego,* and *Introductory Lectures on Psycho-Analysis* were published in London in 1922. Leonard and Virginia Woolf, as owners and directors of the Hogarth Press, agreed to publish the International Psycho-Analytical Library in 1924, and the *Standard Edition* of Freud's work, translated and edited by James Strachey, a lengthy project, was begun in that year by the Press in association with the Institute of Psycho-Analysis. *The Ego and the Id* came from the Hogarth Press in English in 1927. Popular Freudianism probably took hold in Britain with Penguin who published *Psychopathology of Everyday Life*, post-1938 and rather late for Lawrence. Otherwise, Freud was known in Britain through pupils, enthusiasts and practitioners like David Eder and Barbara Low.[3] Her niece, author Ivy Low, wrote enthusiastically of *Sons and Lovers* 'This is a book about the Oedipus complex!',[4] a response to which Lawrence was always hostile given the redescription of his novel in Freudian terms, about which he was largely ignorant. Through Frieda Weekley he had some acquaintance with psychoanalysis: 'I never read Freud, but I have learned about him since I was in Germany' (*Letters*, II, p. 80).[5] Later, of course, he was able to articulate the extent to which he differed from Freud.

Freud's relation to his medium had to be one of control. As

Frederick Hoffman notes in his book *Freudianism and the Literary Mind*,[6] Freud himself habitually modified his own language, giving new inflections to established terms as his ideas changed. Other psychoanalysts, like Jung, would also adapt Freud's terms to suit their own intellectual needs and theories. The terms themselves reflected a variety of positions. Hoffman describes the initial lay-reponse to Freud:

> It is not at all surprising that the writers, of the twenties at least, should have been a bit confused about the exact meaning of Freudianism. The writer brought to the confusion his own preconceptions and prejudices. Many of the young intellectuals of the twenties confused the issue further by accepting Freudian terms immediately upon hearing them, or by attaching at the most a summary sketch of their meaning. Thus repression as Freud defined it lost much of its original meaning in a discussion; but it gained new cultural ingredients from the particular area in which it found an audience.
>
> (*Freudianism and the Literary Mind*, p. 88)

At the heart of the problem was the elusive psyche. The terms required to define it have to be descriptive and metaphorical: the concepts themselves are acknowledged to be dynamic and difficult to express. It is a commonplace that Freud, resistant to a technical vocabulary, had no choice but to use metaphor, principally that of the Unconscious which made it possible to speak about that 'territory' which is not available for direct examination. Lawrence's language of 'flows', 'circuits' and 'vibrations' to which I shall return, and Freud's metaphors of exchange from one agency to another, indicate the prevalence of a certain kind of metaphoric language for expressing the individual's psychic profile. But with Freud the emphasis is on analogy, as it is not with Lawrence. Lawrence was sensitive to Freud's need for a metaphorical standpoint but he was also critical of what might be called Freud's 'models', what have come to be thought of as his conceptual apparatus. By the same token words like 'ego', 'super-ego' and 'id' have ceased to be perceived as metaphors: we no longer notice their original meanings because of what they have come to stand for. There are many words in Lawrence that function like this (although purely within the intimate space of his own writing), words like 'blood-consciousness', for instance,

by which Lawrence intends to describe a non-deliberate responsiveness and, crucially, something which happens elsewhere than
in the head. The head is, after all, the *locus* of the Freudian psyche.
Hoffman says that 'Understanding anything is not a cognitive
act; it is the *undeliberate functioning* of ourselves as organic and
individual beings' (p. 166, my italics). As a construction, 'blood-
consciousness' is one of those fruitful Lawrentian paradoxes,
related to the more general role of metaphor in his writing: the
paradox which informs the attempt to put non-verbal experience into language, the basis of Lawrence's aesthetics. Such words
belong to a specifically Lawrentian lexicon and the focus will
increasingly be on his metaphoricity as the only way to describe,
or redescribe, what we are accustomed to think of as unconscious functioning.

    In the 1920s it was quite modish to talk about psychoanalysis,
which meant Freud, a state of affairs to which Lawrence satirically refers in the Introduction to *Fantasia of the Unconscious*.
Acknowledging this, Hoffman's point, however, is that the real
significance of psychoanalysis in the culture was not fully recognized. In his fiction, and specifically in his books on the unconscious, Lawrence at least reflects the cultural significance of
Freud; and Lawrence himself was in possession of a related interest in the instinctual life, in human relationships, in the development of child consciousness – which was the projected theme
of *Fantasia of the Unconscious* – and in 'unconscious' modes of
human being. However, among his contemporaries, few were
ready for a mature debate on the general significance of psychoanalysis. The implication is that the modernists had a sense of
Freud on the horizon, and on occasion reference was made to
this horizon, but on the whole a gulf persisted which today can
be read as a deep-lying, if not to say unconscious, resistance to
his theories. Lawrence's unease with contemporary attempts to
conceptualize the unconscious, to reduce it to a number of fixed
metaphors, makes him more genuinely post-Freudian in his perceptions than many of the British writers of the time. In 1977
one critic wrote 'When I look back at *Psychoanalysis and the Unconscious* from the perspective of contemporary theory and practice, I see how close Lawrence was in 1921 to aspects of theory
that are central for interpreters now.'[7] The theorists cited in this
context, as in an important sense prefigured by Lawrence, include Marion Milner, D.W. Winnicot and J.-B. Pontalis.[8] In the

1970s Gilles Deleuze and Félix Guattari engaged skilfully with a corpus of thought and a corpus of *language* in Lawrence, in a context which points up the radical tenor of Lawrence's aversion to Freudian psychoanalysis.[9] Certainly Lawrence's books on the unconscious in some part articulate his own resistance to Freudian concepts and are important for that reason. More specifically, in their discursive mode and consciously metaphorical language, they allow us to focus tightly on the whole question of metaphor, and its relation to knowledge, in Lawrence.

Lawrence's books allow us to focus on metaphor as a mode of thought, it is true, and it is just as true that Freud in some important respects motivates Lawrence to write in the way he does in these books. J.-B. Pontalis has drawn attention to the difficulties in distinguishing between Freud's 'practical' and his 'theoretical' texts, referring to the complex rhetorical strategies of 'Beyond the Pleasure Principle'.[10] In the context of clinical practice the work of Freud represents a body of propositions which have to be tested empirically yet, as Jacques Derrida and others have shown, his language is a subtle medium, as mobile as any literary text. *Die Traumdeutung* is an open-ended structure like its subject matter, dream. Freud's work, as we expect, shows that a theoretical text is no more a closed structure than is a fiction or a poem. Malcolm Bowie highlights the importance of Freud's language when he remarks that,

> Freud's own technical language, as is now well known, was the product of a daring syncretistic verbal imagination, and it was a triumph of rhetorical ingenuity. Similarly, the underlying mechanisms that he sought to delineate as a basis for his explanations of both normal and pathological mental processes were assembled from a variety of conceptual components; they were schematic and parsimonious despite these varied origins; and they always needed to be made malleable again if they were to handle successfully the shifting complexity of actual clinical cases. Freud as clinician brought a new rhetoric into play, one that spoke not of systems, mechanisms, apparatus or modes of functioning but of autobiographical human speech seized on the wing and in the density of its affective life.[11]

Bowie's concluding statement articulates a sense of language in Freud which Lawrence shared. Lawrence, too, recognized the inadequacy of a 'technical' or conceptual language which established a gulf between the individual and the emotional life. His own language, at best, starts out as non-deliberate, arising from an unconscious, or partly conscious, functioning: the result of the writer's intuitive awareness of its appropriateness (as the vehicle of his 'metaphysic' or personal philosophy) rather than through conscious design. Yet as Michael Black has shown, the repetitive deployment of certain figures, across a range of works, reveals how what arose undeliberately became central to the more conscious articulation of Lawrence's 'metaphysic'. In the first instance, Bowie's 'autobiographical speech seized on the wing and in the density of its affective life' is exactly right. His observations also return us to the fundamental recognition shared by Freud and Lawrence (and Heidegger), and which makes the work of these figures distinctive: each recognizes the need to think metaphorically, but which of them can transform metaphor into a radical 'thinking further'?

Freud's 'new rhetoric' develops because of the urgency of his recognition of the use of metaphor combined with the sense that verbal correspondences for psychic states are always approximations. As he says in 'The Question of Lay Analysis', 'In psychology we can only describe things by the help of analogies. There is nothing peculiar in this; it is the case elsewhere as well. But we have constantly to keep changing these analogies, for none of them lasts long enough' (SE, XX, p. 195). This is a very simple statement of the special dependency of psychoanalysis on figurative language. It is a dependency which underpins the work of Freud and his leading reinterpreter, Jacques Lacan, but it also alerts us to the fact that for a psychoanalyst language is, as Bowie succinctly puts it elsewhere, 'the main source of clinical data' and the analyst's chief 'therapeutic instrument'.[12]

Lawrence does not overtly acknowledge the importance of Freud's conjoining of language and the unconscious. Pervading his texts on the unconscious is his outrage that Freud's authority is based on a negative set of rigid and repressive structures (like Oedipalization) to which individuality is subsumed. In a letter written to Frederick Hoffman, and quoted by him, Frieda Lawrence states that 'Lawrence's conclusion was more or less that Freud looked on sex too much from the doctor's point of view, that Freud's "sex" and "libido" were too limited and mechanical and that the root was deeper' (*Freudianism and the Literary*

Mind, p. 154). I propose to stay with Hoffman for the time being because of his insistence on the theoretical differences between Freud and Lawrence, though *Psychoanalysis and the Unconscious* and *Fantasia of the Unconscious* do not constitute an unproblematic commentary on Freud's ideas. They do not simply circumscribe Freud's writings: Freud is a part of their content, of course, but is far from being Lawrence's only preoccupation. These are books where Lawrence is determined to communicate *his* version of unconscious functioning, and in that debate Freud is utterly marginal. Hoffman's book, one of the first discussions of the relation between Lawrence and Freud and published six years after the death of Freud, was also among the first books to examine seriously the relevance of psychoanalysis to literature. But the title of Hoffman's chapter on Lawrence, 'Lawrence's *Quarrel* with Freud' (my italics), suggests that Lawrence's criticisms of Freud were essentially, if not purely, doctrinal: consequently he does not examine critically the role of *language* in Lawrence's deliberations about psychoanalysis.

Hoffman properly underscores Lawrence's preference for Trigant Burrow, who as a psychologist had moved away from Freud's thinking. Lawrence's review of *The Social Basis of Consciousness* by Burrow is a further statement of his own ideas, or more precisely a re-articulation of his suspicion of theories of the self (Lawrence often uses 'self' and 'ego' interchangeably without attending to distinctions). The anti-subjective Lawrence lays into the 'modern' universal striving for self-consciousness so that all experiences are 'in the head' as he puts it in *Fantasia of the Unconscious*, and the '[i]dolatry of self' which prevents the 'flow' of consciousness 'from within outwards' (*Phoenix*, p. 380). Burrow's privileging of the social group and his emphasis on group analysis rather than the one-to-one relation of analyst and analysand appealed to Lawrence for a time because of its closeness to his own conception of a sympathetic community: 'what must be broken is the egocentric absolute of the individual' (*Phoenix*, p. 379). In contrast, Freud stands out as a single and singular figure of authority, dependent upon the hierarchy which Burrow, and Lawrence, wanted to dismantle and thereby disempower.

By means of comparison Hoffman persists in interpreting the differences between Freud and Lawrence as doctrinal; he only briefly focuses on Lawrence's response to Freud's language as negative:

His [Lawrence's] critical, philosophical works all refer at one time or another to psychoanalytic terms – the unconscious, the oedipus complex, repression, sublimation etc. But his chief reason for reading psychoanalysis was to refute it; or, rather, to find his own explanations for the terms which psychoanalysis had offered him.

(*Freudianism and the Literary Mind*, p. 161)

While Lawrence does challenge psychoanalytic terms it is not merely in order to substitute his own language. Freud is, in his view, a symptom of a universal malaise in human consciousness and Lawrence's response is not simply to re-invest Freudian terms with new meaning. Hoffman proceeds by enumerating the points on which Lawrence disagreed with Freud – making the unconscious conscious, and Freud's assessment of the mother-son relationship chief among them. It is true that in his books on the unconscious Lawrence does of course reject Freud's concept of infantile sexuality precisely because Freud breaks down 'the sacred mysteries' (Foreword, *Women in Love*, p. 485) into elements which unmask the mechanisms of psychosis. In chapters of *Fantasia of the Unconscious* called 'Education and Sex in Man, Woman and Child' and 'The Birth of Sex', Lawrence concentrates on the psychosexual, but from within the context of his own system of thought where the subject is precisely not neurotic or psychotic. Readers are familiar with the idea that Lawrence's resistance to Freud's theories has been construed as a repression of something he recognizes in his own relations with his mother. Quite apart from psychoanalytic interpretations of *Sons and Lovers*, texts like the recently located poem, 'Death-Paean of a Mother', reinforce such tired speculations.[13] Lawrence's response to the reading of his third, and most overtly autobiographical, novel as an Oedipal drama is something which I shall address presently. In assessing Lawrence's response to Freud, Hoffman's theme is also the familiar one that Lawrence rejected intellectualism especially when it obstructed and denied the unconscious life of the individual, but that he owed Freud a debt inasmuch as the latter recognized the importance of the unconscious at all: 'For the metaphor of the unconscious, which Lawrence substituted for the notion of the soul, he was grateful to the psychologist. The incest-motive and its associate, the oedipus complex, puzzled Lawrence, and forced him to re-explain, in terms of a highly original version of biology' (*Freudianism and the Literary Mind*, p. 167).

This is perhaps to lend too much weight to the sense of Freud as an intellectual adversary of Lawrence: clearly everything which Lawrence achieved after the publication of *Sons and Lovers* was not in response to Freud, even though in the novels he was developing his views on human consciousness through his language. Furthermore, Lawrence's 'metaphysic' was not developed as a rejoinder to Freud. In regarding Freud as the major, indeed the only, point of reference in the books on the unconscious, to which he has frequent recourse, Hoffman fails to pay sufficient attention to this 'metaphysic'. That the Oedipal theory put Lawrence in a vulnerable position because of the character of his relationship with his mother is a separate issue. Neither is Lawrence 're-explaining Freud in terms of biology', which is Hoffman's assessment of Lawrence's discussion of the body in his books on the unconscious. In fact, Lawrence's attempts to renew a sense of the intrinsic relation of body and mind are not a retrograde step, a reversal of Freud's insights, but a sign of his holism, which is in our period gaining more and more credence.

The fact is that in assessing Lawrence's response to psychoanalysis the focus properly returns to language. This is the arena that he sets up in his books on the unconscious by writing them in such a self-consciously metaphorical mode: what is needed is a 'fantasia of' the unconscious rather than a discourse on it. Freud's discourse, metaphorical as it needs to be, falls short because in Lawrence's view it attempts to circumscribe that which ultimately refuses to be circumscribed. Hoffman's discourse is even less metaphorical than Freud's. Hoffman himself, we need to remember, is writing from within a Freudian, or indeed 'analytical', position, and is unable, therefore, to see Lawrence's point: we are able to perceive a certain 'critical blindness' on the part of Hoffman despite his assertions about metaphor. The fundamental difference must be that Hoffman (like Freud) regards metaphor as rhetorical, as a figure, whereas for Lawrence it is the flow of consciousness itself (but not the modernist 'stream'). Hoffman's praise for the 'series of metaphors' devised by Freud for the 'definition, description and analysis of the psychic economy' (*Freudianism and the Literary Mind*, p. 317) would draw Lawrence's fire because it realizes metaphor only as an expressive or discursive instrument. The critical horizon for Hoffman and Freud is interpretation; for Lawrence (and this is no surprise), creativity.

Hoffman (in an Aristotelian gesture) posits a language which is the standard, distinct from the verbal aberrations and ambiguities which reveal the speaker's unconscious preoccupations. The central argument of Lawrence's essays on the unconscious is that the unconscious is simply not quantifiable in such a way. The productive focus in Lawrence is on metaphor itself and not on 'metaphorical equivalents' as Hoffman calls them (p. 320). Freud's discourse is, for Lawrence, negatively symbolic.

The fluent and extensive metaphoricity of Lawrence's own essays on the unconscious must thus be seen as subverting the 'mechanistic' theories of the psychological apparatus expressed by Freud's metaphors, and the consequent construction of the psychoanalytic subject. Freud's error, Lawrence asserts, lies in constructing a theory at all, and sustaining it with 'static', essentially tragic, metaphors like the mythic paradigm represented by Oedipus. Criticizing this reliance on the purely conceptual, Lawrence argues that:

> All theory that has to be applied to life proves at last just another of these unconscious images which the repressed psyche uses as a substitute for life, and against which the psychoanalyst is fighting. The analyst wants to break all this image business, so that life can flow freely. But it is useless to try to do so by replacing in the unconscious another image – this time, the image, the fixed motive of the incest-complex.
>
> (*Phoenix*, p. 378)

As we shall see, this view will gain in currency. Nevertheless Lawrence cannot help – as he implicitly acknowledges – but use Freud's basic terms even while challenging the status of Freud's central theory as a theory. So it is that the works of Lawrence and Freud have a distinctive relation, both of distance and intimacy, to each other.

In *The Interpretation of Dreams* Freud not unexpectedly refers to other authorities as part of the scientific frame of reference for his key work. Lawrence makes a gesture of following the convention. In the Foreword to *Fantasia of the Unconscious* he writes:

> I am no 'scholar' of any sort. But I am very grateful to scholars for their sound work. I have found hints, suggestions for what I say here in all kinds of scholarly books, from the Yoga

and Plato and St. John the Evangel and the early Greek philosophers like Herakleitos down to Frazer and his 'Golden
Bough', and even Freud and Frobenius.

(*Fantasia of the Unconscious*, F&P, pp. 11–12)

The casualness with which Freud is remembered at the end is
itself significant. By listing the range of thought which must figure in *Fantasia of the Unconscious*, even if it does so impercep-
tibly, Lawrence is ostensibly discounting a fixed starting place
for his account. If *Fantasia of the Unconscious* has its origin in
these writings then its beginning is a perpetual drift between
diverse co-ordinates (which would include the first shorter book,
Psychoanalysis and the Unconscious). Lawrence's own travels are
interesting in this regard.

Travel itself is quite a literal dimension and for Lawrence it
both governed and interacted significantly with his reading –
his correspondence frequently shows that on his travels Lawrence's priorities included a library, or some other form of access to literature, with his friends sending books and other reading
matter *poste restante*. Geographical co-ordinates – Lawrence's place
in the world on any given journey – have, therefore, a significant relation to the ones he here proposes in the Foreword. At
these times Lawrence's reading matter was determined by a selec-
tion of texts from a diminished, at best limited, resource, with
chance playing an important part, although Rose Marie Burwell's
research confirms our sense of Lawrence reading profusely.[14] In
the travel-writing Lawrence of course starts with the literal journey,
but the experiences and landscapes he describes are meaningful
at a level other than the purely literal.

In this context a single point of origin as such cannot be identified – forewords are traditionally written last, after the body
of the text is completed, and 'first words' are seldom that.[15] It is
this observation which reveals the fragmented boundaries of *Fantasia of the Unconscious* itself – part Plato, part Freud, part Jung
and others – and shows the incomplete nature of borders generally. In as much as the ever receding references identified in the
Foreword actually defer a beginning, they also postpone the identification of a single subject of the essay. In *Fantasia of the Unconscious* Lawrence ostensibly has so many potential subjects that
one dominant theme is difficult to identify. Within the text he
has also plotted another apparently infinite set of co-ordinates

which he pursues in a multi-layered operation, continually resisting a traditional linear, traditionally logical, structure for his
work (this resistance is also a feature of *Women in Love*). We also
need to remember that Lawrence had begun to articulate his
understanding of 'unconscious' in the Foreword to *Sons and Lovers*,
'Study of Thomas Hardy', 'The Crown' and related texts, long
before he became critically aware of Freud's colonization of the
territory, so to speak. In this light, *Psychoanalysis and the Unconscious* and *Fantasia of the Unconscious* confirm much of Lawrence's
previous thought, but with the introduction of the anti-Freud
polemic which attracts so much of the critical attention.

This is to place *Fantasia of the Unconscious* in particular in relation to Freud's writing into a clearer perspective. The casual reference to Freud, yoked together with Frobenius, is not unexpected
but shows Lawrence denying him the central place that the titles
of these books, particularly the first, imply to the reader (despite apparent 'borrowing' from Jung's English titles, Jungian
practice is barely the issue). So, despite any suggestion of his
centrality, Freud is being marginalized. Inevitably we observe
the tone which Lawrence adopts when he does refer explicitly
to Freud. The opening pages of *Psychoanalysis and the Unconscious*
are declamatory. Freud is the 'psychiatric quack'; the 'psychoanalytic gentleman' (in other words the perfect *bourgeois*); Lawrence
identifies an unmistakeable 'Freud look' (clearly not visionary);
psychoanalysts are accused of subversively establishing themselves as healers – which smacks of mysticism – physicians, which
implies the authority of science, and finally apostles; their 'doctrine' has been subtly 'inoculated into us'; 'Psychoanalysis is out,
under a therapeutic disguise, to do away entirely with the moral
faculty in man' (*Psychoanalysis and the Unconscious*, F&P, pp. 201–
2). It sounds like a conspiracy theory. In *Fantasia of the Unconscious* Lawrence recants a little, opening with an apology to
psychoanalysis and qualifying his opinions. After this Freud is a
presence in the essay, but is infrequently named.

The conspicuous omission of Freud's name in a text which is
nominally a response to his ideas is matched with Lawrence's
quasi-biological description of the plexuses and eight dynamic
centres of feeling. This structure, described at the end of *Psychoanalysis and the Unconscious* as providing the 'great centres of
the unconscious' (p. 249), is now proposed implicitly as a substitute for Freud's system. With this comes Lawrence's message

that any dismissal of his 'centres', the infamous 'plexuses' and 'ganglia', should be accompanied by a comparable willingness to question the acceptance of Freud's 'myths'. The anatomical basis of consciousness described by Lawrence is a transformation of his negative conception of the 'self-conscious ego' as a 'framed gap' in 'The Crown': 'There are myriads of framed gaps, people, and a few timeless fountains, men and women . . . Myriads of framed gaps! Myriads of little egos' (in *Reflections*, p. 274). In *Fantasia of the Unconscious* the description of the embryonic cell in the womb forces the reader back to a comparable awareness of boundaries – we recognize primitive cell structure as a nucleus inside a space defined by a boundary – and, furthermore, reinforces Lawrence's enduring theme of individuality:

> And yet, from the moment of conception, the egg-cell repudiated complete adhesion and even communication, and asserted its individual integrity. The child in the womb, perfect a contact though it may have with the mother, is all the time also dynamically polarized against this contact. From the first moment, this relation in touch has a dual polarity, and, no doubt, a dual mode. It is a fourfold interchange of consciousness, the moment the egg-cell has made its two spontaneous divisions.
> (*Fantasia of the Unconscious*, F&P, p. 72)

Here the metaphors which build on conception and growth, underpinned by the language of dual structures, articulate Lawrence's real interest in the birth of the self. The diaphragm, organs, are further literal divisions, which yet speak to this preoccupation. In a study which privileges the linguistic over the philosophical, George Lakoff and Mark Johnson describe how 'container metaphors'are used to construct subjectivity:

> We are physical beings, bounded and set off from the rest of the world by the surface of our skins, and we experience the rest of the world as outside us. Each of us is a container, with a bounding surface and an in-out orientation. We project our own in–out orientation onto other physical objects that are bounded by surfaces. Thus we also view them as containers with an inside and an outside.
> (*Metaphors We Live By*, p. 29)

As they remind us, these concepts are so extensively entrenched in our thought and language that we tend to be unaware of the frequency with which we use them to articulate the relation between subject and world. Lawrence naturally uses them, but at the same time he is absorbed in questioning the in/out model, a questioning which is the basis of his holism. He can insist that the individual is unique in the world by repeating his formula 'I am I', but he also emphasizes the individual's integral relation or connection with the sensible world (a theme of the travel writing).

The psycho-biology described in Lawrence's essays functions both literally and metaphorically; indeed this is its force. It need not be taken as analogous to Freud's early concentration on positivist science. Indeed, the origin of Lawrence's anatomical plan is fragmented and imprecise: 'Authorized science tells you that this first great plexus, this all-potent nerve-centre of consciousness and dynamic life-activity, is a sympathetic centre' (*Fantasia of the Unconscious*, F&P, p. 28). The authors of this 'science' are not named, but the implication is that they are many and various, so once again origin is defined in terms of a drift between co-ordinates. This is also to omit Freud in particular from the gallery of authors, or authorizers, and this ellipsis becomes a legitimate subject of *Fantasia of the Unconscious*. Lawrence is both focused enough discursively on Freud to disagree with him – inasmuch as Freud's, and Lawrence's, interest in psychoanalysis apparently provides the motivation for writing the book – and capable of omitting that body of theory, and in doing so gainsaying it, almost altogether.

It is almost impossible, given what we think we know of Lawrence's emotional history, or given the attention paid to the details of his family relations, not to speculate how far his dismissal of psychoanalysis is anchored in the fear of being himself unmasked, and that *Fantasia of the Unconscious* in particular constitutes an unconsciously constructed rhetoric of fear.

Lawrence was dismissive of Alfred Booth Kuttner's vulgar psychoanalytical reading of *Sons and Lovers* in 1916.[16] This lack of enthusiasm on Lawrence's part, combined with the tone of his books on the unconscious, is grounded in a dismissal of the Oedipus complex as a psychic structure, or at the very least an attempt to reinterpret it. In the tenth chapter of *Fantasia of the Unconscious*, called 'Parent Love', Lawrence's initial strategy is to hit at what he regards as the 'idealism' of love between the parents and the child (which Freud also reassesses), and particularly the love of mother and son. In this essay he concedes the notion of infant sexuality, but in a way radically different from that encountered by psychoanalysis. It seems that Lawrence takes what he terms Freud's 'conclusion of incest' (*Fantasia*, F&P, p. 121) seriously, but insistently he changes the emphasis to what he calls 'dynamic *spiritual* incest' (p. 120) which describes the familiar Lawrentian thesis of an overwhelming mother's love for her son, causing the arrest in the child of its own sex.[17] The striking thing about Lawrence's 'fantasy' of biology, to which he resorts here as elsewhere, is that it asserts a considerable legislative weight. As Lawrence locates real issues like parent–child relationships within his 'anatomical' model it takes on the role of a censor. In resorting to it all other possibilities are discounted and in effect eliminated, particularly those offered up by 'authorized science'. In particular, Lawrence's sense of the wilful 'spiritual' love of the mother causes in the child 'an exaggerated sensitiveness alternating with a sort of helpless fury; and we have delicate frail children with nerves or with strange whims' (p. 118).

Inevitably one wonders how much this is a portrait of the artist himself, feeling singled out and exposed by Freud's Oedipal theory and its implications. In as much as Freud has provided the terms by which Lawrence's fiction, and by implication Lawrence himself, can be judged Lawrence might well feel that even if the Oedipal theory does not apply to him Freud has somehow made it look as though it does, and the response of Alfred Booth Kuttner, who might well be representative of a substantial body of opinion given the popularity of Freud in some quarters at that time (perhaps more in the United States than in Britain), is proof of this. It is in this highly personal context that Lawrence himself is in danger of feeling given away, and the books on the unconscious may be in part an attempt to resist this degree of exposure. His friends persisted in regarding the fiction as symptomatic: Mabel Dodge Luhan, familiar with Freud's theories although not as familiar perhaps as Frieda Lawrence, subscribed to the view that Lawrence had a 'mother-complex'.[18] Frieda, at an early stage in their relationship, in a letter to Edward Garnett, described Lawrence's love for his mother as Oedipal:

⸺ missed the point in 'Paul Morel'. He really loved
⸺ore than any body, even with his other women,
⸺rt of Oedipus, his mother must have been adorable
⸺ing P.M. again, reads bits to me and we fight like
⸺r it, he is so often beside the point 'but "I'll learn
him to ⸺ a toad" as the boy said as he stamped on the toad.'
(*Letters*, I, p. 449)

Critics have plundered the sources to show Lawrence's resistance to Freud, despite the fact that the Oedipus complex is, or
was, frequently identified as the 'sickness' being shed in *Sons
and Lovers*, Lawrence later finding it necessary to resist Freud's
terms. In *Fantasia of the Unconscious* Lawrence can be seen trying
to reclaim certain terms, specifically 'unconscious', from the
Freudians: other psychoanalytical designations he dismissed as
'so many other catch-words' (*Fantasia*, F&P, p. 129). This theme
of resistance is clearly written in to the novels: Rupert Birkin
could be regarded, in his defensive relations with Ursula
Brangwen, as a resisting device for the author. Birkin's resistance to Ursula recalls Lawrence's documented opposition to Frieda
in the early stages of their marriage, during the writing of 'The
Sisters' and as it became two novels. This theme of resistance is
double-edged. Lawrence's resistance to Freudian structures ap-
plied to his work of fiction need not be because of the suggestion of an autobiographical project focusing on his own neurosis.
An alternative view repudiates Lawrence's blind self-identifica-
tion with Paul Morel, and views the novel as demonstrating
Lawrence's critical distance from the central emotional relationship organizing *Sons and Lovers*, Lawrence having already come
to his *own* conclusions about mother–son relationships. He could,
after all, write with confidence to Edward Garnett in 1913
suggesting that his relationship to his mother was David Garnett's
problem (*Letters*, I, pp. 526–7). Much of Lawrence's resistance,
then, is to the eclipsing of his own insights by Freud's. If Lawrence
had a model in *Sons and Lovers* it is most likely to have been
literary, Hamlet, for instance, or straight from Sophocles rather
than Freud. His other works of fiction do not represent a mother–
son problematic in the central figure with whom Lawrence might
well identify, yet Lawrence is focused enough to examine its effects
in other characters, for instance the David Garnett and Harold
Hobson figures, Terry and Stanley, of *Mr. Noon*.

Still on the diagnostic theme, and without wishing to exaggerate Kuttner's importance, it is worth noting that in his concluding remarks to his essay on *Sons and Lovers* he writes of the 'cure' which the artist effects in himself in writing:

> For Mr. Lawrence has escaped the destructive fate that dogs the hapless Paul by the grace of expression: out of the dark struggles of his own soul he has emerged as a triumphant artist. In every epoch the soul of the artist is sick with the problems of his generation. He cures himself by expression in his art.
>
> ('A Freudian Appreciation', in Salgado, 1969, p. 94)

Kuttner could not have known of Lawrence's now famous statement about the artist shedding his sicknesses in art (in a letter to Arthur McLeod, 26 October 1913, Lawrence wrote 'I felt you had gone off from me a bit, because of *Sons and Lovers*. But one sheds ones [sic] sicknesses in books – repeats and presents again ones [sic] emotions, to be master of them', *Letters*, II, p. 90), but his remark is an interesting trace of Lawrence's deeper idea, even if the reviewer appears to give the artist a *social* consciousness, 'In every epoch the soul of the artist is sick with the problems of *his generation*' (emphasis added). Kuttner at any rate focuses on literature as a privileged order of talking-cure. His position is that Lawrence has, independently of Freud, shown Freud's conclusions to be true. Freud himself famously finds in literature his own theory in place as it were, and seeming to confirm, if not to legitimize, his own thought. As he says, 'It sometimes happens that the sharp eye of a creative writer has an analytic realization of the process of transformation of which he is habitually no more than the tool' (SE, IV, p. 246).

ANTI-OEDIPAL

Kuttner is perhaps too close to Freud or too unfamiliar with Lawrence, judging him on the basis of his third novel as autobiographical, to know how to read him, believing Lawrence to have had such an 'analytic realization' of a Freudian theme. Convinced by Freud's models, Kuttner is hardly in a position to examine what has since been seen as the 'anti-Oedipal' drift in Lawrence.[19]

So far I have drawn attention to the complex relation which Lawrence's writing on the body unconscious has to Freud's conceptions. I have also underlined Lawrence's rejection of Freud and have qualified this by drawing attention to his possible fear of being exposed, unmasked. The genuinely important issue for Lawrence, however, is how Freud's evaluation of human relations, and particularly sexuality, differs from his own. It is time to see exactly how radical Lawrence's objections to Freud were, quite apart from how Freudian conceptions might apply to him. This involves a move from the 'content' of Freud's thought to the central question of 'discourse'.

In my view, Deleuze and Guattari have a point when they argue that Freud's 'conception of sexuality' appals Lawrence exactly because it is just that, a conception, 'an idea that "reason" imposes on the unconscious and introduces into the passional sphere, and is not by any means a formation of this sphere' (*Anti-Oedipus*, p. 323). In a study which, written from within the domain of psychoanalysis, challenges the status of Freud, reassessing him as one of the 'poor technicians of desire . . . who would subjugate the multiplicity of desire to the twofold law of structure and lack' (Michel Foucault, in the preface to *Anti-Oedipus*, pp. xii–xiii), Lawrence is cited as a radical and innovative thinker and one of the first to identify the Oedipal model as both limited and censorious.

Of the two conceptions which Lawrence is seen to challenge, the first is the Oedipal trinity, 'the holy family' as he ironically calls it in *Fantasia of the Unconscious* (Chapter 2), also evoked in the Foreword to *Sons and Lovers*, a description which Deleuze and Guattari revive for one of their chapter-headings (*Anti-Oedipus*, pp. 51–137). The second is the tyranny of the Phallus as 'the despotic signifier prompting the most miserable struggle' (p. 351). It is precisely this 'tyranny' which is the basis of what Lawrence calls 'sex-hatred'. His books on the unconscious might, then, raise questions about whether, for Lawrence, the self-styled champion of 'phallic-consciousness', the Phallus is the first term.

Deleuze and Guattari are with Lawrence inasmuch as they agree that Freud's theory of sexuality is predicated on a negative theory of sex which inhabits, indeed constitutes, the unconscious. Responding to Lawrence's books on the unconscious, they speak for themselves:

Let us keep D.H. Lawrence's reaction to psychoanalysis in mind, and never forget it. In Lawrence's case, at least, his reservations with regard to psychoanalysis did not stem from terror at having discovered what real sexuality was. But he had the impression – the purely instinctive impression – that psychoanalysis was shutting sexuality up in a bizarre sort of box painted with bourgeois motifs, in a kind of rather repugnant artificial triangle, thereby stifling the whole of sexuality as production of desire so as to recast it along entirely different lines, making of it a "dirty little secret," the dirty little family secret, a private theater rather than the fantastic factory of Nature and Production. Lawrence had the impression that sexuality possessed more power or more potentiality than that. And though psychoanalysis may perhaps have managed to 'disinfect the dirty little secret,' the dreary, dirty little secret of Oedipus-the-modern-tyrant benefited very little from having been thus disinfected.

(*Anti-Oedipus*, p. 49)

This identifies the grounds of Lawrence's dissatisfaction with psychoanalytical modes of enquiry. Having done so, Deleuze and Guattari respond as much to Lawrence's language as to the challenge which it embodies. In the statement to follow they alight on Lawrence's metaphor of the 'flow' of human relations, and proceed to quote extensively from the essay 'We Need One Another' (printed in *Phoenix*, pp. 188–95):

Lawrence shows in a profound way that sexuality, including chastity, is a matter of flows, an infinity of different and even contrary flows. . . . Lawrence attacks the poverty of the immutable identical images, the figurative roles that are so many tourniquets cutting off the flows of sexuality: 'fiancée, mistress, wife, mother' – one could just as easily add 'homosexuals, heterosexuals,' etc. – all these roles are distributed by the Oedipal triangle, father-mother-me, a representative ego thought to be defined in terms of the father-mother representations, by fixation, regression, assumption, sublimation – and all of that according to what rule? The law of the great Phallus that no one possesses, the despotic signifier prompting the most miserable struggle, a common absence for all the reciprocal exclusions where the flows dry up, drained by bad conscience and *ressentiment*. '. . . sticking a woman on a pedestal, or the reverse, sticking her beneath notice; or making a "model" house-wife of her, or a "model" mother, or a "model" help-meet. All mere devices for avoiding any contact with her. A woman is not a "model" anything. She is not even a distinct and defi-nite personality. . . . A woman is a strange soft vibration on the air, going forth unknown and unconscious, and seeking a vibration of response. Or else she is a discordant, jarring, painful vibration, going forth and hurting everyone within range. And a man the same.' Let's not be too quick to make light of the pantheism of flows present in such texts as this: it is not easy to de-oedipalize even nature, even landscapes, to the extent that Lawrence could.

(*Anti-Oedipus*, p. 351)[20]

Lawrence's characters do not finish up being merely these 'rep-resentative egos', and to many readers who want something more reductive than Lawrence offers this is a considerable problem.[21] The aspect of the 'metaphysic' being identified here is that which evaluates sexuality as more dynamic than is allowed in the models which more usually represent it. The metaphor of 'flow', which is fundamental to Lawrence and has an important status in the lexicon of his 'metaphysic', is rightly seen as challenging the status of the individual as a subject determined by the Oedipal drama, created within a psychosexual configuration based on the fam-ily. The subject in Lawrence is the constantly (re)created subject. Metaphors of 'flow' in Lawrence embody a linguistic and con-ceptual challenge to Freud's explanations as based on repressive structures which have their basis in an *algebraic* mind-set. One commentator associates Lawrence's language of 'flows' with the feminine;[22] the language of vibrations may owe something to the scientific discourse of Lawrence's day.[23] Whatever its origins, devising psychological types or consigning individuals to cer-tain sex roles goes against this understanding which refuses to concede ground to the subject's past as deterministic. The indi-vidual, for Lawrence, is principally responsive as s/he inhabits the present moment, rather than determined by oedipalization, for instance. Rather than constructing a theorized 'housing' as he perceives Freud to be doing, in the words of Deleuze and Guattari 'the framework of the "dirty little secret"' (*Anti-Oedipus*, p. 350), Lawrence has placed the emphasis metaphorically on figures which escape, in his words, 'algebraic' designations. His figures privilege motion and mobility, principally 'tides', 'efflux', and the operations of these as *process*. The point about Lawrence's 'flows' and 'vibrations' is that they do not constitute a rigid explanatory model, a fixed psychic structure: in fact they try to obliterate any such rationalist paradigms. In his mature work Lawrence's language, and this is the real point, carries the weight of this metaphysical recognition.

So it is that Deleuze and Guattari understand much better than Hoffman, who stays at the doctrinal level, the importance of Lawrence's language in his assessment of the premises of psychoanalysis. If it were otherwise they would not have responded with such immediacy to his dissenting language of 'tides' and 'flows' in his analysis of desire (where it emerges as such), as it erupts in his own metaphors of (the) unconscious. This concentration on Lawrence's metaphors as at once the vehicle for his own thought and critique of psychoanalytic models and their cultural implications, carries this discussion to its next stage; to the particular metaphoricity of Lawrence's books on the unconscious.

METAPHOR AND 'METAPHYSIC' IN LAWRENCE'S BOOKS ON THE UNCONSCIOUS

Psychoanalysis and the Unconscious and *Fantasia of the Unconscious* are among the least discussed of Lawrence's prose works. *Fantasia of the Unconscious*, written second, is commonly printed first because of the British publisher's view, at least recorded in the modern Penguin edition, that it 'represents Lawrence's developed views on the subject, which are more tentatively outlined in *Psychoanalysis and the Unconscious*' (publisher's note, F&P, [p. 10]). In actual fact *Psychoanalysis and the Unconscious* is not as provisional as this suggests.

The evidence is that Lawrence found writing the longer essay, *Fantasia of the Unconscious*, a valuable experience, that it was of considerable importance to him, and that, although subject to revision, it progressed quite quickly in comparison with the novels most of which were radically redrafted either in their entirety, or in large part, until the appropriate form emerged.[24] The fact that the later text is called a 'fantasia' throws the form, as well as the contents, into relief.[25] 'Fantasia' is an old word appropriated by Lawrence. As we know, it was a word that went 'lugubriously to [Lawrence's] bowels' in the drapery shops of the Via Mequeda, Palermo, as the Lawrences made their way to Sardinia (*D.H. Lawrence and Italy*, 'Sea and Sardinia', p. 19). Largely because of Freud, 'the unconscious' now bore to Lawrence implications of a self-indulgent and reductive modernity that he despised. If the word 'fantasia' has negative implications in his later discursive writing, in the text of *Fantasia of the Unconscious* it does not significantly figure. Yet coupled strangely with 'the unconscious' in his title, like 'fantasy' in some mouths it reflects derogatively on the products of the mind – the 'foam' of the over-heated, over-conscious, imagination.

'Fantasia' gives rise to 'fantasy' and 'phantasmagoria' with their suggestions of unrestrained creativity: the highly individualistic is privileged, the imaginary and dream. Although historically 'fancy' was eventually distinguished from 'imagination', 'fantasy' retained its Greek meaning, *phantasiā* signifying the imaginative faculty. Both 'fantasy' and 'fantastic' retain their senses of the extraordinary made visible, and 'phantasm' and 'phantasmagoria' can be heard echoing in the modern word. These meanings exert a linguistic pressure on Lawrence's book. Certainly the sense which some of them bear of mental images, dream images, as 'fanciful' and hallucinatory, accidentally stimulated by external factors and hardly worth serious attention, refers satirically to Freud's analyses of dreams as part of his scientific project, and to his plotting of the unconscious. This said, one can speculate whether Lawrence in a self-critical, or ironic, mood, found it appealing that 'fantasia' eventually gave a name to a literary project which demonstrates his preference for his own 'fantastic' projections given the cosmology, the 'biological psyche' and the discoursing on the family which underpins that work.

Fantasia has also come to signify a musical composition, particularly one with an impromptu, improvised form. Fantasia, therefore, refers to a form where form itself is subsidiary to caprice and desire. The musical usage does have implications for the form of *Fantasia of the Unconscious* with its multiple points of entry and false starts, and the sense that Lawrence wishes himself to communicate, describing the act of writing it, that it is an impromptu and largely spontaneous composition. Obviously there are many modernist instances of texts which explore the interface between music and language without being fantasias: Mallarmé's *Un coup de dés* is one example. Lawrence's *The Trespasser* could also be cited as a text which makes structural and thematic uses of musical allusions, although it is by no means a fantasia. Of course, Lawrence is familiar with a Romantic tradition which asserts a profound relation between music, like dream, and the representation of the unconscious, but he would resist the tendency, evident in Schopenhauer for instance, to establish a hierarchy which accords music a particular value, and the word a lower one. While Freud persistently gives 'phantasy' (*Phantasie*) different and distinctive inflections, Lawrence would respond to the broad conception negatively, as he did to the Freudian notion of dream, particularly given the emphasis on desire and *Wünschphantasie*, because of what Freud does with the underpinning premises of prohibition and repression.[26]

The title of the longer book, then, presents us with two terms in a tense relation to each other; 'fantasia' with its emphasis on the impromptu and free-form, and 'unconscious' defined by psychoanalysis as something determined. Lawrence's book occurs in the space opened up by this tension, or contradiction. This alignment of unexpected terms in such a privileged place as the title is significant not least because it is linked to the important question of oxymoron in Lawrence. Here, it is enough to note how the juxtaposition of 'fantasia' and 'unconscious' in the title represents a challenge to the determinism of Freud, as Lawrence saw it, in the former's assertion that the unconscious could be contained within a set of rational designations. In using the word 'fantasia' Lawrence is suggesting the impossibility of organizing the unconscious within what he regards from the first as meanly iconic and restrictive structures. He is not alone: even given their differences (which are considerable), among his contemporaries, the Dadaists and Surrealists, at least, were exploring the relationship between a spontaneous creativity and the unconscious.[27] Crucially, Lawrence touches on this relationship in the references to his 'demon' in the Preface to *Collected Poems*: 'A young man is afraid of his demon and puts his hand over the demon's mouth sometimes and speaks for him. And the things the young man says are very rarely poetry. So I have tried to let the demon say his say, and to remove the passages where the young man intruded' (*Complete Poems*, p. 28). This is a nice comment both on the value of spontaneity in Lawrence's work, and on the mature interventionist poet. It also throws the supposed spontaneity of *Fantasia of the Unconscious* into relief, so that it begins to look like a programmatized example of literary spontaneity. However, the promise of the title is that Lawrence will draw attention back to the inventive dynamics of language.

Structurally, it remains to be seen whether or not 'fantasia' is an appropriate description of the form that Lawrence's longer book takes. Like *Women in Love, Fantasia of the Unconscious* is more spatial than temporal in structure. Even so, it is less inclined than the novel to progress by degrees towards a conclusion. It draws to a literal end with its fifteenth chapter by commenting on the 'anarchical conclusions' to which 'the Jewish mind insidiously drives us' (p. 181). This gives way to a long meditation on the interaction between men and women in which the focus is on (masculine) power. The chapter sequence of the book seems quite arbitrary. More important than the structure, however, is its language. Two groups of chapters out of the entire fifteen seem to be more closely related thematically than others: an interest in, and critique of, origins is recorded in 'First Glimmerings of Mind' and 'First Steps in Education' in which Lawrence elaborates on his account of child development and education; 'Parent Love', 'The Vicious Circle', 'Litany of Exhortations', nominally on love. There are two acknowledged 'digressions', early on in 'Trees and Babies and Papas and Mamas' – where the focus is partially on presence, a central question, if not to say quality, in Lawrence's writing – and the entire chapter called 'Education and Sex in Man, Woman and Child'. 'Cosmology' is a chapter that sidesteps the general deliberation on human consciousness, and refers back to themes articulated in his essay 'The Two Principles'.[28]

So, to all intents and purposes *Fantasia of the Unconscious* is a collection of essays on a few related themes, the principal one being that referred to as 'child consciousness', with Lawrence concentrating broadly on the biological development of the child and beyond that on family relations. 'The Holy Family', title of the second chapter (as well as of one of Lawrence's paintings), is the trinity of father, mother and child which comprises the basic point of reference throughout the essays, and is also a point of focus for his critique of Freud. Orthodox psychology and conventional social mores provide only rudimentary frames of reference, since Lawrence is highly critical of both. 'Love' and 'knowledge' are familiar themes generally for Lawrence. In both *Psychoanalysis and the Unconscious* and *Fantasia of the Unconscious* he returns to first things in order to explain what he regards as the perversion of these qualities in modern understanding. Orthodox psychology and Freudian psychoanalysis are implicated in that perversion. Tightly focused on the developing individual, but in a mood of resistance to the available discourses and models for explaining subjectivity, Lawrence constructs his own systems – which come to be seen as highly personal metaphors continually unfolding in the course of the essays – plotting a middle way between the body and the psyche, unnecessarily polarized, in Lawrence's view, by Freud.

As for its style, *Fantasia of the Unconscious* is one of several extended works, including *Aaron's Rod* and *Mr. Noon*, where Lawrence continually makes use of direct address, referring to 'dear reader', 'gentle reader', and so on. This is a tendency of particular consequence in Lawrence's writing, as it is a means by which he inverts, and subverts, a literary convention which usually creates a sense of intimacy and community, a feeling of solidarity, with the reader. Lawrence uses the convention to attack the reader and to disturb complacency, often by berating the otherwise passive audience for the smugness of its assumptions. The most extreme examples arise in *Mr. Noon*, as I said in my previous chapter: .

> And so, gentle reader – ! But why the devil should I always *gentle-reader* you. You've been *gentle reader* for this last two hundred years. Time you too had a change. Time you became rampageous reader, ferrocious reader, surly, rabid reader, hellcat of a reader, a tartar, a termagant, a tanger – And so, hellcat of a reader, let me tell you, with a flea in your ear, that all the ring-dove sonata you'll get out of me you've got already, and for the rest you've got to hear the howl of the tom-cats like myself and the she-cats like yourself, going it tooth and nail.
>
> (*Mr. Noon*, pp. 204–5)

So, quite apart from the other signals this sends, this diatribe demonstrates Lawrence's strategic use of a convention. In the Foreword to *Fantasia of the Unconscious*, he sets about dissuading the 'generality' of readers and critics from reading any further.

This, in accord with a rhetorical tradition, encourages the reader to stay with the book. Such gestures make us, if we are already alert to Lawrence's attunement to the relation between language and power, think whether his devices are in fact merely 'rhetorical' and ornamental or whether they are not really intrinsic to his thought.

The shorter and earlier book, *Psychoanalysis and the Unconscious*, is divided into six relatively concise chapters, which rehearse the principal themes of *Fantasia of the Unconscious*, although it is erroneous to regard the former merely as an adumbration of the latter. The first two chapters represent a direct attack on Freud's ideas but thereafter, as I have said, Freud disappears. The content of the book is essentially the same as that of *Fantasia of the Unconscious* but is dealt with much more economically: the expansion in the second essay actually adds very little. Certainly for my purposes *Psychoanalysis and the Unconscious* is much more tightly focused than *Fantasia of the Unconscious*, and much richer in what it communicates about Lawrence's thought on language. *Fantasia of the Unconscious* is, in contrast, subject to genuine repetitions and narrative looseness. In terms of language and content *Psychoanalysis and the Unconscious* would seem to be the more conventional essay, but its significance lies in the fact that a close reading shows it to be the more radically *un*conventional of the two. Although they can be, and have been, overlooked, the central statements on metaphor, as I shall show, are to be found in *Psychoanalysis and the Unconscious*.

Critics are increasingly showing how Lawrence challenges logocentric modes in his writing. This is a response to the linguistic mobility of Lawrence's texts while recognizing that there are certain appointed themes that direct his thought. In the fourth chapter of *Fantasia of the Unconscious*, 'Trees and Babies and Papas and Mamas', which I discussed briefly in Chapter 3, Lawrence refers to his own physical presence, his environment and the act of writing the text which we are reading. Far from being presented as simply a conscious act, writing is described as a 'forgetting' (p. 43). This can be compared to his comments on his hand as it writes the essay 'Why the Novel Matters', apparently without the intrusion of consciousness, or conscious handling. It is a passage which recalls Nietzsche's remark that 'we lack any sensitive organs' by which to perceive the 'inner world':[29]

Why should I look at my hand, as it so cleverly writes these words, and decide that it is a mere nothing compared to the mind that directs it? Is there really any huge difference between my hand and my brain? – or my mind? My hand is alive, it flickers with a life of its own. It meets all the strange universe, in touch, and learns a vast number of things, and knows a vast number of things. My hand, as it writes these words, slips gaily along, jumps like a grasshopper to dot an i, feels the table rather cold, gets a little bored if I write too long, has its own rudiments of thought, and is just as much me as is my brain, my mind or my soul. Why should I imagine that there is a me which is more me than my hand is? Since my hand is absolutely alive, me alive.

('Why the Novel Matters', in *Study of Thomas Hardy and Other Essays*, p. 193)

The orthodox duality of mind and body is here, characteristically, rejected completely. We are being asked to regard the physical hand which writes as more than a mere appendage of the mind which thinks: 'The whole is greater than the part' (*Hardy*, p. 195). The hand, a sentient 'organ', *knows*, a word which Lawrence sometimes italicizes because all the meanings which meet in the word give it special significance for him, but it learns and knows in a way different from the eye, for instance (we are reminded of the emphasis placed in Lawrence on blindness as positive, and Lawrence's preoccupation with touch). Lawrence's interest here is less in the definite properties of objects in the external world, 'the strange universe', than in the hand. The physicality of the hand appeals to Lawrence: the eye, for instance, does not do the 'knowing' in the way the hand does; the eye cannot 'reach out' in the same way as the hand; its physicality is more neutral to Lawrence (less real) than the physicality of the hand. Lawrence, looking down, can see his hand in front of him as physical, as flesh, but additionally regards it as having more than a simply mechanical function. After all, hands, to which there are numerous references not least in Lawrence's early fiction,[30] are 'in touch' both with the world of things and, in writing, with the creative levels within the writer. The 'flow' of writing and language is the 'flow' of thought. Lawrence is after a kind of physicality which is not simply or solely fleshly, corporeal.[31]

Hands figure in Lawrence: the longer passage contrasts, for

instance, with a passing remark about Clara Dawes, watched by Paul Morel, as she makes lace in one of numerous references to hands in *Sons and Lovers*: 'And her arm moved mechanically, that should never have been subdued to a mechanism' (*Sons and Lovers*, p. 304); or the reference to Gudrun's 'perfectly subtle and intelligent hands' which, 'greedy for knowledge', feel Gerald's face in the semi-darkness of 'Death and Love' (*Women in Love*, p. 332). This both mirrors and contrasts with the touch of Ursula on Birkin in the previous chapter, 'Excurse' (*Women in Love*, p. 314; p. 316). Hands reach out to the 'unknown', the undefined, as language does. Lawrence's meditation underlines the percipient and intuitive quality of composition, with the focus sharply on the subliminal dimension of the writing act: the novels, coming 'unwatched', are not formally constructed in accordance with a theory, and in the act of creation the body (blood-conscious) is not separable from the mind. In this example, presence, that entirely positive quality for Lawrence, is given a fundamentally positive connection with writing and language.

The passage quoted from 'Why the Novel Matters' embodies Lawrence's preoccupation with presence. Regarding presence, 'living' for Lawrence must be acknowledged as the richness, specialness or realness of inhabiting the present moment, like the moment of writing. Presence, for Lawrence, is not addressed philosophically: it is the quality of being dynamically present, and, inasmuch as this is one of Lawrence's preoccupations, so the word 'presence' is invested with a particular personal and 'metaphysical' significance in his work. The focus can usefully be shifted to another description of composition. In 'Trees and Babies and Papas and Mamas' the trees of the Black Forest, where Lawrence sits writing *Fantasia*, are characterized by their presentness.[32] He describes them as 'so much bigger than me, so much stronger in life, prowling silent around. . . . Today only trees, and leaves, and vegetable presences' (p. 42). He adds 'They have no faces, no minds and bowels: only deep lustful roots stretching in earth, and vast, lissome life in air, and primeval individuality' (pp. 45–6). If this is the living tree then the dead tree, in the familiar instrumental form of pencil and paper, is no less present, and is implicated early on in the writing both of the passage and the book. Indeed, Lawrence describes himself writing as 'a fool, sitting by a grassy wood-road with a pencil and a book, hoping to write more about that baby. . . . so am I usually stroked into forgetfulness, and into scribbling this book. My tree-book, really' (pp. 42–3). This is a passage in which priority is clearly given once again to writing and presence, but underpinned by that idiosyncratically Lawrentian 'metaphysic'. For Lawrence, human consciousness, that is to say 'verbal consciousness' and consciousness at the deepest non-verbal levels, is often a matter of being purely present. In another context he writes:

> Man struggles with his unborn needs and fulfilment. New unfoldings struggle up in torment in him, as buds struggle forth the midst of a plant. Any man of real individuality tries to know and to understand what is happening, even in himself, as he goes along. This struggle for verbal consciousness should not be left out in art. It is not the superimposition of a theory. *It is the passionate struggle into conscious being.*
>
> (Foreword, *Women in Love*, pp. 485–6)[33]

The English tradition, literary or philosophical, does not give Lawrence the articulation he needs. His uniqueness very largely hangs on this: the language which we can call 'Lawrentian' constitutes a radically different poetics of presence than any he might find in his own culture. Wordsworth might be a comparable figure, but essentially Lawrence's difference underpins the present study. Lawrence is certainly the only modernist writer in English to have a 'metaphysic' that even comes close to being articulated (that is to say, in full). The question of metaphor is so central in reading Lawrence precisely because his 'metaphysic' is rooted in language. In Lawrence especially we can see that metaphor and 'metaphysic' are not separable. 'Metaphysic' is a word which, in relation to Lawrence, should perhaps be kept in inverted commas. The inverted commas, written or 'spoken', show that the word has its own logic; Lawrence's 'metaphysic' both gives rise to, and is delivered by the language of his texts, to the point where the inside/outside polarity of metaphor/'metaphysic' can be dismantled. Often quoted remarks in the Foreword to *Fantasia of the Unconscious* suggest that the philosophy comes after the fiction: 'This pseudo-philosophy of mine – "pollyanalytics", as one of my respected critics might say – is deduced from the novels and poems, not the reverse' (p. 15). Yet there is also the argument that without it the fiction could not be:

And finally, it seems to me that even art is utterly dependent on philosophy: or if you prefer it, on a metaphysic. The metaphysic or philosophy may not be anywhere very accurately stated and may be quite unconscious, in the artist, yet it is a metaphysic that governs men at the time, and is by all men more or less comprehended, and lived. Men live and see according to some gradually developing and gradually withering vision. This vision exists also as a dynamic idea or metaphysics – exists first as such. Then it is unfolded into life and art.
            (Foreword to *Fantasia of the Unconscious*, F&P, p. 15)

Stating the case, and this dictum famously underpins Lawrence's best literary criticism notably in *Studies in Classic American Literature*, Lawrence himself is unable to pull away from the fundamental and complex interaction between the two domains of 'art' and 'metaphysic', poetry and thought. What is important here is the Nietzschean–Lawrentian–Heideggerean idea that metaphor is not only rhetorical-ornamental but is a mode of thought, among other modes. This is not the same as saying metaphor is a tool by which we learn to communicate, but that metaphor is thought, does the thinking, often by breaking away from what one commentator has called 'the official models for analogy'.[34] Such a breaking away means a return to the Poetic. Amongst myriad levels of language, indeed, giving rise to them, metaphor enables a thinking further.

Metaphor itself has been through many transformations since Aristotle consigned a classical theory of metaphor to writing, thereby establishing it as authoritative. I do not suggest that Lawrence has a *theory* of metaphor, but his collapsing of the boundaries between metaphor and 'metaphysic' is the single most important key to an understanding of his language, and hence his 'metaphysic'. The fact is that Lawrence's books on the unconscious spring their first surprise by being so unexpectedly and self-consciously metaphorical. Without adopting Allan Ingram's attitude that, in contrast to the majority of his modernist peers, 'With Lawrence, there is no playfulness . . . for Lawrence, language is there to convey what needs to be conveyed, not to be contemplated and enjoyed as a field of play' (*The Language of D.H. Lawrence*, p. 17), it can be argued that what we have in Lawrence is a continual 'play of language', one which displays a kind of *jouissance*, a joy in metaphor.[35]

These observations may be of use in confronting and dismantling the claim made by another critic that Lawrence's books on
the unconscious constitute 'the last, rather shrivelled attempt of
an author to imitate a grand romantic system of metaphors'.[36]
That this view of an exhausted system is debateable is evinced
in the first instance by *Psychoanalysis and the Unconscious*. There
are passages in *Psychoanalysis and the Unconscious* which speak
both to and about the role and function of metaphor in Lawrence
and which, given that they are not obviously awarded any special
status within the text, are easily overlooked. Considered apart
from the whole, however, they potentially transform our understanding of the relation between metaphor and 'metaphysic' in
his writing, and suggest the importance of the language and mode
of the books on the unconscious in assessing Lawrence as a poet-
thinker. The broad theme of the fifth chapter of *Psychoanalysis
and the Unconscious*, called 'The Lover and the Beloved', is the
developing consciousness. Within this context Lawrence writes:

> It is not merely a metaphor, to call the cardiac plexus the sun,
> the Light. It is a metaphor in the first place, because the
> conscious effluence which proceeds from this first upper cen-
> tre in the breast goes forth and plays upon its external object,
> as phosphorescent waves might break upon a ship and reveal
> its form. The transferring of the objective knowledge to the
> psyche is almost the same as vision. It is root-vision. It happens
> before the eyes open. It is the first tremendous mode of *appre-
> hension*, still dark, but moving towards light. It is the eye in
> the breast. Psychically, it is basic objective apprehension. Dy-
> namically, it is love, devotional, administering love.
>
> (*Psychoanalysis and the Unconscious*, F&P, p. 236)

If it is not merely metaphor to call the cardiac plexus the sun or
'Light' then is it in some way literal, and has Lawrence got a
special investment in distinguishing the metaphorical from the
literal? The capitalization of 'Light' suggests that some distinction is being made between them. When he talks about metaphor
'in the first place' can we say whether Lawrence has a logical
order or an evolutionary order in mind? It is, by virtue of the
questions it raises, a passage which focuses some of the most
central issues ever addressed by Lawrence. As a figure, the
phosphorescent wave resembles the rainbow: the light is not 'in'

the breast, nor is it 'in' the wave. Like the rainbow, the meta-phor of the phosphorescent wave is dependent on *viewpoint*; and on a conjunction of elements, or factors. The figure as a figure also describes how Lawrence wants to be read. It recalls the distinc-tion made between allegory and symbol in *Apocalypse*:

> Allegory can always be explained: and explained away. The true symbol defies all explanation, so does the true myth. You can give meanings to either – you will never explain them away. Because symbol and myth do not affect us only mentally, they move the deep emotional centres every time. The great quality of the mind is finality. The mind 'understands', and there's an end of it.
>
> But the emotional consciousness of man has a life and movement quite different from the mental consciousness. The mind knows in part, in part and parcel, with full stop after every sentence. But the emotional soul knows in full, like a river or a flood.
>
> (*Apocalypse*, p. 142)

The figure of the 'phosphorescent wave' communicates some-thing fundamental about Lawrence's language-sense. Staying with the metaphor, in our 'mind's eye' we can imagine without any difficulty a phosphorescent wave breaking over a ship and in doing so revealing the ship's form. The wave, by its engulfing movement, reveals the ship as present: without the wave we might have missed it altogether. In other words, Lawrence's interest is in what is not directly perceivable, or only perceivable *through* things. The 'ship' came into view through the 'wave'. If something is translated into something conceivable, it is generally done so through concepts, which is never satisfying to Lawrence. The consciousness which Lawrence gives to the hand in 'Why the Novel Matters', discussed earlier, is difficult to 'conceive'. Lawrence's well-rehearsed point is that we only know or perceive 'life' in the living. Seeing it in the living we are aware that it is a con-tinually deferred quality – we pass from living thing to living thing recognizing that each is living but with no fixed sense of what life is. It evades definition in a way which 'body', for ex-ample, does not. The body is present, it bleeds: 'if I cut it [my hand] it will bleed' ('Why the Novel Matters', *Hardy*, p. 193). But we recognize 'life' through 'body'. These distinctions are present in Lawrence's 'wave' metaphor which gives rise to an understanding of language as a medium flowing around a reality which is 'knowable' yet not easily 'conceivable'. The problem, suggests Lawrence, is that people generally take that which is known for reality, an illusion which is created by the habit of seeing language as the limit. Lawrence is searching for ways (in metaphor) of reminding us that language gives us a sign or a 'shape', some form, but not the thing that essentially *is* that shape, or form. The sense is of some force, and with Lawrence, poet-thinker, it is usually language, 'illuminating' or uncovering the object *as present*: writer and reader alike are urged to remember that language is a trace, like a clot of light on a radar screen, revealing the presence of something hitherto undetected and not yet directly 'visible'. The word is not the thing, just as the spot of light on the radar screen is not the thing, but it shows that the thing is present. The important distinction for Lawrence here is between a 'referential' conception of language and the flow of a medium around an object.

To call the cardiac plexus the sun *is* to make a metaphor: the cardiac plexus, or network of nerves around the heart, is not the sun. However, as Lawrence also writes in *Psychoanalysis and the Unconscious*, 'When the ancients located the first seat of consciousness in the heart, they were neither misguided nor playing with metaphor' (*Psychoanalysis and the Unconscious*, F&P, p. 231).[37] The heart is not merely mechanical, argues Lawrence, not merely a valve for pumping blood: it is commonplace to feel physical sensations in the region of the heart – it can be felt to race with excitement, or to pound with fear, for example. It is not accidental that it is traditionally associated with the emotions, specifically love and sexual feelings. The literalness of a consciousness of feeling stirring in the body continually draws Lawrence's attention. As with the heart, so the individual feels fear, panic and misery in the 'pit' of the stomach, in the region of the solar plexus, which is so central to Lawrence. His preoccupation with the physiological dimension of emotional experience arises from its centrality to his 'metaphysic', which is why he constructs what comes to be seen as a peculiarly Lawrentian physiology in the course of writing the books on the unconscious. This preoccupation is part of his dismantling of the body/psyche polarity, which he felt as a cultural given. So, to call the cardiac plexus, associated with the heart (and traditional seat of the emotions), the sun is not merely metaphor – it is because of the sun and the light (capitalized by Lawrence) that we see at all, and the heart 'sees feelingly'.

Here Lawrence turns his attention to vision. His language-sense, imaged as a phosphorescent wave, has been described as revealing the form of something that is present. In the first and longer passage quoted, the transfer of 'objective knowledge' to the psyche is called 'root-vision'. This is 'almost the same as' ordinary vision but there is an important difference. Lawrence, in agreement with classical thought, writes that 'Vision is perhaps our highest form of dynamic upper consciousness', but he adds 'But our deepest lower consciousness is blood-consciousness' (*Fantasia of the Unconscious*, p. 173). At the risk of piling metaphor upon metaphor it is sufficient to say here that 'root-vision' is a form of 'blood-consciousness'. In the human being 'root-vision' is a way that Lawrence has found of describing a special kind of vision, or knowledge, different from mere ocular perception.[38] It is a characteristically Lawrentian compound noun and as such it helps us to focus tightly on the life and function not only of vision, but also of metaphor in his thought. For, joining together so graphically with a hyphen two terms from such diverse realms is itself a kind of metaphor, and Lawrence is undoubtedly conscious of the status of this and his other related constructions, of which 'root-vision' and 'blood-consciousness' are important examples. To be sure, there is some difference between these: with a phrase like 'blood-consciousness' one is not always aware of having two unrelated terms yoked together, such is the extent that the 'consciousness' part of the construction is subsumed to 'blood'. Hence for a great many people the immediate sense is that this is simply another term relating to Lawrence's emphasis on the blood, an assumption which diminishes the force of the word 'consciousness' as part of the construction. In 'root-vision' the difference between the composite words seems greater. The semantic, indeed the logical, difference between the separate elements makes us aware of the unique standing of the construction. It needs to be made clear here that Lawrence's reference in the first example is not to 'blood' in the racial sense, a sense which gives rise to accusations of proto-Nazism. The reference is Biblical with the focus on the blood as the *locus* of life. This is both a constitutive metaphor and a cultural reference, since the idea comes from the Old Testament, and evokes an ancient metaphysic with which Lawrence challenges modern mental-consciousness.

Like 'blood-consciousness', 'root-vision' depends on the meaningful proximity of dissimilar terms and as such recalls the principle of oxymoron.[39] Significantly, with oxymoron, expressivity is derived from the difference between the terms involved rather than resemblance. Traditionally, of course, metaphor is a trope of resemblance, but with the emphasis placed too much on resemblance metaphor is in danger of becoming glorified simile. In Lawrence, as will be seen particularly in *Women in Love*, the potent end of metaphor is often, in fact, oxymoron with its emphasis on semantic and logical difference. It is a trope which is founded on paradox: Lawrence's way of saying the unsayable. Suffice it to say that, as examples like 'blood-consciousness' and 'root-vision' suggest, a sensitivity to the oxymoronic lurks close to the heart of metaphor in Lawrence, at the heart, that is to say, of a style which is both vital and subliminal, subliminal because the oxymoronic implication gets subsumed to metaphor so that its full impact is not conscious. It is a common recognition that experience is already understood through metaphor – this is how the world is perceived (Lakoff and Johnson deal with this form of conceptualizing). In 'root-vision' and 'blood-consciousness', however, new metaphors are being coined for the 'old' familiar experiences that 'ordinary' language generally bypasses.

The attention that he pays to sight, and the way in which vision is addressed in his work, highlights Lawrence's awareness of a philosophical tradition with its roots in pre-Socratic thought. He shares the historical moment with Heidegger who writes in *Being and Time* about the primacy of sight as a sense in the Western philosophical tradition. Both embark, from different intellectual traditions, on critiques of the orthodox position. Heidegger labours to articulate what the passages from *Psychoanalysis and the Unconscious* reveal that Lawrence knows intuitively, and metaphorically, poetically, expresses. This passage from *Being and Time* could serve as Heidegger's conceptualizing definition of Lawrence's understanding:

'Seeing' does not mean just perceiving with the bodily eyes, but neither does it mean pure non-sensory awareness of something present-at-hand in its presence-at-hand. In giving an existential signification to 'sight', we have merely drawn

upon the peculiar feature of seeing, that it lets entities which
are accessible to it be encountered unconcealedly in themselves.
(*Being and Time*, p. 187)

This is a version of the Lawrentian preoccupation and is poetically thought by the 'phosphorescent wave' and, indeed, the
'rainbow' metaphors. This preoccupation, which is with modes
of understanding, also underpins Lawrence's discourse on the
infant. The baby represents a version of being human that is, all
importantly for Lawrence, 'pre-visual'. Yet the baby 'knows', is
constantly stimulated by, and surprised by, 'world'. Lawrence's
description of the exchanges between mother and baby echoes
the language of his phosphorescent wave idea:

> The great magnetic or dynamic centre of first-consciousness
> acts powerfully at the solar plexus. Here the child knows be-
> yond all knowledge. It does not see with the eyes, it cannot
> perceive, much less conceive. Nothing can it apprehend; the
> eyes are a strange plasmic, nascent darkness. Yet from the belly
> it knows, with a directness of knowledge that frightens us and
> may even seem abhorent. The mother, also, from the bowels
> knows her child – as she can never, never know it from the
> head. There is no thought nor speech, only direct, ventral
> gurglings and cooings. From the passional nerve-centre of the
> solar plexus in the mother passes direct, unspeakable efflu-
> ence and inter-communication, sheer effluent contact with the
> palpitating nerve-centre in the belly of the child. Knowl-
> edge, unspeakable knowledge interchanged, which must be
> diluted by eternities of materialization before they can come
> to expression.
> (*Psychoanalysis and the Unconscious*, F&P, p. 221)

In this passage the child 'knows', whereas the mother 'knows
her child'. In his treatment of the child's knowing, Lawrence
minimizes the cognitive element. The child knows 'beyond all
knowledge' with a 'directness' that signifies, to Lawrence's readers,
'consciousness', yet in Lawrence's terms both child and mother
are 'unconscious'. The knowledge each has of the other is unutterable, non-verbal: in resorting to language in order to represent the unutterable, or at the least the conditions of unutterable
knowledge, Lawrence resorts to his biological psyche, to the body

of feeling. 'Ventral' pre-verbal utterance is another reminder of the abdominal centres of the body conscious and unconscious.

In the mature novels Lawrence makes dramatic use of his sense that there are different modes of vision. In fact 'seeing' is a recurrent theme in his fiction, aligned with the trope of blindness. When Tom Brangwen, for instance, first sees Lydia Lensky, seeing her from different distances means that he experiences her differently at each stage. Espying her from a long way away he is almost indifferent, 'he saw a woman approaching. But he was thinking of the horse.' As she passes, 'unseeing', his vision of her changes: 'He saw her face clearly, as if by a light in the air. He saw her face so distinctly, that he ceased to coil on himself, and was suspended. / "That's her," he said involuntarily' (*The Rainbow*, p. 29). Until his proposal of marriage Brangwen sees her on occasions from different distances: from far off, at a relative closeness in the church, in the farm kitchen, with Anna on visits to the farm and 'Gradually, even without seeing her, he came to know her' (p. 39). This 'knowing' is 'root-vision'. In the baby, about which Lawrence writes so much, the capacity to know like this characterizes its specialness. The baby 'knows' things at a very deep level and prior to speech. Such knowledge is instinctive rather than reasoned. In *Psychoanalysis and the Unconscious* Lawrence describes the baby's 'pre-visual discerning . . . pre-visual apprehension' (*Psychoanalysis and the Unconscious*, p. 238).

On the evening of his proposal Brangwen finds Lydia and the baby Anna enclosed within the vicarage window. He sees a vision which, although he does not formulate it in these terms, is Rembrandtesque in its stillness and in the play of light on the child's face:

> The fair head with its wild, fierce hair was drooping towards the fire-warmth, which reflected on the bright cheeks and clear skin of the child, who seemed to be musing, almost like a grown-up person. The mother's face was dark and still, and he saw, with a pang, that she was away back in the life that had been. The child's hair gleamed like spun glass, her face was illuminated till it seemed like wax lit up from the inside.
>
> (*The Rainbow*, p. 42)

This 'Dutch' stillness is not a visual style that characterizes the novel as a whole. One critic has assessed the significance of this vision as the first of five iconographical moments in the novel which arrest the reader's attention and which, when considered in relation to each other, demonstrate the novel's changing, or accelerating, rhythm. He refers to this scene as the novel's 'first icon' which 'in itself and in its social and cultural implications, represents virtually a complete stasis.'[40] This stasis emphasizes the scene's presentness to Tom, the onlooker. Anna, presented in this way, and in contrast to the external turmoil which is usually seen as representing Tom's state of consciousness, represents the 'stabilising relationship' of the marriage and in Tom's attraction to Lydia we witness the inclination of the (early) Brangwens 'to refer and assign to woman' (*The Visual Imagination of D.H. Lawrence*, p. 134).[41] The configuration of mother-and-child is retained from a long tradition, the iconography of the Holy Family referred to so often in Lawrence. There are affinities with the Holy Family even though the child is female, Lawrence always working against its conventional significance. Tom's gaze is not devotional, but it is not neutral either: it is, at the least, contemplative. Neither is he looking at a painting but at a living social grouping. In this, Lawrence may well be anticipating Will Brangwen's dependence on the visual arts as a means of achieving intensity of feeling, and will therefore be comparing Will negatively to Tom's propensity to attend to presence. The question is to what extent this vision is a 'medium' or means to a dimension of feeling which is otherwise inaccessible to the character. Describing Will Brangwen's experience Alldritt rightly says, 'art for Will Brangwen is not a means for better understanding or appreciating reality but rather a means of experiencing the heightened conscious-ness that life does not ordinarily allow' (p. 86). For Tom Brangwen, the vision through the window is a sign that his reality will change. His world will shrink (or expand) to encompass the lives, and life, represented within the window-frame which is not, how-ever, to be understood in terms of either a sentimental 'ideal' or a narrowly reductive domestic routine. Tom has an interactive relation to the 'picture'. He is not unproblematically 'outside' it. In the act of looking he is also participating in it, unconsciously creating the life it represents. Consequently he is both outside it and a part of it. It is comparable to the relation which the reader has with Lawrence's texts: the reader, like Tom Brangwen in this instance, is required to project, as it were, to create a meaning. Crucially, metaphorization in Lawrence is in some sense like projection: it *creates* a sense.[42]

A second passage shows Lydia's significance not as a madonna figure but as a more abstract 'presence', a word which occurs in the description and which asserts the central problem of the difference between the 'knowable' and the 'conceivable'. Whatever the vision through the window might suggest, even if it is a familiar icon, Lydia is fundamentally and always mysterious to Tom quite apart from the cultural and social differences between them:

> She turned into the kitchen, startled out of herself by this invasion from the night. He took off his hat, and came towards her. Then he stood in the light, in his black clothes and his black stock, hat in one hand and yellow flowers in the other. She stood away, at his mercy, snatched out of herself. She did not know him, only she knew he was a man come for her. She could only see the dark-clad man's figure standing there upon her, and the gripped fist of flowers. She could not see the face and the living eyes.
>   He was watching her, without knowing her, only aware underneath of her presence.
>
> (*The Rainbow*, p. 43)

The stillness in which both mother and child were unconscious, and unconscious of Brangwen observing them, has been dispersed by the emotions caused by his 'presence'. In the last sentence Brangwen's vision of Lydia has altered by virtue of proximity and a tacit commitment to 'know' her. While both these scenes have visual properties, the quality of each vision is different. The Rembrandt effect, created in part by distance, has been replaced by a more expressionistic way of seeing. In the first passage the window-frame's more literal function was to single out and isolate the group. In the second passage the featureless figure of Tom is made dark by the light which minutes before had an illuminating function. The distance made possible by the window has dissolved and the essential relationship has been problematized beyond the simple pictorial configuration.

While the focus is principally on his linguistic configurations Lawrence's preoccupation can never be simply with language, because language is always already busy in the event of saying something other. Consequently, it is impossible (or at least inappropriate) to isolate language in Lawrence without also addressing 'metaphysic' and perennial themes like vision, knowledge and presence, and their interaction in his thought. In the next chapter I attend further to Lawrence's sense of 'bodily' seeing, that is to say, of the whole body being implicated in the act of seeing, feeling and knowing. The focus is on what becomes in Lawrence a lengthy meditation on the knowable and conceivable dimensions of physical existence. In debating the interaction between these two 'felt' domains, Lawrence's highly metaphorical language becomes for the reader the 'phosphorescent wave'.

5

Language and the Unconscious: The Radical Metaphoricity of *Psychoanalysis and the Unconscious* and *Fantasia of the Unconscious* II

DISMANTLING THE BODY/PSYCHE MODEL

Lawrence is implicating the psyche *and* the body in his representation of emotional experience and human consciousness. The planes, plexuses and centres of feeling initially set out in *Psychoanalysis and the Unconscious* are *ambivalently* present in the body, and this is very much the point. Lawrence's own grounding of the instinctual life in the configuration of planes, plexuses and ganglia – the upper and lower centres of psychic activity – insists on being taken both literally and metaphorically. Although we are asked to treat the 'biology' literally, as we now expect, it ultimately works metaphorically. Crucially, Lawrence's insistence on the literal dissolves the very distinction on which it rests. The 'solar' plexus, for instance, exists and gets its name from its resemblance to the sun inasmuch as it is a structure of nerves and ganglia radiating from a central network of nerves, but as a metaphor it has a special status of which Lawrence is particularly conscious. Some critics insist on the derivative nature of Lawrence's conception. Christopher Heywood, for instance, suggests that Lawrence was influenced by the studies in physiology of Marie-François Xavier Bichat and Marshall Hall, and draws attention to his knowledge of William James's *The Principles of Psychology*,

Edward Carpenter's *The Art of Creation,* and William Pryses's
The Apocalypse Unsealed.[1] Bertrand Russell, in passing, gives a
further sense of a context for Lawrence's ideas. In a book on
knowledge rather later than Lawrence's he writes:

> The theory of the emotions has been radically transformed by
> the discovery of the part played by the ductless glands. Can-
> non's *Bodily Changes in Pain, Hunger, Fear and Rage* is a book
> whose teaching has come to be widely known, though not more
> so than its importance warrants. It appears that certain secre-
> tions from the glands into the blood are the essential physio-
> logical conditions of the emotions. Some people say that the
> physiological changes correlated with these secretions *are* the
> emotions. I think this view must be received with some caution.
>
> (*An Outline of Philosophy,* p. 174)

Lawrence, not a behaviourist, would have agreed with the final
sentence. Far from being anachronistic, or part of a scientific debate,
Lawrence's 'physiology' as a stage in his metaphorical thought
can be seen as a form that has its own truth and discipline. In
Psychoanalysis and the Unconscious he refers to the 'great sympathetic centre of the breast' as the 'heart's *mind*' (p. 230, my
italics) and to the solar plexus as 'the active human *first-mind*'
(p. 225, my italics). He talks of a knowledge metaphorically called
'the treasure of the heart' (p. 231). This knowledge is formulated as 'objective knowledge, *sightless, unspeakably* direct' (p. 231,
my italics). These are descriptions which, now familiarly, emphasize a non-verbal, far from analytical, kind of knowing. As we
shall see, they also substantiate Lawrence's sense, which I outlined earlier, of there being different modes of vision.

In *Lady Chatterley's Lover* one of Lawrence's themes is the
difference between 'mechanical' vision and vision through desire. Seeing an unsuspecting (and therefore unconscious) Mellors
washing himself, Connie's response is ambivalent, as 'shock' turns
into a 'visionary experience'. She *sees* him for the first time:

> In spite of herself she had had a shock. After all, merely a
> man washing himself! Commonplace enough, Heaven knows!
>   Yet in some curious way it was a *visionary* experience: *it had
> hit her in the middle of her body.*
>
> (*Lady Chatterley's Lover,* p. 66, my italics)

The point about knowledge is made unequivocally a few lines later: 'Connie had received the shock of *vision* in her *womb,* and she knew it. It lay inside her. But with her mind she was inclined to ridicule' (*Lady Chatterley's Lover,* p. 66, my italics). The language looks ahead to the conception of their child and in that sense is perfectly consistent with the events and the relationship that will develop. However, the impact of knowledge 'in the middle of her body' is not such an ordinary reference as it at first seems: 'middle' is a word with a high value in Lawrence's lexicon as it becomes the *locus* of 'emotional consciousness'. In *The Prussian Officer,* for instance, Schöner's self is located at his heart, 'hard there in the centre of his chest was himself, himself' (*The Prussian Officer,* p. 13); in a much later work Ramón tells Kate Leslie that 'Beyond me, at the middle, is the God' (*The Plumed Serpent,* p. 74).[2]

In the passages from *Lady Chatterley's Lover* seeing is returned to the physical centre of the human being, not to the eye as the dedicated organ of sight, but to the body's centre. In the discursive works, notably the books on the unconscious, the breast is more usually given this capacity. In identifying the womb here, Lawrence may be formulating the 'otherness' of one human being to another in terms of a gendered 'seeing'. The common view is that subjectivity lies behind the eyes, but here it is not only Connie's eyes which do the seeing, but the whole body of the woman.

So here the breast and the mind, solar plexus and cardiac plexus, are given a value which the eyes alone do not have as the physical centres of knowing and 'vision'. In *Psychoanalysis and the Unconscious,* looking ahead to the key passage from 'The Lover and the Beloved', he writes:

> The breasts themselves are as two eyes. We do not know how much the nipples of the breast, both in man and woman, serve primarily as poles of vital conscious effluence and connection. We do not know how the nipples of the breast are as fountains leaping into the universe, or as little lamps irradiating the contiguous world, to the soul in quest.
>
> (*Psychoanalysis and the Unconscious,* F&P, p. 231)

This breast/eye metaphor encapsulates the knowledge theme which lurks consistently in the expression of Lawrence's personal

philosophy.[3] It recurs in *The First Lady Chatterley*. Connie veils
her face, up to her eyes, and looks at herself naked in a mirror:

> Her breasts were also eyes, and her navel was sad, closed,
> waiting lips. It all spoke in another, silent language, without
> the cheapness of words.
>
> (*The First Lady Chatterley*, p. 30)

Lawrence omits this idea of the body as a face in the next two
versions of the novel but this does not lessen the significance of
the perceived similarity between the eye and the nipple as sentient organs, and as sentient in related ways. The nipple is posited as a primal, or primordial, eye; 'the eye in the breast'.
Lawrence's suggestion is that the sense-organs themselves do not
perceive, but that perception is *through* them (and for Lawrence
from the breast). In his quite extensive description of sight in
'The Five Senses' (*Fantasia of the Unconscious*, Chapter 5), the phrase
'I go forth' (in the act of seeing) occurs several times. This going
forth to meet something is 'from the centre of the glad breast,
through the eyes':

> The eyes are the third great gateway of the psyche. Here the
> soul goes in and out of the body, as a bird flying forth and
> coming home. But the root of conscious vision is almost en-
> tirely in the breast. When *I go forth* from my own eyes, in
> delight to dwell upon the world which is beyond me, outside
> me, then *I go forth.* from wide open windows, through which
> shows the full and living lambent darkness of my present in-
> ward self. *I go forth*, and I leave the lovely open darkness of
> my sensient [sic] self revealed; when *I go forth* in the wonder
> of vision to dwell upon the beloved, or upon the wonder of
> the world, *I go from the centre of the glad breast*, through the
> eyes, and who will may look into the full soft darkness of me,
> rich with my undiscovered presence.
>
> (*Fantasia of the Unconscious*, F&P, p. 63, my italics)

This foregrounds the passage quoted where Lawrence talks of
the breasts as eyes. Here, the fact that vision and feeling,
knowledge (something encountered, something disclosed), have
a common origin is part of Lawrence's general drift.
Clearly Lawrence is not bound, in his meditations, by biological,

or even evolutionary, imperatives. Instead, he subjects biology to a very specific kind of understanding, which is metaphorical, in order to extend the limits of his enquiry. In this way, he enters the debate about the value of 'seeing' in our culture as a metaphor for 'knowing'. So, when Lawrence discusses the eye in 'The Five Senses' he continues to dwell metaphorically on the concept 'vision', returning to the position taken up in *Psychoanalysis and the Unconscious* represented by the passages on metaphor discussed earlier. The now familiar thesis is that 'the root of conscious vision is almost entirely in the breast' (*Fantasia of the Unconscious*, p. 63). Even cognition in Lawrence is 'thought' metaphorically: Noah's use of the dove to find land as the flood-waters draw back from the earth becomes a metaphor for the cognitive aspect of sight as knowing, or as finding something out that was previously concealed: 'The eyes are the third great gateway of the psyche. Here the soul goes in and out of the body, as a bird flying forth and coming home' (p. 63). In this reference the bird which is sent out and returns home represents the eyes of Noah. The bird goes forth, and is the source of knowledge. The very metaphoricity of this as a description of perception is significant.

The word 'sensual' is also one which is subject to different semantic pressures in this text. Lawrence argues that 'sight is the least sensual of all the senses' (p. 65). This is because, in our cerebral, inquisitive mode 'we strain ourselves to see, see, see – everything, everything through the eye, in one mode of objective curiosity' (p. 65). But he suggests that 'The eyes have, however, their sensual root as well. But this is hard to transfer into language, as all our vision, our modern Northern vision, is in the upper mode of actual seeing' (p. 64). Here the word 'sensual' means something more than the sense of sight as a faculty of perception. It refers to the sensation in the breast (the centre) which is not separable from a 'knowing' which is non-verbal, being 'hard to transfer into language'. Dramatized in Constance Chatterley, the whole body, not just the eye, 'sees'.

Still on the question of vision, Lawrence unpacks his negative interpretation of what he calls the human being's purely, or merely, 'objective curiosity' (in a 'mental-conscious' culture). Talking of the 'savage' Lawrence states that 'What we call vision, that he has not' (p. 64), with the implication that 'he' possesses a mode of seeing which goes beyond mere attention to externals, an attentiveness characterized by its paucity ('we stare endlessly at the outside', p. 65). His mode of understanding is different: the 'savage' possesses 'the eye which is not wide open to study, to learn, but which powerfully, proudly or cautiously glances, and knows the terror or the pure desirability of strangeness in the object it beholds' (p. 64). Romantically, through accessibility to 'strangeness', Lawrence attributes to this blood-conscious figure an 'authentic' mode of seeing which is not available to the 'mental-conscious' modern, and focuses on a non-analytical mode of response. In Lawrence's hierarchy, the 'savage' and the 'modern' individual mean something different by sight, and 'see' differently.

Given these formulations of vision, Lawrence's reader may be guided to ask further questions about the value of 'curiosity' in his vocabulary inasmuch as it turns up when he considers sight. If 'objective curiosity' is used pejoratively, the word 'curiosity' is awarded a positive meaning in *Fantasia of the Unconscious* when it describes the gaze of the animal, the cow, for instance, as different from that of the human being. Lawrence's assertion in *Fantasia of the Unconscious* about the animal recalls the cattle staring at Gudrun dancing in *Women in Love*: 'The eye of the cow is soft, velvety, receptive. She stands and gazes with the strangest intent curiosity. She goes forth from herself in wonder' (*Fantasia of the Unconscious*, p. 64). So, to Lawrence, the 'intent curiosity' of the cow constitutes both a kind of vision and, correspondingly, a kind of 'belonging' different from that experienced by the over-conscious human being. This general perception, which is undeveloped in the prose, underlines the force of Lawrence's conception of the animal as 'other' (addressed brilliantly in the poetry), and further underlines his recognition of the complexity of thinking 'otherness'.[4]

These distinctions in part articulate the middle way which Lawrence plots through the polarized model of body/mind which in his view limits modern understanding, forcing it into the isolated and circumscribed realms of psychology, biology, philosophy and other singular domains. From the examples given it is evident that we cannot say in Lawrence what is purely physical and what is purely unconscious because these extremes are partly dissolved in his language. The very interconnectedness of the physical and non-physical dimensions of human existence is articulated by, and in, the radically metaphorical mode of these short books, *Psychoanalysis and the Unconscious* and *Fantasia of the Unconscious*.

The discussion is supplemented by other observations on bodily presence and human being. In the course of the books on the unconscious Lawrence writes a great deal about physical gesture. As the baby, for instance, strives for its own singularity in relation to the mother Lawrence describes its physical movements in the act of what is also the symbolic rupture of the infant from the mother: 'The child is screaming itself rid of the old womb, kicking itself into a blind paroxysm into freedom, into separate, negative independence' (*Psychoanalysis and the Unconscious*, p. 222). Having achieved a degree of singularity the baby enters a new stage: 'The warm rosy abdomen, tender with chuckling unison, and the little back strengthening itself. The child kicks away, into independence. It stiffens its spine in the strength of its own private and separate, inviolable existence' (p. 223). For 'child' read 'self'. The Lawrentian subject is always subject to re-birth.

The references to kicking recall Gerald Crich in 'Diver' (*Women in Love*, Chapter IV) kicking against the water, asserting his own singularity: 'He was happy, thrusting with his legs and all his body, without bond or connection anywhere, just himself in the watery world' (*Women in Love*, p. 47). This sense of a vital connection between the individual's physical bearing and emotional life is a theme to which Lawrence returns in *Fantasia of the Unconscious*: 'Above all things encourage a straight backbone and proud shoulders. Above all things despise a slovenly movement, an ugly bearing and unpleasing manner' (*Fantasia*, F&P, p. 79). The baby's back, he notes in the first book, 'has an amazing power once it stiffens itself' (*Psychoanalysis*, F&P, p. 223). A derangement of the internal energies, a starving of the emotions or any emotional disorder results in physical weakness: 'How weary in the back is the nursing mother whose great centre of repudiation is suppressed or weak; how a child droops if only the sympathetic unison is established' (p. 224). So, in the sentential voice of authority, Lawrence sets out to convince his reader that a strong back is one sign of the perfect correspondence between self and world, according to the terms of his vitalistic philosophy.[5]

In *Aaron's Rod*, contemporaneous with the earliest versions of the essays on American literature, where the 'biological psyche' is represented, and *Psychoanalysis and the Unconscious*, psychophysical explanations for emotional disturbance are in evidence in quite an explicit way in the narrative. Asking how we know of the importance of the solar plexus as the 'primal affective centre', Lawrence replies 'We feel it, as we feel hunger or love

or hate' (*Psychoanalysis*, F&P, p. 219). This recalls Jim Bricknell
in 'A Punch in the Wind' (*Aaron's Rod*, Chapter VIII). Bricknell
is subject to an insatiable hunger and, in response to Lilly's asking why he eats so much bread, replies that it 'gives the stomach
something to work at, and prevents it grinding on the nerves.'
Unable to feel at the place which Lawrence identifies as the primal
and primary centre of consciousness, Bricknell tells Lilly 'I'm
losing life if I don't [eat]. I tell you I'm losing life. Let me put
something inside me' (*Aaron's Rod*, p. 77). Unable to love, he
crams food into his stomach as a substitute, in order to feel some
sensation in the region of his solar plexus. Starved of the right
kind of feeling he declares that,

> 'I shall die. I only live when I can fall in love. Otherwise I'm
> dying by inches. Why, man, you don't know what it was like.
> I used to get the most grand feelings – like a great rush of
> force, or light – a great rush – right here, as I've said, at the
> solar plexus. And it would come any time – any where – no
> matter where I was. And then I was all right.'
>
> (*Aaron's Rod*, p. 80)

Like Lawrence in *Psychoanalysis and the Unconscious*, Bricknell
is not merely making a metaphor. The 'light' is not literal, of
course, but the force or feeling, the sensation, is real enough.
His experience connects the physical with the emotional and
unconscious life of the individual (in quite a crude way), distinct
from the mechanical aspects of sex. It is Lilly who further recalls
the terms of *Psychoanalysis and the Unconscious* with his holistic
suggestion to Bricknell that an improvement in his posture might
dispel the arrest in feeling which he experiences. 'Body language'
is not a phrase used by Lawrence but clearly both 'body' and
'language' are important and related concepts in his mature work.
Bricknell's 'body language' communicates an arrest in some 'vital' centre. Lilly, ever the pedant, says, '"Then you should stiffen
your backbone. It's your backbone that matters."' Finding Bricknell
impossible to walk with – 'Jim staggered and stumbled like a
drunken man: or worse, like a man with locomotor ataxia: as if
he had no power in his lower limbs' (*Aaron's Rod*, p. 81) – Lilly's
words eventually engender the violent response which gives the
chapter its name. Bricknell, by punching Lilly in the solar plexus
('upon the front of the body', p. 82), proves Lawrence's general

point by winding him and depriving him of speech. It is a comedic definition. Lilly has told Bricknell that it is '"A maudlin crying to be loved, which makes your knees all go rickety."' . . . "you stagger and stumble down a road, out of sheer sloppy relaxation of your will"' (p. 82). In Bricknell, Lawrence dramatizes that part of his 'metaphysic' which refers to the body's centres of feeling. In Anne Fernihough's view modernism itself constitutes an attempt to heal the mind/body division to which Lawrence is so sensitive, evidenced in his treatment of Bricknell.[6] There is also Lawrence's particular importance in offering his own critique of the polarization of the psychic and the physical in modern understanding. As we have seen, Lawrence's thought is not unproblematically a response to Freud and perhaps his own 'metaphysic' approaches the body/psyche polarity more critically than the movement which we think of as modernism, anyway a highly diverse phenomenon.

I have concentrated on the centrality of vision and on Lawrence's sense of vision as 'efflux', a quality of understanding which flows through the eyes rather than from them: it is the whole body which 'sees'. The 'flow' rises in either the breast or the solar plexus. It is a 'flow' which, in Deleuze and Guattari vein, disrupts the conventional division between the body and the psyche (the non-physical body), dissolving the distinctions between them in language. We possess a language for articulating the biological functions, the psychological faculty and its operations. Lawrence, in these books, strives to find a way of saying what is not said (and therefore not entertained) by such scientific and exclusive discourses. To date, the metaphoricity of his books on the unconscious has been largely ignored, and yet in that metaphoricity is grounded *Lawrence's* idiosyncratic definition of unconsciousness (paradoxically how we 'know' and 'see' anything, and how we 'feel') articulated as, in part, a 'bodily' facility in an argument which relieves the body of its duller, more mechanical character. With a different emphasis from the clinicians, Lawrence regards unconscious life as dependent on a certain level of metaphoricity for its articulation. So while I have latterly concentrated on sight, for instance, it has been with metaphor consistently in view. There is, however, another mode of 'seeing' or visualizing which is rooted in the unconscious: that is the domain of dream, which can only be reported in language and metaphor.

DREAM

Dream is, like language, a radically metaphorical form of expression. I suspect that this is the basis of its interest for Lawrence, and the reason why he devotes a good deal of attention to dreams and dreaming in *Fantasia of the Unconscious*. There Lawrence discusses what he presents as common dream images. However, these images – the raging horses and the bull for instance – described in the 'Sleep and Dreams' chapter of *Fantasia of the Unconscious* (F&P, pp. 170–1), occur very effectively in the fiction not as dreams but as 'actual' phenomena, yet charged with psychic meaning (the running horses at the end of *The Rainbow*, pp. 451–4; the bull being loaded onto a boat in *The Plumed Serpent*, pp. 431–2). We are, then, invited to contrast Lawrence's use of dream in fiction with his use of these powerful symbols. The question that arises from such a contrast is why is dream, which is not so effectively used in his fiction, such a flat quality for Lawrence?

The Interpretation of Dreams is Freud's near-definitive work on the aetiology and nature of dreams as manifestations of the unconscious. Lawrence's most extended response to it occurs in 'Sleep and Dreams' (*Fantasia of the Unconscious*, Chapter 14). Although his resistance to Freudian determinism is manifest in that chapter, here too Lawrence's opposition to Freud is not the primary purpose of the argument. The genuine importance of the chapter on dreams – although Lawrence analyses generic rather than actual dreams – is that dreams provide an occasion for Lawrence to think about metaphor as the expression of what cannot otherwise be said.

Commentators invariably look for influences on Lawrence from the world of contemporary psychology when considering his discourses on dream.[7] Lawrence himself divides dreams into two main categories. The first of these deals with dreams as the result of somatic stimuli while the other is a uniquely Lawrentian category, that of 'true soul-dreams' (*Fantasia of the Unconscious*, F&P, p. 166). While he pays more than lip-service to Freud's contention that wish-fulfilment is the origin and cause of dreams, Lawrence lends more support to the argument that dreams are chiefly the result of somatic stimuli. To emphasize somatic sources for dreams is to hold the Freudian conception up as 'myth':

The image of falling, of flying, of trying to run and not being able to lift the feet, of having to creep through terribly small passages, these are direct transcripts from the physical phenomena of circulation and digestion. It is the directly transcribed image of the heart which, impeded in its action by the gases of indigestion, is switched out of its established circuit of earth-polarity, and is as if suspended over a void, or plunging into a void: step by step, falling downstairs, maybe, according to the strangulation of the heart-beats. The same paralytic inability to lift the feet when one needs to run, in a dream, comes directly from the same impeded action of the heart, which is thrown off its balance by some material obstruction. Now the heart swings left and right in the pure circuit of the earth's polarity. Hinder this swing, force the heart over to the left, by inflation of gas from the stomach or by dead pressure upon the blood and nerves from any obstruction, and you get the sensation of being unable to lift the feet from earth: a gasping sensation.

(*Fantasia of the Unconscious*, F&P, pp. 165–6)

Lawrence has, of course, no real interest in physical or external disturbances which might affect the dreamer. His concentration on dream images ultimately becomes a sort of preliminary sketch for the work in *Apocalypse* on symbols. Otherwise, his interest is in a very specific sort of commerce between the body and the psyche, and his favourite theme. 'Most dreams', he argues,

are stimulated from the blood into the nerves and the nerve-centres. And the heart is the transmission station. For the blood has a unity and a consciousness of its own. It has a deeper, elemental consciousness of the mechanical or material world. In the blood we have the body of our most elemental consciousness, our almost material consciousness. And during sleep this material consciousness transfers itself into the nerves and to the brain.

(*Fantasia of the Unconscious*, F&P, p. 166)

Dreams, then, are rooted in the blood and 'blood-consciousness' and the heart, Marconi-style, 'transmits' the signals to the psyche – 'in sleep the transfer is made through the dream-images which are mechanical phenomena like mirages' (p. 166).

Lawrence's further distinctions include dreams which affect the soul ('By the unconscious we do mean the soul. But the word *soul* has been vitiated by the idealistic use', Psychoanalysis, F&P, p. 215) and dreams which are so much flotsam. 'Soul dreams' are mechanical up to a point, like those already described; connected to the emotions but not a cipher as Freud suggests. Characteristically, Lawrence describes dreams as the product of the exchange and resistance between the centres of feeling in the individual, and the tension between automatism and 'the living, wakeful psyche' which is here conflated with 'the living soul' (*Fantasia*, F&P, p. 169). Then comes a direct criticism of psychoanalytical practice: 'We have to be very wary of giving way to dreams. It is really a sin against ourselves to prostitute the living spontaneous soul to the tyranny of dreams, or of chance, or fortune or luck, or any of the processes of the automatic sphere' (p. 170). Lawrence's interest is not principally in the dream, but in dreaming as another kind of vision. Here it is mechanical and automatic, negative qualitites for Lawrence:

> As we sleep the current sweeps its own way through us, as the streets of the city are swept and flushed at night. It sweeps through our nerves and our blood, sweeping away the ash of our day's spent consciousness towards one form or other of excretion. This earth-current actively sweeping through us is really the death-activity busy in the service of life. It behoves us to know nothing of it. And as it sweeps it stimulates in the primary centres of consciousness vibrations which flash images upon the mind. Usually, in deep sleep, these images pass unrecorded; but as we pass towards the twilight of dawn and wakefulness, we begin to retain some impression, some record of dream-images.
>
> (*Fantasia of the Unconscious*, F&P, p. 163)

In this description dreams are the product of a purging activity which is essential to mental and physical health. This passage, in keeping with the whole, is highly metaphorical, reminiscent of the novels rather than a discursive essay. Street-sweeping as a metaphor for mental and physical purgation (a kind of excretion) predominates here, but the language speaks to the Lawrentian preoccupation with 'tides' and 'flows'. The reader is reminded of how fundamental the concept of the 'flow' is to Lawrence, and how it invests all his thought on the psyche. It is the 'flushing' and 'sweeping' current which results in the visual dimension of sleep. The metaphor of the phosphorescent wave identified his medium as a 'sea' of language flowing around the object. Here it is a deep-lying metaphor in his description of the main activity of sleeping. The street-sweeping references continue into the next passage, with the repetition of 'sweeping' and variations of tense as Lawrence finds rhymes and alliterative instances to make this a self-conscious point of style. The deliberate repetition of sweep, swept, sweeping, sweeps, in quite a lengthy passage recalls the style of echo and restatement for which Lawrence was criticized in *The Rainbow,* and which he himself identifies in the Foreword to *Women in Love* as 'natural' to the writer; but is it here 'frictional'?

Oxymoronic constructions are very much a part of this consciously metaphorical style: we have the watery 'earth-current' and 'death-activity' which is 'busy in the service of life'. As before, the hyphenated constructions acquire a special significance. Considered separately, the words 'earth' and 'current', 'death' and 'activity' have no special or particular charge different from their familiar meanings. Yet the 'earth-current'/'death-activity' are quite significant abstractions. The hyphens galvanize ordinary words into some special relation because, as Lawrence sees it, language is ordinarily limited. The hyphens are an attempt to mould 'ordinary' language into new forms which institute a new way of knowing (and, here, a new way of representing the creative unconscious). There is also an effect of reification, in which the words, whilst not being the thing, are seeking to form a 'thing'. The same can be said of dream.

As the passage continues Lawrence, writing about dream, manages a discrete critique of mainstream modernism about which he is so disparaging in 'The Future of the Novel': 'It is self-consciousness picked into such fine bits that the bits are most of them invisible, and you have to go by smell' (*Hardy*, p. 152). The unselective content of the dream serves implicitly as a model for what is to Lawrence bad fiction:

Usually also the images that are accidentally swept into the mind in sleep are as disconnected and as unmeaning as the pieces of paper which the street-cleaners sweep into a bin from the city gutters at night. We should not think of taking all these papers, piecing them together, and making a marvellous book of them, prophetic of the future and pregnant with the past. We should not do so, although every rag of printed paper swept from the gutter would have some connection with the past day's event. But its significance, the significance of the words printed upon it, is so small that we relegate it into the limbo of the accidental and meaningless. There is no vital connection between the many torn bits of paper – only an accidental connection. Each bit of paper has reference to some actual event: a bus-ticket, an envelope, a tract, a pastry-shop bag, a newspaper, a handbill. But take them all together, bus-ticket, torn envelope, tract, paper-bag, piece of newspaper, and handbill, and they have no individual sequence, they belong more to the mechanical arrangements than to the vital consequence of our existence. And the same with most dreams. They are the heterogeneous odds and ends of images swept together accidentally by the besom of the night-current, and it is beneath our dignity to attach any real importance to them.

(*Fantasia of the Unconscious*, F&P, pp. 163–4)

Of course, several of Lawrence's important contemporaries, working in visual media, did think of utilizing ordinary found objects, like those described here, to great effect in collage and construction. That does not shake Lawrence's faith in his distinction between 'vital' and merely 'accidental' connections with objects of this kind. By *Kangaroo* he seems to have had a change of heart. In 'Bits' (*Kangaroo*, Chapter 14), the Lawrence-figure, Richard Lovat Somers, reading the anecdotal entries of the Sydney *Bulletin*, is given to think, 'It was not mere anecdotage. It was the momentaneous life of the continent. There was no consecutive thread. Only the laconic courage of experience' (*Kangaroo*, p. 272). In 'Bits' Lawrence himself makes something significant of the newspaper items chanced upon, which leaves us to wonder whether he is being a little refractory in the passage from *Fantasia of the Unconscious*. However else it is read, the expertly constructed central metaphor in the passage also speaks volumes about Lawrence's suspicions that Freud, in particular, labours in the gutter of human activity, that his interests are gutter-interests. But the passage is most revealing in the bearing it has on Lawrence's use of dream in his fiction.

In the final chapter of *Aaron's Rod*, called 'Words', a considerable amount of the narrative is given over to Aaron's dream. It is too long to quote in full, but a summary of its principal elements is adequate for my purposes. Continuity between diverse scenes is provided by the figure of Aaron, here a split subject. In part the dream foreshadows the words of Lilly to follow: on the self, the 'dream-Aaron' having a 'second self', an 'invisible, *conscious* self'; on there being a 'flesh-and-blood Aaron' which is 'palpable or visible', to which the 'second self' is other (*Aaron's Rod*, p. 287). In the dream, Aaron is in a strange country from which he passes into a labyrinthine realm of rooms and corridors populated with tin-miners and their wives. With a dreamer's knowledge Aaron knows that they are to eat a man, realized as 'a man's skin stuffed tight with prepared meat' (p. 286), whom the dreamer sees receding into the distance, down a dream corridor. Then 'Aaron' undergoes a Hadean journey:

> The next thing he could recall was, that he was in a boat. And now he was most definitely two people. His invisible, conscious self, what we have called his second self, hovered as it were before the prow of the boat, seeing and knowing, but unseen. His other self, the palpable Aaron, sat as a passenger in the boat, which was being rowed by the unknown people of this underworld. They stood up as they thrust the boat along. Other passengers were in the boat too, women as well, but all of them unknown people, and not noticeable.
>
> (*Aaron's Rod*, p. 287)

The ambivalence of a dream-ego is communicated using the split self: in a dream the dreamer is both present and not present; s/he sees and knows things about the dream and dream-world which are not there in the phenomenal world to see and know. The 'corporeal' Aaron fails to notice his naked elbow being struck hard as the boat passes stakes standing erect in the water. The 'invisible' Aaron wills him to notice, and the boatmen cry warnings in the second instance in the dream of an incomprehensible language, the first having been spoken by the people of the room-country. The boat reaches a city, 'A lake-city, like Mexico' (the reference is to Mexico City and looks ahead to *The Plumed Serpent*) where the dream resolves itself into weakly mythic forms: the dream Aaron sees a figure of Astarte sitting by a roadside bearing eggs and bread in her open lap. In an early version of

Lawrence's essay on Nathaniel Hawthorne, Astarte is the symbol of the subversively sensual woman also designated Magna Mater and Syria Dea.[8] At this point the dreamer wakes up. The major elements include a series of alien and underworld locations, unknown languages, a chthonic community, a journey over water to a city, an 'edible' man and a fertility goddess, with the split self of Aaron presiding. Aaron's unfulfilling domestic life is encoded in the dream, and his inconstancy, as well as the hostility to women's sexual identity which is inscribed not least in the last dialogue in the book between Aaron and Lilly. The anxiety content of the dream seems to come from the fear of personal pain. The nurturing 'invisible' Aaron hears the warnings from the chorus of boatmen but is inactive. The 'palpable' Aaron is oblivious to pain and warnings of pain: he is 'unfeeling'.

Despite his remarks that dream-images are accidental and 'as unmeaning as the pieces of paper which the street-cleaners sweep into a bin from the city gutters at night' (*Fantasia*, F&P, p. 164), Lawrence does palpably employ dream in his fiction, as well as writing passages that might as well be dream, or indeed, uncanny texts like the whole of 'The Woman Who Rode Away'. Certainly in *Aaron's Rod* he does seem to be 'taking all these papers, piecing them together, and making a marvellous book of them, prophetic of the future and pregnant with the past' (p. 164). Whatever Lawrence's motives, the dream in *Aaron's Rod* is in danger of being seen as one of the novel's flaws, an inadequate representation of the novel's concerns. Perhaps it works as a comment on Aaron's past, but it provides neither an insightful commentary on the novel nor an extension of Lawrence's consideration of non-verbal modes of understanding. It is, rather, an unwieldy narrative within a narrative. It may be a response to Lawrence's sense that at this point in his narrative he needs a visionary, or a poetic, interjection. As a symptom, Aaron's symptom, it accords with Lawrence's views in 'Sleep and Dreams' that only those dreams which are genuinely rooted in the individual's deepest levels of consciousness are significant. Lawrence concedes (paradoxically) that:

Only occasionally they [dreams] matter. And this is only when something threatens us from the outer mechanical or accidental death-world. When anything threatens us from the world of death, then a dream may become so vivid that it arouses

the actual soul. And when a dream is so intense that it arouses
the soul – then we must attend to it.

(Fantasia of the Unconscious, F&P, pp. 164–5)

In conceding this Lawrence may well be conceding everything.
Aaron's dream occurs in the night following the destruction of
his flute, by which time, as Lawrence promised some of his first
confidantes about this novel, 'Aaron had been through it all'
(*Aaron's Rod*, p. 289).[9] At the end of 'The Broken Rod' (*Aaron's
Rod*, Chapter XX) Lawrence describes Aaron as 'quite dumb-
founded by the night's event: the loss of his flute. Here was a
blow he had not expected. And the loss was for him symbolistic.
It chimed with something in his soul: the bomb, the smashed
flute, the end' (p. 285). In this context of foregrounded anxiety it
is quite fitting that Aaron dreams, although Lawrence never quite
succeeds in overcoming the artificiality of the dream within his
narrative. A year after beginning *Aaron's Rod* he had written to
Katherine Mansfield saying 'It seems to me, if one is to do fiction now, one must cross the threshold of the human psyche'
(*Letters*, III, p. 302). This may be a general statement about modernism or a more specific statement of Lawrence's own preoccupation. Aaron's dream is a poor, rather literal, attempt to suit
the artistic action to the word. It fails to throw events into relief
in any significant sense, existing at the edge of the narrative and
separate from it. It also fails to raise questions about the framing function of dreams. Aaron himself wakes from the dream,
tries to assign meaning to the fragments he recalls and, failing,
dismisses it in order to assess the end of his literal (and metaphysical) journey, and to consider the possibilities of the new
phase of his life into which he has been projected by the loss of
his flute. There may be at work in Lawrence the memory of his
treatment of the will in his long essay 'The Reality of Peace',
where the metaphor is of the will at the helm as the subject is
borne upon the stream. Aaron has had, throughout, to negotiate
various currents. Even given Lawrence's artistic dilemma as he
prepares to include a 'dream' narrative, Aaron's dream-images
are too much of a literalized language under a merely notional
heading of dream. There are other instances in Lawrence's fiction where dream is deployed and where it arguably creates more
aesthetic problems than it solves. Ellen March's dreams in *The
Fox*, for example, are skilfully constructed but are, arguably,

actually unnecessary. They could be viewed as surplus to requirements, acts of crude symbolism, because the moment March actually sees the 'fox' she is 'unconscious' and, therefore, does not need to dream. For Lawrence, perhaps for any writer, the insertion of 'dreams' into a narrative creates the possibility of instances which are unworkable as dream-language: at once bad metaphor and weak frame.

So the dream at the end of *Aaron's Rod* is arguably a device characterized by imaginative paucity, or obviousness, leaving us to confront a meaningful paradox in Lawrence. When he uses dream, as here, the structure which is meant to be meaningful (the dream) actually loses its force. This is in sharp contrast, however, to those scenes in Lawrence which are charged with meaning and, while being in important respects dream-like, are not in fact dreams; yet they seem to have an equally deep source. Instances include the horses at the end of *The Rainbow* and the bull scenes in *The Plumed Serpent*. We have to consider why these are effective where the description of a dream is not, or is less so. It may be because an authentic dream resists the translation into language, into writing. What is written down as representing dream is always already interpreted by the writer, and, as some commentators have observed, repression has begun its work.[10] In Lawrence's 'dream-like' scenes, like the horses in *The Rainbow*, there is an unconscious in operation. This is why critics continually feel the need to interpret such scenes, in effect to fix a meaning. The horse-scene, for instance, like a real dream, is infinite; potentially, its meanings continually unfold. A text which purports to contain a dream is not rigorously or critically coming to terms with this infinity, which is why Aaron's 'dream' is inadequate. As a narrative it fails to come to terms with a 'real' dream's radical metaphoricity. The horse scene in *The Rainbow*, however, is uncanny (*unheimlich*) in the way a dream is uncanny: a quality which can elude the transcription of 'dream' in the fiction. The significance of Ursula's encounter with the 'actual' horses is essentially a matter of her projection. This is also the case in 'St. Mawr' where all the characters apart from the groom project their different meanings onto the horse. The object, there the horse, awaits inscription. This is common in Lawrence and usually skilfully done. But where dream is his conscious subject Lawrence's insistence is on the mechanistic and automatic nature of both the dream and the dream-work.

In 'Sleep and Dreams' he not only makes reference to, but also attempts to codify, a number of dream images or motifs. The figure of the mother is one of these. Lawrence:

> The truth is, every man has, the moment he awakes, a hatred of his dream, and a great desire to be free of the dream, free of the persistent mother-image or sister-image of the dream. It is a ghoul, it haunts his dreams, this image, with its hateful conclusions. And yet he cannot get free. As long as a man lives he may, in his dreams of passion or conflict, be haunted by the mother-image or sister image, even when he knows that the cause of the disturbing dream is the wife. But even though the actual subject of the dream is the wife, still, over and over again, for years, the dream-process will persist in substituting the mother-image. It haunts and terrifies a man.
>
> Why does the dream-process act so? For two reasons. First, the reason of simple automatic continuance. The mother-image was the first great emotional image to be introduced in the psyche. The dream-process mechanically reproduces its stock image the moment the intense sympathy-emotion is aroused. Again, the mother-image refers only to the upper plane. But the dream process is mechanical in its logic. Because the mother-image refers to the great dynamic stress of the upper plane, therefore it refers to the great dynamic stress of the lower. This is a piece of sheer automatic logic. The living soul is *not* automatic, and automatic logic does not apply to it.
>
> But for our second reason for the image. In becoming the object of great emotional stress for her son, the mother also becomes an object of poignancy, of anguish, of arrest, to her son. She arrests him from finding his proper fulfilment on the sensual plane. Now it is almost always the object of arrest which becomes impressed, as it were, upon the psyche. A man very rarely has an image of a person with whom he is livingly, vitally connected. He only has dream-images of the persons who, in some way, *oppose* his life-flow and his soul's freedom, and so become impressed upon his plasm as objects of resistance.
>
> (*Fantasia of the Unconscious*, F&P, pp. 167–8)

Quite apart from the seductions of autobiography, this describes exactly Richard Lovat Somers' dream in *Kangaroo*, after Jack Callcott's briefing about the Diggers. The context is the belief of the (deceased) mother and the wife in the man, a belief which is tested in his pursuit of the 'impersonal business of male activity' (*Kangaroo*, p. 96) located in a masculine community characterized by cultishness, a *locus* of male bonding which of necessity excludes the woman. Harriett Somers remains grounded in the 'intimate' and 'personal' life between man and woman that Lawrence initially represented as an 'authentic' relationship, and articulates both her distrust of the 'man's business' and her hurt at being pushed to the margins. Somer's dream, aligned with the description from *Fantasia of the Unconscious*, is about the resistant, oppositional female *and* about his need for validation from both his mother and his wife:

> But Somers knew from his dreams what she was feeling: his dreams of a woman, a woman he loved, something like Harriett, something like his mother, and yet unlike either, a woman sullen and obstinate against him, repudiating him. Bitter the woman was, grieved beyond words, grieved till her face was swollen and puffy and almost mad or imbecile, because she had loved him so much and now she must see him betray her love.
>
> (*Kangaroo*, p. 96)

Both descriptions, of course, manifest anxieties about female emotional power and about a perceived need in Lawrence, also viewed as problematic, to seek validation from loved women whose identities as mother and wife merge: he had already described his wife to Katherine Mansfield as 'the devouring mother' (*Letters*, III, p. 302). In 'Sleep and Dreams', the metaphor of projection, in the cinematic meaning of the word, of stock images flashing into the mind, connects with Lawrence's metaphors in *Psychoanalysis and the Unconscious* for the functioning of language. In his thesis, dreams are thrown up out of the psyche to indicate the presence of an anxiety: a whole complex of anxieties must rely for their expression on a limited medium, a limited number of stock-images. The analogy with language is manifest.

I propose in the next few pages to consider some of Lawrence's examples and his explanations. First is the 'dream' of raging horses, a description which needs quoting at length:

> For example, a man has a persistent passionate fear-dream about horses. He suddenly finds himself among great, physical horses,

which may suddenly go wild. Their great bodies surge madly round him, they rear above him, threatening to destroy him. At any minute he may be trampled down. Now a psychoanalyst will probably tell you off-hand that this is a father-complex dream. Certain symbols seem to be put into complex catalogues. But it is all too arbitrary. Examining the emotional reference we find that the feeling is sensual, there is a great impression of the powerful, almost beautiful physical bodies of the horses, the nearness, the rounded haunches, the rearing. Is the dynamic passion in a horse the danger-passion? It is a great sensual reaction at the sacral ganglion, a reaction of intense, sensual, dominant volition. The horse which rears and kicks and neighs madly acts from the intensely powerful sacral ganglion. But this intense activity from the sacral ganglion is male: the sacral ganglion is at its highest intensity in the male. So that the horse-dream refers to some arrest in the deepest sensual activity in the male. The horse is presented as an object of terror, which means that to the man's automatic dream-soul, which loves automatism, the great sensual male activity is the greatest menace. The automatic pseudo-soul, which has got the sensual nature repressed, would like to keep it repressed. Whereas the greatest desire of the living spontaneous soul is that this very male sensual nature, represented as a menace, shall be actually accomplished in life. The spontaneous self is secretly yearning for the liberation and fulfilment of the deepest and most powerful sensual nature. There may be an element of father-complex. The horse may also refer to the powerful sensual being in the father. The dream may be a love of the dreamer for the sensual male who is his father. But it has nothing to do with *incest*. The love is probably a just love.

(*Fantasia of the Unconscious*, F&P, pp. 170–1)

Lawrence's terms, 'danger-passion', 'automatic dream-soul', 'automatic pseudo-soul' and its antithesis, the 'living spontaneous soul', demand attention. Once again the arena for the implicit challenge to Freud, and in particular the Oedipal drama, is linguistic and involves the conscious setting up of quite different terms. Here the unconscious, or what passes in Lawrence for the unconscious, is framed in a new set of metaphors. Whether or not the reader finds his opinions palatable, Lawrence has developed in his work justification for terms that are positively idiosyncratic and imaginative, and of course metaphorical. The theme in this description is the tension and interplay of the mechanical and the automatic with the 'unharnessed' spontaneous self; the interplay of 'death-modes' and 'life-modes' in the individual. Lawrence's certainty as to what the horses signify here, a repressed male sensuality, does not alter the ambiguity of the horses that frighten Ursula towards the end of *The Rainbow*. The real point of interest in terms of artistic choices is that the horses do not appear to Ursula in a dream. Similarly, the kicking and rearing horse of the passage from *Fantasia of the Unconscious* is non-dream in 'St. Mawr'. This distinction forces the necessary comparison in Lawrence's fiction between dream, projection and vision. As one of the strongest animal scenes in the fiction, we know that the horses in *The Rainbow* are charged with psychic meaning but the reader has to labour hard to extract that meaning. This is a good stratagem on Lawrence's part: a dream would have the effect of closing off the significant substance from the narrative. Indeed, this is conventionally how dreams function in fiction. In making the horses at the end of *The Rainbow* 'real', their significance is pervasive rather than circumscribed. It is always difficult to say exactly what the horses signify and this is very much the point. If they appeared in a dream the expectation would be the possibility of extracting and attaching to them a specific meaning because even striking dreams, incorporated into a fiction, can seem too deliberate and too self-conscious, demanding a systematic interpretation. A visionary mode of representation, which characterizes *The Rainbow*, for instance, forces the reader to project in a more subtle way than might otherwise be the case.

Lawrence himself falls prey to a reductiveness. His interpretation, in *Fantasia of the Unconscious*, of the horses as a dream-image (not a symbol in a work of fiction) refers only to a masculine mode of consciousness, or perhaps, a mode of masculine consciousness. In this context the horses in *The Rainbow* could be interpreted as representing an arrested male 'sensuality' (Lawrence's choice of 'sensual' is interesting, as a word that is interrogated in the dream-of-horses passage) which menaces Ursula, who has throughout emphasized her fundamental singularity to the point of crisis in her relationship with Skrebensky. Fortunately, the finality of such an interpretation is prevented by the ambiguous quality of the experience. In this connection we can think of 'St. Mawr' particularly as discussed by David Cavitch. His interpretation accords with Lawrence's statement that 'the great sensual male activity is the greatest menace', but it is very reductive:

> Lou's responses to St. Mawr overtly express her unconscious sexual anxieties, and that is why the horse is like a revelation to her. She lives in the thrall of male aggression – her aversion to what she believes is real sex is the only explanation of the 'spell' of 'nonentity' over her life – and St. Mawr expresses symbolically the intense ambivalence of her fear and her anticipation of violation by a man. The horse is not a figure of simple sexual potency but of dangerously overwrought sexual inhibition.
>
> (*D.H. Lawrence and the New World*, p. 156)

Furthermore, Cavitch argues, the sexual fear which is thematized in the story is Lawrence's own, and the conclusion is duplicitous because Lawrence is battling with his own notion of male power: 'The story is inadequate intellectually to its complex materials, because Lawrence does not rationally understand what his story reveals' (p. 163). This last assertion represents an attempt to psychoanalyse Lawrence rather than to 'read' him; not only is the real point lost, but the approach is the source of much crude misreading. The horse's significance rests in each onlooker, and each onlooker's own emotional history. If St. Mawr is a symbol, he works better as a 'real' horse than as a dream element: the story makes us work at understanding his complex significance. If St. Mawr simply appeared in a dream, like the dream at the conclusion of *Aaron's Rod*, the dream convention itself would transform him into that literalized language and his force would be lost.

The second dream-image which Lawrence isolates in *Fantasia of the Unconscious* is the bull, which again speaks to the mapping of the sensual body:

> The bull-dream is a curious reversal. In the bull the centres of power are in the breast and the shoulders. The horns of the head are symbols of this vast power in the upper self. The woman's fear of the bull is a great terror of the dynamic upper centres in man. The bull's horns, instead of being phallic,

represent the enormous potency of the upper centres. A woman
whose most positive dynamism is in the breast and shoulders
is fascinated by the bull. Her dream-fear of the bull and his
horns which may run into her may be reversed to a significance of desire for connection, not from the centres of the lower,
sensual self, but from the intense physical centres of the upper body: the phallus polarized from the upper centres, and
directed towards the great breast centre of the woman. Her
wakeful fear is terror of the great breast-and-shoulder, upper
rage and power of man, which may pierce her defenceless lower
self. The terror and the desire are near together – and go with
an admiration of the slender, abstracted bull loins.

(*Fantasia of the Unconscious*, F&P, p. 171)

Lawrence rather disingenuously ignores what is actually encoded
here. Characteristically, he reinscribes a traditional symbol with
his own meaning rather than showing any real interest in the
dream as dream. This 'decoding' activity works precisely against
his more measured judgment elsewhere about giving symbols
meanings. In this part of *Fantasia of the Unconscious*, at any rate,
Lawrence is going against his later stated intuitions in *Apocalypse* that 'The true symbol defies all explanation, so does the
true myth' (p. 142). In these passages on dream-motifs, Lawrence comes close to dealing in allegory, one of his least favourite modes of understanding. Elsewhere, he properly articulates
his insight that the whole process of seeing one thing as standing for another is crude. These more dogmatic passages in *Fantasia of the Unconscious*, the superficial pontificating, need to be
distinguished from that which is more useful and more characteristic in Lawrence. The sexual subtext in the bull passage, the
theme and figures of masculine power, violence and a desire for
violence, are clear enough, even while Lawrence tries to gainsay
the phallicism of the bull's horns. It is unsurprising that in his
dream-bestiary the woman should have 'dream-fear of the bull'.
    Always in Lawrence the decoding operation is underpinned
by a highly personal formulation; of otherness, of a masculine
principle, versions of masculine sexuality, where the underlying
theme is the relation between 'the woman' and this principle.
Superficially, the mystery is why Lawrence should set out to
address dream at all, unless to underline his point about the
limited psyche with its reliance on the most impoverished store

of stock images; to work against the hegemony of the psychoanalytic conception; to extend his own discourse on knowledge
and the nature of human knowing. But here is 'the superimposition of a theory': dream according to Lawrence's rigid formulations regarding the psyche (in his meditation on dream he largely
avoids the word 'unconscious'). In the fiction, the delimitation
of dream as something separate and symbolic runs against the
grain of the 'metaphysic'. The problem with dream as a narrative mode, in Lawrence, rests precisely in its literalness and indeed, in his hands, dream is in danger of becoming too much a
literalized language, although never as literalized as some of the
interpretative schemes in *Fantasia of the Unconscious* itself.

Bulls and visions come together in *The Plumed Serpent* but not,
and this is very much the point, as dream. Towards the end of
the novel Kate Leslie watches a bull and a cow being loaded
onto a boat. The cow goes fairly easily but her mate is less ac-
commodating:

> Then two peons passed a rope loosely round the haunches of
> the bull. The high-hatted farmer stepped on to the planks, and
> took the nose-ring again, very gently. He pulled softly. The
> bull lifted its head, but held back. It struck the planks with an
> unwilling foot. Then it stood, spangled with black on its white-
> ness, like a piece of the sky, immobile.
>
> The farmer pulled once more at the ring. Two men were
> pulling the rope, pressing in the flanks of the immovable, pas-
> sive, spangled monster. Two peons, at the back, with their heads
> down and their red-sashed, flexible loins thrust out behind,
> shoved with all their strength in the soft flanks of the mighty
> creature.
>
> And all was utterly noiseless and changeless; against the
> fulness of the pale lake, this silent, monumental group of life.
>
> (*The Plumed Serpent*, p. 432)

The men and the animals initially form a 'silhouette frieze' against
the background of the water, and the entire scene has a distinctive visual quality which is summed up in the description 'It
was near, yet seemed strange and remote' (p. 431) and, later,
'All so still and soft and remote' (p. 433). Indeed, these sentences,
and the whole narrative, impose on the actual scene the quality
of dream: the loading of the cow and bull onto the boat seems

to take place at a remove from the world inhabited by Kate who looks on but is not dreaming. If she were, the scene would have to bear an extra and specific significance. As it is, the reader responds to it by recognizing that it is forceful and charged with meaning but without being directed to regard it as significant in a diagnostic way. Compared with the long dream in *Aaron's Rod* this scene is not too self-aware, indeed it is beautifully observed in a way the other cannot be: it is both part of the world occupied by Kate and invested with a remoteness which, in part, derives from its being 'real' rather than 'imagined'.

In this episode the narrative requires the reader to participate in Kate's attentiveness in a way that dream would not. The significance, then, is not so much in the event itself as in the quality of attention to the paradoxically near but distant scene. This accords, and contrasts, with the first chapter of the novel where bulls are again associated with the idea of spectacle. At the bull-fight the baited bull strikes out at a redundant horse whose function is to be sacrificed to the show. The spectacle draws the gaze of a highly charged crowd. The scene of violence is mediated through Kate's eyes:

> Kate had never been taken so completely by surprise in all her life. She had still cherished some idea of a gallant show. And before she knew where she was, she was watching a bull whose shoulder trickled blood goring his horns up and down inside the belly of a prostrate and feebly plunging old horse.
>
> The shock almost overpowered her. She had come for a gallant show. This she had paid to see.
>
> (*The Plumed Serpent*, p. 16)

The different conscious, or stated, responses of the expatriate Europeans and Americans in the audience point up the difference between seeing as an experiential function, and seeing as knowing, or more accurately as the feeling which alerts Kate to the fact that she would rather not attend the bull-fight any longer. Her companions need the voyeuristic thrill which might in their barren epistemology indicate an authentic experience – the 'frantic effort to *see* – just to *see*' (p. 28): for them seeing provides what passes for an insider's access to the quite excluding ritual. Kate is given a different perspective, and gives thanks that she is not the many-eyed Argus.

Just as in the episode where Tom Brangwen's gaze is focused on the scene of Lydia Lensky and the baby Anna, so the scene of the cow and bull being loaded onto the boat has implications for us in the way we read Lawrence. The reading process is never a simple and hygienic standing-back from the language. Neither is it a conscious engagement with a language that self-consciously makes the point about the reader participating in a text that resists easy consumption. The level of readerly interaction and creativity is more subtle than that might allow. The reader is both at a remove from the action, as is Kate in the bull scenes, and busy in the creation of its meaning. Much in Lawrence is both 'strange and remote' and yet 'near'; qualities of both 'vision' and dream.

Lawrence's discourse on dreams thus cuts across and into his more interesting thought on vision and representation. In the first place dreaming is the result of 'flows' of activity in the body; the 'sweeping' current, the 'earth-current' (*Fantasia*, F&P, p. 163). Lawrence's refusal to 'attach any real importance' (p. 164) to dreams highlights his deep-seated resistance to any tendency to regard dreams as representations from 'the' unconscious. Judging him from his fiction, it is alien for Lawrence to think that the vigorous unconscious, ('soul-dreams'), should manifest itself in neat fables precisely because they invite a hermeneutic exercise which transforms unconscious production into regulated and limited structures of meaning. We can see from the fiction, if not from the discursive writing, that such a transformation is in Lawrence's view restrictive, placing what Deleuze and Guattari regard as the production of desire in harness. The following passage underlines the Deleuzian–Guattarian parallel with Lawrence. It is argued that in current psychoanalytical practice:

The whole of desiring-production is crushed, subjected to the requirements of representation, and to the dreary games of what is representative and represented in representation. And there is the essential thing: the reproduction of desire gives way to a simple representation, in the process as well as theory of the cure. The productive unconscious makes way for an unconscious that knows only how to express itself – express itself in myth, in tragedy, in dream.

But who says that dream, tragedy, and myth are adequate to the formations of the unconscious, even if the work of transformation is taken into account? . . . It is as if Freud had drawn back from this world of wild production and explosive desire, wanting at all costs to restore a little order there, an order made classical owing to the ancient Greek theater.

(*Anti-Oedipus*, p. 54)

This shows exactly why Lawrence responded aggressively to what he perceived as the banality of his critics (and admirers) reading *Sons and Lovers*, for instance, as an ordered representation of 'his' neurosis, and why he felt misread. The question asked by Deleuze and Guattari is implicitly asked by Lawrence in his chapter 'Sleep and Dreams'. His way of resisting the classical or mythic framing of the dynamic unconscious is to contrast what he understands as Freudian 'dream-meaning' (*Fantasia*, F&P, p. 167) with his own understanding, articulated in a language of 'flows'. His emphasis is on the blood: once again we are in a position to ask how literal Lawrence is being when he explains nightmares by referring to 'an arrest of the mechanical flow of the system' (p. 165), an arrest which affects the organs, stimulating dreams. There is a literalness, but there is also an ambivalence, one which Deleuze and Guattari, partly accidentally, help to bring into clearer focus. The 'physical flow' and the 'mechanical flow' (pp. 165–6) on which Lawrence concentrates are not merely literal: we have to understand 'the friction of the night-flow' (p. 167), for instance, metaphorically before we begin to fathom the complexity of Lawrence's repudiation of psychoanalysis. This return to metaphor, to language, is in Lawrence an entirely radical way of confronting the unconscious formulated by Freud as an ordered phenomenon, articulated in terms of classical myth, where Oedipus is the principal term. Its current value would seem to be the way in which Lawrence's poetic thought is seen to nourish certain post-Freudian positions.

CONCLUDING REMARKS: LANGUAGE AND THE UNCONSCIOUS

I suggested earlier that *Psychoanalysis and the Unconscious* and *Fantasia of the Unconscious* constitute, not a theory of the unconscious, but the most extended treatment of Lawrence's version of the inextricability and interconnectedness of the body, language and unconscious functioning. This is not anything that Lawrence states as such, but it is a conviction that is rooted in the metaphoricity of the books. Furthermore, it is precisely this metaphoricity that enables Lawrence to (re)-figure some of the assumptions of psychoanalysis. Metaphor is the way Lawrence argues past Freud, as it were, and institutes his own sense of the dissenting value of the Poetic. At the root of this is his rejection of the authority of Oedipus in Freudian thought and, crucially, his rejection of what Lawrence called the 'algebraic' tendency to interpret only ever according to one system, the better to solve the very real problems which have taken hold at the deepest levels of the human unconscious.

As I have suggested, Lawrence's metaphoricity embodies the iconoclastic and what has been represented as the 'anti-Oedipal' direction of his own understanding. It is fair to say, with Deleuze and Guattari, for whom Lawrence is a radical theorizer of desire, that Lawrence 'speaks by virtue of the flows of sexuality and the intensities of the unconscious' (*Anti-Oedipus*, p. 115). To say so is implicitly to recognize the importance of Lawrence's metaphorical language as a 'speaking' that offers a challenge to the rigidity of Freudian formulations, and to the moral and cultural authority (of which Lawrence was suspicious) reserved for psychoanalysis. In their book, Deleuze and Guattari return to Lawrence's language, referring appropriately to *Psychoanalysis and the Unconscious* in particular, in order to point up the force of his 'flow' as a subversive medium under its own momentum:

> flows ooze, they traverse the triangle, breaking apart its vertices. The Oedipal wad does not absorb these flows, any more than it could seal off a jar of jam or plug a dike. Against the walls of the triangle, toward the outside, flows exert the irresistible pressure of lava or the invincible oozing of water . . . . We are all libidos that are too viscous and too fluid – and not by preference, but wherever we have been carried by the deterritorialized flows. . . . Who does not feel in the flows of his desire both the lava and the water?
> (*Anti-Oedipus*, p. 67)

What Deleuze and Guattari do with this, in terms of extending and developing their thesis of schizoanalysis is outside the purview of the present study. Of interest and immediate relevance is the way they resort to a highly metaphorical mode and language in order to gain access to the processes of human desire. They recognize in Lawrence a fellow revolutionary poet-thinker.

The unconscious that Lawrence apprehends in these books is not, then, the construct posited by Freudian psychoanalysis. The mode and language of *Psychoanalysis and the Unconscious* and *Fantasia of the Unconscious* are implicated in a very particular way, as I have suggested, in disempowering what are viewed as the authoritarian structures of Freudian thought. We are now in a position to recognize the real force of the word 'fantasia' in the title of the longer book: the language and structure of the book, as spontaneous as it can reasonably be, is in itself a 'flow' of language breaking across the more formal limitations that its stated subject, the unconscious, would usually demand. Metaphor and 'metaphysic', Lawrence's personal philosophy, have been shown to coincide radically in these books.

6

Undulating Styles: *The Rainbow*

There still remains a God, but not a personal God: a vast shimmering impulse which wavers onwards towards some end, I don't know what – taking no regard of the little individual, but taking regard for humanity. When we die, like rain-drops falling back again into the sea, we fall back into the big, shimmering sea of unorganised life which we call God. We are lost as individuals, yet we count in the whole.

(*Letters*, I, p. 256)

For we are all waves of the tide. But the tide contains the waves.

('The Crown')

Evidently the wealth of critical writing on Lawrence, and in particular on his mature fiction, means that the main ideas are continually laid down and augmented, and Lawrence's style almost always, rightly, receives critical attention. That there are right ways and wrong ways of approaching his language is something which is implicitly taken up in this study. Lawrence is, of course, recognizably a highly metaphorical writer and his work has much to communicate about the necessarily metaphorical nature of understanding. If Lawrence can be seen 'thinking metaphorically' in his discursive writing, to what extent is the poetic character of his thought available to us in his fiction? While I would be reluctant to say that *The Rainbow* is 'about' language any more than the books on the unconscious, or indeed *Women in Love*, are 'about' language, directly, my intention here is to examine metaphoricity in *The Rainbow* as the proper vehicle for Lawrence's thought in the context of a significant work of fiction. This will not prove to be another mode entirely, different

117

utterly from that of the subsequent novel, *Women in Love*, for instance, but a specific modulation of Lawrence's 'metaphysic', broadly speaking. To make a metaphor is not the same as 'thinking metaphorically': *The Rainbow* embodies its own mode of thinking metaphorically which communicates what it is really 'about'. The discussion opens with a concentration on something which is on the face of it quite local, on the wave-imagery of the novel as representing a tangible body of metaphor within the work. This is with a view to focusing on the question of how an instance of metaphor within a narrative can also come to be seen as the language of the whole novel. Essentially it will emerge that without the 'wave' in *The Rainbow* there is no novel. So that even at this point it is possible and appropriate to talk about *The Rainbow*'s 'engulfing' medium.

There is nothing in the first paragraph of *The Rainbow* to suggest the radical view of language that will emerge in the course of the novel. It unproblematically sets the scene after a traditional model, and the debt to Hardy has often been noted, but we cannot talk benignly about influences on Lawrence who was, in his discursive writing, a perceptive theorizer of the novel genre. In his mature fiction Lawrence turned the novel form into the arena of his critique of the ideals and aesthetic orthodoxies which were habitually represented within that form. His art-speech ('Artspeech is the only truth') also constituted a critique of the excessively aestheticized, excessively self-reflexive modern novel, a form which, in his view, revealed a lack of artistic integrity. The tendency in modern fiction which it represented provoked Lawrence's criticism partly because it seemed to him to pay lipservice to Nietzsche's view in *Human, All Too Human* that 'artists of all ages have raised to heavenly transfiguration precisely those conceptions which we now recognize as false' (p. 220) but stopped short of a genuinely philosophical critique of those conceptions. In the process of re-reading, we are forced to recognize how Lawrence's radically metaphorical prose reveals *his* awareness of the distance between himself and the traditions of the past, a distance that he can strategically develop.

The second paragraph, and successive relatively short paragraphs leading into the distinctive 'prologue' of *The Rainbow* begin to suggest that the narrative language itself will have a specifically Lawrentian ontological bearing. The 'wave which cannot halt' (*The Rainbow*, p. 9) has been set in motion. It refers to a structure of repetition just as evident in the narrative language as in terms of the action. The characteristic rhythm of the evenly spaced nouns, and repetition of sounds represented in the often quoted sequence 'the pulse of the blood of the teats of the cows beat into the pulse of the hands of the men' (p. 10) gives rise to a kinaesthetic language which signals the wave-like quality of the entire narrative: the continuous ever-changing nuances of the language imitate, as far as language can, a fluid wave-form, rhythmic, repetitive, with a suggestion of motion (through tempo). Another example of Lawrence's repetitive style is afforded by the meeting of Ursula and Skrebensky in 'The Bitterness of Ecstasy' (*The Rainbow*, Chapter XV, pp. 412–16). Here the continual repetition of 'dark' and 'darkness' occurs in contexts which sometimes relate to this persistent image of the wave: 'The thought of walking in the dark, far-reaching water-meadows, beside the full river, transported her. Dark water flowing in silence through the big, restless night made her feel wild' (p. 412); 'The deep vibration of the darkness could only be felt, not heard'; 'He seemed like the living darkness upon her, she was in the embrace of the strong darkness' (p. 413). As Ursula becomes more 'conscious' she perceives the town – 'It rests upon the unlimited darkness, like a gleam of coloured oil on dark water, but what is it? – nothing, nothing' (pp. 414–15). This interpretation is projected onto the people she encounters as she travels home in solitude: 'But in reality each one was a dark, blind, eager wave urging blindly forward, dark with the same homogeneous desire' (p. 415). Through the rhythms established by repetition like this, Lawrence is drawing on what Nietzsche called the primeval union of music and poetry which 'deposited so much symbolism into rhythmic movement . . . that we now *suppose* it to speak directly *to* the inner world and to come *from* the inner world' (*Human, All Too Human*, p. 215). So it is that Lawrentian modernism exhibits *its* interest in the relation between the work of art and the experience of feeling. As many commentators have pointed out, rhythm is one of the primal forms of expression within Lawrentian poetics.

There is an ebb and flow between the paragraphs of the first pages of this novel that helps to establish the point about undulating styles. Taking the first section of the book as a prologue, it is likely that the reader is drawn in by the language: not only does it define a certain mode of 'being-in-the-world' as has often

been remarked, it does so seductively. Whether this state is claus-
trophobic or suffocating for the Brangwens, seemingly saturated
by their environment, is not the initial point. That point rests in
the reader's awareness of the language having a special quality.
Ontological difference at this early stage is largely the difference
between Brangwen-male and Brangwen-female. The language
describing the existence of the Brangwen male is distinctive and
different from the tone which describes the yearning outwards
of the women, who are in comparison more 'conscious'. Once
again it is the general rather than the individual terms which
are an important part of the difference: there are no named individuals at this stage, only male and female. Difference is implied in the minute changes of style (the inflectional changes)
even within a relatively small space. The reader is encouraged
to be sensitive to subtle modulations in the narrative language
exemplified in the difference between the paragraphs quoted below.
The paragraph-break is the moment of change, of the subtlest
transition:

> It was enough for the men, that the earth heaved and opened
> its furrow to them, that the wind blew to dry the wet wheat,
> and set the young ears of corn wheeling freshly round about;
> it was enough that they helped the cow in labour, or ferreted
> the rats from under the barn, or broke the back of a rabbit
> with a sharp knock of the hand. So much warmth and gener-
> ating and pain and death did they know in their blood, earth
> and sky and beast and green plants, so much exchange and
> interchange they had with these, that they lived full and sur-
> charged, their senses full fed, their faces always turned to the
> heat of the blood, staring into the sun, dazed with looking
> towards the source of generation, unable to turn round.
>
> But the woman wanted another form of life than this, some-
> thing that was not blood-intimacy. Her house faced out from
> the farm-buildings and fields, looked out to the road and the
> village with church and Hall and the world beyond. She stood
> to see the far-off world of cities and governments and the active
> scope of man.
>
> (*The Rainbow*, pp. 10–11)

A quality of repetition persists where 'the woman' is the focus
but it is appropriately of a different order. Such tonal difference

is pronounced by the obvious contrast to the more 'ordinary' language of a line which is often quoted by critics to signal a decisive change in narrative interest: 'About 1840, a canal was constructed across the meadows of the Marsh Farm . . .' (p. 13). This, in the simple past tense of completed action, offers the most obvious contrast stylistically with either of these earlier modulations and is itself part of the 'wave' of language 'which cannot halt'.

It is generally recognized that these linguistic modulations signal to the reader when a particularly significant moment of feeling or experience is about to be entered upon. *The Rainbow* is indeed characterized by memorable passages which might serve to typify the book to the wide community of its readers. These episodes are largely triumphs of language and include the novel's 'prologue'; Tom Brangwen with the infant Anna feeding the cattle on the night of Lydia's confinement; Anna and Will stacking sheaves; Ursula's 'epiphanic' moment on looking into her college microscope; her encounter with the horses. The placing of these episodes within the narrative results in each being on the crest of a structural wave, being in some senses of the nature of a crescendo, the products of an increasing of verbal and rhythmic force. The emphasis need not be on the fact alone of heightened language, but on the strategic function of this heightened language.

The description of Will Brangwen in the cathedral provides a case in point:

> Here the stone leapt up from the plain of earth, leapt up in a manifold, clustered desire each time, up, away from the horizontal earth, through twilight and dusk and the whole range of desire, through the swerving, the declination, ah, to the ecstasy, the touch, to the meeting and the consummation, the meeting, the clasp, the close embrace, the neutrality, the perfect, swooning consummation, the timeless ecstasy. There his soul remained, at the apex of the arch, clinched in the timeless ecstasy, consummated.
>
> And there was no time nor life nor death, but only this, this timeless consummation, where the thrust from earth met the thrust from earth and the arch was locked on the keystone of ecstasy. This was all, this was everything. Till he came to himself in the world below. Then again he gathered himself together,

in transit, every jet of him strained and leaped, leaped clear in
to the darkness above, to the fecundity and the unique mystery, to the touch, the clasp, the consummation, the climax of
eternity, the apex of the arch.

(The Rainbow, pp. 187–8)

To some readers this sort of writing loses much of its credibility
because the double meanings are too clumsily spelled out and
sexual inference dominates at the expense of the text's more serious project. It is the linguistic climax to a relatively long passage. The 'wave' of language can be heard building up as Will
and Anna approach the cathedral and as they enter. Indeed, the
wave metaphor which will dominate is at first generated visually, by the sequence of arches moving up to the altar. So, what
begins as a visual image, is later felt as a crescendo. The context
is, therefore, extremely important inasmuch as it will ultimately
offer the best explanation both of the passage and of Will's experience. Anna too is revealed to us through her experience of the
cathedral, and through her judgement of what it means to Will.

Not surprisingly, given that water and waves are a far from
arbitrary choice as a metaphor in Lawrence, the context, when it
offers an explanation of Will's emotional commitment to the
cathedral, does so like this:

His soul would have liked it to be so: here, here is all, complete, eternal: motion, meeting, ecstasy, and no illusion of time,
of night and day passing by, but only perfectly proportioned
space and movement clinching and renewing, and passion surging its way in great waves to the altar, recurrence of ecstasy.

(The Rainbow, p. 188)

There are three distinct levels of language here. First, the sup-
plementary association of 'waves of feeling' can have the effect
of transmitting Will's experience into cliché. This is not necessarily inappropriate since feeling, for Will, is always mediated
by some external object, usually a work of art or architecture,
and he struggles hopelessly for something original, which cannot be faked, in his own artistic projects. Being aware of Will's
cliché leads into a more particular awareness of the fact that
Lawrence is here making creative use of a body of already existing, or dead, metaphor in common usage. So the second level is

the use of deep-lying metaphor already in language, quite apart from cliché. And yet cliché can have the effect of reviving a tired or dead metaphor if the ground is prepared. Often a pun is the means to this revival. In this passage the language is inflected towards both, that is to say towards cliché and towards a 'deep' level of common metaphor in the language. These discriminations are very interesting for Lawrence.

The third more difficult level is Lawrence's overall view of language, which is implicit and emergent. A 'thinking about' and a 'listening to' language is only possible from within language itself: one of the questions Lawrence implicitly poses is whether there is a place 'beyond' language. It is only the concentrated metaphoricity in Lawrence which helps him to 'think' this through. In the passage quoted, the wave is also a model for a kind of sentiment. Waves have now become a common figure for the course of feeling represented by contact with the cathedral. The syntax in this short passage has an impressionistic function, imitating as closely as possible wave-repetition and wave-rhythm. Anna's resistance is articulated in related terms: 'She was not to be flung forward on the lift and lift of passionate flights, to be cast at last upon the altar steps as upon the shore of the unknown' (p. 188). Anna's refusal to be cast (re-born) on this 'shore' is presented as a failure. The terms recall the figure in 'Study of Thomas Hardy' who must 'give himself naked to the flood' if he is to 'live' (*Hardy*, p. 19), but in contrast, this figure is heroic. These tiny instances remind us how one figure (metaphorical), like the 'wave', leads inevitably to another: 'dive' ('Diver'), shore, 'unknown'.[1] The description of Anna, resisting, also contains an element of readerly resistance bearing in mind the common experience of some of Lawrence's readers who feel that he is evidently saying something of importance although it is often difficult to pinpoint his meaning.

This language culminates in the longer passage which is given over wholly to Anna's desire to go against the current she perceives in Will:

So that she caught at little things, which saved her from being swept forward headlong in the tide of passion that leaps on into the Infinite in a great mass, triumphant and flinging its own course. She wanted to get out of this fixed, leaping, forward-travelling movement, to rise from it as a bird rises with wet, limp feet from the sea, to lift herself as a bird lifts its breast and thrusts its body from the pulse and heave of a sea that bears it forward to an unwilling conclusion, tear herself away like a bird on wings, and in the open space where there is clarity, rise up above the fixed, surcharged motion, a separate speck that hangs suspended, moves this way and that, seeing and answering before it sinks again, having chosen or found the direction in which it shall be carried forward.

(*The Rainbow*, p. 189)

The oxymoronic suggestiveness of 'fixed, surcharged motion' and the 'fixed, leaping, forward-travelling movement' in a sentence that drastically postpones its own conclusion, speak to the mode of *The Rainbow* itself with its great wave of language. The references are to the complex movement of the wave as perpetually mobile and yet eternally, fixedly, running along the same course. Anna imagines herself temporarily detached from the enveloping wave of experience, the Brangwen experience that characterizes the novel's opening, but ultimately recognizes that she will be carried forward as part of it, creating it as child follows upon child. It is inappropriate, and impossible, for her to imagine the 'isolation unbearable' that Gudrun, for instance, feels in 'Water-Party', as the direct result of being separate (*Women in Love*, p. 182). However, while Anna is content to return to a condition in which she will again be 'carried forward', the 'separate speck that hangs suspended', which she momentarily desires to be, recalls both the moon, a principal image in *The Rainbow* and *Women in Love*, and the star that moves without connection. In this, Anna can be seen to anticipate the mode of *Women in Love*, as will Ursula as she becomes increasingly more individuated, but it is here a fleeting projection.

Where water is more literal in the text, moving the action of the novel on, related issues are thrown into relief. The death of Tom Brangwen is a case in point. The water has come, 'in little waves', to claim him:

Still he wrestled and fought to get himself free, in the unutterable struggle of suffocation, but he always fell again deeper. Something struck his head, a great wonder of anguish went over him, then the darkness covered him entirely.

In the utter darkness, the unconscious, drowning body was

rolled along, the waters pouring, washing, filling in the place. The cattle woke up and rose to their feet, the dog began to yelp. And the unconscious, drowning body was washed along in the black, swirling darkness, passively.

(The Rainbow, p. 229)

In the first place this passage communicates the physical force of the element, and Tom's vulnerability in its presence. Part of the initial fascination that the sight holds for Tom (in many respects a Noah figure) is the strangeness of there being water in the place where usually there is none. He is compelled to meet the 'running flood' which has such force in the novel partly because of its Biblical overtones. Tom's drowning anticipates both the 'Diver' and 'Water-Party' episodes of *Women in Love.* In drowning, he becomes barely distinguishable from the whole, becoming part of the continually moving flood and part of the darkness outside. In his final moments of consciousness his struggle is to 'get himself free' (which is momentarily Anna's impulse at the cathedral). His failure to do so marks his ultimate unity with the whole. The manner of his death reinforces our sense, nourished at the novel's opening, of the inseparability of the Brangwens from their world. In death, Tom merges with his environment, with which he nevertheless had an instinctive connection as an 'unconscious' Brangwen: the 'freedom' evinced by the 'wave' is the freedom to be a part of the whole, within the larger milieu. The individual and the background become one, which is the mode, the specifically linguistic mode, of *The Rainbow.*

In all the passages identified so far there is always the hand that writes the tale. In none of the passages outlined above is the character's consciousness simply or ingenuously represented. The consciousness of individuals – first the unspecified Brangwens differentiated principally by gender, then specific characters – is communicated, but not principally because they divide 'the gift of speech' (*Twilight in Italy,* p. 107). The narrative language comes in waves as the music does at Fred Brangwen's wedding, so that it is possible to talk about 'the deep underwater' of the novel (*The Rainbow,* p. 295). The description of the 'one great flood heaving slowly backwards to the verge of oblivion, slowly forward to the other verge, the heart sweeping along each time, and tightening with anguish as the limit was reached, and the movement, at crisis, turned and swept back' (pp. 295–6), applies to the narrative as much as to the dance and dancers.[2] The 'flood' of language in *The Rainbow*, heaving between the great tide of oblivion and the individual wake of heightened consciousness, describes how the novel itself progresses. In the longer passage relating to Anna Brangwen quoted above, it is the 'forward-travelling movement' that she has to escape. This movement is inherent in the structure of generation and succession within *The Rainbow*. It is in the quite different simultaneity and frictionality of styles in *Women in Love*, with its insistent oppositional language, that this 'wave' is eventually halted.

'Undulating' as a description of the stylistic structure of *The Rainbow* refers to waves as distinct from other waterish metaphors such as the rainbow itself. The rainbow, formed by light reflecting from minute droplets of water, is also a far from arbitrary image for Lawrence. Two poems, 'The Rainbow' and 'Rainbow', (*Complete Poems*, p. 692; pp. 818–20) give an indication of the double significance to him of the rainbow as a phenomenon. The latter recalls the condition of Tom and Lydia Brangwen as married, separate but meeting 'to the span of the heavens' (*The Rainbow*, p. 91). But 'The Rainbow', among Lawrence's last poems, relates more closely to the implied connection between water and consciousness, and provides a more subtle expression of Lawrence's poetics:

> Even the rainbow has a body
> made of the drizzling rain
> and is an architecture of glistening atoms
> built up, built up
> yet you can't lay your hand on it,
> nay, nor even your mind.
>
> (*Complete Poems*, p. 692)

In the poem, the complex quality of the rainbow's presence is foregrounded. The rainbow is embodied by the conjunction of light and water but it amounts to more than its twin elements. Lawrence might ask how to understand what a rainbow *is* rather than simply its cause, which is easy to comprehend. The idea of 'rainbow' depends on the idea of 'light', and who, asks Lawrence, can explain the idea of light? The poem speaks of continuity and change, the twin dynamic of fixity and transformation that underpins *The Rainbow*. It speaks of the present moment as transient – what is more elusive than the present moment, and yet what more urgent? In the poem the rainbow is the only kind of 'architecture' to retain, for the onlooker, a sense of exaltation, what Nietzsche called 'the proximity of the divine' (*Human, All Too Human*, p. 218), in contrast to the forced and vulnerable ecstasy represented in the stone building beloved of Will Brangwen. The divine, the religious, revisits the poet through the embodiment of the rainbow. The religious itself figures largely within Lawrence's poetic in the vivid tension between an ahistorical present and primordial forms which continue to speak within the present, for Lawrence. The rainbow's denial of a past – a rainbow is an architectural form without a history – is countered by the archaic symbolism in the Judaeo-Christian context consciously evoked by Lawrence, of the bow set in the sky. This sign of God's covenant that he would not destroy Creation again, as he did in the Flood, finds many significances in Lawrence's work through his language, and through indirectly mythic figures (Tom/Noah). In this way history and the fleeting present co-exist, as they must in his novel.

LANGUAGE AS METAPHOR

Rehearsing these points it is evident that the use of water as a stylistic analogy is a far from arbitrary choice on my part, the image deriving from Lawrence. Lawrence, it has already been ascertained, speaks 'by virtue of flows'. These, for instance, are his more general comments on the novel in the ninth chapter of *Lady Chatterley's Lover*:

> And here lies the vast importance of the novel, properly handled. It can inform and lead into new places the flow of our sympathetic consciousness, and it can lead our sympathy away in recoil from things gone dead. Therefore, the novel, properly handled, can reveal the most secret places of life: for it is in the passional secret places of life, above all, that the tide of sensitive awareness needs to ebb and flow, cleansing and freshening.
> (*Lady Chatterley's Lover*, p. 92)

While this addresses the novel form, the *locus* of Lawrence's most overt critiques of modernity, and the testing-ground for his own modernism, it also speaks of language. The explicit image of 'cleansing' as a function of language in *Lady Chatterley's Lover* is an idea which is more subliminally written in to the language of the earlier novels. Language is the appropriate medium if the intention is to 'clean out' ingrained conceptions of what is 'normal', 'natural' and 'right' in human relations and attitudes, the challenge to idealism and a programme of orthodoxies that characterizes Lawrence's work. One of Lawrence's goals is not just to question such conceptions analytically but to modify and transform them by a continual, gradual, barely recognizable process.

Apart from this explicit image of cleansing, water is an image of psychic activity, as in the earlier references to dream, and this is particularly true in *The Rainbow*. The choice of water is again hardly arbitrary: the psychologist's metaphor, William James's 'stream of consciousness', so significant to the modernists, grows out of a collective sense of the continuousness of thought. In *Psychoanalysis and the Unconscious* Lawrence was ironic about this conception because of its links with psychoanalysis. In 'Introduction to Pictures' he transformed it into a term of 'blood-consciousness' in his characteristic affirmation of the body:

> All the cells of our body are conscious. And all the time, they give off a stream of consciousness which flows along the nerves and keeps us spontaneously alive. While the flow streams through us, from the blood to the heart, the bowls [sic], the viscera, then along the sympathetic system of nerves into our spontaneous minds, making us breathe, and see, and move, and be aware, and *do* things spontaneously, while this flow streams as a flame streams ceaselessly, we are lit up, we glow, we live.
>
> (*Phoenix*, p. 767)

So water in Lawrence, distinct from the modernist 'stream', is an effective image of consciousness *and* language because of its special qualities as a pervasive medium. It is not always the engulfing image of *The Rainbow* where 'water' and 'wave' jointly become an image of the evolving psyche: Tom Brangwen is conscious of water, yet unconscious of the 'wave'. The opening of the novel depicts Ursula's forebears in psychological terms and the often rehearsed movement throughout the book towards individuation (represented in Ursula herself) is sustained princi-

pally by the water and wave imagery. It would be inappropriate for Lawrence to incorporate an external model of consciousness as visible as the aestheticized Jamesian 'stream' into his novel,
as to do so would seriously undermine his own sense of psychic
evolution, a central theme in *The Rainbow*, and run counter to
his own language-sense.

It is this implicit language-sense that makes any external theory
irrelevant. The wave imagery in *The Rainbow* does not constitute
a linguistic representation of a current theory of consciousness.
Yet the wave, what one commentator has called the '"tidal"
rhythms' of the novel,[3] reveals the extent to which Lawrence is
thinking metaphorically about language as a medium for consciousness. The effect of this thinking metaphorically is not the
self-consciously aestheticized text of 'high' modernism. Rather,
it is a sign of the Heideggerean suggestion in Lawrence that 'to
talk about language is presumably even worse than to write about
silence' ('Language', in *Poetry, Language, Thought*, p. 190). His
thinking is implicit rather than explicit, as suits the nature of
the subject.

In this lies the significant contrast between Lawrence, a central but not a programmatic modernist, and his contemporaries.
James Joyce and Virginia Woolf, for instance, despite their intrinsic differences, represent a more conscious approach to language and consciousness than Lawrence, and one which is more
evidently related to Symbolist innovations. The central text in
this regard is *Ulysses* with its decisive influence on the artistic
imagination for the rest of the century. Joyce's stream of consciousness techniques completed the move of 'consciousness' as
a novelistic preoccupation to a centre-stage position in the early
twentieth century. With Joyce in mind, Virginia Woolf famously
considered the 'shower' of thoughts in 'an ordinary mind on an
ordinary day', and added that 'For the moderns . . . the point of
interest, lies very likely in the dark places of psychology' ('Modern
Fiction', in *The Common Reader*, pp. 149–52). Lawrence begged to
differ.

The subject in modernist fiction is recognizable by his or her
linguistic contours; in Woolf and Joyce, for instance, subjectivity
does indeed lie behind the eyes. In this way language becomes
a legitimate subject of their novels as each writer consciously
pulls away from that which Woolf designates a 'materialist' mode
of fiction, at least in the English novel (p. 147). Lawrence uses

the term 'materialism' in a related context in 'John Galsworthy'. Complaining about the lack of individuals in Galsworthy's *oeuvre* and reading his imaginative output symptomatically, Lawrence writes, 'When one reads Mr. Galsworthy's books, it seems as if there were not on earth one single human individual. They are social beings, positive and negative. . . . the tragedy today is that men are only materially and socially conscious' ('John Galsworthy', in *Hardy*, pp. 212–13).

In *Ulysses* the relation of Homer's *Odyssey* to Joyce's fiction is metaphorical given the extent of substitution and transposition. By the same token it is the *Odyssey*'s externality which is significant, the most obvious framework upon and around which Joyce's text is constructed. There can be no expectation of an equivalent framework in Lawrence where the central metaphor of a work, as in *The Rainbow*, arises wholly from within; an implicit 'structure' of thought. In Lawrence's view, a purely structural and thematic use of a culturally significant text is never more than a matter of making mechanical equivalents, and 'mechanical' is a word which he would use to describe a modernist grasp of consciousness.

Joyce and Woolf are to a significant extent responding to, and contributing to, a specific historical moment. Their work brings into relief the relation between a tradition and a counter-tradition. Because Lawrence's language-consciousness is not so directly informed by the response which their work manifests, in him the focus must inevitably be on an emergent and highly personal view of language which can only be inferred from the metaphorical levels in his texts. While he is aware of the distance between his own language and 'metaphysic' and a distinct literary tradition, he does not make that distance a principal and conscious preoccupation in his own work. This is clearly one of the reasons for aligning Lawrence on one level with figures like Freud, or more obviously Nietzsche, because of the forcefulness of the recognition in the latter, for instance, of metaphorical discourse as the necessary vehicle of thought. It is a commonplace to say that neither consciousness nor language can be discussed non-metaphorically. Lawrence is a writer who subtly exemplifies the reasons why this should be the case. Nietzsche is more analytical about the whole question of metaphor, his point of view being that the language we use gives us various models of reality, which is the case in an individual context as well as a cultural one. The highly metaphorical language of Lawrence's nominally 'discursive' books, where the reader might expect a barely metaphorical style, underlines this point. Water as a metaphor for consciousness is not simply illustrative in an *ad hoc* way, therefore, but arises intrinsically from Lawrence's language-sense. It is worth briefly considering, in the light of this statement, some fundamental attributes of water. Naturalistically, water has properties which distinguish it from the other elements. Water falls as rain, for example, and is present on the earth as such. Nevertheless, rain which has fallen can dry up or go underground, leaving no immediately identifiable trace to suggest that it has been there at all (apart from in memory). This transitory quality of water is artistically very useful to Lawrence. Water occurs underground, lying at subterranean levels, or it can be invisible, present on, under and above the earth in different forms. Scientifically, this is the 'indestructibility of matter' that Lawrence refers to in 'The Crown' in the course of his critique of 'rational' explanations. Interestingly, his considerations become linguistic, 'We don't know what we mean, ultimately, by *conservation,* or *indestructibility*' (in *Reflections on the Death of a Porcupine,* p. 287).

Even if we do not move beyond the crudest of analogies, these features help to attend to Lawrence's thought about language and the fact that language itself is only ever ambivalently 'present'. Yet it is the medium that empresents 'world'. References in *The Rainbow* reveal clearly enough that Lawrence is attuned to the analogy: it occurs in other contexts, slightly transformed, as in 'Study of Thomas Hardy' and 'The Crown', although it is only in *The Rainbow* that it bears consistently on questions of language. It came to Lawrence 'unwatched' because at some deep level he was conscious of it.

In 'The Marsh and the Flood' (*The Rainbow,* Chapter IX) Tom Brangwen meditates aloud on the changeable quality of water:

Th' rain tumbles down just to mount up in clouds again. So they say. There's no more water on the earth than there was in the year naught. That's the story, my boy, if you understand it. There's no more today than there was a thousand years ago – nor no less either. You can't wear water out. No, my boy: it'll give you the go-by. Try to wear it out, and it takes its hook into vapour, it has its fingers at its nose to you. It turns into cloud and falleth as rain on the just and unjust.
(*The Rainbow,* p. 227)

This is not simply Tom rambling. In the first place his words recall one of Lawrence's favourite *topoi*, the Creation, with the world created from the separation of the waters (the waves draw back and reveal presence: this is a recurring idea in Lawrence). On another level, its being in a continually changing state makes water extremely interesting and appropriate for Lawrence who will throughout *The Rainbow* use water to talk about something else. The 'living event of actual speech'[4] is foregrounded metaphorically in Tom's soliloquy. Speech leaves no physical traces. What has been heard is lodged temporarily in the memory of the listener. 'Dry up' as a vulgar euphemism for 'don't say any more' indicates that the homology between water and speech is lodged, to a degree, in collective consciousness. This shifts the focus to 'dead' metaphor; to an existing body of metaphor which, as Lawrence reminds us, is increasingly pertinent. 'Dry up' is part of the common stock of metaphors in English but it is entirely apposite for Lawrence's view of language here.

It can be asked of both speech and water, 'Where does it come from?', a single point of origin, a neutral state, being difficult to isolate in each, yet both constitute a physical event. We have in Lawrence a subconscious alertness to the inventiveness and appropriateness of a certain level of metaphor in a 'philosophical' context and to philosophical ends. The reader is open to the suggestion that the water/speech equivalent is serviceable up to a point. What it does not do is take account of the view of language in terms of particular categories, of language as a sociopolitical construct for example, of language as discourse; but this is because the emphasis in Lawrence is on the whole body of language rather than its particular social configurations.

In the early discursive writing Lawrence introduces the language of water explicitly ('Study of Thomas Hardy', 'The Crown'). By *The Rainbow* the significance of that language for Lawrence is operating at subliminal levels, and is the more effective for doing so. I hope by this to suggest the extent to which Lawrence is operating metaphorically, and that the implications of the particular metaphor in hand are far-reaching, not least in the context of *The Rainbow*. Earlier in this study, the idea of the 'phosphorescent wave' derived from *Psychoanalysis and the Unconscious* was developed as a metaphor for language as process, underlining the radar effect of a phosphorescent wave that reveals the presence of an object in its entirety without necessarily disclosing its details. The wave's phosphorescence gives rise to a luminous moment set apart from the more familiar repetitive character of waves. Its importance as an image of consciousness and language lies in its revelation of the presence of something in an instant, and yet the revelation itself is part of an immense and sweeping process. Elsewhere in the discursive essays this association is part of the general currency of Lawrence's thought.[5]

So far the emphasis has been explicitly on language as a medium. No formal view of language has been proposed by Lawrence, and yet his language-consciousness is evident, emerging through the text's central metaphor. It has been stressed how far what is expressed here is a view of language which is derived from the text rather than from an external source. The real significance of the novel is in the language and in *its* action. With this in mind I propose to deal much more consciously than Lawrence with the wave-water dynamic, gradually moving towards an understanding of the Lawrentian individual in *The Rainbow* who must inevitably be seen in the context of this vast metaphor.

A wave looks on the surface as though it is moving and breaking at a point which lies at some distance from its beginning. The surface of the water, like the space of water observed by Ursula in 'The Bitterness of Ecstasy' (*The Rainbow*, Chapter XV), appears to be mobile, a kinaesthetic form. Projecting, she looks out over the 'tender sea, with its lovely swift glimmer' (p. 401); later she sees it 'running' to burst, breaking and receding. The undulating, repetitive surface has its own rhythm. Beneath the surface of the wave, however, a different condition exists. Wave-formation occurs because of a force spreading through a medium, here water, and causing a local displacement of the medium. Water particles oscillate in response to the disturbance, and this motion makes the wave visible on the surface, as areas of water rise above and return to the general level. The pattern is of swells and troughs alternating. Therefore, on the surface the effect is of a mobile body of water moving to the shore in response to a natural phenomenon like the wind, for example, but beneath the surface water particles are being displaced and are not moving laterally very far at all. So, in macro and micro terms, while there is a sense of continual movement on the surface, there is also always the point of minimal movement below.

This emphasis on structures and altered states is how waves relate (metaphorically, not literally) to 'allotropic' states, so

significant for Lawrence in the famous description of the relation of diamond and coal to carbon: a metaphor which underpins his readers' expectations of his construction of the subject
in fiction, and yet one to which he never expected them to have
such conscious access. Despite its various forms, in the immediate context, water is the 'radically-unchanged element'. This sup-
plements the fact that a wave is composed of countless water
particles, and cannot be what it is without these particles, which
makes it a good image of the Lawrentian individual in *The Rainbow*. As the great and sweeping wave is composed of minute
particles indistinguishable from the whole, so the individual in
The Rainbow is a part of the greater life, an element at home in
the external world. The individual consciousness is submerged
in the novel's language, which also sustains it.

The 'wave' metaphor is established on the first page of *The
Rainbow* with 'the wave which cannot halt' and is unpacked in a
number of related images, and a related language, as the novel
proceeds. These include 'the deep underwater of the dance' which
absorbs the couples 'waving intertwined in the flux of music'
(p. 295); the language of the episode in the cathedral; Ursula's
apprehension of people in 'The Bitterness of Ecstasy' ('each one
was a dark, blind, eager wave urging blindly forward', p. 415);
her own association with the wave in Skrebensky's eyes (p. 444).
These associations are often implicit – like the 'splash' of the
sheaves being stacked by Anna and Will (p. 115) – poetic, and
bear the thought.[6] This 'wave' is deeply implicated in the differences between *The Rainbow* and *Women in Love*, and refers to the
life of the single word in *The Rainbow*. It is useful to begin by
imagining a human figure treading water just off-shore. A wave
builds up and lifts the figure in its swell so that the figure is
raised, in the area of water s/he inhabits, above the general level.
As the wave 'passes', the figure is let down (in a trough) to that
same general level until the next wave, when the action is repeated. The figure has not in fact been carried forward by or on
the wave, but is rising and falling with the water level and is
consequently staying in roughly the same place. The wave therefore
passes around the figure, that is to say it passes in spite of the
figure. Inasmuch as the force which causes the wave might be
felt by the individual it could be said to pass through, and not
just around the figure. This constitutes a very literal representation of an engulfing medium. In *Women in Love*, in contrast, the

distance between the individual and the background is more explicit. At some point a gulf has opened up between them so that the Lawrentian individuals do not 'belong' in that novel as they do in *The Rainbow*. The drama of this split, this rupture, is contained in the double meanings of the word 'cleave' in *Women in Love*, which simultaneously (and oxymoronically) designates a splitting away from something *and* an adhering to something. In the dance of the three women at Breadalby, for instance, Gudrun's 'cleaving' is mentioned repeatedly (*Women in Love*, pp. 91–2), and for the most part it is the condition of the individual in that novel to be apart without achieving positive singleness.

Women in Love memorably offers its own image of a human figure in water in the form of Gerald Crich swimming in the lake in 'Diver'. The configuration here is not of belonging to the milieu but of being a thing apart. Gerald Crich pushes himself through the water of the lake. Physically in the water, he is isolated from it, a foreign body in the midst of a medium which is in Lawrence's words 'uncreated', wilfully following his own trajectory. He does not have an effortless unity with the watery medium, or the larger scene, but is fundamentally and literally 'separate' from it: this represents the disjunctive relationship of Lawrentian character to world which characterizes *Women in Love*, quite different from *The Rainbow*'s 'belonging'. Gerald occupies a world that is different from the world of *The Rainbow* which is always richly, and sometimes suffocatingly, 'present'. In swimming, Gerald agitates the water of the lake in a way which the figure in my example, off-shore, does not: Gerald's relation to the water is 'frictional', a word Lawrence uses in the articulation of his own aesthetic in *Women in Love* (Foreword, *Women in Love*, p. 486). The condition of the individual is once again thrown into relief, but so too is the condition of the word in the novel.

It is difficult not to talk about the language of Lawrence's fiction without eventually arriving at the problematics presented by certain key words. They are distributed evenly throughout the important philosophical narratives comprising the Lawrentian lexicon. Critical focus is habitually on the key words 'presence', 'reality' and 'knowledge'. Different commentators have subjected these words to different pressures. Michael Bell calls them 'verbal motifs' which constitute a 'speculative discourse' within the narrative of *The Rainbow*.[7] They are words which Lawrence deploys so that, at appropriate moments, they take on a psychological and ontological weight that they do not ordinarily possess. Once again context is crucial. So, like some critics before him, Bell has focused on a philosophical vocabulary within the narrative of a particular novel.[8] Regarding 'presence', 'reality' and 'knowledge' he draws attention to the fact that in *The Rainbow* Lawrence 'uses these terms in contradictory clusters so that their normal meaning is challenged, modified or reversed. Or else he uses the word singly but with an odd inflection that leads us to construct its significance anew in context. The effect of this is progressively to impart a constitutively psychological factor into the existential claims of these terms' (p. 73). So, as motifs, they represent a special mode of Brangwen subjectivity. The understated recognition here is also that the oxymoronic consciousness which permeates Lawrence's narratives comes into view. Indeed, the oxymoronic in Lawrence, and particularly in *Women in Love*, deserves greater critical attention than it has received precisely because it invests Lawrence's language, in its very grain, with a philosophical specificity that speaks indirectly of the novel's 'metaphysic'. There is more at stake in Lawrence's oxymoronic consciousness than simply rhetoric. Regarding these key words, and their deployment, we need to confront the oxymoronic at a level which is below rhetoric but not below language.

If words like 'reality' are characterized in Lawrence's narratives chiefly by the opposing meanings they are sometimes made to bear, it is a sign of the oxymoronic functioning at even deeper levels in the text than we previously suspected. Where the reader encounters a reversal of meaning in a single word which is used repeatedly, s/he is justified in identifying an oxymoronic movement of meaning within that word. Indeed, this is one of the effects of deploying the same word more than once in a relatively brief passage: consciously or unconsciously the reader responds to a new suggestion, a different meaning. Such a deployment of words is typical of Lawrence's modernism. The day-to-day meaning of the word is still accessible, and in play, but interacting with the 'Lawrentian' modulation. Indeed, we respond to the Lawrentian sense largely because of our familiarity with the everyday 'proper' sense. The example of Tom Brangwen and Lydia Lensky, strangers, passing on the road, and Tom's response, is frequently cited in the debate on these key words in Lawrence[9] and I shall refer to it again this time to point up the oxymoronic force of 'reality':

She had passed by. He felt as if he were walking again in a far world, not Cossethay, a far world, the fragile reality. He went on, quiet, suspended, rarified. He could not bear to think or to speak, nor make any sound or sign, nor change his fixed motion. He could scarcely bear to think of her face. He moved within the knowledge of her, in the world that was beyond reality.

(*The Rainbow*, p. 29)

Suddenly conscious of her presence, Tom is transported into 'the fragile reality' of what will be *their* world. In the second use of the word, their world, of which he has had a sensation, is 'beyond reality', so reality in the second instance means the quotidian Tom-alone world. The novel contains many such examples of these shifting semantic sands. In the first instance, placing the word 'reality' next to itself in a context like this where each time it signifies differently, is oxymoronic, and by the same token, an oxymoronic dynamic is being identified in the *single* word. Lawrence's point is that the single word 'reality' potentially contains both its 'proper' meaning, and its reverse. My suggestion is that the double deployment of this word, in the manner described, is oxymoronic, not because two different elements are brought together in unusual proximity (which is how we usually understand oxymoron) but because the same word is repeated in a context where its meaning is reversed, so that deploying the same word more than once creates the oxymoron. By extension, in using the word singly, its oxymoronic quality is implicitly present as a possibility. The oxymoronic dynamic is thus the play of opposing meanings within the key word. The suggestion is that meaning has an oxymoronic tendency rather than a centripetal or centrifugal one, which are the usual models of meaning on offer. This understanding, which underpins the 'metaphysic' of *Women in Love*, is potentially present in *The Rainbow*, although the latter presents us with a far less analytical medium.

Whether the critical enterprise is to point up, as Michael Bell does, the ontological pressure which Lawrence exerts on single words, or whether it is to target their metaphorical significance, these key words continue to attract the attention of critics. They are words that are ideally placed to focus the questions of self, being, world and language which increasingly preoccupy

Lawrence's readers. Some brief examples are sufficient to demonstrate their importance.

In 'The Cathedral' (*The Rainbow*, Chapter VII) the word 'reality' occurs repeatedly in a context which expressly underlines the fact that it does not signify the phenomenal world, but Will Brangwen's fragile 'world' as it is embodied by the church architecture. It is a word which does not enter the immediate narrative until Anna's remarks have interfered with his illusions about the cathedral's absolute value for him. We have Will's 'beloved realities' and the 'mysterious world of reality' (p. 190), the 'reality' which is an 'order' or system for him, within the church where 'all reality gathered' (p. 191). In plain terms 'reality' is the wrong word except that it is appropriate for Will, and constituted by him. Anna's experience, the language used to describe her sense of things, underlines the contradictions in play in the word: in the different reality of child-birth and child-rearing she puts off 'all adventure into unknown realities' (p. 191). This last formulation is tentatively oxymoronic, and points up the contradictory play of meaning which pervades the book but without bearing the 'metaphysic' as it will do in *Women in Love*. Each character occupies different realities and subjectivity is understood as this difference. Although the reader can deduce the meaning of the word in context, the whole question of definition is far from conscious in *The Rainbow*. The characters do not struggle with definitions because, as has often been pointed out, they do not live verbally: they inhabit a silence, Heidegger's *Stille*. This is a further significant point of contrast with the extremely verbal novel, *Women in Love*.

An example from *Women in Love* serves to show how extremely the function of these key words has changed in that novel. Once again the word which I have singled out for consideration is 'reality'. The broad context is 'Excurse' (*Women in Love*, Chapter XXIII). Ursula 'sees' Birkin, as he paradoxically leaves the scene, in these terms:

> Even as he went into the lighted, public place he remained
> dark and magic, the living silence seemed the body of reality
> in him, subtle, potent, indiscoverable. There he was! In a strange
> uplift of elation she saw him, the being never to be revealed,
> awful in its potency, mystic and real. This dark, subtle reality
> of him, never to be translated, liberated her into perfection,

her own perfected being. She too was dark and fulfilled in silence.

(Women in Love, p. 319)

The emphasis on 'indiscoverability' and untranslatability in relation to the word 'reality' is significant.[10] Where 'reality' occurs for a second time it is very difficult to decide whether it is the word or the experience which is 'never to be translated'. The meaning of this passage is palpably more difficult to grasp than that in the passages above from *The Rainbow*. The word 'indiscoverable' and the phrase 'never to be translated', far from explaining the meaning of 'reality', highlight inexpressibility. Ultimately the reader is left to question, rather than decide, what it is that they refer to. That the language is apparently begging questions, that it is in relation to *The Rainbow* more problematic, is not a weakness of style in *Women in Love*, but points to Lawrence's preoccupation in that novel with the limitations of language. *Women in Love* is making the whole question of meaning more conscious, which is, I take it, Michael Ragussis's point in *The Subterfuge of Art*. Yet in the context of any discussion on his language, language itself is not overtly the subject: the subject is what Lawrence's language-sense both is and what it points to.

As the play with 'reality' foregrounds, in *The Rainbow* meaning is constituted as part of the sentence which is itself constituted as part of a broader context. The focus here is on emergent meanings rather than lexical or 'proper' meaning. Different critics of course approach key words in the fiction differently and in the end their viewpoints are likely to have an accumulative value. To sum up my position, in the passages from *The Rainbow* where the key words are explained by their context an emergent oxymoronic dynamic can be identified as continually present in the life of the word. While oxymoron is part of the 'frictional' mode of *Women in Love*, in that novel words have a more exploratory or experimental, a more conscious, function than in *The Rainbow*. In *Women in Love*, as the example about Birkin quoted above shows, the reader cannot unproblematically alight on a meaning and pass on, because it is not here the function of the sentence, or the larger context, to provide such easy access to meaning. In examining these differences between the two novels it has been useful to cite examples which deal with the individual, like the episode of Gerald swimming, and the moment of Tom's seeing Lydia on the road. I propose next to consider further the relation of language and the individual, principally in *The Rainbow*, which is something my examination has been working towards.

LANGUAGE AND THE INDIVIDUAL

The question of individuality furthers the fundamental point about 'belonging' and 'disjunction' made by my analysis of the condition of the word in each novel. The water images in both *Women in Love* and *The Rainbow* underline the different treatment of individuality and 'belonging' in the books. A brief passage from 'The Novel' underscores the significance of the concept of 'belonging' to Lawrence. Constructing his argument he turns to consider the furniture in the private space where he sits and writes: 'That silly iron stove somehow belongs. Whereas this thin-shanked table doesn't belong. It is a mere disconnected lump, like a cut-off finger' (*Hardy*, p. 183). This indirectly describes the condition of the individual in *The Rainbow* and *Women in Love* respectively: the Brangwens *belong* in the same way Lawrence's stove *belongs* in its immediate milieu. In *Women in Love* belonging is more problematic, with the Lawrentian figures only too conscious of their lack of meaningful connection with their world, but the Lawrentian figures in *The Rainbow* experience a more complex kind of freedom than those in *Women in Love*. They are 'free' within an enveloping milieu. Their consciousness is not separable from that whole environment. So they are not existentially 'free' as the 'astral' figures of *Women in Love* may aspire to be, but in that novel such 'freedom' itself is shown to be problematic.

This issue of freedom is most thoroughly identified in *The Rainbow*'s Ursula, seen first in the context of the family before the narrative shifts to the details of her personal experience. The wave image continues to operate, remaining a prominent feature of the novel's 'actual' landscape. Away with her family, Ursula watches a wave at sea. The description communicates the event of an 'actual' wave, and Ursula's sense of it as symbolizing her condition:

Then came a time when the sea was rough. She watched the water travelling in to the coast, she watched a big wave running unnoticed, to burst in a shock of foam against a rock, enveloping all in a great white beauty, to pour away again, leaving the rock emerged black and teeming. Oh, and if, when the wave burst into whiteness, it were only set free!

(*The Rainbow*, p. 402)

Ursula's response is to a deep, sweeping, eternal life that the wave represents to her and which is central to *The Rainbow*. But it is also a commonplace that in Ursula Lawrence represents the move towards individuation which distinguishes the end of the novel from its beginning. The image of the wave pulling away from the rock, and the fact that the rock is left singular and distinct from the 'enveloping' water, foregrounds the violent separateness which is an issue in *Women in Love*. At the beginning of 'Moony', for instance, Ursula's metaphysical state is described in the same language, but a shift has taken place: 'One was a tiny little rock with the tide of nothingness rising higher and higher. She herself was real, and only herself – just like a rock in a wash of flood-water. The rest was all nothingness. She was hard and indifferent, isolated in herself' (*Women in Love*, p. 244). In the passage quoted from *The Rainbow* Ursula identifies herself with the wave. In the passage from 'Moony' she is distressed to find herself identifying now with the rock. Her projections speak volumes about her altered state.

It is worth highlighting one more example from Ursula's experience. Consider the force of the water and wave imagery in the episode which describes Ursula's encounter with the horses in the final chapter of the novel. Ursula leaves the house in an attempt to dispel the 'tumult' within her while she waits to hear from Skrebensky, 'that her course should be resolved' (*The Rainbow*, p. 450). It is not accidental that she is placed in 'the chaos of rain' (p. 450), and Lawrence goes to some lengths to establish her watery context: she sees Willey water at a distance through low cloud; 'the hawthorn trees *streamed* like hair on the wind' (p. 450, emphasis added). At this point she feels inside the rain. Her field of vision, which is to become filled with the oppressively close flanks and hooves of the horses, is taken up momentarily with the 'visionary' colliery before 'the veils closed again. She was glad of the rain's privacy and intimacy' (p. 450).

At this point she is enclosed, 'encircled' (p. 450), by and within the environment, but there is a strong sense in the language of her resistance to this enveloping milieu:

> She turned under the shelter of the common, seeing the great veils of rain swinging with slow, floating waves across the landscape. She was very wet and a long way from home, far enveloped in the rain and the waving landscape. She must beat her way back through all this fluctuation, back to stability and security.
>
> (*The Rainbow*, p. 451)

The final sentence looks ahead to other Lawrentian figures who beat their way through a watery environment, notably Gerald Crich. Consequently it is another statement which anticipates Ursula's individuation in *Women in Love*, in terms of her separation from the engulfing world of *The Rainbow*. In the next line she is 'a solitary thing' herself going 'through the wash of hollow space' (p. 451). It is significant that it is here the individual who presses on and goes 'through' the world, and this in itself identifies Ursula's fundamental difference from the other Brangwens of *The Rainbow*: if Ursula is now a conscious and 'solitary thing' pushing through her world, the early Brangwens especially were people through whom consciousness, language, that is to say life itself, passed. By this stage Ursula propels herself along her own trajectory: 'She would go straight on, and on, and be gone by' (p. 451). Any sense of anything passing through Ursula now, in this encounter, is equated with pain and resistance. For a moment the 'wave' is transformed into the horses:

> But the horses had burst before her. In a sort of lightning of knowledge their movement *travelled through her*, the quiver and strain and thrust of their powerful flanks, as they burst before her and drew on, beyond.
>
> (*The Rainbow*, p. 452, emphasis added)

The horses are now part of the water, while she is separate. They are also a mid-term between the driving rain (as pervasive) and Ursula herself (as becoming singular). Like water, they crash down upon her 'thunderously about her, enclosing her' in a 'burst transport' (p. 453). After this Ursula herself is 'dissolved like water' with 'limbs like water' (p. 453), before her individuation is articulated finally as a separation from the wave of experience:

> As she sat there, spent, time and the flux of change passed away from her, she lay as if unconscious upon the bed of the stream, like a stone, unconscious, unchanging, unchangeable, whilst everything rolled by in transience, leaving her there, a stone at rest on the bed of the stream, inalterable and passive, sunk to the bottom of all change.
>
> (*The Rainbow*, p. 454)

So it is that the individuation of Ursula is completed in terms of the 'wave' and, ultimately, her being separate from it. The significance of the horses is not purely what they might represent in Ursula, which is a common critical assumption, but lies, at least equally, in their relation to the water.

The water images in *Women in Love* provide a different perspective on the same theme, stressing the individual's isolation. In 'Water-Party' water is a boundary, a surface, a dividing line between two worlds; it is the isolating flood. In 'Moony' it is a mirror and a screen. In 'Water Party' the human figures are '*on* the water' (*Women in Love*, p. 178, emphasis added). The *under*water of the lake is a hostile and mysterious world: diving in it for the bodies of his sister and her potential rescuer, Gerald, far from being a part of the scene, is 'gone' (*Women in Love*, p. 181), he is absent. The extent of the isolation of the human figures in *Women in Love*, of their separation from the larger scene, or sweep, of life, is summed up in Gudrun's experience as she waits for Gerald to surface for the second time:

> She was so alone, with the level, unliving field of the water stretching beneath her. It was not a good isolation, it was a terrible, cold separation of suspense. She was suspended upon the surface of the insidious reality until such time as she should disappear beneath it.
>
> (*Women in Love*, p. 182)

'Reality' here is not the whole, but a subtle and treacherous world with which she has a troubled connection: far from implying 'belonging', the word 'insidious' (*insidere*) signifies a being 'in' something, like captivity, rather than *The Rainbow*'s 'being a part of' something. Alienation, loss and separation are the central ideas rather than integration with the broader natural world which we perceive even at the moment of Tom Brangwen's death. What follows is not a statement of integration but of deprivation and ultimately, bereavement: 'everything was drowned within it [the water of the lake], drowned and lost' (*Women in Love*, p. 185). The flood which kills Tom and the drowning in 'Water-Party' are significant as events but they are also subtle metaphors for 'belonging' and alienation respectively. The different perspectives which they represent on individuality and 'belonging' underline the fundamental differences between the two novels. The world which is a projection of Gudrun in the passage above seems to be a fragment or part of the whole, but it resists definition or contextualization. The best that can be said is that the whole world is now conceived of as fragmented: the world under the lake's surface; the worlds above it; worlds experienced by the highly conscious Lawrentian characters as individuals; the underworld of the mines; and the abstract cosmology of Birkin's 'star-equilibrium'.

It is now possible to see fully how the water image in each book is linked to the style of each. The 'wave' of *The Rainbow* incorporates the whole, and all the Lawrentian figures fit into the broader scheme. In *Women in Love* the human figures are 'suspended', a recurrent word in the novel which in its literal sense reinforces their lack of connection with a background. *The Rainbow* on the other hand presents, in its language and action, a complex image of freedom within an engulfing but sustaining medium. This is to underline Lawrence's sense of a 'living continuum' which is so apposite for *The Rainbow*:

> Paradoxical as it may sound, the individual is only truly himself when he is unconscious of his own individuality, when he is unaware of his own isolation, when he is not split into subjective and objective, when there is no *me or you*, no *me or it* in his consciousness, but the *me and you*, the *me and it* is a living continuum, as if all were connected by a living membrane.
>
> ('"John Galsworthy", Fragment of an early draft',
> in *Hardy*, p. 249)[11]

7

'The Tension of Opposites': The Oxymoronic Mode of *Women in Love*

... an unconscious artist often puts the wrong words to the right feeling.

(*Letters*, I, p. 102)

The philosophical importance of *Women in Love* is grounded not so much in referential statement as in its complex and sophisticated metaphoricity. It has this in common with the books on the unconscious. Certainly, in the novel, at least five years in the making, metaphor moves significantly away from its merely rhetorical function. One of the novel's achievements is the extent to which its specific concerns are embodied in its language, and by the same token it represents Lawrence's alertness to the philosophical qualities of his medium.

If *Women in Love* did not exist the general view of Lawrence's language would be very different. If either of the major novels existed in isolation, if we had *The Rainbow* without *Women in Love* or vice versa, we would have a very different sense of Lawrence's language. It cannot be presupposed, as my previous discussion suggests, that the novels share an identical mode of language: indeed, the conceptions of language that each novel embodies are radically different. So, in the first place, it is crucial to realize that Lawrence does not have a fixed or prescriptive view of language that characterizes his *oeuvre*. The critical emphasis should be placed on positive difference rather than continuity.

In holding this view I differ from Michael Ragussis for whom *Women in Love* is unequivocally the representative text: it has the advantage, from Ragussis's point of view, of being about language and problems of expression. The way in which language is given thematic status there is very alluring and it would seem that Ragussis has been seduced by what language is, and what it does, in *Women in Love*, so that he does not at any stage question its representativeness.[1] However, the emphasis need not be so much on what is stated, but on what is evident at the subliminal, sub-textual levels.

In fact *Women in Love* is representative, but it is not typical. It is a novel that exemplifies Lawrence's major habitual preoccupations and tendencies: his exploration of personal relations, his re-evaluation of masculinity, his critique of Western culture, the development of his 'metaphysic' and his highly metaphorical style. In this chapter I propose to concentrate on this metaphoricity (which is not separable from the other tendencies) because it is here, and in other matters of language, that the atypicality of *Women in Love* resides. Why, for instance, does Lawrence engender such a radically metaphorical language in *Women in Love*? Is it because he is continually trying to get a complex and difficult conception of otherness into his sights? If so, language is the only medium in which this is even a possibility.

If there is a difficulty in saying that with Lawrence metaphor expands to include the whole of language, that difficulty resides in distinguishing what seems generally true of language from what is specific to Lawrence. Lawrence, like Nietzsche, is recognizably an individual stylist, and in him the question of metaphor goes beyond bare style. In particular, oxymoron is a dynamic, potent, form of metaphor for Lawrence, in large part because it makes something positive out of difference and opposition, rather than resemblance. The tension between two unrelated terms brought suddenly into proximity, to recall Paul Ricoeur's definition of oxymoron, is, in Lawrence, 'frictional', a word which, in his lexicon, has sexual overtones but which more properly refers to language and questions of style. In oxymoron, friction is generated (and meaning created) by the semantic or more properly, the logical, disparity between the two terms brought together. It is a type of metaphor which does not 'invent relations' so much as rely on our sense of logic.[2] Yet the emphasis does not fall entirely on this principle of opposition. Structurally, oxymoron comprises two contradictory elements brought into a new relation to each other. In *Women in Love* it is this *structure* which resonates with significance because of its resemblance to

the structure of the central metaphysical image of the novel, Rupert
Birkin's description of 'star-equilibrium' as a way of describing
two individuals in a union where mutual self-definition is, at
least notionally, one of the terms. The critical focus in the present
chapter will be, sometimes implicitly and sometimes explicitly,
on the homology between the structure of oxymoron and this
central image of *Women in Love*, in order to underline the fact
that the 'metaphysic' which gives rise to this conception is being expressed at a structural level within the book's language.

First, in the discussion to follow I begin by addressing the
simultaneity and 'friction' of styles that characterize *Women in
Love* and underpin its difference from *The Rainbow*. Such simultaneity is important for Lawrence in this novel because it helps
him break down certain oppositions, for instance, internal/ex-
ternal (subjective value is understood within the 'external' in
Lawrence). Lawrence is after a more radical conception of the
other: his sense of it is not of the merely 'objective', what the
camera, for instance, records. These discriminations are made
available to us in Lawrence's language. My focus, then, is consistently on the Poetic. The metaphorical in Lawrence's writing
constitutes what Ricoeur calls in *The Rule of Metaphor*, a 'thinking more': 'Metaphor is living by virtue of the fact that it introduces the spark of imagination into a 'thinking more' at the
conceptual level' (p. 303). Much of this 'thinking more' occurs at
subliminal levels within Lawrence's fictional narratives. Here the
implied parallel with Martin Heidegger is again foregrounded.
A great deal of effort and sophistication went into Heidegger's
saying some of the same things as Lawrence but his discourse,
although it is radically metaphorical, is more 'conscious' than
Lawrence's.

I then concentrate on the *rhetoric* of love in this novel, examining how Lawrence's critique of 'love' in *Women in Love* takes
him to the unconscious levels of metaphor at work in human
understanding. In this novel Lawrence has pulled together the
threads of his critique of romantic love begun in his earlier works.
In doing so, he has moved away from the habitually oxymoronic
rhetoric of love, which externalizes the emotion, and instituted
a different, and highly personal, conception of the love-relation,
the oxymoronic nature of which is much more radically a part
of the general quality both of the language and of the experience.

THE SIMULTANEITY OF STYLES IN *WOMEN IN LOVE*

Simultaneity is a word that broadly describes the mode of *Women in Love*, and in this respect the novel can be contrasted with *The Rainbow*. The difference between them is principally a question of language. Great variations of language occur in *The Rainbow* but these variations are part of the vast sweep, or 'wave', of language which is that novel: the sweeping metaphorical *process* of *The Rainbow* is not reproduced in *Women in Love*.

In *The Rainbow* the reader typically recognizes moments, or episodes, as being particularly important because in them the style reaches a certain pitch of intensity. There are many instances of this. One example is provided in 'Childhood of Anna Lensky' (*The Rainbow*, Chapter III) where the emotional connection between Tom Brangwen and Lydia Lensky is properly forged after two years of married life. A contributory factor is Tom's encounter with his brother's mistress, which gives rise to his contemplation of the emotional paucity of his own existence. In the resulting encounter with Lydia the language moves to the genuine emotional intensity of their maturing marriage, recalling the language of the Foreword to *Sons and Lovers* in its deployment of the language of blindness, transfiguration and rebirth:

> Blind and destroyed, he pressed forward, nearer, nearer, to receive the consummation of himself, be received within the darkness which should swallow him and yield him up to himself. . . . She was the doorway to him, he to her. At last they had thrown open the doors, each to the other, and had stood in the doorways facing each other, whilst the light flooded out from behind on to each of their faces, it was the transfiguration, the glorification, the admission.
>
> (*The Rainbow*, pp. 90–1)

Attention is drawn to the difference in the language at the moment of intensest feeling from the kind of language that preceded it. The intensely metaphorical tone is the 'foreign language' Lawrence felt he was using as the novel developed. Of 'The Sisters' (the first working title), he complained, 'it's like a novel in a foreign language I don't know very well – I can only just make out what it's about' (*Letters* I, p. 544). Eight months later he wrote to Edward Garnett about 'The Wedding Ring', as he now called

novel, calling them 'disorienting', and argues that they show Lawrence's attempt to pull away from the 'old stable *ego*' and to show every individual as 'nonindividualized', an 'a-psychological, mass of life and death energies'.[3] Bersani, whose theme is desire, focuses on details of narrative language which indicate personal crises in the lives of the characters. The emphasis can also usefully be on the simultaneity of a number of modes, like those outlined in the long quotation above, which characterize the whole narrative, and not only moments of extremity in feeling. Birkin's self-adjusting consciousness in this passage is recalled later on in 'Snow' (*Women in Love*, Chapter XXX) where Gudrun, absorbed in, and by, her vision of the mountainous landscape, and recoiling from Gerald, stands on the threshold between two 'worlds': 'She closed her eyes, closed away the monotonous level of dead wonder, and opened them again to the everyday world. / "Yes," she said briefly, *regaining her will with a click*' (*Women in Love*, p. 402, my italics). If we are reminded of Birkin here we also notice the contrast between his subtly shifting modes of consciousness and Gudrun's: Birkin's consciousness is effortlessly self-adjusting where with Gudrun the change is obviously a matter of a more relentless will. Whatever Birkin is saying, at some deeper level he is responding, in Lawrence's terms, positively and instinctively to Ursula. This contrasts with Gudrun's machine-like change: 'click' is a word which evokes a mechanism. So, when these descriptions recall each other they do so by way of both similarity *and* contrast.

In 'Water-Party' (*Women in Love*, Chapter XIV), Gudrun's alienation is examined in relation to her sister in the cameo of the 'mythic' beech-grove. Seeking attention, a 'connection' (p. 165) with Ursula, she dances, in a description which is recognizably 'Lawrentian':

Gudrun, looking as if some invisible chain weighed on her hands and feet, began slowly to dance in the eurythmic manner, pulsing and fluttering rhythmically with her feet, making slower, regular gestures with her hands and arms, now spreading her arms wide, now raising them above her head, now flinging them softly apart, and lifting her face, her feet all the time beating and running to the measure of the song, as if it were some strange incantation, her white, rapt form drifting here and there in a strange impulsive rhapsody, seeming to be lifted on a breeze of incantation, shuddering with strange little runs. Ursula sat on the grass, her mouth open in her singing, her eyes laughing as if she thought it was a great joke, but a yellow light flashing up in them, as she caught some of the unconscious ritualistic suggestion of the complex shuddering and waving and drifting of her sister's white form, that was clutched in pure, mindless, tossing rhythm, and a will set powerful in a kind of hypnotic influence.

(*Women in Love*, p. 166)

I have written 'Lawrentian' in inverted commas because this kind of repetitive and metaphorical language is recognizably and uniquely of Lawrence, with its distinctive sentence structure and verbal rhythm. Lawrence is aware that readers will have no difficulty in visualizing a woman dancing, but their gaze might well be the uncomprehending, the curious, gaze of the nearby cattle. The tendency to provide an image for what is written is challenged again by the non-visual, or more properly anti-visual, language. Gudrun is depersonalized, communicated kinaesthetically through a catalogue of depersonalizing metaphors: 'fluttering', 'waving', 'drifting'; she is also a (modernist) 'white form'. The level of metaphoricity employed prevents the description from delineating the merely physical dimension of Gudrun, as Lawrence plays the writer's trick of calling on some other mode of vision within us which responds to the language. This passage is not just about Gudrun dancing, clearly, but in fact highlights many of the levels of the novel which the present chapter addresses. In particular the metaphorical language works against expectations of a description that visualizes the scene. Lawrence draws attention to Ursula's eyes. These do not in themselves do the seeing: Ursula does that *through* them and perceives an 'unconscious ritualistic suggestion' for which the language is the vehicle. She cannot say that she perceives it: she, too, is 'unconscious'. Only the metaphorical density of the passage communicates significance to the reader: referential language, a visual description of the dance with its basis in verisimilitude, could not do it so effectively *and* bring the focus back to language.

Gudrun's dances in 'Water-Party' are details rather than the explicit focus of the chapter, yet *Women in Love* is almost entirely made up of such details. Here is a fundamental difference from *The Rainbow* where any comparable intensity of language

frequently indicates intensity of personal feeling and has monu-
mental significance within the overall structure of the book. Tom
Brangwen and Gudrun Brangwen are both exceptional, both derive
from Lawrence's dismantling of the subject and yet both have a
different 'metaphysical' significance from each other. Tom's spontaneous self is much more a part of the whole linguistic background of 'his' novel than Gudrun in the context of 'hers'. She
is, as in the dance, 'suspended', at a remove from her immediate environment, or scene. The 'metaphysic' of the earlier novel
stresses the inseparability of individual from scene, whereas in
Women in Love a gulf has opened up between them.

This example is part of the expanding context where Lawrence
draws attention to what he calls in 'Introduction to these Paintings' 'intuitional awareness' (*Phoenix*, p. 558) as a facet of the
sensual body, which, claims Lawrence, modern fiction, and modern
thought about subjectivity, on the whole bypasses. The complex
nature of the interaction between at least three states is examined. These states are purely sensual physicality, physicality which
is not just sensual, and 'intuitional awareness'. Examination of
these different states in Lawrence's writing demands the simultaneity of different styles: the swift but subtle changes from 'plain'
metaphor in some instances to a more difficult, sometimes more
opaque, metaphoricity foreshadowed in the examples already
given. In *Women in Love*, uniquely, these changes are rapid and
challenge the reader to 'think more'. If in *The Rainbow* the reader
knows by the narrative tone that a significant episode has been
reached, in *Women in Love* the language acts as less of a guide.
In a critique of *The Rainbow* fairly substantial passages can be
isolated to make a point about its language, but with *Women in
Love* the metaphorical levels are more elusively distributed: single
phrases signal subliminal levels of thought at work across the
entire narrative and interacting with further levels. The difficulty
lies in isolating such phrases from the whole *and* retaining their
significance.

The constantly changing levels of significance in the narrative
can be seen in the way the 'physical' frequently and surprisingly contrasts with the 'visual'. The novel has the characters
continually participating in primarily physical activities: there
are many instances of dancing and swimming; there is physical
conflict ('Gladiatorial', 'Breadalby', 'Snowed Up'); there are the
sexual encounters; the 'ecstasy of physical motion' described in

'Snow' (p. 421), events that are given a special status by the language that describes them. None of these activities is *merely* physical. A less athletic episode than any of these, in 'Class-room' (*Women in Love*, Chapter III), helps to make the point. Birkin is watched by Ursula: 'She seemed to be standing aside in arrested silence, watching him move in another, concentrated world. His presence was so quiet, almost like a vacancy in the corporate air' (p. 36). As the note to this passage in the Cambridge edition of the novel records, 'corporate' is a strange choice of word.[4] The reference is not a side-swipe at the stifling air of the educational authority which they shall both eventually relinquish at the end of 'Excurse'. 'Corporate air' sounds like a contradiction in terms, one of the oxymorons which are so fundamental in articulating the metaphysical specificity of this novel. This is because a pertinent play on body resonates from 'corporate' and as a metaphor it is exactly right. 'His presence was so quiet, almost like a vacancy in the corporate air': the continual interaction of the physical and non-physical, the visualizable and the non-visualizable (for how is 'presence' in Lawrence's sense visualized?) is common in Lawrence. That this interaction has a special significance in *Women in Love* helps to focus the subtle relation in Lawrence between the general (the body of language and thought identified with Lawrence as a broad index of his style) and the particular (the force of language in this novel distinct from the rest).

If simultaneity of styles is one distinctive characteristic of *Women in Love*, the 'friction' of styles is another, related, feature. In this novel, again in contrast to *The Rainbow*, words operate 'frictionally', having a 'frictional' relation to each other and to the immediate context. This is the word that Lawrence uses to describe the style of *Women in Love* in the Foreword, written after the novel, although *The Rainbow* was not necessarily far from his thoughts:

> In point of style, fault is often found with the continual, slightly modified repetition. The only answer is that it is natural to the author: and that every natural crisis in emotion or passion or understanding comes from this pulsing, frictional to-and-fro, which works up to culmination.
>
> (Foreword, *Women in Love*, p. 486)

In this context 'frictional' is obviously sexual, but here it is linked, crucially, to language which is what Lawrence is actually talking about. His theme is repetition, but he arrives at a statement about understanding arising from a frictional movement, a 'to-and-fro', which must characterize what is generally agreed to be his most dialogic novel. His statement allows itself to be read metaphorically: word and context in *Women in Love* move against each other. Indeed, this frictional relation of word and context is at the heart of meaning in *Women in Love*, part of its oxymoronic dynamic, and what is called elsewhere in Lawrence's writing 'the tension of opposites'. The fact that the metaphor in the Foreword bears a sexual meaning makes it additionally useful in underlining a specific problem to do with how Lawrence is read: what happens constantly in Lawrence studies is that a subject, and here it is sex, distracts from what in a work of fiction is actually the deeper subject, namely language. This study is preoccupied with precisely this problem, and with a reading of Lawrence which depends on this recognition.

It is Lawrence who moves from a reference to repetition, to friction. Hence, a relationship between them, 'in point of style', is derived from his own sense of his language. If the principal issue is language, the 'frictional to-and-fro' recalls that other statement which underpins Lawrence's aesthetic, notionally in the poetry of 'Birds, Beasts and Flowers', but in fact generally. This statement recalls the language of conflict, of positive and necessary antagonism, in the earlier philosophical writing, particularly the opening of 'The Crown':

'Homer was wrong in saying, "Would that strife might pass away from among gods and men!" He did not see that he was praying for the destruction of the universe; for, if his prayer were heard, all things would pass away – for in the tension of opposites all things have their being –'

(Complete Poems, p. 348)

This 'tension of opposites' already touched on, this emphasis on 'strife', speaks to the 'frictional to-and-fro' of the Foreword. It is the understanding that organizes, indeed gives rise to, the complex narrative of *Women in Love*. The Ursula–Birkin relationship, for instance, must be left unconcluded, as its survival depends on the immediacy of the friction between the two of them. There are moments of agreement, 'culmination', high points, but not closure. The Gudrun–Gerald relationship, predicated as it is on the need for conclusive declarations either of love or hate, predicated as it is on the need for finality, perishes. These couples demonstrate, respectively, positive friction and negative friction. The negative friction felt between Gudrun and Gerald manifests itself in increasingly brutal shows of mastery, symptomatic of their highly conscious urges to control. Where the critical focus is on language, a frictional style, as it is in the Foreword to *Women in Love*, the 'tension of opposites' surfaces in the oxymoronic language and structures of the book.

The debate on structures of opposition at a linguistic level in Lawrence gives rise to a further concentration on the dualities or bipolarities which can be seen to be organizing his thought very early on, in the first version of 'The Crown' and the discursive writing of that period. The relationship, what Heidegger would call the 'intimacy', between any two factors figures in Lawrence and is not to be understood as synthesis. Focused on opposition, Lawrence's concentration is typically on separateness, nearness, and the distance that 'nearness' paradoxically implies, between the two elements or bodies that figure at any point in his thought. A Heideggerean notion of intimacy can be derived from a passage in his lecture called 'Language' which is anticipated in its essentials by Lawrence. Heidegger embarks on a critique of the prevailing view that 'language is expression'. He does so by offering a reading of George Trakl's poem 'A Winter Evening'. The poem provides him with a means of discussing the '*neighbouring*' of 'world' and 'thing'. It is a critique which retraces some of the steps taken by Lawrence, although Lawrence has no investment in articulating his 'metaphysic' so consciously. This is Heidegger on the relation of 'world' and 'thing':

> The intimacy of world and thing is not a fusion. Intimacy obtains only where the intimate – world and thing – divides itself cleanly and remains separated. In the midst of the two, in the between of world and thing, in their *inter*, division prevails: a *dif-ference*.
>
> ('Language', in *Poetry, Language, Thought*, p. 202)

His highly self-conscious hyphenation of 'dif-ference' (*Unter-Schied*), makes the point graphically. This model frequently comes into play in Lawrence who is, like Heidegger, and in Heidegger's words, not interested in the *'empty* unity of opposites' ('The Origin of the Work of Art', in *Poetry, Language, Thought,* p. 49, my italics). In that essay the relation of world and earth is one of 'striving' that finishes up as 'intimacy' (p. 49): that is to say, Heidegger asserts a tense oppositional dependency between the two elements, the closest of 'opponents', a relation which Paul Ricoeur later identifies between the two linguistic elements of oxymoron, a metaphor that speaks loudly in Lawrence's poetics in 'the tension of opposites in which all things have their being.' Within his lexicon of phrases like 'blood-consciousness' and 'root-vision', for instance, Lawrence is not simply seeking to substitute for an existing word, like 'instinct' or 'consciousness', his own construction. The point is, with Lawrence, that his metaphor, for example 'blood-consciousness', *bears* the thought dynamically. To return to Heidegger's formula, 'language speaks' in the tension, the strife and the 'intimacy' between the linguistic elements 'blood' and 'consciousness', held near *and* at a distance at the point at which 'division prevails'. 'In the *struggle,*' claims Heidegger 'each opponent carries the other beyond itself' (p. 49, my italics).[5]

At a superficial level this pronouncement also bears upon Lawrence's treatment of personal relations. In *Women in Love* an examination of personal relations means a very particular concentration on striving and strife (incorporating Heidegger's sense of self-assertion, and Lawrence's of rebirth) in such a way which returns us inevitably to questions of language. The work of art, the poetic, is the proper ground for the enquiry: 'This struggle for verbal consciousness should not be left out in art. . . . *It is the passionate struggle into conscious being'* (Foreword, *Women in Love,* p. 486). The return to the poetic is precisely because of Lawrence's recognition that, in the words of Hölderlin, 'poetically, man dwells', precisely the words which stimulate Heidegger's meditation (*Poetry, Language, Thought,* pp. 211–29). The paradigm that recurs in Heidegger's thought, and in Lawrence's, is not necessarily one of reciprocity between two 'domains' (Heidegger's word), but of what is called 'neighbouring'. This word 'neighbouring' shares the force of 'frictional' in Lawrence's lexicon inasmuch as it denotes a separation and distance between the 'domains': without distance, nearness ('neighbouring') is not possible. This model works for the neighbouring of poetry and thought in Heidegger: 'Poetry and thinking meet each other in one and the same only when, and only as long as, they remain distinctly in the distinctness of their nature' (*Poetry, Language, Thought,* p. 218). The neighbouring of poetry and thought inheres in Lawrence's poetic prose as it does (although not identically), for Heidegger in the poetry of Hölderlin and Trakl. The closeness of their ideas on 'neighbouring' underlines the accord between Lawrence and Heidegger. In short, Lawrence is interested in questioning some of the orthodoxies that prevail about language in a way that recalls Heidegger's conscious interrogation of the same orthodoxies. When his interest seems to be elsewhere, for instance in *Women in Love* when his concentration on personal relations becomes a concentration on 'love', Lawrence eventually brings the critical focus radically back to language.

'LOVE'

Love is . . . a difficult, complex maintenance of individual integrity throughout the incalculable processes of interhuman polarity.
(*Psychoanalysis and the Unconscious,* F&P, pp. 245–6)

It is useful for Lawrence that 'love' is a familiar word and an apparently simple and traditional one. In his book *Rational Love* Warren Shibles' view is that 'The word "love" is very familiar. This is unfortunate. It suggests that we know more about love than we really do.'[6] Lawrence would not agree that the familiarity of the word is so unfortunate, indeed on one level its simplicity makes it a highly suitable word for him to address. The etymology of 'love' does not reveal a very different sense from its current meaning. In some contexts older meanings would not pose a problem for Lawrence at all, but in *Women in Love* it is addressed as a problematic term precisely because it is simultaneously an ancient and 'natural' word *and* one with a distinctively modern and sublimative inflection. 'Love' is a word Lawrence must get behind in the course of his literary career, and his consciousness of the word's literary-historical past is the first step on the way. Rupert Birkin is the character in *Women in Love* whose radicalism lies in his interrogation of a tradition of European loving which has its roots in a literary form, principally through romance and the novel, and it is Lawrence's consciousness of literary representations of love which provides a starting-point. In his interrogation of 'love', a potentially very narrow field, Birkin is asking the question asked by Nietzsche; the question continually and implicitly addressed by Lawrence: 'Is language the adequate expression of all realities?'[7] For Birkin, 'love' has become a 'herd' word and his response is to submit it to a critique underpinned by moral terms. To use the word 'love' with its old meanings intact reminds him that to use language at all is 'to lie according to a fixed convention'.[8]

In his early novels Lawrence consciously and actively resists the Wagnerian ethic derived from the remotest courtly love tradition. This is the substance of Lawrence's critique of 'romance' which he worked out in its essentials in his early career. In the early novels he sets out to demolish the historical tradition with varying degrees of success. In *The Trespasser*, for instance, he is himself both inside and outside the Wagnerian tradition. It is not until *The Rainbow* that he has pulled away from that ethic altogether, as he finds a language which can better articulate his own representations. The treatment of love in *Women in Love* in particular has an important relation to its treatment in much of Lawrence's discursive writing on sexuality from the Renaissance to the modern day, and with his critique of the sentimental novel and ethics. This sense of an implicit historical synopsis working in the term 'love' is central to what follows.

Lawrence's position, uniquely, is his dissolution of the received conceptions and expectations which conventionally delimit heterosexual love, which he describes in 'Morality and the Novel' as the principal human relationship (*Hardy*, p. 175), although his views altered as he thought the question through. His interest, represented overtly in Rupert Birkin's discourse, is on love as a cultural construct and one that is constructed *in* language. The problem for Lawrence is the problem identified in a very different context by his contemporary, C. S. Lewis, in his critique of courtly love, that the expression, the *rhetoric*, of love comes to be seen as genuinely representing the emotion when in fact it is rather creating that emotion.[9] For Lawrence, the gulf which persists between the genuine feeling, which is not easily defined, and its literary-historical representation begs to be closed. If the rhetoric of love threatens to maintain that gulf, Lawrence's purpose is to bring a different conception of love back to language.

This is his position. A split has opened up between the 'natural'

emotion 'love' which has to do with the growth of specific feelings in people, and the artificial language of love, for instance,
in literature. The cultural construct becomes naturalized, is taken
to be the thing itself, and 'love' as 'natural', existing prior to
language, is to all intents and purposes effaced. It is lost to, and
because of, a highly artificial language which persists in making
a set of 'timeless' assertions. Lawrence's critique of romance is
grounded in his sensitivity to this artifice. A rhetoric of oxymoron,
a language of contradiction and opposition, frequently, traditionally, accompanies expressions of love. Love, in the West, is a
conception in which oxymoron is implicated, and in Lawrence's
view negatively so. There are grounds for seeing that, in his own
representations of love, the oxymoronic is given a more dynamic
significance. Traditionally, the *rhetoric* of oxymoron, which is so
overt in poetry, creates and sustains the rupture between language and love, what Lawrence would call the thing itself.
    'Love' is therefore culturally constructed as problematic, founded
as it seems to be on a proliferating ground of oppositions and
contradictions. Lawrence's alertness to the rhetoric of oxymoron
and its implications in a romance tradition motivates in his own
thought a rather different oxymoronic consciousness. As in all
things in Lawrence, the problem of 'love' must be brought back
to language, indeed to 'art-speech'. Birkin is the central mouthpiece for this and the relation between the sexes which is described metaphorically as 'star-equilibrium' (*Women in Love*,
p. 319), is obviously the pivotal conception in Lawrence's critique of romantic love properly developed in *Women in Love*.
    In 'star-equilibrium' Lawrence makes the hyphenated construc-
tion bear a great deal of the 'metaphysical' weight, as he will in
the writing of *Fantasia of the Unconscious* (with 'root-vision', 'blood-
consciousness', and so on), and in this context, as there, the construction has a unique and striking force. The reader responds
to it, with varying degrees of enthusiasm, as a description of
relations between lovers and as a particular instance of 'Lawrentian'
language. Crucially, in this example the metaphor and the idea
it embodies radically, if crudely, coincide. They do so in this
way: in 'star-equilibrium' two normally unrelated (verbal) elements are brought into a specific relationship which is concretized
by the graphic presence of the hyphen. However, in bringing
these elements into mutual proximity the hyphen also simultaneously holds them apart. We see the verbal elements neigh-

bouring each other without yet understanding the logic of the construction. 'Star-equilibrium' is *not* an oxymoron, yet in its own internal logic (the proximity of the two verbal elements), the *structure* of oxymoron is imitated. Hence, there is a profound homology, of which Lawrence does not have to be conscious, between the structure of oxymoron and the structure of 'star-equilibrium' as Rupert Birkin's way of talking about 'love'. This makes 'star-equilibrium' a linguistic structure that resembles the central 'metaphysical' idea it describes. It does so by bringing two elements into the relation described and simultaneously holding them apart so that each retains a separateness in relation to the other. This is, crucially, a linguistic equivalent to Birkin's ideal of male and female relationships.

By reading from within Lawrence's stated philosophy we can configure the relationship between the two verbal elements as positively 'frictional'. The context of love and, ultimately, marriage makes this possible. Lawrence typically refers to the sexual in terms of the cosmic. In 'A Propos of *Lady Chatterley's Lover*', for example, he assures his reader that 'there is no marriage apart from the wheeling sun and the nodding earth, from the straying of the planets and the magnificence of the fixed stars' (*Phoenix II*, p. 504). Both the terms of Birkin's metaphor, and the structure, form a particular and significant coincidence. 'Verbal consciousness' and 'the passionate struggle' are embodied in Birkin's speech at this point; indeed, the passionate 'frictional' struggle is at the heart of the art-speech of *Women in Love*. The linguistic elements in the novel are subject to the 'frictional to-and-fro' of the Foreword. The positive frictionality of this configuration, particularly as expressed in the Foreword where 'passion' and 'understanding' are aligned, is contrasted with 'the nervous negative reaction' of masturbatory 'modern sex' ('"white" sex') discussed in 'A Propos of *Lady Chatterley's Lover*' (pp. 507–8), and foregrounded in the Foreword to *Women in Love* by the reference to 'the degradation, the prostitution of the living mysteries in us' (p. 485). In *Aaron's Rod* the positively frictional is embodied in the rubbing down of the sick Aaron by Lilly: that encounter speaks directly to Lawrence's philosophy of positive contact *and* a degree of detachment (*Aaron's Rod*, p. 96).

The astral metaphor predominates wherever Birkin makes a serious attempt to cast his ethic or 'metaphysic' into words. These are the strongest terms in which love's conventional rhetoric of oxymoron is implicitly challenged. This is Birkin's appeal to Ursula: '"What I want is a strange conjunction with you –" he said quietly: " – not meeting and mingling; – you are quite right: – but an equilibrium, a pure balance of two single beings: – as the stars balance each other"' (*Women in Love*, p. 148). What is being rejected is the oxymoronic language of a (male) lover experiencing the desirable pain of love, as well as the loss of self-identity of either party in the course of the relationship. The kind of romantic love that has the effect of consuming both bodies, making them notionally inseparable, relieving them of their singularity, has no positive place in Birkin's conception. The same terms he uses here describe the bullying relationship, as Ursula sees it, between the tom-cat Mino and the she-cat. Birkin argues that '"with the Mino, it is the desire to bring this female cat into a pure stable equilibrium, a transcendent and abiding rapport with the single male. – Whereas without him, as you see, she is a mere stray, a fluffy sporadic bit of chaos"' (*Women in Love*, p. 150). Ursula's cleaving to the negative term 'satellite' (p. 150) points up the misogynous sub-text in his description. Birkin, against his better judgement as it turns out, is anthropomorphizing as he interprets what he views as the male's superiority over the 'fluffy' she-cat. However, Ursula's response also underlines the usual reception of Lawrence's more radical ideas, in his view typically misunderstood. It could be argued that Birkin's critique of romantic love is not the basis for another misogynous creed, as Ursula suspects. Inasmuch as he is challenging masculinist conceptions of love, and given that the principal thesis of 'star-equilibrium' is the mutual separateness of each individual 'in love', rather than the gendered superiority of one over the other, he insists on being heard as offering a radical alternative. But Ursula is right to be suspicious.

Birkin continues to restate his theory using the same metaphor as before: '"One must commit oneself to a conjunction with the other – forever. But it is not self-less – it is a maintaining of the self in mystic balance and integrity – like a star balanced with another star"' (p. 152). If his terms are to be believed, this commitment is not necessarily that of marriage or 'pseudo-marriage' and, as the closing argument of the novel makes clear, Birkin perceives that many such conjunctions can be achieved and can thrive simultaneously in the course of a single life. Ursula, at the end, is ironically perceived as subscribing uncritically to the received idea: the word 'love' is never as problematic to her as it is to Birkin. He articulates the kind of love he associates with her desires and which Lawrence regards as the contemporary view. Birkin: '"I tell you, you want love to administer to your egotism, to subserve you. Love is a process of subservience with you – and with everybody. I hate it"' (p. 153). Embedded in his philosophy is what Lawrence articulates elsewhere as the hegemony of the ego in Western society. Lawrence/Birkin is, on the face of it, anti-ego. In 'Man to Man' (*Women in Love*, Chapter XVI) Birkin is to articulate the egoism of love as 'a lust for possession, a greed of self-importance in love. She wanted to have, to own, to control, to be dominant' (p. 200). This perceived desire for control in the woman, and the anxiety it gives rise to, is written into the other remarks in the novel about love as 'a dance of opposites' (p. 153) which is how Birkin describes Ursula's conception, also calling her relation with Will 'a love of opposition' (p. 367), where opposition takes on negative significance.

The themes of polarization and relation, central too in the description of family relations in *Fantasia of the Unconscious*, are then more explicitly introduced. The notion of separateness is qualified by a new emphasis on difference and interaction. Although Birkin is always in danger of sounding tedious and monologic, the 'metaphysic' that he articulates has a fundamentally dialogic basis. Using terms which rehearse the language and conceptions of the discursive essays, particularly *Fantasia of the Unconscious*, Lawrence argues that men and women are not simply different but are 'fulfilled in difference' (*Women in Love*, p. 201). In that difference they are 'perfectly polarised' (p. 201). Interaction between the poles rather than dependence on the part of either in relation to the other avoids the 'self-abnegation of love' (p. 201). Birkin's creed nominally challenges the erasure of self-identity in 'love', even if concern about his own masculine identity, 'singleness' is a better word in the context, motivates his critique. This enduring fear of self-abnegation is derived from Lawrence's awareness of the literary-historical origins of the modern conception of love: on it he builds the extensive re-evaluation of masculinity that underpins the fiction. Birkin's complaint concerns the cultural re-invention of love and the consequent loss, as he sees it, of 'separate being' (p. 201), that is of intrinsic difference, for both men and women in love.

By making 'love' the subject of metaphysical speculation

Lawrence is consciously destabilizing the word and the values it usually bears. The linguistic structure of 'star-equilibrium' embodies an attempt to destabilize the conventional conception of love. Lawrence/Birkin has effectively dismantled 'love' by uncovering new words which reveal the standard conception as an artifice. The newly realized relation in Lawrence of metaphor and 'metaphysic' is consequently underlined.

Love always has an object. Prior to Lawrence the physical condition of love is effaced in language. It is never linguistic, but merely written about or spoken of. Lawrence's uniqueness is to make the physical dimension of love a linguistic matter: this is implicit in Birkin's language although Birkin is never conscious of the fact; his language simply covertly attests to this, as it does to the strength of oxymoronic structures in the articulation of his desire. Importantly, the subliminality of this oxymoron-effect in Lawrence's prose contrasts with the deliberately oxymoronic rhetoric that more conventionally fashions love poetry.

Such rhetoric might more usually keep the language at a considerable distance from 'love' as an experience. By destabilizing a common conception like 'love', which is not a metaphor in broadly understood terms, Lawrence is removing the sense of rhetorical oxymoron in the literary tradition, and pushing the oxymoronic quality back into the nature of the thing itself. The relation of two lovers, Lawrence argues, must ultimately be oxymoronic in order to escape the disintegrative consequences of a state that is conventionally *only* expressed or conceptualized as oxymoron. Lawrence's conception is therefore of separate entities in a dialogic relation. In the relationships on offer, jealousies and discord stem from a resistance to this dialogism and betray an unconscious cleaving to the conventional, or orthodox, conception.

The oxymoronic narrative of *Women in Love*, in the very grain of its language, represents the sense that there is no getting 'outside' love. A problem which Birkin never confronts, however, is that 'star-equilibrium' is also a construction, an artifice. The problem is one that Lawrence enjoys, that of casting something which is non-linguistic (love) into language. As Birkin identifies in his references to an age in which love was conceived differently, a pre-conscious epoch sometimes alluded to in Lawrence's discursive writing, 'love' was nevertheless present. This would be a difficult assertion either to contradict or support. A particular conception of love need not be in place, argues Birkin, but people still love. As it is, conceptions of love surround and envelop the subject too closely and completely ever for there genuinely to be an 'outside' or 'beyond'. Less abstractly, a critic like Lewis can point to a tradition and a language, a discourse, which sustains the rupture between the feeling and the language, precisely the split which Lawrence, with his experiential language, dislikes so much and to a considerable degree writes against. The rupture between love as a feeling and 'love' as a construction is something he draws attention to, so that, like Birkin, he can attempt a critique of the conception as part of his critique of his culture.

Ursula's insistence at the end of the novel on Birkin's not being able to achieve the relationships he desires because of 'perversity' (p. 481) reinforces a sense in the novel of the very real difficulties of challenging any conception that has entered the collective consciousness as 'natural'. However flawed it may be in its conception and in its expression, 'star-equilibrium' sets out to destabilize the legitimate and official conception ('love'), which is why Birkin's positive subversiveness is underlined as the novel closes.

It could be argued that Lawrence has simply returned 'love' to oxymoron rather than genuinely destabilizing the familiar conception. Is he in fact only restating the conventional view, that is to say, the view that persists at the point of origin of romantic love, that 'love' is oxymoronic and, therefore, only bringing us back to standard clichés about 'love' (where cliché itself bears a kind of poverty)? The answer to this rests in Lawrence's own subliminally oxymoronic language. In contrast to the tradition where the rhetoric of oxymoron is overt and easily available to the reader, the oxymoronic nature of Lawrence's conception is covertly embedded within his narrative. The homology between the conception and structure of 'star-equilibrium', that I have represented as significant, is far from explicit in *Women in Love* but this does not rob it of its relevance. On the contrary, Lawrence's point is partly that the explicit has a distancing function which his own language resists. To sum up, the oxymoronic is veiled and subliminal within the narrative *and at the same time* is the central structuring element of the whole. Once again metaphor and 'metaphysic' are demonstrably not separable. 'Love' is one of those conceptions that Lawrence modifies at the level of language. There is another level where love and metaphor have a distinctive relation. This is where 'love' becomes difficult to define except by metonymy, synecdoche or synonym. The once popular and commercialized formula 'love is . . .', followed by a phrase intended to represent the familiar experience, has a certain symptomatic value representing the general need to say what 'love' is (it becomes a fixed notion) in terms of collective agreement. This formula never extends to say what love is not when the romantic myth, popularly sustained by the commercialized form, fades. Where a definition is sought 'love' is commonly defined in relation to something else. In *Rational Love* Warren Shibles, offering a general truth, says 'any definition given of love is only a metaphor which is expanded and so should not be taken literally' (p. 20). The 'only' in his statement is too negative and he consequently throws out too much. Part of the interest of 'love', as Birkin's dilemma shows, is that we can only approach an understanding of it through metaphor. As I have said, 'love' is no more of a metaphor than any other word but metaphor is profoundly implicated in its meaning for us.

Does the value of 'love' therefore change? This question might force us to look again at those places in the novel where the word 'love' previously seemed innocuous enough. The title becomes more problematic than it at first seemed. Michael Ragussis rightly draws attention to its ambiguity: 'It is only in the course of reading the novel that [the reader] begins to realize he did not understand the title at all' (*The Subterfuge of Art*, p. 191). Reading the novel, it is soon apparent that the principal emphasis is not unequivocally on the intransitive construction 'in love' in the sense in which it has been an habitual preoccupation of poets and novelists. The title seems in the first place as descriptive as *Sons and Lovers* or *Lady Chatterley's Lover*, or any of Lawrence's other titles which refer to personal relations. Although on the face of it the title does refer to the relationships of Ursula and Gudrun Brangwen, the talk which characterizes these relationships brings the word 'love' sharply into focus as problematic.

Indeed, the phrase 'women in love' begins to resonate like the phrases 'women in work' or 'women in politics', signifying a female 'trespass' into predominantly masculine domains. Romantic love originally represented the male point of view, indeed, constituted the male myth. Casting 'women in love' in the light of these other phrases has the effect of pushing 'love' further from the romantic ideal. 'Love' in this novel is combative in the first place. The relationships between the two couples are conducted egotistically. In both *The Rainbow* and *Women in Love* Ursula is represented as independent and, therefore, it is suggested, modern: she is a woman who desires to be 'in work'. In love she is prepared to participate only in a relationship that leaves her with her own sense of self, which Birkin interprets as egoism, but at the same time subscribes to a received romantic conception of 'love' believing it to be 'natural'. She challenges any idea of love as a construct and therefore questions the notion of an alternative to the emotion she 'feels'. Ursula: '"You can't have two kinds of love. Why should you!"' (*Women in Love*, p. 481). She is represented as making sense of the emotion only in terms of the myth. Given the way she fights her corner, however, it is evident that in her public and personal lives her horizons are political, more truly so than are Gudrun's who, as an artist, situates herself outside the common boundaries. Ursula is, in this sense, an extension of *The Rainbow*'s Winifred Inger. Winifred Inger is as significant as Skrebensky in Ursula's development, but her response to the break with Ursula is barely considered. She is kept marginal by Lawrence. However, Winifred's sexuality is deeply related to the questions of 'otherness' and 'polarity' which have been raised here and, in general, Lawrence's treatment of homosexuality and bisexuality may be seen in these broader, philosophical terms. New research by Mark Kinkead-Weekes, particularly on the unpublished writing to have survived on Whitman, represents recently uncovered work which suggests 'the culmination of Lawrence's self-examination about homosexuality' (*D. H. Lawrence: Triumph to Exile 1912–1922*, p. 453).[10] This writing, contemporaneous with the revisions of *Women in Love*, would seem to show considerable cross-fertilization of ideas and language between these texts, as Lawrence continues to examine and change his position on same sex (male) relationships (remember the 'Prologue' to *Women in Love*, abandoned by Lawrence) and heterosexual marriage. The nominal point of interest for Lawrence is the quality (the anti-egotistical quality) of the human relationship and not only its sexual configuration. This, at least, seems to be Birkin's position. Once again the real subject is not simply sex. In the particular instance of Winifred Inger and Ursula a cosmic metaphor serves to define the relation between them: not that of positive polarity which is intrinsically part of the 'metaphysic' of the later novel, but of a sun and its 'satellite', the word with which Ursula will berate Birkin in the sister novel. Ursula and Winifred's early relationship is captured in, 'the girl sat as within the rays of some enriching sun' (*The Rainbow*, p. 312). The relation between them is not the unity of two bodies posited in the relation of Tom Brangwen and Lydia Lensky, the 'established polarity' of the 1919 essay on Whitman,[11] or the (related) balanced singleness as desired by Birkin, but a wavering and uneven relation that modulates continually between unity and separation: this is represented in the swimming scene where 'the bodies of the two women touched, heaved against each other for a moment, then were separate' (*The Rainbow*, p. 314).

When Ursula herself enters the world of work as a school-teacher in the chapter of *The Rainbow* pointedly entitled 'The Man's World' (*The Rainbow*, Chapter XIII), the problem of her female status in a predominantly male preserve (although educated women traditionally became school-teachers), is accentuated in the narrative: 'She tried to approach him [the headmaster] as a young bright girl usually approaches a man, expecting a little chivalrous courtesy. But the fact that she was a girl, a woman, was ignored or used as a matter for contempt against her' (*The Rainbow*, p. 351). Lawrence treats the subject of Ursula's employment ironically, and not only to underline her naivety. She wants her pupils to 'love' her: 'She dreamed how she would make the little, ugly children love her. She would be so personal. Teachers were always so hard and impersonal. There was no vivid relationship' (p. 341). In the dialogues of *Women in Love* the mature Ursula apprehends love differently of course, and those dialogues in which she participates so fiercely throw the love-experiences of *The Rainbow* into relief. It is only Birkin who, despite his 'critical blindness', forces them both into a further consciousness of the politics of love and language. Lawrence is explicit about the resulting relationship in 'Excurse': 'She was next to him, and hung in a pure rest, as a star is hung, balanced unthinkably . . . he too waited in the magical steadfastness of suspense' (*Women in Love*, p. 319). By the end of *Women in Love* 'love' is not reduced to an intelligible quantity, an unproblematic marriage (or even the 'blood-marriage' of 'A Propos of *Lady Chatterley's Lover*'), or a separation, but is distinguished by the contradictions, oppositions and mobility that it has helped to focus throughout the novel.

Warren Shibles argues that '"I love you," may become "I understand you," in order to distinguish the term love from related terms and to gain insight into the word "love"' (*Rational Love*, pp. 20–1), but simple substitutions like this do not engender the profound critique that Lawrence finds necessary. In part Shibles's problem (which has a representative value) is the one the characters are struggling with as they endeavour to define the word, or define themselves in relation to the conception they carry about with them in their heads. In 'Flitting' (*Women in Love*, Chapter XXVII), for instance, Ursula wants exaggerated verbal declaration, 'overstatement', from Birkin. Even so, the words she hears 'sounded like lies': when Birkin, 'whispering with truth', says he loves her, 'it was not the real truth.' Conscious of the split between 'I' and 'you' he contemplates 'This I, this old formula of the ego' as 'a dead letter'. In the longer description from which this comes, Ursula's ignorance, indeed her limitation, is emphasized with the repeated formula, 'she could not know', and towards the end of the episode the narrative voice describes a 'new, superfine bliss, a peace superseding knowledge' (p. 369). Modern knowledge is suddenly obsolete. Birkin, typically in the novel, draws attention to the linguistic, and to the possibility (the fantasy?) of a condition that both precedes and transcends the modern split between mind, body and spirit that so preoccupies Lawrence. In 'A Propos of *Lady Chatterley's Lover*' he was to write that 'In the blood, knowing and being, or feeling, are one and undivided: no serpent and no apple has caused a split' (*Phoenix II*, p. 505).

This moment of reconciliation in *Women in Love* occurs towards the end of the principal conflict between Ursula and Birkin. After this they continue to argue, but with the confidence that some basic understanding has been reached. In 'Mino' Birkin has already struggled to articulate that which is 'beyond love', that is beyond the received view, and has engendered the usual contest. He is thrown into considerable confusion. For this man, who hates his own metaphors, 'love', or the conception he prefers to 'love', resides for him in a place beyond the lexicon. In the end, his desire for silence suggests that language, the available rhetoric of love, is inadequate: 'And it is there I would want to meet you – not in the emotional loving plane – but there beyond, where there is no speech and no terms of agreement' (*Women in Love*, p. 146). His words suggest his philosophical profundity: what he cannot speak of he must consign to silence.[12] He is in need of a different language for his different conception of love, but the point is that love is still, on an important level, linguistic. Birkin

d of a transcendental condition but, perhaps because
poet, it seems to him that it resists being contained
ive forms.

debate on love is taken up again in the conflict between
Gerald and Gudrun. One of Birkin's themes, as he dismantles
the word, has been that what 'love' really means is 'hate'. Gerald
and Gudrun operate within this opposition. For them 'love' and
'death' are also keenly associated terms. Appropriately enough
'Death and Love' (*Women in Love*, Chapter XXIV) is the title of
the chapter in which Gerald makes his way to Gudrun's bed-
room, his boots soiled with the mud from his night visit to his
father's grave, a son-lover within the family space defined by
Beldover. Gerald, who is cast initially in an heroic mould even
if he is to represent the destructive impersonal forces of indus-
trialized society, sets out on his journey to Gudrun (her legen-
dary counterpart is a husband-slayer) on a quest for renewal at
a time paradoxically both of loss (of the father) and gain (of the
family business, his public identity confirmed). Although 'death'
in Lawrence's chapter-heading is prophetic inasmuch as Gerald
eventually perishes and inasmuch as the relationship with Gudrun
is represented as disintegrative (Gerald's dependency on Gudrun
as the vehicle, if not the medium, of his rebirth, is fatal not least
to the relationship, and a far cry from the kinds of intimate polarity explored through Birkin and Ursula), in the immediate
context the reference is to the dead father. The death of the parent
here is significant, as it is at the end of *Sons and Lovers* where
Paul Morel contemplates joining his mother *in* the grave: 'He
wanted her to touch him, have him alongside with her. / But
no, he would not give in' (*Sons and Lovers*, p. 464). In calling his
chapter 'Death and Love' Lawrence associates two terms which
are very closely associated, again oxymoronically, in the European psyche. Romantic tradition is stocked with characters who
literally and metaphorically die for love. The irony of the chapter depends to some extent on this association which inhabits
the narrative of Gerald as he accompanies Gudrun home from
Shortlands: 'fatal elation' and 'fatal exuberance' usher in descriptions where passion and sensation are couched in the language
of death (pp. 329–30). Unhappy liaisons have a central place in
literature, of course. Lawrence's early novels subscribe to this
convention while the mature works turn to the developing critique of 'love'. It is perhaps worth noting that, in the episode
that takes them to the bridge, Gerald seeks selfishly, in a self-

conscious impulse that is masturbatory, to use Gudrun for his immediate relief in a description where Birkin's favourite metaphor is usefully distorted: 'If he could put his arm round her, and draw her against him as they walked, he would equilibriate himself.' Gudrun has previously been represented as setting herself up as functional, having assured him that '"You must use me if I can be of any help"' (*Women in Love*, pp. 325–6).

In the mountains, Gudrun and Gerald act out the final stages of their conflict. Gudrun, now become 'elemental' (p. 441) and 'diabolic' (p. 442) taxes Gerald with the concept 'love'. The question becomes ostensibly one of semantics:

'You know you never *have* loved me, don't you?'
'I don't know what you mean by the word "love",' he replied.
(*Women in Love*, p. 442)

Gerald's appeal to the question of meaning here is defensive. In the course of this exchange the word 'love' is used repeatedly, and by denying knowledge of the word as Gudrun uses it Gerald attempts to protect himself both from the force of the emotion and from the consequences of ever having loved, or of ever having gone through the motions of loving, Gudrun at all. He never displays with her the unconscious sympathy that he displays in his involuntary clutching of Birkin's hand in 'Gladiatorial'. Gudrun, cast as an agent of destruction, or as one critic puts it 'modernist villain',[13] demonstrates her power by forcing a declaration of love from Gerald:

'Say you love me,' she pleaded. 'Say you will love me for ever – won't you – won't you?'
But it was her voice only that coaxed him. Her senses were entirely apart from him, cold and destructive of him. It was her overbearing will that insisted.
'Won't you say you'll love me always?' she coaxed. 'Say it, even if it isn't true – say it Gerald, do.'
'I will love you always,' he repeated, in real agony, forcing the words out.
She gave him a quick kiss.
'Fancy your actually having said it,' she said, with a touch of raillery.
He stood as if he had been beaten.
(*Women in Love*, p. 443)

Gerald's declaration of love while he is 'in real agony' provides a further ironic slant on love's oxymoronic rhetoric. This scene highlights the relation between speech, lies and power which is given a high profile in the novel. Formerly it is Birkin who wants to prevent the utterance of 'love' until the old meaning has gone from it, while Gudrun enjoys hearing the old meaning evoked within the framework of mutual antagonism, or negative friction, that characterizes her relationship with Gerald. Here, silence and speech, in league with an oppressively orthodox conception of 'love', alternately become repressive instruments of the will.

The modern lovers are Gerald and Gudrun, Gerald and Pussum, Pussum and Halliday, Loerke and Leitner, and Gudrun and Loerke, 'modern' because of the insistent egoism of each participant. Occasionally in *Women in Love* two characters achieve a momentary equilibrium, but on the whole this state is elusive and the individuals remain for the most part locked into states of negative (egotistical) singleness. In 'Death and Love', for instance, Gudrun and Gerald are 'such strangers – and yet they were so frightfully, unthinkably near' (p. 330). In 'A Chair' (*Women in Love*, Chapter XXVI) the young man's 'slinking singleness' (p. 359) is represented, projecting him as a potential Aaron Sisson, who walks out on his family. In 'Flitting', thinking about marriage as a social institution, Gudrun sees herself as 'free' (p. 374) and as 'one of the drifting lives that have no root' (p. 376), that is to say without even the impersonal connection desired by Birkin. Birkin's trajectory as he leaves Britain with Ursula is represented as positive, in contrast to the Futuristic descent of Gerald and Gudrun following a different trajectory on the toboggan in 'Snow' (*Women in Love*, Chapter XXX). There the star metaphor is given negative significance: their movement is described as 'a fall to earth, in a diminishing motion' (p. 420). Only in the relationship between Ursula and Birkin, because of its dialogic foundations, is romantic idealism even remotely dismantled in order to achieve a suggestion of an alternative conception of the other. The oxymoronic rhetoric of love acquires a new meaning as a result of Lawrence's critique: it is now no longer an external rhetoric but the implicit nature of the experience.

OXYMORON: 'THE TENSION OF OPPOSITES'

In *D.H. Lawrence: Language and Being*, Michael Bell contrasts the image of star-equilibrium with the rainbow and arch imagery of *The Rainbow*, arguing that the 'architectural' stability of the arch represents an intrinsic solidity which is absent from the idea of the star with its 'openness on all sides' (p. 98). This perception can be extended by emphasizing the *two*-star or *two*-body structure of 'star-equilibrium' in the light of what has already been said about the oxymoronic mode of this novel and Lawrence's oxymoronic spirit generally.[14] This extends to the relation between the two novels, *The Rainbow* and *Women in Love*, themselves the products of a radical split. 'Star-equilibrium' represents Birkin's desire to be simultaneously single *and* exist meaningfully in relation to an other. The image does contrast with the more 'architectural' constructions of the sister novel, including the rainbow with its high arch and two ends rooted firmly in the earth. The stars in Birkin's metaphor are, however, not entirely free-floating bodies. In the phenomenal world, in a spiral galaxy (Lawrence's model), the complex tensions set up by gravity keep the stars in motion and determine the attraction–repulsion relation of each body to the other. Without these tensions the cosmos would either collapse into itself, or its elements would simply drift apart. There is the homology between the structure of oxymoron and the structure of the metaphor, 'star-equilibrium': they have in common two separate elements held apart (and together) by dynamic forces, as well as being in a balanced relation. The linguistic construct creates this tension, signified by the hyphen in the written text where the hyphen is both bridge and yoke. In this way, as I have said, a linguistic structure unconsciously echoes the novel's central metaphysical image.

The 'metaphysic' of impersonal duality that Birkin/Lawrence struggles to make conscious in his encounters with Ursula is therefore represented at a deeper subliminal and linguistic level than might be expected. The structure of oxymoron reproduces the fundamental metaphysical principle, which itself assists in the dismantling of certain orthodoxies, which Birkin struggles to articulate through his cosmic metaphor, and which is extended throughout the novel. In resorting to metaphor Birkin is endeavouring to make something conscious by using language as a descriptive medium – he has a comparison view of metaphor[15] which means that the relation he wants with Ursula is expressed almost as a simile in that they must become *like* two stars – whereas the 'metaphysic' actually gets expressed at a much less conscious level. Consequently, the relation between the language and 'metaphysic' of the novel is unequivocally established, but not by Birkin, at least not directly. The habitually separate levels of metaphor and 'metaphysic' merge as the structures of language mediate the philosophy.

So it is that the linguistic structure of the book is identical to its philosophical, or metaphysical, premises. As Paul Ricoeur, one of the major theorists of metaphor, says, 'Things that until that moment [of being brought together] were "far apart" suddenly appear as "closely related"' (*The Rule of Metaphor*, p. 194). The suggestion is not that Lawrence has singled out oxymoronic structures for particular attention: to insist on this goes against the grain of the argument. It is difficult to say how consciously achieved the oxymoronic suggestion of phrases like 'star-equilibrium' and 'blood-consciousness' is, for instance. In orthodox terms, of course, they are *not* oxymorons, but both enjoy the creative conjunction of their composite elements, both being metaphorical expressions of quite complex levels, bearing the weight and emphasis of Lawrence's latest position. Lawrence is evidently sensitive to what Ricoeur calls 'the complex expression at play in oxymoron' (p. 194). The point is that somehow these forms have been arrived at, that they are incongruous and yet distinctive, and special to Lawrence. Put crudely, he has something to say and the extent of his linguistic sensitivity is vital to the saying of it. This is most likely the origin of constructions like 'star-equilibrium', 'root-vision' and 'blood-consciousness'. At the same time, these Lawrentian metaphors effectively concretize Lawrence's mode of thought in a way that makes this available to examination.

Oxymoron, then, participates in the collapse of the boundary between metaphor and 'metaphysic' in Lawrence's thought, because Lawrence's language-sense and philosophy are ultimately not separable. This collapse is of particular importance in *Women in Love* whose 'frictional' mode of language this is. To Ricoeur, who tends to regard metaphors as isolated occurrences within a narrative, the tension, or explicit contradiction, in oxymoron is significant only inasmuch as it points to a metaphorical meaning which 'solves', that is to say brings to an end, the problem of contradiction itself. For him, 'The metaphorical meaning as such is not the semantic clash but the new pertinence that answers its challenge' (p. 194). But the artist need not dispense with metaphorical structures quite so finally. A metaphor need not be an isolated occurrence, a mere stage on the way to understanding: Lawrence's writing shows how, as a tendency, metaphor becomes a process, a mode of thought, distinct from other modes. His use of the oxymoronic in this novel begs to be taken as a sign of his deep-lying linguistic response to his own 'metaphysic', different from a consciously articulated philosophy. It is an indication of the extent to which he is 'at home' in language, to recall the Heideggerean formulation that in language, and specifically poetry, we 'dwell'. It remains to distinguish between the oxymoronic as a tendency in Lawrence, and 'oxymoron' as a conventional, separable, figure of speech. There is no need in Lawrence to attempt to uncover a metaphorical meaning that *solves* the problem of contradiction when the fact of oxymoronic contradiction, or more specifically the positive friction between the composite elements, is what is important, at least in this novel, as well as the notion of these elements in a balanced relation.

While it is the *structure* of oxymoron, rather than instances of the actual metaphorical expression, which is at the heart of *Women in Love*, I propose to examine the first instance in the novel of an oxymoronic statement, and to draw out its significance within the text as a whole, before discussing parts of the 'Diver' chapter (*Women in Love*, Chapter IV), which is particularly rich in oxymoronic expressions.

There is a subliminal message in the first few pages of the novel which alerts us to the possibility of Lawrence innovating with the relationship between metaphor and reference. Early on in 'Sisters', in the context of the sisters' conversation on marriage, Gudrun's physical response to Ursula's words is ambiguous:

> 'You wouldn't consider a good offer?' asked Gudrun.
> 'I think I've rejected several,' said Ursula.
> '*Really*!' Gudrun *flushed dark*.
> (*Women in Love*, pp. 7–8, final emphases added)

The description of Gudrun shows that in physical terms she has experienced a sensation akin to a *frisson*. The phrase 'flushed dark' is oxymoronic and in many ways a signature of Lawrence.

The semantics of 'flushed' with its glowing, reddish connotations evidently challenge the semantics of 'dark', although 'dark' also belongs to that special group of words which have meaning in the context of the psychic life as in the phrase 'the dark sun', often viewed as the exemplar of Lawrentian oxymoron. Had Lawrence written of Gudrun that she 'flushed deeply' the sense would have been different. Gudrun's response is to all intents and purposes generated from the centres of feeling described in Lawrence's books on the unconscious. It is entirely appropriate that in the narrative she should 'flush' – a physical sign of the blood – 'dark', something which is not so evidently physical, but related more (in Lawrence's lexicon) to the emotions. The same formula occurs in *The Rainbow*: the young Baroness Skrebensky has the effect of making Will Brangwen 'flush darkly by assuming a biting, subtle class-superiority' (*The Rainbow*, p. 185). Here it is a formula which has not yet acquired the structural and symbolic significance that it has in *Women in Love*, but it is nevertheless deeply embedded in Lawrence's unconscious: evidently he is a writer who is drawn to the oxymoronic, and the other novels furnish us with examples, but in *Women in Love* the homology outlined between metaphor and 'metaphysic' underlines the particular significance of the oxymoronic in this novel. The enigma in 'flushed dark' cannot be easily solved, 'for metaphors imply riddles',[16] at least not without recourse to what we already know about Lawrence's relation to language.

There is a related moment in 'Snow' as the characters pass through the wintry landscape on their way to the lodge: 'Up and up, gradually, they went, through the cold *shadow-radiance* of the afternoon, silenced by the imminence of the mountains, the luminous, dazing sides of snow that rose above them and fell away beneath' (*Women in Love*, p. 400, my italics).[17] 'Shadow-radiance' functions like 'flushed dark'. Hyphenated, it recalls constructions like 'root-vision' and 'blood-consciousness', though less 'noticeable', but where they are metaphors for states of being and knowing, 'shadow-radiance' communicates the numinous scene. Visualizing what Lawrence means is difficult, although the terms which are offered relate to an a priori understanding of a mountain landscape. Like 'flushed dark', 'shadow-radiance' can be compared and contrasted with oxymoronic expressions in everyday linguistic exchange. 'Shadow-radiance' does not communicate commonly felt experience as effectively, and universally, as the quotidian example: the difference is that Lawrence's term, uniquely, throws its own elements into question. His is a construction which questions the 'kodak-objectivity' discussed at length in the essays on art and wherever Lawrence interrogates the merely optical as a sense. 'Flushed dark' and 'shadow-radiance', like the 'cold-burning mud' of the Chinese goose drawing (p. 89), are linguistic structures which sustain the idea of an anti-visual aesthetic in Lawrence; a particular quality of his art-speech.

The landscape of 'Snow' is characterized by 'imminence'. The mountain lodge is at the centre of a snowy expanse which is metaphorically 'an open rose' (p. 400). The paragraph rendering the scene is dense with similes: the lodge, the only man-made landmark, is 'like a dream'. This reference is strategic: 'like a dream' goes a long way to explaining the special nature of the language and also alludes to the metaphoric mode of *Women in Love*. It is a repeated note in the novel: in 'Mino', Ursula, travelling in a tram-car on her way to see Birkin, 'seemed to have passed into a kind of dream world, absolved from the conditions of actuality' (p. 144). This contrasts with the more literal understanding of dream narratives as in, for example, *Aaron's Rod*. Ursula's 'dream world', as we expect, is a temporary absolution from quotidian limitations. The implicit division is between the social sphere and the private world of the self. In 'Snow' the language does partly describe a dream-scape, a world which is fundamentally different from that of Beldover; one where Gudrun can become a crystal and 'pass altogether into the whiteness of the snow' (p. 420). The 'terrible waste of whiteness' (p. 400) that characterizes the landscape here stands for disintegrative, resistant, repellant modern consciousness as it does in Lawrence's references to frictional, masturbatory, '"white" sex' in 'A Propos of *Lady Chatterley's Lover*'. As in a dream the 'actual' world is present only as a 'shadow-world' (p. 410). Journeying to the same landscape Ursula 'visualizes' her childhood and life and consigns it to a past for which she has no further use. Generally speaking, therefore, the language of the novel is dream-like in the dimensions it imagines. It delimits an elusive world which is both alien and familiar, a far cry from incorporating an 'actual' dream into the plot on grounds of symbolic continuity.

Also as in a dream the scene in 'Snow' is simultaneously many things. The protagonists are, for instance, 'in the *heart* of the mountains' (p. 398, emphasis added), which is unambiguous in itself as a metaphor from popular parlance. However, we know from *Psychoanalysis and the Unconscious* how much the heart is implicated in Lawrence's thought. Here, the mountains are invested with a special uncanny significance. The drama of feeling ends there. The silence in the mountains has the stifling effect of 'surrounding the heart with frozen air' (p. 399); the peaks become 'the heart petals of an open rose' (p. 400). The repetition of 'heart' is in keeping with the 'hair' and 'navel' imagery and the description of the station platform and lodge interior as 'naked'. The language recalls the 'heart of the world' passage in *The Trespasser* where Helena, listening to the actual heart-beats of Siegmund, contemplates the possibility of an unconscious impersonal force in the world: 'Had the world a heart? – Was there also deep in the world a great God thudding out waves of life, like a great Heart, unconscious? (*The Trespasser*, pp. 79–80).

In these instances the oxymoronic mode has been able to negotiate a shift to the visionary as opposed to the visual; a further discrimination explored by the language. It is a feature of oxymoron that it demands that several meanings be apprehended simultaneously. Consider, for instance, the oxymoronic structures which occur in a cluster in the opening paragraph of the 'Diver' episode, and what they communicate about the subliminal levels at work in the narrative. In an ordinary language context oxymoron does not generally take care to conceal itself, being a clever and pertinent formula for expressing a felt condition, like a 'bittersweet' experience. We are usually aware of its poetic force in the ordinary communicative act because opposites are not normally combined meaningfully, and where they occur appositely they have a special power. The following passage would most likely be read as both 'naturalistic' and typically 'Lawrentian'. While the language here is highly oxymoronic it most usually passes unremarked:

> The atmosphere was grey and translucent, the birds sang sharply on the young twigs, the earth would be quickening and hastening in growth. The two girls walked swiftly, gladly, because of the soft, subtle rush of morning that filled the wet haze. By the road the blackthorn was in blossom, white and wet, its tiny amber grains burning faintly in the white smoke of blossom. Purple twigs were darkly luminous in the grey

air, high hedges glowed like living shadows, hovering nearer, coming into creation. The morning was full of a new creation.

(*Women in Love*, p. 46)[18]

Here the use of oxymoron is not overt, but at the same time the oxymoronic is an important characteristic of the language, for example in the repeated formula of 'wet . . . burning'. Again this is not strictly oxymoron, but phrases using the formula do partake of the oxymoronic in bringing together terms and ideas which bear opposing meanings. The first sense of an oxymoronic tension that raises questions about resemblance, or verisimilitude, occurs with the reference to the blackthorn in blossom. Naturalistically the blossom is 'wet' while the pollen is metaphorically 'burning' in the 'white smoke' of the flower. The metaphor of the blossom as 'smoke' puts the literalistic 'wet' on the defensive. If noticed, the struggle between the naturalistic and the metaphorical language can raise consciousness about ways of naming. If it passes unnoticed it may be meaningful at some other subliminal level, whence it came. The problem of meaning is resolved in the interaction of the two expressions: Lawrence succeeds in representing the physical quality of the blackthorn and its unconscious vitality, if we can speak of it as such, rather than sacrificing one for the other in the narrative, the 'kind of marriage between ideas and experience' to which Ragussis refers (*The Subterfuge of Art*, p. 180). Lawrence returns to the idea of a 'burning' landscape a little later on, using Hermione as a mouthpiece: 'Isn't the young green beautiful? So beautiful – quite burning' (p. 50). Coming from Hermione any ambiguity is heightened. Her verbal response seems incongruous.

Two more related constructions follow on almost immediately from the reference to the blackthorn: 'Purple twigs were darkly luminous in the grey air, high hedges glowed like living shadows'. 'Darkly luminous' is representative, corresponding, for instance, to the negative imagery of Lawrence's poem 'Bavarian Gentians' (*Complete Poems*, p. 697; p. 960), the poetry representing the more available oxymoronic spirit of Lawrence's language. Attention was earlier drawn to the force of 'dark' in the context of Gudrun's experience. It is a word which is recognized as having a high value in Lawrence's personal lexicon, along with words like 'quick' and 'motionless'. Having 'darkly' and 'luminous' neighbouring one another is highly effective. It could be argued that the 'purpleness' of the twigs introduces a naturalistic quality which reduces the efficacy of the oxymoronic, at the least forcing the status of the oxymoron into question. My sense of it, however, is that the oxymoronic mode dominates, and that Lawrence's language is not simply evoking a rural scene visually. This is another of Lawrence's unconscious landscapes.

The terms used to relate to the vegetation have a physicality, but their artistic importance also resides in the way they highlight the play of the noumenal and the numinous in Lawrence. Principally through metaphor and metaphorical expressions like those examined here, Lawrence's language interrogates the status of the conditioned reality of empirical observation, in its relation to the world of noumena. It is in this context that metaphor in Lawrence enacts questions of being and knowing, which plain language is not accustomed to do. The numinous is the vital generative force suggested by Lawrence's description of a world that ultimately resists being rendered naturalistically.

The second instance of oxymoronic language in this passage is related to the first. The hedges 'glowed' like 'shadows', a description which functions in a way similar to 'darkly luminous'. Glow signifies light, brilliance and heat, concepts which have a positive value to Lawrence for whom they suggest 'presence', if not what he calls elsewhere 'quivering momentaneity' ('Poetry of the Present', *Complete Poems*, p. 183). 'Living shadows' is more ambiguous. In the first place the phrase is part of a simile wherein 'high hedges glowed like living shadows', but 'glowing' shadow is again naturalistically challenging if the reader stops to consider the effect of the detail. There is no need to make sense of the enigma, to recall Ricoeur's formulation. Like the purpleness of the twigs, the greyness of the air and the rush of the morning, 'living shadows' contributes to the physical sense of the time, place and space. Further than that, the simple metaphor is part of a *relational* aesthetic. The presence of shadow depends upon the presence of an object and the presence of light, just as the rainbow's luminescence depends upon the conjunction of light and water.

It is an image to which Lawrence returns in 'Breadalby' (*Women in Love*, Chapter VIII). Hermione and some of her guests take a swim in one of Hermione's terraced ponds:

They all dropped into the water, and were swimming together like a shoal of seals. Hermione was powerful and unconscious

in the water, large and slow and powerful, Palestra was quick
and silent as a water rat, Gerald wavered and flickered, a *white
natural shadow*. Then, one after the other, they waded out, and
went up to the house.

(Women in Love, p. 101, my italics)

It is quite difficult to decide, in the immediate context at least,
whether this description of Gerald is a positive or a negative
image: Lawrence may indeed be playing with the idea of positive and negative images in the photographic sense, as an extension of his thought on 'kodak' vision. Clearly the language is
highly visual and highly figurative. While 'wavered' and 'flickered' signify an unconscious mode of being, Gerald is also 'white',
a stark figure embodying the extremity of modern consciousness.

So it is that the oxymoronic quality of some of Lawrence's
constructions helps to bring the novel's mode of language to light.
In an ordinary-language context we are invited to establish a
degree of semantic proximity, which will bring the distant terms
of the oxymoron close together in a meaningful way. In the chapter
called 'Diver' the fundamental difference between the oxymoron
in an ordinary language context and the oxymoronic in Lawrence
is obvious. Both generate meaning by bringing unlike terms together, but Lawrence's expressions are context-specific as well
as being what creates the context. Because of this characteristic
the metaphorical expressions in 'Diver', unlike any number of
oxymorons from the store-house of ordinary language expressions, would lose their force away from this context. This reinforces the point that metaphor, in these immediate phrases, is
inseparable from the 'metaphysic', the overall philosophical context. Not only are the examples from 'Diver' poetic, they are
specifically features of the radical grammar of *Women in Love*.
So, what kind of objectification is this, and how central to
Lawrence's aesthetic?

They are indeed among the apictorial features of 'Diver'. They
vividly recreate because, paradoxically, they do not 'resemble'
the object. The reader's reception of the opening scene is largely
unconscious. It is not imperative for the reader to isolate these
stylistic features, even though to do so is to confront Lawrence's
language-sense. This is not a conscious rhetoric on Lawrence's
part. The related question of resemblance is important. The language which introduces Gerald to the scene swimming in the

'uncreated water' of the lake is one of many indications that
pictorialism is not Lawrence's primary concern. There are several anti-visual passages running close upon each other which
serve to dramatize the noumenal within the landscape, of which
this is one. The description of the lake as 'all grey and visionary'
(p. 46) is a further sign: 'visionary' is an unusual word in this
context giving the lake a presence which is not altogether physical. At times, but only at times, *Women in Love* shares in the
'visionary' mode which is more characteristic of *The Rainbow*.

This style of 'rendering' the world of experience is more exaggerated in the descriptions of Gerald whose human frame, and
by inference his humanity, is shed for something more abstract.
Making his appearance in 'Diver', he is depersonalized from the
outset:

> Suddenly, from the boat-house, a white figure ran out, fright-
> ening in its swift sharp transit, across the landing-stage. It
> launched in a white arc through the air, there was a bursting
> of the water, and among the smooth ripples a swimmer was
> making out to space, in a centre of faintly heaving motion.
> The whole otherworld, wet and remote, he had to himself. He
> could move into the pure translucency of the grey, uncreated
> water.
>
> (*Women in Love*, p. 46)

To describe Gerald diving as 'a white arc' is to continue the
process of his alienation. It is also a compelling image, a featureless version of the rainbow. Whereas the infinitely coloured
rainbow has a primordial charge, the white arc is a stark modernist construction of pure form. Rather than polarizing the naturalistic and the abstract, Lawrence has them interacting, thereby
stressing their relationship. Neither is evoked for its own sake.
It is worth adding that Gerald swimming is also an element, but
a single one, in a state of equilibrium. The episode is mediated
through the eyes of Gudrun and Ursula who as yet can only
regard Gerald as being outside their immediate world. This gulf
is emphasized in the narrative: 'He waved again, with a strange
movement of recognition across the difference'. Elsewhere the
lake is 'his separate element'. Gerald feels his 'possession of a
world to himself', and 'exulted in his isolation in the new element, unquestioned and unconditioned ... without bond or con-

nection anywhere, just himself in the watery world' (p. 47). The word 'unconditioned' continues the signification of a noumenal world which informs these 'naturalistic' descriptions.

The opposition of 'motion/motionless' points up the elemental differences at this stage between Gerald, depersonalized, and Gudrun, whose individuality has been emphasized from the beginning of the novel, externally with regard to her distinctive clothing, and internally in her responses to her environment. Gerald is motion, a word which in Lawrence's lexicon signifies a male principle: 'among the smooth ripples a swimmer was making out to space, in a centre of faintly heaving motion' (p. 46); 'The sisters stood watching the swimmer move further into the grey, moist, full space of the water, pulsing with his own small, invading motion' (pp. 46–7); 'she stood watching the motion on the bosom of the water'; 'In the faint wash of motion, they could see his ruddy face'; and the solipsistic, masturbatory 'He loved his own vigorous, thrusting motion' (p. 47). Each repetition of the word reinforces the idea of flow, of a fluid interplay of elements rather than Gudrun's 'finality'. Gerald is perceived as little more than movement, *and* fundamentally a thing apart from his environment. Even in this cameo Lawrence takes the opportunity to explore his own thesis on self-sufficient male freedom and singleness, yet representing through Gerald narcissism, a self-consciousness not accommodated by Lawrence's 'metaphysic'. In contrast to Gerald, Gudrun is 'motionless' a word which communicates both her physical stasis as she becomes absorbed in the object before her, and the psychic profile of their future relationship, suggested linguistically by the opposition of motion/motionless. We are not given to expect anything like 'star-equilibrium' between them because the language does not suggest it. Her absorption is of the kind which is implied in 'Sisters' (*Women in Love*, Chapter I) when, on seeing Gerald for the first time, she conceives of the 'arctic light that envelopes only us two' (p. 15). The infinity of white 'arctic' light is a further sign of purest modern consciousness, an image of over-exposure that opposes the dark space of Birkin's astral vision. At its best, as Birkin insists, the 'metaphysic' of 'star-equilibrium' accommodates a plurality of relations, not the couple in isolation. This is a shift from his own first terms when he declared to Gerald, 'First person singular is enough for me' (p. 56). At a relatively early point in the novel we are invited to consider whether this is crass egotism and selfishness, or a statement of positive singleness emerging from a critique of what is proposed as the inauthentic feeling sustaining *Egoïsme à deux*.

Although the word is not Lawrence's, at least not here, Gudrun's heart is indeed 'contracted' to Gerald, something that is evident from 'Sisters' and finalized in 'Sketch-Book': 'The bond was established between them, in that look, in her tone' (p. 122). This bond is the alternative to the social arrangement of marriage which Gudrun later disparages, the contract into which Ursula and Birkin enter, having first 'read the terms' (p. 148). Gudrun's bond bears a sense of the two being 'contracted', a word that also recalls physical recoil from something. In the light of what we know of the 'metaphysic' of *Women in Love* we can see that Lawrence has instituted a whole network of puns: Gudrun wonders, 'Am I *really singled* out for him in some way?' (p. 15, final emphasis mine); watching Gerald in the wash of the water, and feeling herself held back, she 'felt herself as if *damned*, out there on the highroad' (p. 47, my italics).

Punning is conventionally regarded as having more to do with the superimposition of linguistic levels than with oxymoron with *its* dependence on the pertinent juxtaposition of meanings. Its general significance is communicated succinctly by Jonathan Culler in the context of his assessment of a work very different from Lawrence's: the pun 'displays the infinite play of differences by which a word sends us off to other words instead of linking directly with a world'.[19] This is nevertheless pertinent to *Women in Love* given the extent to which the central quartet debate meanings, although language mediates something specific in Lawrence as well as being about the play of signification. Lawrence may indeed be suggesting that the dynamic of meaning, even in a single word (like 'love' for example), is oxymoronic rather than either purely centripetal (tending towards other meanings as with puns) or purely centrifugal (tending towards a world). Out of these thoughts emerges the question whether pun is in fact in a profound sense related to oxymoron? Certainly a punning consciousness characterizes Lawrence's language.[20] A pun is effective because it aligns two separate meanings, and as soon as this is said a rhetorical similarity with oxymoron emerges. Both tropes are predicated on difference, although in the case of oxymoron difference is very clearly 'the tension of opposites'. Jean-Jacques Lecercle, also examining a very different writing practice from Lawrence's, concludes that 'Puns *are* close to metaphors': he identifies a legislative tendency attached to them, suggesting that because the expansion of meaning in pun is limited (usually to two meanings, in contrast to the complex creativity of metaphor), puns act as a controlling device, bringing order (i.e. a restricted field of linguistic play) to a text which is constantly the site of the excessive production of meaning.[21] This focus on the creativity of metaphor is appropriate and sustains the notion of metaphor (aside from pun) as a kind of projection: confronted with it, the reader is invited to begin the process of interpretation from within a rich textual field. Metaphor and pun: without wishing to push their similarities too far, the fact of their kinship, in the context of Lawrence's language at any rate, suggests that important contiguity of language and thought already alluded to.

To concentrate on an oppositional dynamic of meaning, even within single words, is to realize that the 'frictional to-and-fro' on a linguistic level in Lawrence generates meaning. It is a phrase that describes the tension of opposites which institutes the *'struggle* for verbal consciousness' that characterizes Lawrence's art-speech, and lies at the heart of Lawrentian modernism.

CONCLUSION

The oxymoronic tendency in the language of this novel coincides with the philosophy of relationships articulated by Birkin. At this time Lawrence was developing other modes of expression, the 'body language' of the early versions of *Studies in Classic American Literature*, for example, and shifting his position on personal relations the whole time (*Aaron's Rod*, with its rejection even of Birkin's notions of heterosexual and same-sex relationships, was begun as *Women in Love* and the American essays were revised). There is no fixed position that Lawrence consistently occupies. Productively for his critics, he remains a writer whose interest in certain extremely complex questions to do with identity, sexuality, gender and the heterosexist paradigm, the self, relationality, surfaces in a genuine curiosity about modes of understanding which impacts subtly on his writing practice, his treatment of, and relationship with, his own medium.

In conclusion, it is worth reiterating that the statements on repetition in the Foreword to *Women in Love* do refer to a significant degree to the language of *The Rainbow*, which is most probably the source of Lawrence's remarks on his own repetitive style. Nevertheless, the modes of language in each novel clearly differ, and by attending to the various levels of metaphor within the individual works it is possible to see the extent to which *Women in Love* is to a considerable degree a subtilization of modes of language present in *The Rainbow*. Both novels, more than the others, bear the weight of Lawrence's recognition that metaphor is not simply expressive, but both do so differently. The style of each is linked to the 'metaphysic' of each.

The *un*conscious modality of *Women in Love*, in particular, is thrown into relief by the conscious metaphoricity of Lawrence's books on the unconscious. The way its thought is embodied in its narrative language, particularly the way it partakes of the oxymoronic, and its critique of the *merely* rhetorical makes it crucial to a consideration of Lawrence thinking metaphorically, indeed poetically, in the context of a major work of fiction. Hence, while *Women in Love* is about themes and issues which continually preoccupy Lawrence in his writings, its linguistic specificity helps us to grasp the profound role of metaphor within his poetics. Yet, central as it is, *Women in Love* is far from covering all the stylistic possibilities available to Lawrence. It is not the work in which we are presented with Lawrence's final word on language, but a stage in his thinking about language and the values it bears – like the other novels it came, in a significant measure, 'unwatched'. As I have suggested, while, of the novels, it is most explicitly concerned with language as a theme, it does not represent a *theory* of language, or a theory of meaning, which is rehearsed and reproduced elsewhere. To say so, and to bear in mind its differences from what I have called the 'engulfing' medium of *The Rainbow*, is to highlight the fact that in Lawrence we are aware of different modes of language, and further, that through these radically dissimilar works an understanding of the diverse levels of creativity within language emerges. Each work's particular tone is available through attention to metaphor, which is no *simply* rhetorical figure in Lawrence.

Considering *The Rainbow* my immediate emphasis is on the pervasively metaphorical language, which is to underline something very distinctive about that novel within Lawrence's *oeuvre*. The kind of repetition indicated there, which is part of a vast metaphorical process, contrasts sharply with the 'continual, slightly modified repetition' described in the Foreword to *Women in Love* as a 'pulsing, frictional to-and-fro'(*Women in Love*, p. 486), and yet, crucially, as I suggest, is its source. 'Frictional' there, implies the resistance of one body against another in the context of a sexual encounter; it describes a momentary, local, resistance, and in doing so suggests the relation of the verbal elements in oxymoron, as I have indicated, a profound type of metaphor for Lawrence. 'Frictional' is a word which Lawrence used again and again, exploiting the different levels of meaning in the word as they disclosed themselves to him. Towards the end of *The Plumed Serpent*, for instance, the word is given purely negative connotations. As in the Foreword to *Women in Love* it refers to the sexual, but here sex and speech are seen in the first place as being too conscious and too sensational. Of Kate and Cipriano it is written that:

> He was aware of things that she herself was hardly conscious of. Chiefly, of the curious irritant quality of talk. And this he avoided. Curious as it may seem, he made her aware of her own old desire for frictional, irritant sensation. She realized how all her old love had been frictional, charged with the fire of irritation and the spasms of frictional voluptuousness.
>
> (*The Plumed Serpent*, p. 421)

This often-quoted passage is charged with a sexual language signifying a sex-consciousness that no character could voice in *The Rainbow*, and announces a view of female sexuality that gave rise to critical responses which ushered in a period of significant re-evaluation of Lawrence's work from the 1970s.[22] 'Friction' does here refer to Lawrence's horror of the clitoris and women's demand for satisfaction, something which has its first crystallization in *The Rainbow*, in the last sexual episode, for example, between Ursula and Skrebensky (*The Rainbow*, p. 444). Kate Leslie is represented here as questioning the 'law' which has always told her where, literally, her bodily pleasures reside. As she thinks it through, a gulf opens up between sexual pleasures and the sexualized body: this is the route Lawrence chooses to make female orgasm seem undesirable, in the last analysis, to her. The language of the passage from *The Plumed Serpent*, and the Foreword to *Women in Love*, represents modes of consciousness

188 D.H. Lawrence: The Thinker as Poet

which contrast with that of the *The Rainbow* represented here, for instance, in the description of the Brangwens 'feeling the pulse and the body of the soil, that opened to their furrow for the grain, and became smooth and supple after their ploughing, and clung to their feet with a weight that pulled like desire' (*The Rainbow*, p. 10). In this language the sexual is less personal: it exists at a much deeper, prolonged, sustained and more unconscious level than the former. In this we are referred to the subterranean sweep of *The Rainbow*, to language and consciousness as process. The 'slightly modified repetition' of *Women in Love*, in contrast, effectively focuses that novel's preoccupation with language, where what Lawrence sees as the problem of being so 'conscious' is inseparable from the problem of being so verbal. It is the problem which the main characters, in their different ways, discuss. In *The Rainbow*, language essentially rolls on, unconscious, impersonal, undulant.

How does this point up the difference between the mode of language in *Women in Love* compared to *The Rainbow*? I have emphasized how metaphor in these texts does not have a merely rhetorical function, but sustains the thought. At the same time, the metaphorical quality of the language of the one novel is strikingly different from that of the other. Hence, despite a common basis in Lawrence's thought, the novels do not share an identical 'metaphysic'. I have suggested that there is a subtle correlation between the condition of the individual in each novel and the condition of the word. For instance, my model of the figure in water (not Gerald Crich) also describes the condition of specific single words, key words for Lawrence, in *The Rainbow*. Like the figure in my example who is a part of the continuous flood, these key words, like 'reality', 'presence', that are central to the thought, have a whole set of meanings, and often *opposing* meanings, passing through them. Crucially, no difficulty is experienced in understanding what these particular words mean where they occur in *The Rainbow* because their context makes 'sense' of them. Context in *The Rainbow*, therefore, has an explanatory function. In *Women in Love*, however, while the same vocabulary remains important, the context fails to provide a stable meaning and, against expectation, often forces plain meaning into question. The importance of context is discussed briefly by Paul Ricoeur who makes a useful distinction in pointing out that words 'acquire an actual meaning only in a sentence'. Words listed in a dictionary, he adds, are only 'lexical entities' having 'merely potential meanings'. Indeed, metaphor is a 'contextual change of meaning' and not a lexical one (*Hermeneutics and the Human Sciences*, pp. 169–70). Ricoeur is talking about metaphor at a rhetorical level, and about the smallest units of 'proper' sense. However, his words apply obliquely in the present context as *The Rainbow* dramatizes his point (which is a general one), at least with regard to Lawrence's key words: 'presence' and 'reality', it is generally recognized, change their meaning within the narrative according to context. In *Women in Love*, on the other hand, actual meanings are in crisis. In *Women in Love* it is the word which 'pushes through' the narrative language around it, giving rise to the 'frictional' quality of that language, a quality which now speaks to more than the linguistic. Instead of the word seeming fixed and having language (sense) passing through it (the sweeping wave of *The Rainbow*), it is more active: it interrogates by 'disturbing' and as I observed earlier, destabilizing, its surroundings. This has repercussions for the values created in that language.

This chapter has traced a route through specific themes in Lawrence's novel and has arrived, inevitably, back at language. The principal focus has been on Lawrence's ability to close the distance between language and what it describes, and the radical ways in which the metaphorical levels within the language contain the thought. The critique of 'love' subtly underpinning *Women in Love* most ably demonstrates this, but it is equally apparent in the way Lawrence recovers a special kind of seeing from ordinary optical seeing, and a special kind of physical being from the purely physical. In this sense *Women in Love* is Lawrence's most philosophical novel in contrast to the highly 'novelistic' *The Rainbow*: within its own narrative language, philosophically and structurally, *Women in Love* deals in the most penetrating fashion with the central problems of language and rhetoric.

8

'Forbidden Metaphors': Lawrence and Language

We are now in a position to consider Lawrence's view of language in a broader, more analytical context. Towards the end of 'On Truth and Lies in a Nonmoral Sense' Nietzsche makes a statement which anticipates a modernist idea of language. It also contains a directive for the poet-thinker:

> The free intellect copies human life, but it considers this life to be something good and seems to be quite satisfied with it. That immense framework and planking of concepts to which the needy man clings his whole life long in order to preserve himself is nothing but a scaffolding and toy for the most audacious feats of the liberated intellect. And when it smashes this framework to pieces, throws it into confusion, and puts it back together in an ironic fashion, pairing the most alien things and separating the closest, it is demonstrating that it has no need of these makeshifts of indigence and that it will now be guided by intuitions rather than by concepts. There is no regular path which leads from these intuitions into the land of ghostly schemata, the land of abstractions. There exists no word for these intuitions; when man sees them he grows dumb, or else he speaks only in forbidden metaphors and in unheard-of combinations of concepts. He does this so that by shattering and mocking the old conceptual barriers he may at least correspond creatively to the impression of the powerful present intuition.
>
> (*Philosophy and Truth*, p. 90)

It is the iconoclasm of this passage, combined with the positive effects of restructuring the 'framework' intuitively and in the 'ironic' way described, which anticipates certain kinds of modernist practice, particularly in the last sentence. It is the 'liberated intellect', no longer governed by concepts, which must break down and recreate differently the 'framework'. The entire essay, which is barely more than a creative sketch where Nietzsche can lay down some first terms, is a dialectic between rational man and intuitive man, and towards the end it seems to be approaching a sense of art and philosophy as interacting more than they have done traditionally.

Heidegger also raises questions which are central to modernist poetics. This statement from Nietzsche may be compared with some of the positions in Heidegger's lecture 'The Nature of Language',[1] partly because of this concentration on the interconnectedness of art and philosophy, and because the starting point for Nietzsche's reflections is metaphor ('we possess nothing but metaphors for things – metaphors which correspond in no way to the original entities', *Philosophy and Truth*, p. 83). The discourses with which Heidegger concerns himself are poetry and thought, attributing a different language to each. They do not function alone, and many other modes of language exist, but the languages of poetry and thought have already in part been privileged in the culture. Hence, Heidegger like Nietzsche ascribes a sort of initiative to thought and to poetry, but not the same initiative in both. Certainly Heidegger rejects the view that language is merely the instrument of thought, a position shared by Lawrence. These thinkers start from the position, then, that human understanding does not occur *only* through deduction. In the course of his lecture, Heidegger draws attention to a fundamental distinction between the language of poetry and the language of thought, and in so doing describes the situation in which philosophers, as thinkers, find themselves:

Poetry and thought, each needs the other in its neighborhood, each in its fashion, when it comes to ultimates. In what region the neighborhood itself has its domain, each of them, thought and poetry, will define differently, but always so that they will find themselves within the same domain. But because we are caught in the prejudice nurtured through centuries that thinking is a matter of ratiocination, that is, of calculation in the widest sense, the mere talk of a neighborhood of thinking to poetry is suspect.

('The Nature of Language', in *On the Way to Language*, p. 70)

Heidegger's position here is very close to Nietzsche's in 'On Truth and Lies in a Nonmoral Sense'. The onto-theological tradition which Heidegger seeks to leave behind speaks inauthentic poetry. His assessment of the tradition indirectly reminds us of Nietzsche's distinction between rational and intuitive man (*Philosophy and Truth*, pp. 90–1). Heidegger and Nietzsche have in common the belief that poetic language is in itself a 'thinking' which is free from the limits of ratiocination (poetry is a kind of questioning different from that which is the principal mode of Western metaphysics). Like Lawrence, although not in the manner of Lawrence, Heidegger's own later prose tends towards the poetic, partly in response to his radical apprehension of poetry and thought sharing a 'neighbourhood'. In 'Language' he states that 'The opposite of what is purely spoken, the opposite of the poem, is not prose. Pure prose is never "prosaic." It is as poetic and hence as rare as poetry' (*Poetry, Language, Thought*, p. 208). Heidegger's notion of the 'nearness' of the 'domains' of poetry and thought is felt in the imaginative etymologies that stage a nostalgia for 'thinking' in his writing.

In his use of language Heidegger, as poet-thinker, can be seen 'playing with seriousness', to recall Nietzsche's formulation (*Philosophy and Truth*, p. 91). His style shows how radically he has moved from regarding thinking as a matter of ratiocination. We are reminded of his difficult thesis, '*Language speaks*' ('Language', in *Poetry, Language, Thought*, p. 190). The play of actual and potential meanings that he institutes signals the 'speaking' of language. In his own words, 'It is not a matter here of stating a new view of language. What is important is learning to live in the speaking of language' (p. 210). As we expect, he is not about to theorize metaphor. The reference is more properly to the subject's 'dwelling in' language, the poetic ('dwelling' is at the heart of Heidegger's thought on 'Being', towards which the whole movement in Heidegger tends: in his essay 'Building Dwelling Thinking' he labours to communicate the continuity of the three concepts in the title).[2] What his critics might call his 'primitivism' develops out of his sense of an impoverished language and a correspondingly diminished capacity in man to *dwell*: 'everyday language is a forgotten and therefore used-up poem, from which there hardly resounds a call any longer' (p. 208). The artist, and Lawrence is exemplary, may be attuned to Heidegger's recognition. Heidegger himself foregrounds his own creativity with meanings: his insistence is that we let ourselves be reached by the challenge to thought offered by the Poetic. The artist (intuitive man) of course already knows this. The philosopher can be seen coming to this understanding.

Because of his thesis, much of Heidegger's language resists a clearly demarcated analytical register. Hence the special urgency of the question as to whether he can actually be 'translated'. The answer would conceivably focus on the apparent arbitrariness with which Heidegger proceeds. To what extent can levels of thought that turn on a complex play of metaphor be expressed non-metaphorically, or be substituted by other metaphors? An implicit distinction here, at work in Lawrence's writing, is that between metaphor and metaphoricity. The continuous production and proliferation of meaning can be traced in a work, but the value of the exercise will not be on the fact of dissemination but on understanding-as-metaphorical, which the serious business of word-play like Heidegger's signals. Heidegger enacts, in his own terms, a form of 'authentic hearing' (p. 209). If by this stage the differences between the language of poetry and the language of thought have become in any way polarized, even in the process of considering their nearness, or alternatively have begun to seem indistinguishable, Heidegger provides the following meditation:

> We must discard the view that the neighborhood of poetry and thinking is nothing more than a garrulous cloudy mixture of two kinds of saying in which each makes clumsy borrowings from the other. Here and there it may seem that way. But in truth, poetry and thinking are in virtue of their nature held apart by a delicate yet luminous difference, each held in its own darkness: two parallels, in Greek *para allelo*, by one another, against one another, transcending, surpassing one another each in its fashion. Poetry and thinking are not separated if separation is to mean cut off into a relational void. The parallels intersect in the infinite.
> ('The Nature of Language', in *On the Way to Language*, p. 90)

The nearness, the proximity, of poetry and thought itself depends on the difference ('dif-ference') of the two 'neighbourhoods'. 'The Nature of Language' is a statement of Heideggerean 'intimacy'.

Lawrence shares, if not Heidegger's style, this view of the

closeness of the two domains; shares the sense of the relation of each to the other. Heidegger seems to be a little surprised (although this surprise is probably strategic) at the sense of the concealed richness of language which he initially derives from poetry. But his own language, his own meaning, depends precisely on this richness. As a philosopher he is writing, not about language – he remarks that linguists, philologists, psychologists and analytic philosophers have done this practically to saturation point – but, in what is more than simply a poetic gesture, he is giving language the space to reveal language-sense. He repeats that his experience with language must be a thinking one. If Heidegger as a philosopher is responding to the need to slough off an acculturated ratiocinative mode of thinking precisely because it fails to think, then the artist is in a similar position when s/he recognizes the need to shatter and mock 'the old conceptual barriers' (*Philosophy and Truth*, p. 90). A modernist consciousness of language is something to do with this recognition.

So there is in Lawrence's language (and in the particular inflections of the works examined in this study), precisely such a neighbourly nearness, to use Heidegger's terms, between poetry and thought. The Heideggerean recognition in Lawrence distinguishes him from his modernist contemporaries for whom radical practice may be construed as not so much a philosophical question of language, but a question of technique. There is in Joyce, Richardson, Eliot and Pound, for example (as producers of some of the 'high' modernist master narratives), that kind of modernist consciousness which might actually impede the real 'neighbouring'. We cannot help but be aware, particularly in his mature writing, of his language-*sense*, and the metaphorical basis of understanding in Lawrence, even while metaphor only takes us part of the way to anyone's 'truth'. Given their nearness, a principal difference between Lawrence and the later Heidegger is that Heidegger must in the end say something about language, which Lawrence is not constrained, explicitly, to do. The important thing about Lawrence, whatever can be said 'locally' about his handling of language, is that language itself is the legitimate subject of his texts because in them the 'neighbouring' about which Heidegger speaks is not obstructed by a concern with modes which are in the end principally self-reflexive. In taking this position I have not sought to justify Lawrence to Heidegger, or to use Heidegger to make Lawrence seem philosophically legitimate. To talk of the Heideggerian dimension of Lawrence is simply to underscore this observation: the 'philosopher', since Nietzsche, seems to be reaching, or reaching for, a consciousness of language which the creative writer intuitively possesses. Deleuze indirectly states the case using a metaphor which Lawrence would perhaps have approved: 'Language quivers in all its limbs, and we discover at this point the principle of a poetic understanding of language itself: it is as if language were carving a line to stretch – both abstract and infinitely varied.'[3]

Many of Lawrence's essays, and particularly the books on the unconscious, provide a context where Lawrence is consciously bringing something particular about language, a poetic understanding of it perhaps, to notice. In these instances, a *barely* metaphorical style simply is not conscious enough for Lawrence's purposes. We can recall one of the central puns of *Fantasia of the Unconscious*, a text where Lawrence exploits the levels of meaning in the simple word 'solar'. The solar plexus is so-called because of the resemblance between the radial network of nerves at this point in the body, and the sun's rays radiating from its centre. Lawrence brings the life-giving force of the sun to bear on his assessment of the solar plexus as the *locus* of the self; it is 'where you *are*. It is your first and greatest and deepest centre of consciousness' (*Fantasia*, F&P, p. 28, my italics). It is a word that also, pleasingly for Lawrence, echoes 'soul', a notion preferred by him to psychoanalytical designations for the unconscious. He also makes a play on 'sympathetic'. The 'autonomic' nervous system, controlling the voluntary actions of certain organs including the heart, is organized according to 'sympathetic' and 'parasympathetic' systems. The solar plexus constitutes, as Lawrence says, part of the network of sympathetic nerves, so he plays on 'sympathetic' as characterizing the feelings. Both meanings are brought to bear on his statement that the solar plexus is a 'sympathetic centre' (p. 28) as he seeks to close the gap between the physical and the emotional. It also informs the value of the 'middle' of the body, the centre, the metaphorical 'heart', in Lawrence's thought.

In the same kind of discussion, a play on the notion of a blood tie between child and parent is also instituted, turning on the idea of emotional and physical connection. The navel is a site of physical connection with, and rupture from, the mother, but Lawrence is insistent on the 'tie of blood' (p. 29) with the father as having a special quality, in some sense competing with the significance of the literal flow which connects the mother and foetus. This 'tie of blood' does not bear a racial or ethnic meaning; what is meant is 'lifeblood' which gives rise to a mode of consciousness different from that which informs debates on racial difference. Father and child are subject to 'unknowable communications':

> On the contrary, the true male instinct is to avoid physical contact with a baby. It may not even need actual presence. But, present or absent, there should be between the baby and the father that strange, intangible communication, that strange pull and circuit such as the magnetic pole exercises upon a needle, a vitalistic pull and flow which lays all the life-plasm of the baby into a line of vital quickening, strength, knowing. And any lack of this vital circuit, this vital interchange between father and child, man and child, means an inevitable impoverishment to the infant.
> The child exists in the interplay of two great life-waves, the womanly and the male.
>   (*Fantasia of the Unconscious*, in F&P, p. 33)

The metaphors of pull and flow, of 'life-waves', challenge and threaten to dismantle the 'old conceptual barriers' governing the family dynamic, particularly inasmuch as it is set up by psychoanalysis. Blood and milk are the more literal waves of life on which the infant depends. Between the father and child the 'vitalistic pull and flow' is a non-literal equivalent of the flow of maternal milk. As Deleuze and Guattari suggest, it is the infinite and subversive 'flow' of response which institutes an implicit critique of the Oedipal relation, that which Lawrence is challenging here. '[T]he womanly and the male' stand principally for the parent figures, recalling, in the fiction, Tom and Lydia Brangwen framing the world of the child Anna. In this description from *Fantasia of the Unconscious*, Lawrence is attempting to remap the paternal relationship as, in the same book, he remaps the maternal body and the sexual body, shifting the emphasis from the usual *loci* of desire and sensation. Part of what he is attempting to do in the books on the unconscious is question the ways in which desire and identity have been culturally mapped onto the body.

These simple examples have a representative function. For Lawrence, there are no non-metaphorical equivalents in which the same could be said: the metaphorical language is not just ornamental but bears the understanding without becoming simply the vehicle of meaning. Throughout Lawrence, the language subverts, tells against, unitary, univocal systems of understanding. He is not, after all, writing a textbook. He, and we, would not expect *Fantasia of the Unconscious* to answer the general need for textbooks on child psychology, sex, or family relations. The point is that metaphor is a condition of finding something out: it is a medium of knowledge. The barely, or routinely, metaphorical (Heidegger's 'used-up poem') effectively fails as a mode of thought, being limited to a more blandly expressive function.

In fact, Lawrence can be more exploratory with metaphor in texts like his books on the unconscious because there he is free from the demands of fiction. Writing 'discursively' Lawrence takes advantage of the absence of a certain type of narrative in order to focus more consciously on the metaphorical, and to be more experimental with it (or from within it) as a mode of understanding. This is how language comes into view, in the books on the unconscious, as a legitimate subject of Lawrence's writing. This is also true of the fiction; but there the exigencies of fiction being different from those of the 'discursive' texts, the question of language is subtilized and assimilated to other narrative purposes.

So far the emphasis has been on a view of language in Lawrence which Heidegger principally helps to throw into relief. A brief comparison with a different kind of philosophical thought can extend the horizons of the debate further. Paul Ricoeur has methodically examined the relation between text and metaphor, representing metaphor as in some senses a 'work in miniature' (*Hermeneutics and the Human Sciences*, p. 167). Reading the later Heidegger enables Ricoeur to re-examine the relation between thinking and poetry, particularly, and appropriately, 'the very dialectic between the modes of discourse in their proximity and in their difference' (*The Rule of Metaphor*, p. 313). On the way he has articulated misgivings about Heidegger's position, but concedes that his philosophy 'gives new life' 'even to a kind of despair of language resembling that found in the next to last proposition in Wittgenstein's *Tractatus*' (p. 313), a statement that might, for some, raise questions about Ricoeur's reading of Wittgenstein.

With Heidegger and Lawrence defining the parameters of the approaches to language represented in this study, Ricoeur's interjection is sometimes useful, the issue unproblematically breaking down into two basic approaches. These are 'creativity' (Lawrence and Heidegger) and 'interpretation' (Ricoeur). It is evident from *The Rule of Metaphor* that Ricoeur is not, in quite the same way as Heidegger and Lawrence, exploring minutely the relation between these categories, that gives rise to their difference. It is Ricoeur who, despite his emphasis on the creative power of metaphor in the context of 'redescription', stays with the comparative hygiene of interpretation, a position exemplified in the 'sequel' study, *Time and Narrative*, where his readings of Woolf, Proust and Mann approach the mediocre. If *The Rule of Metaphor* is marked by the scarcity of reference to literature, *Time and Narrative* is disappointing in its quite superficial treatment of it. There, interpretation is indeed fundamentally elucidation and reduction. Indeed, Ricoeur's acts of interpretation could be usefully contrasted with those of Heidegger and Lawrence neither of whom, evidently, offers a methodology adaptable for critical practice.[4] What emerges with Ricoeur, in my view, is a theoretical distance from the text, and therefore from language (a distance not comparable with Heidegger's strategic defamiliarisation), and this distance, also a feature of *The Rule of Metaphor*, characterizes his critique. In itself it constitutes a, perhaps unconscious, resistance to the 'dwelling in' and therefore 'thinking in' poetry which we expect in Heidegger and Lawrence. Perhaps, having chosen 'interpretation' over 'creation', the Poetic itself is beyond Ricoeur's reach; indeed it is barely an issue for him, in spite of Heidegger's assertion, of which he is well aware, that '[w]e encounter language everywhere' ('Language', in *Poetry, Language, Thought*, p. 189). The argument that Ricoeur's theme in *Time and Narrative* is time, not language, is particularly weak, given the writers that he chooses, that is to say given the crucial importance of 'style' in each of them.

By way of contrast, Lawrence's critical astuteness is famously represented in *Studies in Classic American Literature*. Here Lawrence (whose position on any number of issues alters from version to version of the essays) is reading to 'get somewhere' but without the reductiveness exhibited at times by Ricoeur, for instance. In contrast to the critical ideals of his day Lawrence's aim is never closure; neither is he interested in critical detachment. Elizabeth Wright, discussing Lawrence's 'psychoanalyti-cal' reading of the Americans correctly concludes that 'the value of Lawrence's reading is bound up with the effect the text has had upon him'.[5] His starting point in the published book is his view of language as a positively duplicitous medium, and the 'psychoanalytical' recognitions, if that is the appropriate desig-nation (although his perspectives do not emerge from psycho-analytic theory), grow out of this understanding. We confront Lawrence's acknowledged creativity in reading the American writers as well as being alert to the related question of his ana-lytical astuteness. Certain implications for Lawrence's readers are bound up with his representations of 'art-speech', which pro-vide one of the few occasions when his alertness to the mobile and subversive properties of language is exhibited rather than implicit. *Studies in Classic American Literature* is, of course, the text where Lawrence famously articulates his dictum about 'art-speech'; where he characterizes art as 'subterfuge', and drives a wedge between the artist and the tale. He has famously remarked that:

> The artist usually sets out – or used to – to point a moral and adorn a tale. The tale, however, points the other way, as a rule. Two blankly opposing morals, the artist's and the tale's. Never trust the artist. Trust the tale. The proper function of a critic is to save the tale from the artist who created it.
>
> Now we know our business in these studies; saving the Ameri-can tale from the American artist.
>
> (*Studies in Classic American Literature*, pp. 8–9)

The study's lasting significance lies in the fact that, typically, Lawrence's interpretations expand rather than reduce. The ob-servation in the passage quoted has its roots in 'Study of Thomas Hardy', in Lawrence's comments on the artist's 'metaphysic', a term which he is creating for his own purposes in the study of Hardy:

> Yet every work of art adheres to some system of morality. But if it be really a work of art, it must contain the essential criti-cism on the morality to which it adheres. And hence the antinomy, hence the conflict necessary to every tragic conception.
>
> The degree to which the system of morality, or the metaphysic,

of any work of art is submitted to criticism within the work
of art makes the lasting value and satisfaction of that work.

('Study of Thomas Hardy', in *Hardy*, p. 89)

Enacted in the work of art is a dynamic conflict between ortho-
doxy ('some system of morality') and a highly personal 'sensuous understanding' which embodies a critique of that 'system'
or 'theory'. Lawrence arrives at this position through a reading
of Hardy which characteristically sets Hardy's superficial alle-
giance to the social system against his 'feeling':

> His feeling, his instinct, his sensuous understanding is, how-
> ever, apart from his metaphysic, very great and deep, deeper
> than that perhaps of any other English novelist. Putting aside
> his metaphysic, which must always obtrude when he thinks
> of people, and turning to the earth, to landscape, then he is
> true to himself.
>
> (p. 93)

It is reasonable for the reader, given this cue, to ask when is
Lawrence true to himself in his fiction? Is it in the non-analytical tenor of his language in those fictions which are significantly
the expressions of his 'metaphysic', different from the more conscious metaphoricity of the 'discursive' prose? He was not out
to 'subdue' his 'art' to a 'metaphysic', but his *oeuvre* gives voice
to his 'theory of being and knowing' which jostles in each text
with his 'living sense of being'. Perhaps, after all, the question
is redundant. Lawrence's style is the result of a specific kind of
friction, the struggle to admit tension into his work, *and* to rec-
oncile opposing tendencies:

> It is the novelists and dramatists who have the hardest task in
> reconciling their metaphysic, their theory of being and know-
> ing, with their living sense of being. Because a novel is a mi-
> crocosm, and because man in viewing the universe must view
> it in the light of a theory, therefore every novel must have the
> background or the structural skeleton of some theory of be-
> ing, some metaphysic. But the metaphysic must always *subserve*
> the artistic purpose beyond the artist's conscious aim. Other-
> wise the novel becomes a treatise.
>
> (p. 91, emphasis added)

The 'metaphysic' does not legislate from within the work of art, but helps it into the open. 'Art-speech' ('the only truth') works in opposition to 'the superimposition of a theory' (Foreword, *Women in Love*, p. 486), in opposition to the falsification which occurs in the artist trying to adhere to some conscious scheme, aesthetic or social. It is a subversive property of the artist's medium. Properly 'heard', 'art-speech' unmasks the artist's superficial allegiances which take him beyond himself and the integrity of his own inner voice: Hardy's belief, in spite of himself, in a social machine, for instance, in opposition to his own 'sensuous understanding' when he turns to the pre-conscious earth.

The emphasis on 'art-speech', which tends to get most critical attention, need not be at the expense of other perceptions. The *American* context of the 'art-speech' remarks itself raises important questions not least because the essays on American fiction have their provenance in that period of Lawrence's writing which might be characterized as 'European', and they foreshadow the challenge to European culture, European epistemologies, consistently written into Lawrence's work after *Women in Love* as part of his extensive, highly personal, explorations of cultural difference. The extent of that challenge, and its relation to Lawrence's thinking on complex kinds of otherness, can only usefully be ascertained by examining the representations of European and non-European identities in the fiction and discursive writing post-*Women in Love* (perhaps especially in *The Plumed Serpent*, his 'American novel', *Letters*, IV, p. 260).

Though he is opinionated, part of Lawrence's skill as a critic is keeping the specificity of the text being discussed, whether a novel or an Etruscan tomb, in view. His signature is easy to find within the literary criticism: the comments on 'blood-knowledge' and 'mind-knowledge', 'blood-consciousness' versus 'mind-consciousness' in his critique 'Nathaniel Hawthorne and *The Scarlet Letter*' (*Studies*, Chapter 7), are a case in point if the focus is on familiar constructions which, we recognize, have a specific personal value within Lawrence's critical vocabulary.[6] These are the 'forbidden metaphors', the 'unheard-of combinations' which announce Lawrence's credentials as modernist thinker. More broadly, in all the essays, in all available versions of them, Lawrence's shifting positions, his voice, thought and priorities are tangible. Yet it is fair to say that Lawrence's aim is not to restrict the field over which his thought ranges by means of a number of

controlling concepts. It is more important that the field of thought
is opened up: finding these concepts appropriate is not the same
as imposing them. Like Heidegger in his highly idiosyncratic
readings of German poetry, Lawrence's response is the result of
'inhabiting' the text; of responding, as Elizabeth Wright suggests,
to the effect the work has on him. He does not have to write
explicitly about language in order for him to write from 'in' language: 'in' as in being 'at home' in. At the beginning of *Studies
in Classic American Literature* the (Heideggerean as well as
Lawrentian) metaphor of 'listening' to language complements the
Heideggerian notion of language 'speaking' or 'saying' itself.
Lawrence puts this complex recognition quite informally: 'It is
hard to hear a new voice, as hard as it is to listen to an unknown language. We just don't listen. There is a new voice in
the old American classics. The world has declined to hear it,
and has babbled about children's stories' (*Studies*, p. 7).

The notion of listening to an unknown language is one formulation of reading creatively. Comments in 'The Spirit of Place'
(*Studies*, Chapter 1) underline his suggestion that what is needed
is to touch, as far as possible, whatever resides at the unconscious levels of creativity in the essays. As Lawrence performs
it, it is the opposite of a hygienic, perhaps 'Ricoeurean', distance.
The question to be turned back to Lawrence is whether he lets
the narratives 'give' of their own 'metaphysic', particularly bearing
in mind his own requirements. The writers, in Lawrence's readings, are by turns irresponsible (in relation to their art), hypo-
critical, naive, or, like Benjamin Franklin, the American is a
'recreant European' (*Studies*, p. 26) battling, like Lawrence, with
an 'old' and persistent mode of consciousness. When the artists
succeed in the battle, they do so by loosening their conscious
grip on their material, by writing from a less conscious level;
moving 'in the *gesture* of creation . . . usually unconscious' (*Studies*,
p. 26, emphasis added). The *Studies in Classic American Literature*
represent Lawrence's own relation to this unconscious, or half-
conscious, level. In short, Lawrence the reader of the American
texts is not simply outside them, but is creating himself in reading them, and expanding their significance for us as he does so.
This truly dialectical process shows his reader how to read
Lawrence as he reads the Americans.

The 'recreant European' is an interesting, Eurocentric, formulation. In it, once again, Lawrence is articulating the notion of

the split, the intimacy and the strife, between 'American' and 'European' modes of consciousness. This intimate split interests him more than the arguably more available cultural differences. It shares similarities with the model of relationship between the 'savage' and the mental-conscious 'modern' polarized elsewhere in Lawrence. The pattern of this split, this division which is not wholly a division, operates at the macro and micro levels in his work: it is the oppositional structure of intimacy exemplified in the structure of oxymoron dynamically at work in Lawrence's art-speech; and in the ontological, political and cultural distinctions which give rise to 'American' and 'European' as, for Lawrence, workable (but unequal) categories. The context is once again complex kinds of otherness and Lawrence's apprehension of this as something to be addressed throughout his *oeuvre*.

This chapter makes explicit my sense that while Lawrence is a writer who engages on several levels with metaphoricity – in the act of writing rather than self-consciously addressing the distinctive nature of a trope – he is apart from more recent commentators on metaphor, not least Paul Ricoeur, whose distance from language contrasts with Lawrence's immersion in it. Perhaps these later commentators, so fixed on questions of metaphor, ultimately avoid language. In contrast, Lawrence's language-sense has to do with our, and his, relation to its totality. While Lawrence is not in a position, of course, to criticize Ricoeur, Ricoeur's 'distance' typifies a relation to language which Lawrence's work subtly challenges. It is Lawrence's confrontation with the 'untranslatable' that paradoxically stimulates language into thought.

This study has dealt not with Lawrence's aims in writing but with his alertness to language, which is variously conscious and subliminal. The consciously metaphorical language of the early philosophical essays and the books on the unconscious has led, through the major fiction, to a recognition of Lawrence's sensitivity to metaphor as a mode of understanding among other modes. If we looked for this in Lawrence, that is to say if we looked for equivalences between his style and a *theory* of language, we might miss it. And arguably we would miss it because his language on the face of it seems unphilosophical. A determination to find in his language a theory *of* language might mean a concentration on the *rhetorical* which would be to misconstrue the real weight of metaphoricity in his work.

Notes

1 INTRODUCTION: THINKING METAPHORICALLY

1. Reprinted in *Martin Heidegger: Poetry, Language, Thought*, Martin Heidegger Works, general editor, J. Glenn Gray, trans. and introduction by Albert Hofstadter (New York: Harper and Row, 1971), 1–14. This translation of *Aus der Erfahrung des Denkens* is Albert Hofstadter's. See, *Poetry, Language, Thought*, pp. xi–xii.
2. Ibid., p. 12.
3. There is currently a mature debate concerned with the nature of Lawrence's attunement to aspects of modern German philosophy. Important studies in this field which herald radical re-readings of Lawrence as a modernist with Heideggerean affinities include, Michael Bell, *D.H. Lawrence: Language and Being* (Cambridge: Cambridge University Press, 1992) and Anne Fernihough, *D.H. Lawrence: Aesthetics and Ideology* (Oxford: Clarendon Press, 1993). Michael Bell's emphasis is principally ontological; Anne Fernihough's is principally on Lawrence's aesthetics and its intellectual contexts. My emphasis, via Heidegger, is on the poetic, and principally Lawrence's alertness to the efficacy of metaphor as a mode of thought.
   Another recent study, Robert E. Montgomery's *The Visionary D.H. Lawrence: Beyond Philosophy and Art* (Cambridge: Cambridge University Press, 1994), establishes its argument by examining the influence of German post-Kantian thought on Lawrence, but without extending the debate to Heidegger. It can usefully be read alongside Patrick Bridgewater, *Nietzsche in Anglo-Saxony: A Study of Nietzsche's Impact on English and American Literature* (Leicester: Leicester University Press, 1972), and Colin Milton, *Lawrence and Nietzsche: A Study in Influence* (Aberdeen: Aberdeen University Press, 1987).
4. F.R. Leavis sets up a relation between language (art) and thought in Lawrence in his attention to the way texts work and what they do: it is a position which is in a sense well established, but still needs examining. Part of my intention is to use words which have been in critical use since Leavis but which need to be reclaimed; to be shifted away from Leavis's concentration on values, and in particular his inability to re-think his own.
5. *Study of Thomas Hardy and Other Essays*, ed. Bruce Steele, The Letters and Works of D. H. Lawrence, general editors, James T. Boulton, Warren Roberts et al. (Cambridge: Cambridge University Press, 1985). This volume is hereafter referred to as *Hardy*.
6. 'The Crown', in *Reflections on the Death of a Porcupine And Other Essays*, ed. Michael Herbert, The Letters and Works of D.H. Lawrence, general editors, James T. Boulton, Warren Roberts et al. (Cambridge:

Cambridge University Press, 1988), p. 280. The volume is hereafter referred to as *Reflections*.

7. The provenance and early composition history of the first essays, which became *Psychoanalysis and the Unconscious*, is examined in Mark Kinkead-Weekes, *D.H. Lawrence: Triumph to Exile 1912–1922* (Cambridge: Cambridge University Press, 1996) pp. 541–62, vol. 2 of *The Cambridge Biography: D.H. Lawrence 1885–1930*, 2 vols to date (1991–). In the present study, unless it is stated otherwise, reference to both books on the unconscious, *Psychoanalysis and the Unconscious* and *Fantasia of the Unconscious*, will generally be to their dates of publication rather than composition.

8. *The Complete Poems of D.H. Lawrence*, collected and edited with an introduction and notes by Vivian de Sola Pinto and Warren Roberts (Harmondsworth: Penguin Books, 1977), p. 418. Hereafter referred to as *Complete Poems*. 'The sensual body' is a common term of reference in Lawrence's writing, see, for instance, *The Symbolic Meaning: The Uncollected Versions of 'Studies in Classic American Literature'*, ed. Armin Arnold, with a preface by Harry T. Moore (Arundel: Centaur Press, 1962), pp. 140, 153, 157, 259, where the context is ostensibly literary criticism. Hereafter referred to as *The Symbolic Meaning*.

9. D.H. Lawrence, 'for in the tension of opposites all things have their being', *Complete Poems*, p. 348.

10. Friedrich Nietzsche, 'On Truth and Lies in a Nonmoral Sense', in *Philosophy and Truth: Selections from Nietzsche's Notebooks of the Early 1870s*, ed. and trans. Daniel Breazeale (Englewood Cliffs, NJ: and London: The Humanities Press, 1979), p. 90. Hereafter referred to as *Philosophy and Truth*.

2   THINKING POETICALLY IN THE EARLY DISCURSIVE WRITING

1. *Sons and Lovers*, ed. Helen Baron and Carl Baron, The Cambridge Edition of the Letters and Works of D.H. Lawrence (Cambridge: Cambridge University Press, 1992). Appendix I, Foreword to *Sons and Lovers*, pp. 465–73.

2. For details of the dates of composition and publication of all of Lawrence's works, see Paul Poplawski, *The Works of D.H. Lawrence: A Chronological Checklist*, with a foreword by John Worthen, supplement to *The Journal of the D.H. Lawrence Society 1994–5* (Nottingham: The D.H. Lawrence Society, 1995).

3. See, Michael Black, *D.H. Lawrence: 'Sons and Lovers'*, Landmarks of World Literature series, general editor, J. P. Stern (Cambridge: Cambridge University Press, 1992), pp. 94–9, p. 98.

4. 'And the Word was made flesh, and dwelt among us, (and we beheld his glory, the glory as of the only begotten of the Father,) full of grace and truth' (John i.14).

5. Lawrence: 'Böcklin – or somebody like him – daren't sit in a café except with his back to the wall. I daren't sit in the world without

a woman behind me. . . . a woman I love sort of keeps me in direct communication with the unknown, in which otherwise I am a bit lost' (*Letters*, I, p. 503). This notion is restated later: 'Let him [a man] have a woman to whom he belongs, and he will feel as though he had a wall to back up against, even though the woman be mentally a fool. No man can endure the sense of space, of chaos, on four sides of him. . . . He dare not leap into the unknown save from the sure stability of the unyielding female' ('Study of Thomas Hardy', in *Hardy*, p. 58).

6. Matthew xvii. 1–9; Mark ix. 2–10.
7. In *England, My England and Other Stories*, ed. Bruce Steele, The Cambridge Edition of the Letters and Works of D.H. Lawrence, general editors, James T. Boulton, Warren Roberts et al. (Cambridge: Cambridge University Press, 1990), pp. 92–107.
8. References in Lawrence's work to 'hands' is related to this emphasis on 'touch'.
9. 'Listening' to the 'speaking of language' is the Heideggerean formulation that seems most appropriate to Lawrence. See Martin Heidegger, 'Language', in *Poetry, Language, Thought* (New York: Harper & Row, 1971), p. 197.
10. Mark Kinkead-Weekes, in *D.H. Lawrence: Triumph to Exile 1912–1922* (Cambridge: Cambridge University Press, 1996), pp. 438–57, represents the arguments of early versions of those essays, notably a 1919 version of the Whitman essay, which did not, indeed for reasons of content, could not, achieve publication at the time. These versions have only recently surfaced (see *Triumph to Exile*, p. 450).
11. For an extended discussion of the description of Lawrence's encounter with the old woman, and its relevance to '[t]he "metaphysic" of *The Rainbow*', see Michael Bell, *D.H. Lawrence: Language and Being* (Cambridge: Cambridge University Press, 1992), pp. 57–60.
12. References in 'The Crown' to the ego were added in the revisions of 1925.

3 THE SENSUAL BODY IN LAWRENCE'S EARLY DISCURSIVE WRITING

1. See Mark Kinkead-Weekes, *From Triumph to Exile 1912–1922* (Cambridge: Cambridge University Press, 1996), pp. 438–57.
2. This anticipates Lawrence's writing on symbol and myth in *Apocalypse and the Writings on Revelation*, ed. Mara Kalnins, The Letters and Works of D.H. Lawrence, general editors, James T. Boulton, Warren Roberts, et al. (Cambridge: Cambridge University Press, 1980), p. 142. References in the text are to *Apocalypse*.
3. The web metaphor, in this context, was in currency before Lawrence's adaptation of it, developed in 'The Birth of Consciousness' chapter of *Psychoanalysis and the Unconscious*, pp. 217–18. See, for instance, James Sully, *The Human Mind. A Textbook of Psychology*, 2 vols (New York: Appleton, 1892), p. vi.

4. See, for instance, 'The Crown', section III, 'The Flux of Corruption', in *Reflections on the Death of a Porcupine*, pp. 270–8.
5. See textual apparatus for 'The Crown', in *Reflections on the Death of a Porcupine*, p. 471; the changes relate to 'The Crown', pp. 282, 283.
6. Lawrence: 'Why were we driven out of Paradise? Why did we fall into this gnawing disease of unappeasable dissatisfaction? Not because we sinned. Ah no. All the animals in Paradise enjoyed the sensual passion of coition. Not because we sinned, but because we got our sex into our head' (*Fantasia*, F&P, p. 85); 'Seeking, seeking the fulfilment in the deep passional self; diseased with self-consciousness and sex in the head . . . the unhappy woman . . . turns to her child' (*Fantasia*, F&P, p. 125); 'And, I ask you, what good will psychoanalysis do you in this state of affairs? . . . Father complex, mother complex, incest dreams: pah, when we've had the little excitement out of them we shall forget them as we have forgotten so many other catch-words. And we shall be just where we were before: unless we are worse, with *more* sex in the head, and more introversion, only more brazen' (*Fantasia*, F&P, p. 129); 'The awful process of human relationships, love and marital relationships especially. Because we all make a very, very bad start today, with our idea of love in our head, and our sex in our head as well. All the fight till one is bled of one's self-consciousness and sex-in-the-head. . . . But one fights one's way through it, till one is cleaned: the self-consciousness and sex idea burned out of one, cauterized out bit by bit, and the self whole again, and at last free' (*Fantasia*, F&P, p. 138). Reference is to D.H. Lawrence, *'Fantasia of the Unconscious' and 'Psychoanalysis and the Unconscious'* (Harmondsworth: Penguin Books, 1971; repr. 1986). The volume is referred to as F&P in the text.
7. The reference which resonates in the statement 'I used to be afraid' is to the description of the ash tree in 'The Young Life of Paul', *Sons and Lovers*, pp. 82–107, p. 85. Michael Black examines this connection, and the recurrence of references in Lawrence's writing to the 'bristling' forest; Michael Black, 'A Kind of Bristling in the Darkness: Memory and Metaphor in Lawrence', *The Critical Review* (Canberra), 32 (1992), 29–44.
8. Other references in 'Life' to the blind man reinforce its importance. See also my remarks concerning 'The Blind Man' in Chapter 2.
9. Gerald Doherty regards Lawrence as 'an ardent deconstructer of logocentric modes of completion and closure'. He concludes his analysis with an examination of the 'performative rhetoric' of *Women in Love*, focusing on 'Moony' and 'Excurse'; Gerald Doherty, 'White Mythologies: D.H. Lawrence and the Deconstructive Turn', *Criticism*, 29, no. 4 (Fall, 1987), 477–96, pp. 477, 493. For a related critique of the sister novel see; Gerald Doherty, 'The Metaphorical Imperative: From Trope to Narrative in *The Rainbow*', *South Central Review*, 6, no. 1 (Spring 1989), 46–61.
10. Linda Ruth Williams, *Sex in the Head: Visions of Femininity and Film in D.H. Lawrence* (Hemel Hempstead: Harvester Wheatsheaf, 1993), p. 60.

Lawrence: 'I'm like Carlyle [John Morley], who, they say, wrote 50 vols. on the value of silence' (*Letters*, I, p. 504).

11. This is the metaphor adopted by Heidegger in his discourse on the relation between poetry and thought: 'The parallels intersect in the infinite'; Martin Heidegger, 'The Nature of Language', in *On the Way to Language*, trans. Peter D. Hertz (New York: Harper & Row, 1971), p. 90. See also Chapter 8 of the present study.

12. 'The Crown: 1915 Variants', Appendix II, *Reflections on the Death of a Porcupine*, p. 470.

13. Lawrence states that the creative impulse of the human male is 'the prime motivity' (*Fantasia of the Unconscious*, F&P, p. 18).

14. Lawrence may have been prompted to think of this example by Van Gogh's representation of peasant shoes, as Heidegger was in 'The Origin of the Work of Art'.

15. Reference is to Gilles Deleuze and Félix Guattari, *Anti-Oedipus: Capitalism and Schizophrenia*, trans. Robert Hurley, Mark Seem, and Helen R. Lane, preface by Michel Foucault (1972, London: The Athlone Press, 1984, repr. 1990). Their engagement with Lawrence is addressed at greater length in Chapter 4 of the present study.

16. In *Fantasia of the Unconscious* Lawrence exploits Einstein's language, instituting a play on 'relativity'.

17. Michael Black examines the critique of contemporary attitudes to the body instituted by Lawrence, particularly his exposure of the equivalence of sex and excretion in the culture: Lawrence characterizes the Freudian unconscious as constituted notionally by 'heaps of excrement, and a myriad repulsive little horrors spawned between sex and excrement' (*Psychoanalysis and the Unconscious*, F&P, p. 203). See references to the 'dirty little secret' of sex in this study, Chapter 4 § 'Anti-Oedipal'. Black also discusses the relationship between the narrating consciousness and the reader in *Mr. Noon*; Michael Black, 'Gilbert Noon, D.H. Lawrence, and the Gentle Reader', *The D.H. Lawrence Review* 20, no. 2 (1988), 153–78. Another account of the narrator-reader relationship is given in Williams, *Sex in the Head: Visions of Feminity and Film in D.H. Lawrence*, pp. 61–2.

4 LANGUAGE AND THE UNCONSCIOUS I

1. Lascelles Abercrombie, *Thomas Hardy: A Critical Study* (London: Martin Secker, 1912).

2. See, for instance, David Ellis, 'Lawrence and the Biological Psyche', in *D.H. Lawrence: Centenary Essays*, ed. Mara Kalnins (Bristol: Bristol University Press, 1986), pp. 89–109; James Cowan, *D.H. Lawrence's American Journey: A Study in Literature and Myth* (London: Case Western Reserve University Press, 1970), pp. 15–24. Evelyn Hinz, comparing the style and structure of the two books argues for the 'scientific' mode of *Psychoanalysis and the Unconscious* in contrast to the 'archetypal' mode of *Fantasia of the Unconscious*; Evelyn Hinz, 'The Beginning and the End: D.H. Lawrence's *Psychoanalysis*

and *Fantasia'*, *The Dalhousie Review*, 52 (1972), 251–65.
3. I am grateful to Michael Black for his information on the early publishing history of Freud in Britain.
4. Edward Nehls, ed., *D.H. Lawrence: A Composite Biography*, 3 vols (Madison: University of Wisconsin Press, 1957–9), I, p. 215.
5. For a representation of the ideas, principally on sexuality and community, which Frieda communicated to Lawrence at the beginning of their relationship, see Turner, Rumpf-Worthen and Jenkins, *The D.H. Lawrence Review*, special issue, 'The Otto Gross–Frieda Weekley Correspondence', 22, no. 2 (1990).
6. Frederick J. Hoffman, *Freudianism and the Literary Mind*, 2nd edn (Baton Rouge, Louisiana: Louisiana State University Press, 1957).
7. Murray M. Schwartz, 'D.H. Lawrence and Psychoanalysis: An Introduction', *The D.H. Lawrence Review*, 10, no. 3 (Fall 1977), 215.
8. For a critique of 'Lawrence and the British Object-Relations School', see Anne Fernihough, *D.H. Lawrence: Aesthetics and Ideology*, pp. 77–82. For book-length studies of Lawrence's relationship to various psychoanalytic schools, see David Cavitch, *D.H. Lawrence and the New World* (New York: Oxford University Press, 1969); Daniel J. Schneider, *D.H. Lawrence: The Artist as Psychologist* (Kansas: University Press of Kansas, 1984); Daniel A. Weiss, *Oedipus in Nottingham: D.H. Lawrence* (Seattle: University of Washington Press, 1962).
9. Gilles Deleuze and Félix Guattari, *Anti-Oedipus: Capitalism and Schizophrenia*. Referred to in the text as *Anti-Oedipus*. See also the 'sequel', *A Thousand Plateaus: Capitalism and Schizophrenia*, trans. and foreword by Brian Massumi (London: The Athlone Press, 1988, rpt. 1992).
10. Cited in Jeffrey Mehlman, 'Trimethylamin: Notes on Freud's Specimen Dream', in *Untying the Text: A Post-Structuralist Reader*, ed. Robert Young (Boston, London and Henley: Routledge & Kegan Paul, 1981), pp. 177–88, p. 179.
11. Malcolm Bowie, 'A Message from Kakania: Freud, Music, Criticism', in *Modernism and the European Unconscious* ed. Peter Collier and Judy Davies (Cambridge: Polity Press; Oxford: Basil Blackwell, 1990), p. 15.
12. Malcolm Bowie, *Lacan*, Fontana Modern Masters, ed. Frank Kermode (London: Fontana, 1991), p. 84.
13. Published for the first time in *The D.H. Lawrence Review*, 22, no. 1 (Spring 1990), 111–12. MS held in the D.H. Lawrence Collection, University of Nottingham.
14. See Rose Marie Burwell, 'A Checklist of Lawrence's Reading', in *A D.H. Lawrence Handbook*, ed. Keith Sagar (Manchester: Manchester University Press, 1982), pp. 59–125. See also Rose Marie Burwell, 'A Catalogue of D.H. Lawrence's Reading from Early Childhood', *The D.H. Lawrence Review*, 3, no. 3 (Fall 1970), special issue, 'D.H. Lawrence's Reading', 193–330.
15. In 'Poetry of the Present' (Introduction to the American edition of *New Poems*, 1918), Lawrence writes, in relation to *Look! We Have Come Through!*, 'But is it not better to publish a preface long after the book it belongs to has appeared? For then the reader will have

had his fair chance with the book, alone' (*Complete Poems*, p. 186).
16. Alfred Booth Kuttner, 'A Freudian Appreciation', *Psychoanalytic Review*, 1916, repr. in *D.H. Lawrence: Sons and Lovers*, ed. Gamini Salgado, Casebook Series, general editor, A. E. Dyson (London: Macmillan, 1988), pp. 69–94.
17. Judith G. Ruderman's account of the mother figure in Lawrence is interesting, written at a time when critical interpretations of Lawrence were being rigorously revised, particularly by women; Judith G. Ruderman, '*The Fox* and the "Devouring Mother"', *The D.H. Lawrence Review*, 10, no. 3 (Fall 1977), 251–69.
18. Mabel Dodge Luhan, *Lorenzo in Taos* (London: Martin Secker, 1933), p. 49.
19. The discussion to follow is informed by the response of Gilles Deleuze and Félix Guattari to Lawrence in their book *Anti-Oedipus: Capitalism and Schizophrenia*.
20. 'Lawrence, Miller, and then Laing were able to demonstrate this in a profound way: it is certain that neither men nor women are clearly defined personalities, but rather vibrations, flows, schizzes, and "knots"', *Anti-Oedipus*, p. 362; see pp. 365–6.
21. Birkin, in dialogue with Ursula, briefly becomes a figure of the reductive reader in the 'Flitting' chapter of *Women in Love*: '"Gudrun!" exclaimed Birkin. "She's a born mistress, just as Gerald is a born lover – *amant en titre*. If as somebody says all women are either wives or mistresses, then Gudrun is a mistress"' (*Women in Love*, p. 371). Helen Corke noticed the same reductiveness in an immature Lawrence: 'I hate Lawrence's precise classification, "You are not the wife and mother type – you must be *femme de plaisir*." It is not true. It is one of his rare stupidities'; Helen Corke, *D.H. Lawrence: The Croydon Years*, introduction by Warren Clark (Austin: University of Texas Press, 1965), p. 14.
22. Catherine Stearns aligns Lawrence with Hélène Cixous and Luce Irigaray in an attempt to 'write the body'; Catherine Stearns, 'Gender, Voice and Myth: The Relation of Language to the Female in D.H. Lawrence's Poetry', *The D.H. Lawrence Review*, 17, no. 3 (Fall, 1984), 233–42, p. 238.
23. Bertrand Russell notes that, 'Physical science, more or less unconsciously, has drifted into the view that all natural phenomena ought to be reduced to motions', *The Problems of Philosophy*, Opus series, general editors, Christopher Butler, Robert Evans and John Skorupski (Oxford: Oxford University Press, 1912, repr. 1980), p. 13.
24. Recent scholarship on new editions of Lawrence's works reveals the extent to which Lawrence was a meticulous reviser of his own writing.
25. The working title of the MS was 'The Child and the Unconscious'. In a letter of 8 October 1921 Lawrence tested Seltzer's opinion on this title or, alternatively, 'Child Consciousness' (*Letters*, IV, p. 93). He also described it to Amy Lowell as 'Harlequinade of the Unconscious' (*Letters*, IV, p. 97). Later the title was revised to *Fantasia of the Unconscious* (*Letters*, IV, p. 103).

26. See J. Laplanche and J.-B. Pontalis, *The Language of Psycho-Analysis*, introduction by Daniel Lagache, trans. Donald Nicholson-Smith, The International Psycho-Analytical Library, ed. M. Masud R. Khan (1967, London: The Hogarth Press and the Institute of Psycho-Analysis, 1973), pp. 314–19.

27. Frederick Hoffman sees Lawrence as a mediating figure between the practitioners of Dada and the Surrealists, and 'The New Apocalypse' poets of the 1940s. They shared with Lawrence 'his opposition to external or impersonal ordering of their minds' and approved his shift 'from a clinical to a mythological point of view'; Frederick J. Hoffman, 'From Surrealism to "The Apocalypse": A Development in 20th Century Irrationalism', *Journal of English Literary History*, 15 (1948), 147–65.

28. See *The Symbolic Meaning*, pp. 175–89.

29. Friedrich Nietzsche, *The Will To Power*, a new translation by Walter Kaufmann and R. J. Hollingdale, ed. with a commentary by Walter Kaufmann, with facsimiles of the original manuscript (New York: Vintage Books, 1968), p. 283.

30. See Michael Black, *D.H. Lawrence: The Early Fiction. A Commentary* (London: Macmillan, 1986). The extensive index-entry for 'hand, hands' indicates its importance within Lawrence's thought about the body, incorporating the association with 'touch' and, therefore, a non-analytical mode of 'knowledge'.

31. In *D.H. Lawrence: Language and Being*, Michael Bell notes the '"independent" intelligence' of the hand in this passage (p. 90). Patricia Hagen, 'The Metaphoric Foundations of Lawrence's "Dark Knowledge"', *Texas Studies in Language and Literature*, 29 (Spring 1987–Winter 1987), 365–76), discussing the same example, talks about the 'guiding intelligence' which is 'inherent in the organism' as opposed to the machine (p. 369). She underlines Lawrence's refusal to consider this 'intelligence' as distinct from the body or any other part of human functioning. T.H. Adamowski, 'Self/Body/Other: Orality and Ontology in Lawrence', *The D.H. Lawrence Review*, 13, no. 3 (Fall 1980), 193–208, argues that Lawrence 'begins with a body that *finds itself conscious*' (p. 197). Barbara Hardy, also citing the writing hand passage, calls it one of Lawrence's 'apparently casual but intense pieces of critical self-consciousness', see, Barbara Hardy, 'D.H. Lawrence's Self-Consciousness', in *D.H. Lawrence in the Modern World*, ed. Peter Preston and Peter Hoare (London: Macmillan, 1989), pp. 27–46; p. 37.

32. Comparing the typescripts of *Fantasia of the Unconscious*, David Ellis suggests that Lawrence was not in Ebersteinburg, but Sicily, when he wrote this 'digression'; David Ellis and Howard Mills, *D.H. Lawrence's Non-Fiction: Art, Thought and Genre*, pp. 74–5, p. 180 n. 13.

33. Michael Ragussis notes that 'verbal consciousness' is a phrase used by both Lawrence and Freud, arguing that 'The dialectic between patient and analyst becomes replaced in Lawrence by another kind of dialectic . . . "art-speech"'; Michael Ragussis, *The Subterfuge of Art:*

Language and the Romantic Tradition (Baltimore and London: Johns Hopkins University Press, 1978), pp. 4–5.

34. Helen Haste, *The Sexual Metaphor* (Hemel Hempstead: Harvester-Wheatsheaf, 1993), p. 37.

35. I particularly like the pun on *'jouissance'* noted in the introduction to Julia Kristeva, *Desire in Language: A Semiotic Approach to Literature and Art*, ed. Leon S. Roudiez, trans. Thomas Gora, Alice Jardine, and Leon S. Roudiez (Oxford: Basil Blackwell, 1981), p. 16, as *'j'ouïs sens'*, 'I heard meaning'. This also recalls the Heideggerean formulation that when we 'dwell' in language we hear the 'speaking' of language.

36. Daniel Albright, *Personality & Impersonality: Lawrence, Woolf and Mann* (Chicago and London: University of Chicago Press, 1978), p. 24.

37. This sentiment is adumbrated in 'The Two Principles': 'The ancients said the heart was the seat of understanding. And so it is: it is the seat of the primal sensual understanding, the seat of the passional self-consciousness' (*The Symbolic Meaning*, p. 187).

38. In *Fantasia of the Unconscious*, it becomes the trees' way of 'seeing'. In 'Introduction to *Memoirs of the Foreign Legion*' the peasant encountered by Lawrence speaks 'as a tree might speak' (*Phoenix II*, p. 322).

39. See Paul Ricoeur on oxymoron in 'The Work of Resemblance', Study 6 of *The Rule of Metaphor: Multi-disciplinary Studies of the Creation of Meaning in Language*, trans. Robert Czerny, with Kathleen McLaughlin and John Costello, SJ (1975, London: Routledge & Kegan Paul, 1986), pp. 173–215; pp. 194–5. Ricoeur's distinctions are referred to at greater length in Chapter 7 of the present study.

40. Keith Alldritt, *The Visual Imagination of D.H. Lawrence* (London: Edward Arnold, 1971), p. 130. Further references to this study follow quotations in the text.

41. Alldritt may have meant to write 'defer' rather than 'refer'.

42. Lawrence was conscious of requiring a certain creative response from his readers. To Edward Garnett, one of Lawrence's principal 'readers', of 'The Wedding Ring' he wrote that, 'I have a different attitude to my characters, and that necessitates a different attitude in you' (*Letters*, II, p. 182).

5 LANGUAGE AND THE UNCONSCIOUS II

1. Christopher Heywood, '"Blood-Consciousness" and the Pioneers of the Reflex and Ganglionic Systems', in *D.H. Lawrence: New Studies*, ed. Christopher Heywood (London: Macmillan, 1987), pp. 104–23.

2. See Michael Black, *D.H. Lawrence: The Early Philosophical Works. A Commentary* (London: Macmillan, 1991), pp. 55–6, 97–100.

3. Railing against a system of education underpinned by rationalism and arguing for more spontaneous, intuitive modes of understanding than he, an ex-teacher, finds in place, Lawrence writes of his 'intuitive man' that he need not 'cut off his head and try to de-

velop a pair of eyes in his breasts. But . . .' (*Fantasia of the Unconscious*, F&P, p. 83).

4. Reference was made in my previous chapter to Heidegger's critique of the primacy of sight in Western thought in *Being and Time*. It is interesting to note that the discussion develops in a section of that study called 'Curiosity'; Martin Heidegger, *Being and Time*, trans. John Macquarrie and Edward Robinson (Oxford: Basil Blackwell, 1962; repr. 1973), I, 5, §36, pp. 214–17.

5. The emphasis in the books on the unconscious on posture and bearing, and the implicit relation between mood and the physical body, recalls other philosophies which insist on the interaction of body and mind for total mental and physical well-being. For instance, the psycho-physical programme developed by F.M. Alexander, which attracted interest in the 1930s (see Aldous Huxley, *Ends and Means: An Enquiry into the Nature of Ideals and into the Methods employed for their Realization* (London: Chatto & Windus, 1937), pp. 223, 326), introduces the concept of 'use', which refers to good posture and muscle control leading to good physical and mental health. Few of the ideas behind this and related philosophies which challenge the polarization of mind and body would have sounded strange to Lawrence had he been aware of them. Regarding the levels of physical communication between the mother and baby, one of the leading exponents of the Alexander Principle in Britain has written that, 'From the moment of birth the helpless child is dependent on the handling and the ideas of its mother. It is picked up jerkily or smoothly, crossly or kindly: its head and back are supported carefully or ignorantly. It lies face down or face up, according to fashion. It is allowed to yell or it is picked up on demand. It connects with the mother, on breast or bottle, and as it suckles, it likes to gaze long and deep into the mother's eyes, with a unified visual connection which it may never know again. But in the main, its connection is kinaesthetic, through muscles and movement, and it is quick to pick up feelings of tension, timidity or rejection from the bodily rather than the visual contact: and especially from the mother's hands, since another person's hands are a most powerful stimulus towards good or bad USE' (Wilfred Barlow, *The Alexander Principle* (London: Victor Gollancz, 1990), p. 161). The baby is fundamentally, in Lawrence's terms, 'pre-visual'. The Alexander Principle describes a programme, which Lawrence does not set out to do. Kinaesthesia is also central to Lawrence's thinking on the child, although exponents of the Alexander Principle might sceptically detach themselves from Lawrence's views here: 'For a child's bottom is made occasionally to be spanked. The vibration of the spanking acts directly upon the spinal nerve-system, there is a direct reciprocity and reaction, the spanker transfers his wrath to the great will-centres in the child, and these will-centres react intensely, are vivified and educated' (*Fantasia of the Unconscious*, F&P, p. 50). Less provocatively, there is the recognition in *Fantasia* that bad posture reveals something about the individual's sense of self: 'So, weak-chested,

round-shouldered, we stoop hollowly forward on ourselves. It is the result of the all-famous love and charity ideal, an ideal now quite dead in its sympathetic activity, but still fixed and determined in its voluntary action'(*Fantasia of the Unconscious*, F&P, p. 53). Without transforming Lawrence into a therapist, these examples emphasize a broad context within which Lawrence's views are meaningful, without suggesting that those views constitute a programme.

6. See Anne Fernihough, 'The Tyranny of the Text: Lawrence, Freud and the Modernist Aesthetic', in *Modernism and the European Unconscious* ed. Peter Collier and Judy Davies (Cambridge: Polity Press; Oxford: Basil Blackwell, 1990), p. 50.

7. Daniel Schneider, for instance, in *D.H. Lawrence: the Artist as Psychologist*, cites Piaget, Freud and Jung.

8. 'Nathaniel Hawthorne I', *The Symbolic Meaning*, pp. 139–44.

9. Discussing *Aaron's Rod* with Earl and Achsah Brewster, they thought that the protagonist should go through 'the whole cycle of experience'. Lawrence agreed that his was the most likely course for Aaron to take: 'Aaron had to go to destruction to find his way through the whole cycle of experience'; Edward Nehls, ed., *D.H. Lawrence: A Composite Biography*, II, pp. 58–9.

10. As Robert Young, summarizing the insights of Jeffrey Mehlman and Barbara Young, succinctly puts it, 'if interpretation is repression, then repression *is* interpretation', *Untying the Text*, p. 178.

6 UNDULATING STYLES: *THE RAINBOW*

1. For a sense of how the 'wave' is profoundly related to 'creation' in Lawrence's thought, see Michael Black, *D.H. Lawrence: The Early Philosophical Works* (London: Macmillan, 1991), pp. 347–50; see 'wave' in the word-index. See also 'The Crown', in *Reflections on the Death of a Porcupine*, pp. 262– 6, concluding, "'Till, new-created, I am thrown forth again on the shore of creation, warm and lustrous, goodly, new-born from the darkness out of which all time has issued' (p. 266).

2. Genesis viii.15–ix.17 is an important source of this imagery, as for the beginning of *The Rainbow*.

3. Tony Pinkney, *D.H. Lawrence*, Harvester New Readings (Hemel Hempstead: Harvester-Wheatsheaf, 1990), p. 94.

4. Paul Ricoeur, *The Rule of Metaphor* (London: Routledge, 1986), p. 62.

5. See *Twilight in Italy*, pp. 116–17; see also 'The Crown', in *Reflections on the Death of a Porcupine*, pp. 255, 258–9, 278, 470.

6. They form a network of associations in Lawrence's thought with, for instance, the references to 'shore', and 'flood'. 'Waves' of generation in the seed–germinate–flower cycle, is also implied.

7. Michael Bell, *D.H. Lawrence: Language and Being* (Cambridge: Cambridge University Press, 1992), p. 73.

8. See especially, Michael Ragussis, *The Subterfuge of Art: Language and the Romantic Tradition*, Chapter 8, 'The New Vocabulary of *Women in Love*: Speech and Art-Speech', pp. 172–225; John Worthen, *D.H.*

Lawrence and the Idea of the Novel (London: Macmillan, 1979), p. 61.
9. See, for example, Bell, *D.H. Lawrence: Language and Being*, p. 73; Diane S. Bonds, *Language and the Self in D.H. Lawrence*, Studies in Modern Literature, no. 68, ed. A. Walton Litz and Keith Cushman (Ann Arbor, Michigan: UMI Research Press, 1987), p. 66.
10. In an early version of 'The Spirit of Place' Lawrence writes, 'The present reality is a reality of untranslatable otherness' arguing that one characteristic of modernity is that 'we must learn to think in terms of difference and otherness' (*The Symbolic Meaning*, p. 17). This is in the context of his introduction both to the cultural importance of American fiction, and to his sense of a different consciousness of self and being in the 'new' world compared to the 'old', by which is meant Europe.
11. Published under the editorial title 'The Individual Consciousness v. The Social Consciousness', in *Phoenix: The Posthumous Papers of D.H. Lawrence*, ed. with an introduction by Edward D. McDonald (London: Heinemann, 1936; repr. 1970), p. 761.

7 'THE TENSION OF OPPOSITES'

1. Michael Ragussis, *The Subterfuge of Art: Language and the Romantic Tradition* (Baltimore and London: Johns Hopkins University Press, 1978). This is a comparative study in which Lawrence is aligned with his precursors among the Romantics. Michael Bell's chief preoccupation in *D.H. Lawrence: Language and Being* (Cambridge: Cambridge University Press, 1992) is also Lawrence's 'struggle with language' (p. 5). Bell's is one of the most extensive recent examinations of this 'struggle', where the novels in particular are subjected to close critical scrutiny.
2. See Paul Ricoeur, *The Rule of Metaphor* (London: Routledge, 1986), Study 6, 'The Work of Resemblance' §4 'In Defence of Resemblance', pp. 193–200.
3. Leo Bersani, 'Lawrentian Stillness', in *A Future for Astyanax: Character and Desire in Literature* (Boston and Toronto: Little, Brown, 1976), pp. 164–7.
4. The note describes an entry in the *OED* which accounts for an obsolete use of the word meaning 'embodied, material'; *Women in Love*, ed. David Farmer, Lindeth Vasey and John Worthen, The Cambridge Edition of the Letters and Works of D.H. Lawrence (Cambridge: Cambridge University Press, 1987), p. 533.
5. Heidegger's own creativity comes into view here with his definitions of 'striving' and 'difference': 'But we would surely all too easily falsify its nature if we were to confound striving with discord and dispute . . . In essential striving, rather, the opponents raise each other into the self-assertion of their natures' (*Poetry, Language, Thought*, p. 49); 'The word difference is now removed from its usual and customary usage. What it now names is not a generic concept for various kinds of differences' (p. 202). See pp. 202–3.

6. Warren Shibles, *Rational Love* (Whitewater, Wisconsin: Language Press, 1978), p. 19. Further references to this study are given after quotations in the text.

7. Friedrich Nietzsche, *Philosophy and Truth: Selections from Nietzsche's Notebooks of the Early 1870s*, ed. Daniel Breazeale (New Jersey and London: The Humanities Press, 1979), p. 81.

8. Ibid., p. 84.

9. C.S. Lewis, *The Allegory of Love: A Study in Medieval Tradition* (Oxford: Oxford University Press, 1936; repr. 1979).

10. This material will in all likelihood not be available for general examination until the publication of the Cambridge University Press edition of the *Studies in Classic American Literature*.

11. Quoted in Mark Kinkead-Weekes, *D.H. Lawrence: Triumph to Exile 1912–1922* (Cambridge: Cambridge University Press, 1996), p. 455.

12. See *Tractatus Logico-Philosophicus. The German Text of Ludwig Wittgenstein's Logisch-philosophische Abhandlung*, with a new translation by D.F. Pears and B.F. McGuinness, and with an introduction by Bertrand Russell FRS (London: Routledge & Kegan Paul; New York: The Humanities Press, 1961), p. 151.

13. Tony Pinkney, *D.H. Lawrence* (Hemel Hempstead: Harvester-Wheatsheaf, 1990), p. 93.

14. Ginette Katz-Roy considers the function of oxymoron in Lawrence's poetry as a locally available instance of 'paradoxical expression'; Ginette Katz-Roy, 'The Process of Rotary Image-Thought' in D.H. Lawrence's *Last Poems*, *Etudes Lawrenciennes*, no. 7 (1992), 129–38, pp. 132–3.

15. See Max Black, *Models and Metaphors: Studies in Language and Philosophy*, (Ithaca, New York: Cornell University Press, 1962), pp. 35–7.

16. Aristotle, *Rhetoric*, Bk III, 1405^b 1, 5.

17. In association with 'luminous', 'dazing' is arguably a curious choice of word. One can speculate whether Lawrence meant to write 'dazzling'.

18. For preliminary observations on the importance of oxymoron in Lawrence's writing, see Fiona Becket, 'Expressionism in *The Rainbow* and *Women in Love*', unpublished MA paper, University of Warwick, 1986. See also Michael Bell, *D.H. Lawrence: Language and Being*, pp. 110–11.

19. Jonathan Culler, *Structuralist Poetics: Structuralism, Linguistics and the Study of Literature* (London, Melbourne and Henley: Routledge & Kegan Paul, 1975), p. 107.

20. Michael Bell draws attention to the difference between the 'sexual suggestiveness' of *The Rainbow* and the 'punning spirit' of *Lady Chatterley's Lover*; Bell, *D.H. Lawrence: Language and Being*, pp. 214, 222–3.

21. Jean-Jacques Lecercle, *Philosophy of Nonsense: The Intuitions of Victorian Nonsense Literature* (London and New York: Routledge, 1994), pp. 63–8, 66.

22. See Kate Millett, *Sexual Politics* (London: Virago, 1977, reprinted, 1985), pp. 237–93, p. 240. See also Simone de Beauvoir, *The Second*

Sex, trans. H.M. Parshley (1949, Harmondsworth: Penguin Books, 1972, repr. 1975), pp. 245–54. Book-length studies include Anne Smith, ed., *Lawrence and Women* (London: Vision, 1978); Carol Dix, *D.H. Lawrence and Women* (London: Macmillan, 1980); Hilary Simpson, *D.H. Lawrence and Feminism* (London and Canberra: Croom Helm, 1982); Sheila MacLeod, *Lawrence's Men and Women* (London: Paladin, 1987); Carol Siegel, 'Lawrence among the Women: Wavering Boundaries', in *Women's Literary Traditions, Feminist Issues: Practice, Politics, and Theory*, ed. Kathleen M. Balutansky and Alison Booth (Charlottesville and London: University Press of Virginia, 1991); A defensive note is sounded in David Holbrook, *Where D.H. Lawrence was Wrong about Women* (Louisburg: Bucknell University Press, 1992). Linda Ruth Williams, *Sex-in-the-Head: Visions of Feminity and Film in D.H. Lawrence* (Hemel Hempstead: Harvester-Wheatsheaf, 1993). Critics continue to re-evaluate Lawrence's sexual politics, see for instance, *Etudes Lawrenciennes*, no. 12 (Summer 1995), special issue 'Sex and Gender'.

8 'FORBIDDEN METAPHORS'

1. Martin Heidegger, 'The Nature of Language', in *On the Way to Language* (New York: Harper & Row, 1982), pp. 57–108.
2. Martin Heidegger, 'Building Dwelling Thinking', in *Poetry, Language, Thought* (New York: Harper & Row, 1971), pp. 143–61.
3. Gilles Deleuze, 'He Stuttered', in *Gilles Deleuze and the Theater of Philosophy*, ed. Constantin V. Boundas and Dorothea Olkowski (New York and London: Routledge, 1994), pp. 24–5.
4. As Gerald L. Bruns points out in *Heidegger's Estrangements: Language, Truth, and Poetry in the Later Writings* (New Haven and London: Yale University Press, 1989), p. 6, there is not an *'analytique heideggerienne'*.
5. Elizabeth Wright, *Psychoanalytic Criticism: Theory in Practice*, New Accents, general editor, Terence Hawkes (London and New York: Routledge, 1989), pp. 49–55; p. 55.
6. The terms are more extreme in the early versions of the Hawthorne essays, 'Nathaniel Hawthorne I' and Nathaniel Hawthorne II', in *The Symbolic Meaning*, pp. 133–58, 159–72.

Bibliography

PRIMARY SOURCES: D.H. LAWRENCE

Where available the *Cambridge Edition of the Letters and Works of D.H. Lawrence* under the general editorship of James T. Boulton and Warren Roberts has been used.

This study makes special reference to:

The Rainbow, ed. Mark Kinkead-Weekes, Cambridge: Cambridge University Press, 1989.
Women in Love, ed. David Farmer, Lindeth Vasey and John Worthen, Cambridge: Cambridge University Press, 1987.
'Fantasia of the Unconscious' and *'Psychoanalysis of the Unconscious'*, Harmondsworth: Penguin Books, 1977; rpt. 1986.

Others

Fiction

Aaron's Rod, ed. Mara Kalnins, Cambridge: Cambridge University Press, 1988.
England, My England and Other Stories, ed. Bruce Steele, Cambridge: Cambridge University Press, 1990.
The First Lady Chatterley, Harmondsworth: Penguin Books, 1973.
'The Fox', 'The Captain's Doll', 'The Ladybird', ed. Dieter Mehl, Cambridge: Cambridge University Press, 1992.
John Thomas and Lady Jane, Harmondsworth: Penguin Books, 1973.
Kangaroo, ed. Bruce Steele, Cambridge: Cambridge University Press, 1994.
Lady Chatterley's Lover, ed. Michael Squires, Harmondsworth: Penguin, 1994.
The Plumed Serpent (Quetzalcoatl), ed. L. D. Clark, Cambridge: Cambridge University Press, 1987.
The Prussian Officer and Other Stories, ed. John Worthen, Cambridge: Cambridge University Press, 1983.
Sons and Lovers, ed. Helen Baron and Carl Baron, Cambridge: Cambridge University Press, 1992.
The Trespasser, ed. Elizabeth Mansfield, Cambridge: Cambridge University Press, 1981.

Non-fiction

Apocalypse and the Writings on Revelation, ed. Mara Kalnins, Cambridge: Cambridge University Press, 1980.
Phoenix: The Posthumous Papers of D.H. Lawrence, ed. Edward D. McDonald, London: Heinemann, 1936; rpt. 1970.
Phoenix II: Uncollected, Unpublished and Other Prose Works by D.H. Lawrence, ed. Warren Roberts and Harry T. Moore, London: Heinemann, 1968.
Reflections on the Death of a Porcupine and Other Essays, ed. Michael Herbert, Cambridge: Cambridge University Press, 1988.
Sea and Sardinia, in *D.H. Lawrence and Italy*, Harmondsworth: Penguin Books, 1985.
Studies in Classic American Literature, Harmondsworth: Penguin Books, 1977; rpt. 1983.
Study of Thomas Hardy and Other Essays, ed. Bruce Steele, Cambridge: Cambridge University Press, 1985.
The Symbolic Meaning: The Uncollected Versions of 'Studies in Classic American Literature', ed. Armin Arnold, Arundel: Centaur Press, 1962.
Twilight in Italy and Other Essays, ed. Paul Eggert, Cambridge: Cambridge University Press, 1994.

Poetry

The Complete Poems of D.H. Lawrence, ed. Vivian de Sola Pinto and Warren Roberts, Harmondsworth: Penguin Books, 1977.
'Death-Paean of a Mother', *The D.H. Lawrence Review* 22.1 (Spring 1990): 111–12.

Letters and Biographies

The Letters of D.H. Lawrence, ed. James T. Boulton et al., 8 vols, Cambridge: Cambridge University Press, 1979– .
Kinkead-Weekes, Mark, *D.H. Lawrence: Triumph to Exile 1912–1922*. Cambridge: Cambridge University Press, 1996. Vol. 2 of *The Cambridge Biography, D.H. Lawrence 1885–1930* by David Ellis, Mark Kinkead-Weekes and John Worthen. 2 vols to date, 1991– .
Worthen, John, *D.H. Lawrence: The Early Years 1885–1912*, Cambridge: Cambridge University Press, 1991. Vol. 1 of *The Cambridge Biography, D.H. Lawrence 1885–1930*, by David Ellis, Mark Kinkead-Weekes and John Worthen. 2 vols to date, 1991– .
Nehls, Edward, *D.H. Lawrence: A Composite Biography*, 3 vols, Madison: University of Wisconsin Press, 1957–9.

SECONDARY SOURCES

D.H. Lawrence

Adamowski, T.H, 'Being Perfect: Lawrence, Sartre, and *Women in Love*', *Critical Inquiry* 2 (Winter, 1975): 345–68.
────── 'Self/Body/Other: Orality and Ontology in Lawrence', *The D.H. Lawrence Review* 13.3 (Fall 1980): 193–208.
Albright, Daniel, *Personality and Impersonality: Lawrence, Woolf and Mann*, Chicago and London: University of Chicago Press, 1978.
Alldritt, Keith, *The Visual Imagination of D.H. Lawrence*, London: Edward Arnold, 1971.
Andrews, W.T., 'D.H. Lawrence's Favourite Jargon', *Notes & Queries* 211 (March 1966): 97–8.
Arcana, Judith, 'I Remember Mama: Mother-blaming in *Sons and Lovers*' Criticism', *The D.H. Lawrence Review* 21.2 (Summer 1989): 137–51.
Auden, W.H., *The Dyer's Hand and Other Essays*, London: Faber and Faber, 1963.
Balbert, Peter and Phillip L. Marcus, eds., *D.H. Lawrence: A Centenary Consideration*, Ithaca and London: Cornell University Press, 1985.
Baldanza, Frank, 'D.H. Lawrence's Song of Songs', *Modern Fiction Studies* 7.2 (Summer 1961): 106–14.
Bell, Michael, *D.H. Lawrence: Language and Being*, Cambridge: Cambridge University Press, 1992.
Bersani, Leo, *A Future for Astyanax: Character and Desire in Literature*, Boston and Toronto: Little, Brown, 1976.
Berthoud, Jacques, 'The Rainbow as Experimental Novel', *D.H. Lawrence: A Critical Study of the Major Novels and Other Writings*, ed. A.H. Gomme, Hossocks: Harvester Press; New York: Barnes & Noble, 1978, 53–69.
Bickerton, Derek, 'The Language of *Women in Love*', *Review of English Studies* (Leeds) 8.2 (1967): 56–67.
Bien, Peter, 'The Critical Philosophy of D.H. Lawrence', *The D.H. Lawrence Review* 17.2 (Summer 1984): 127–34.
Black, Michael, *D.H. Lawrence: the Early Fiction*, London: Macmillan, 1986.
────── *D.H. Lawrence: The Early Philosophical Works. A Commentary*, London: Macmillan, 1991.
────── *D.H. Lawrence: 'Sons and Lovers'*, Landmarks of World Literature series, gen. ed. J. P. Stern, Cambridge: Cambridge University Press, 1992.
────── 'Gilbert Noon, D.H. Lawrence, and the Gentle Reader', *The D.H. Lawrence Review* 20.2 (1988): 153–78.
────── 'A Kind of Bristling in the Darkness: Memory and Metaphor in Lawrence', *The Critical Review* (Canberra) 32 (1992): 29–44.
────── 'Visiting the Bottom of the Monstrous World: Allusion as Metaphor in Lawrence', *The Cambridge Quarterly* 24.2 (1995): 133–51.
Bloom, Harold, ed., *D.H. Lawrence's 'Women in Love'*, Modern Critical Interpretations, New York, New Haven, Philadelphia: Chelsea House Publishers, 1988.
Bonds, Diane S., *Language and the Self in D.H. Lawrence*, Studies in Modern

Literature 68, ed. A. Walton Litz and Keith Cushman, Ann Arbor, Michigan: UMI Research Press, 1987.

Bridgwater, Patrick, *Nietzsche in Anglo-Saxony: A Study of Nietzsche's Impact on English and American Literature*, Leicester: Leicester University Press, 1972.

Brown, Keith, ed., *Rethinking Lawrence*, Milton Keynes and Philadelphia: Open University Press, 1990.

Burns, Aidan, *Nature & Culture in D.H. Lawrence*, London: Macmillan, 1980.

Burwell, Rose Marie, 'A Catalogue of D.H. Lawrence's Reading From Early Childhood', *The D.H. Lawrence Review* 3.3 (Fall 1970): 193–330.

—— 'A Checklist of Lawrence's Reading', *A D.H. Lawrence Handbook*, ed. Keith Sagar, Manchester: Manchester University Press, 1982, 59–125.

Carter, Frederick, *D.H. Lawrence and the Body Mystical*, London: Denis Archer, 1932.

Cavitch, David, *D.H. Lawrence and the New World*, New York: Oxford University Press, 1969.

Clarke, Colin, *River of Dissolution: D.H. Lawrence and English Romanticism*, London: Routledge & Kegan Paul, 1969.

Cohn, Dorrit, 'Narrated Monologue: Definition of a Fictional Style', *Comparative Literature* 18.2 (Spring 1966): 97–112.

Corke, Helen, *D.H. Lawrence: The Croydon Years*, Austin: University of Texas Press, 1965.

Cowan, James C., *D.H. Lawrence's American Journey: A Study in Literature and Myth*, Cleveland: Case Western Reserve University Press, 1970.

—— *D.H. Lawrence and the Trembling Balance*, University Park and London: The Pennsylvania State University Press, 1990.

Cushman, Keith, and Denis Jackson, eds., *D.H. Lawrence's Literary Inheritors*, London: Macmillan, 1991.

Daleski, H.M., *The Forked Flame: A Study of D.H. Lawrence*, London: Faber and Faber, 1965.

Davies, Alistair, 'Contexts of Reading: The Reception of D.H. Lawrence's *The Rainbow* and *Women in Love*', *The Theory of Reading*, ed. Frank Gloversmith, Brighton: Harvester Press; New Jersey: Barnes & Noble, 1984, 199–222.

Davis, William A., 'Mountains, Metaphors, and Other Entanglements: Sexual Representation in the Prologue to *Women in Love*', *The D.H. Lawrence Review* 22.1 (Spring 1990): 69–76.

Dillon, M.C., 'Love in *Women in Love*: A Phenomenological Analysis', *Philosophy and Literature* 2.2 (Fall 1978): 190–208.

Dix, Carol, *D.H. Lawrence and Women*, London: Macmillan, 1980.

Doherty, Gerald, 'White Mythologies: D.H. Lawrence and the Deconstructive Turn', *Criticism* 29.4 (Fall 1987): 477–96.

—— 'The Metaphorical Imperative: From Trope to Narrative in *The Rainbow*', *South Central Review* 6.1 (Spring 1989): 46–61.

Draper, R.P., ed., *D.H. Lawrence: The Critical Heritage*, The Critical Heritage Series, gen. ed. B.C. Southam, London: Routledge & Kegan Paul, 1970; rpt. 1972; rpt. with corrections, 1979.

Ellis, David, 'Lawrence and the Biological Psyche', *D.H. Lawrence:*

Centenary Essays, ed. Mara Kalnins, Bristol: Bristol Classical Press, 1986, 89–109.

Ellis, David and Howard Mills, *D.H. Lawrence's Non-fiction: Art, Thought and Genre*, Cambridge: Cambridge University Press, 1988.

Fernihough, Anne, 'The Tyranny of the Text: Lawrence, Freud and the Modernist Aesthetic', *Modernism and the European Unconscious*, ed. Peter Collier and Judy Davies, Cambridge: Polity Press; Oxford: Basil Blackwell, 1990, 47–63.

—— *D.H. Lawrence: Aesthetics and Ideology*, Oxford: Clarendon Press, 1993.

Fleishman, Avrom, 'Lawrence and Bakhtin: Where Pluralism Ends and Dialogism Begins', *Rethinking Lawrence*, ed. Keith Brown, Milton Keynes: Open University Press, 1990, 109–19.

Ford, George H., *Double-Measure: A Study of the Novels and Stories of D.H. Lawrence*, New York: Holt, Rinehart and Winston, 1965.

Freeman, Mary, *D.H. Lawrence: A Basic Study of his Ideas*, New York: Grosset & Dunlap, 1955.

—— 'Lawrence and Futurism', *D.H. Lawrence: 'The Rainbow' and 'Women in Love'*, ed. Colin Clarke, Casebook Series, gen. ed. A. E. Dyson, London: Macmillan, 1969, 91–103.

Furbank, P.N., 'The Philosophy of D.H. Lawrence', *The Spirit of D.H. Lawrence: Centenary Essays*, ed. Gamini Salgado and G.K. Das, London: Macmillan, 1988, 144–53.

Gibbons, Thomas, '"Allotropic States" and "Fiddle-bow": D.H. Lawrence's Occult Sources', *Notes & Queries* 233.3 (September 1988): 338–41.

Goldberg, S.L., 'The Rainbow: Fiddle-bow and Sand', *Essays in Criticism* 11.4 (1961): 418–34.

Gordon, David J., *D.H. Lawrence as a Literary Critic*, New Haven and London: Yale University Press, 1966.

—— 'Women in Love and the Lawrencean Aesthetic', Stephen J. Miko, ed., *Twentieth Century Interpretations of 'Women in Love': A Collection of Critical Essays*, Englewood Cliffs, NJ: Prentice-Hall, 1969, 50–60.

—— 'Sex and Language in D.H. Lawrence', *Twentieth-Century Literature* 27.4 (Winter 1981): 362–75

—— 'D.H. Lawrence's Dual Myth of Origin', *Sewanee Review* 89 (Winter 1981): 83–94.

Green, Martin, *The von Richtofen Sisters: The Triumphant and the Tragic Modes of Love*, London: Weidenfeld and Nicolson, 1974.

Greiff, Louis K., 'Bittersweet Dreaming in Lawrence's The Fox: A Freudian Perspective', *Studies in Short Fiction* 20.1 (Winter 1983): 7–16.

Hagen, Patricia L., 'The Metaphoric Foundations of Lawrence's "Dark Knowledge"', *Texas Studies in Language and Literature* 29 (Spring 1987–Winter 1987): 365–76.

—— 'Astrology, Schema Theory, and Lawrence's Poetic Method', *The D.H. Lawrence Review* 22.1 (Spring 1990): 23–37.

Hamalian, Leo, ed., *D.H. Lawrence*. Contemporary Studies in Literature, series editors Eugene Ehrlich and Daniel Murphy, New York: McGraw–Hill Book Company, 1973.

Hardy, Barbara, 'D.H. Lawrence's Self-Consciousness', *D.H. Lawrence in the Modern World*, ed. Peter Preston and Peter Hoare, London: Macmillan, 1989, 27–46.

Hayles, Nancy Katherine, 'The Ambivalent Approach: D.H. Lawrence and the New Physics', *Mosaic* 15.3 (September 1982): 89–108.

Hayles, N. Katherine, 'Evasion: The Field of the Unconscious in D.H. Lawrence', *The Cosmic Web: Scientific Field Models and Literary Strategies in the Twentieth Century*, Ithaca: Cornell University Press, 1984. 85–110. Rpt. in *D.H. Lawrence: Critical Assessments*, ed. David Ellis and Ornella De Zordo, 4 vols, Mountfield: Helm Information, 1992. Vol. 4, 'Poetry and Non-fiction; The Modern Critical Response 1938–92: General Studies', 650–70.

Heywood, Charles, ed., *D.H. Lawrence: New Studies*, London: Macmillan, 1987.

Hinz, Evelyn J., 'The Beginning and the End: D.H. Lawrence's *Psychoanalysis* and *Fantasia*', *The Dalhousie Review* 52 (1972): 251–65.

——— 'Sons and Lovers: The Archetypal Dimensions of Lawrence's Oedipal Tragedy', *The D.H. Lawrence Review* 5.1 (Spring 1972): 26–53.

Hochman, Baruch, *Another Ego: The Changing View of Self and Society in the Work of D.H. Lawrence*, Columbia, South Carolina: University of South Carolina Press, 1970.

Hoffman, Frederick J., 'From Surrealism to "The Apocalypse": A Development in 20th Century Irrationalism', *Journal of English Literary History* (1948): 147–65.

——— *Freudianism and the Literary Mind*, 2nd edn, Louisiana: Louisiana State University Press, 1957.

Holbrook, David, *Where D.H. Lawrence was Wrong about Women*, Louisburg: Bucknell University Press, 1992.

Hortmann, Wilhelm, 'The Nail and the Novel: Some Remarks on Style and the Unconscious in *The Rainbow*', *Theorie und Praxis im Erzöhlen des 19. und 20. Jahrhunderts: Studien zur englischen und amerikanischen Literatur zu Ehren von Willi Erzgröber*, ed. Winfried Herget, Klaus Peter Jochum and Ingeborg Weber, Tübingen: Narr, 1986, 167–79.

Hough, Graham, *The Dark Sun: A Study of D.H. Lawrence*, London: Gerald Duckworth, 1956; rpt. 1970.

Howe, Marguerite Beede, *The Art of the Self in D.H. Lawrence*, Athens: Ohio University Press, 1977.

Humma, John B., 'D.H. Lawrence as Friedrich Nietzsche', *Philological Quarterly* 53.1 (January 1974): 110–20.

——— *Metaphor and Meaning in D.H. Lawrence's Later Novels*, Columbia: University of Missouri Press, 1990.

Hyde, G.M., *D.H. Lawrence*, Macmillan Modern Novelists, gen. ed. Norman Page, London: Macmillan, 1990.

Ingersoll, Earl, 'Staging the Gaze in D.H. Lawrence's *Women in Love*', *Studies in the Novel* 26.3 (Fall 1994): 268–80.

Ingram, Allan, *The Language of D.H. Lawrence*, The Language of Literature Series, gen. ed. N. F. Blake, London: Macmillan, 1990.

Jewinski, Ed, 'The Phallus in D.H. Lawrence and Jacques Lacan', *The D.H. Lawrence Review* 21.1 (Spring 1989): 7–24.

Jones, Carolyn M., 'Male Friendship and the Construction of Identity in D.H. Lawrence's Novels', *Literature and Theology* 9.1 (March 1995): 66–84.

Journet, Debra, 'D.H. Lawrence's Criticism of Modern Literature', *The D.H. Lawrence Review* 17.1 (Spring 1984): 29–47.

Kalnins, Mara, ed., *D.H. Lawrence: Centenary Essays*, Bristol: Bristol Classical Press, 1986.

Katz-Roy, Ginette, 'The Process of "Rotary Image-thought" in D.H. Lawrence's Last Poems', *Etudes Lawrenciennes* 7 (1992): 129–38.

Kermode, Frank, *Lawrence*, London: Fontana, 1973.

Kiely, Robert, 'Accident and Purpose: "Bad Form" in Lawrence's Fiction', *D.H. Lawrence: A Centenary Consideration*, ed. Peter Balbert and Phillip L. Marcus, Ithaca and London: Cornell University Press, 1985, 91–107.

Kinkead-Weekes, Mark, 'The Marble and The Statue: The Exploratory Imagination of D.H. Lawrence', *Imagined Worlds: Essays on some English Novels and Novelists in Honour of John Butt*, ed. Maynard Mack and Ian Gregor, London: Methuen, 1968, 371–418.

———— 'Eros and Metaphor: Sexual Relationship in the Fiction of Lawrence', *Lawrence and Women*, ed. Anne Smith, London: Vision, 1978, 101–21.

———— 'The Marriage of Opposites in *The Rainbow*', *D.H. Lawrence: Centenary Essays*, ed. Mara Kalnins, Bristol: Bristol Classical Press, 1986, 21–39.

Kuttner, Alfred Booth, Untitled review of *Sons and Lovers*, *New Republic*. 10 April 1915, 2: 255–7. Rpt. in *D.H. Lawrence: The Critical Heritage*, ed. R.P. Draper, The Critical Heritage Series, gen. ed. B.C. Southam, London: Routledge & Kegan Paul, 1970; rpt. 1972; rpt. with corrections, 1979, 76–80.

———— 'A Freudian Appreciation', *Psychoanalytic Review*, July 1916. Rpt. in Gamini Salgado, ed., *D.H. Lawrence: 'Sons and Lovers'*, Casebook Series, gen. ed. A.E. Dyson, London: Macmillan, 1969, 69–94.

Langman, F.H., '*Women in Love*', *Essays in Criticism* 17.2 (April 1967): 183–206.

Lawrence, Frieda, *Not I, But the Wind*, London and Toronto: William Heinemann, 1935.

Leavis, F.R., *Thought, Words and Creativity: Art and Thought in Lawrence*, London: Chatto & Windus, 1976.

———— *D.H. Lawrence: Novelist*, Harmondsworth: Penguin Books in association with Chatto & Windus, 1955.

Lerner, Laurence, *The Truthtellers: Jane Austen, George Eliot, D.H. Lawrence*, London: Chatto & Windus, 1967.

Levenson, Michael, '"The Passion of Opposition" in *Women in Love*: None, One, Two, Few, Many', *Modern Language Studies* 17.2 (Spring 1987): 22–36.

Lodge, David, 'Lawrence, Dostoevsky, Bakhtin: Lawrence and Dialogic Fiction', *Rethinking Lawrence*, ed. Keith Brown, Milton Keynes: Open University Press, 1990, 92–108.

Luhan, Mabel Dodge, *Lorenzo in Taos*, London: Martin Secker, 1933.

Macleod, Sheila, *Lawrence's Men and Women*, London: Paladin, 1987.
Michaels-Tonks, Jennifer, *D.H. Lawrence: the Polarity of North and South Germany and Italy in his Prose Works*, Studien zur Germanistik, Anglistik und Komparatistik 42, Bonn: Bouvier, 1976.
Miko, Stephen J., ed., *Twentieth Century Interpretations of 'Women in Love': A Collection of Critical Essays*, Englewood Cliffs, NJ: Prentice-Hall, 1969.
—— *Toward 'Women in Love': The Emergence of a Lawrentian Aesthetic*, New Haven and London: Yale University Press, 1971.
Milton, Colin, *Lawrence and Nietzsche: A Study in Influence*, Aberdeen: Aberdeen University Press, 1987.
Montgomery, Robert E., *The Visionary D.H. Lawrence: Beyond Philosophy and Art*, Cambridge: Cambridge University Press, 1994.
Moore, Harry T., *The Life and Works of D.H. Lawrence*, London: George Allen & Unwin, 1951.
—— 'The Prose of D.H. Lawrence', *D.H. Lawrence: The Man Who Lived*, ed. Robert B. Partlow Jr and Harry T. Moore, Carbondale and Edwardsville: Southern Illinois University Press, 1980, 245–57.
Moynahan, Julian, *The Deed of Life: The Novels and Tales of D.H. Lawrence*, Princeton, Princeton University Press, New Jersey and London: Oxford University Press, 1963.
Padhi, Bibhu, 'Lawrence's Idea of Language', *Modernist Studies* 4 (1982): 65–76.
Partlow, Robert B. Jr and Harry T. Moore, eds., *D.H. Lawrence: The Man Who Lived*, Carbondale and Edwardsville: Southern Illinois University Press, 1980.
Pinion, F.B., 'The Extension of Metaphor to Scene and Action, Chiefly in Lawrence's Early Novels', *The Spirit of D.H. Lawrence: Centenary Studies*, ed. Gamini Salgado and G.K. Das, London: Macmillan, 1988, 32–45.
Pinkney, Tony, *D.H. Lawrence*, Harvester New Readings, Hemel Hempstead: Harvester-Wheatsheaf, 1990.
Poplawski, Paul, *The Works of D.H. Lawrence: A Chronological Checklist*, Foreword by John Worthen, Supplement to *The Journal of the D.H. Lawrence Society 1994–5*, Nottingham: The D.H. Lawrence Society, 1995.
Preston, Peter, and Peter Hoare, eds., *D.H. Lawrence in the Modern World*, London: Macmillan, 1989.
Ragussis, Michael, *The Subterfuge of Art: Language and the Romantic Tradition*, Baltimore and London: Johns Hopkins University Press, 1978.
Ramey, Frederick, 'Words in the Service of Silence: Preverbal Language in Lawrence's *The Plumed Serpent*', *Modern Fiction Studies* 27.4 (Winter 1981/2): 613–21.
Reddick, Bryan D., 'Point of View and Narrative Tone in *Women in Love*: The Portrayal of Interpsychic Space', *The D.H. Lawrence Review* 7.2 (Summer 1974): 156–71.
Renner, Stanley, 'Sexuality and the Unconscious: Psychosexual Drama and Conflict in *The Fox*', *The D.H. Lawrence Review* 21.3 (Fall 1989): 245–73.
Robinson, Ian, 'D.H. Lawrence and English Prose', *D.H. Lawrence: A Critical Study of the Major Novels and Other Writings*, ed. A.H. Gomme,

Hassocks: Harvester Press; New York: Barnes & Noble, 1978, 13–29.

Ross, Charles L., 'Art and "Metaphysic" in D.H. Lawrence's Novels', *The D.H. Lawrence Review* 7.2 (Summer 1974): 206–17.

Ruderman, Judith G., '*The Fox* and the "Devouring Mother"', *The D.H. Lawrence Review* 10.3 (Fall 1977): 251–69.

Sagar, Keith., ed., *A D.H. Lawrence Handbook*, Manchester: Manchester University Press; New York: Barnes & Noble, 1982.

———— *D.H. Lawrence: Life into Art*, Harmondsworth: Penguin Books, 1985.

Sale, Roger, 'The Narrative Technique of *The Rainbow*', *Modern Fiction Studies* 5.1 (Spring 1959): 29–38.

Salgado, Gamini., ed., *D.H. Lawrence: 'Sons and Lovers'*. Casebook Series, gen. ed. A.E. Dyson, London: Macmillan, 1969; rpt. 1973.

———— 'Taking a Nail for a Walk: On Reading *Women in Love*', *The Modern English Novel: The Reader, The Writer and The Work*, ed. Gabriel Josipovici, London: Open Books, 1976, 95–112.

———— and G.K. Das, eds., *The Spirit of D.H. Lawrence: Centenary Studies*, London: Macmillan, 1988.

Sanders, Scott, *The World of the Major Novels*, London: Vision, 1973.

Schleifer, Ronald, 'Lawrence's Rhetoric of Vision: The Ending of *The Rainbow*', *The D.H. Lawrence Review* 13.2 (Summer 1980): 161–78.

Schneider, Daniel L., 'The Symbolism of the Soul: D.H. Lawrence and Some Others', *The D.H. Lawrence Review* 7.2 (Summer 1974): 107–26.

———— *D.H. Lawrence: The Artist as Psychologist*, Kansas: University of Kansas Press, 1984.

———— *The Consciousness of D.H. Lawrence: An Intellectual Biography*, Kansas: University of Kansas Press, 1986.

Schorer, Mark, '*Women in Love* and Death', *D.H. Lawrence: A Collection of Critical Essays*, ed. Mark Spilka, Englewood Cliffs, NJ: Prentice-Hall, 1963, 50–60.

Schwartz, Murray M., 'D.H. Lawrence and Psychoanalysis: An Introduction', *The D.H. Lawrence Review* 10.3 (Fall 1977): 215–22.

Siegel, Carol, 'Lawrence among the Women: Wavering Boundaries in Women's Literary Traditions', *Feminist Issues: Practice, Politics, and Theory*, ed. Kathleen M. Balutansky and Alison Booth, Charlottesville and London: University Press of Virginia, 1991.

Simpson, Hilary, *D.H. Lawrence and Feminism*, London and Canberra: Croom Helm, 1982.

Sinzelle, Claude, 'Skinning the Fox: A Masochist's Delight', *D.H. Lawrence in the Modern World*, ed. Peter Preston and Peter Hoare, London: Macmillan, 1989, 161–79.

Sklenicka, Carol, *D.H. Lawrence and the Child*, Columbia and London: University of Missouri Press, 1991.

Smith, Anne, ed., *Lawrence and Women*, London: Vision, 1978.

Squires, Michael, 'Recurrence as a Narrative Technique in *The Rainbow*', *Modern Fiction Studies* 21.2 (Summer 1975): 230–6.

———— 'D.H. Lawrence's Narrators, Sources of Knowledge and the Problem of Coherence', *Criticism* 37.3 (Summer 1995): 469–91.

Squires, Michael, and Keith Cushman, eds., *The Challenge of D.H. Law-

rence, Madison, Wisconsin: University of Wisconsin Press, 1990.

Stearns, Catherine, 'Gender, Voice, and Myth: The Relation of Language to the Female in D.H. Lawrence's Poetry', *The D.H. Lawrence Review* 17.3 (Fall 1987): 233–42.

Stewart, Garrett, 'Lawrence, "Being," and the Allotropic Style', *Novel* 9 (1975–6): 217–42.

Stewart, Jack F., 'Dialectics of Knowing in *Women in Love*', *Twentieth-Century Literature* 37.1 (Spring 1991): 59–75.

Swigg, Richard, *Lawrence, Hardy, and American Literature*, London: Oxford University Press, 1972.

Turner, John, Cornelia Rumpf-Worthen, Ruth Jenkins, trans., 'The Otto Gross–Frieda Weekley Correspondence', Special issue, *The D.H. Lawrence Review* 22.2 (Summer 1990).

Vickery, John B., 'D.H. Lawrence and the Fantasias of Consciousness', *The Spirit of D.H. Lawrence*, ed. Gamini Salgado and G.K. Das, London: Macmillan, 1988, 163–80.

Vitoux, Pierre, 'The Chapter "Excurse" in *Women in Love*: Its Genesis and the Critical Problem', *Texas Studies in Language and Literature* 17 (1975–6): 821–36.

Vivas, Eliseo, *D.H. Lawrence: The Failure and Triumph of Art*, Evanston, Illinois: Northwestern University Press, 1960.

Weiss, Daniel A., *Oedipus in Nottingham: D.H. Lawrence*, Seattle: University of Washington Press, 1962.

Whelan, P.T., *D.H. Lawrence: Myth and Metaphysic in 'The Rainbow' and 'Women in Love'*, Studies in Modern Literature 88, gen. ed. A. Walton Litz, Ann Arbor and London: UMI Research Press, 1988.

—— 'The Hunting Metaphor in *The Fox* and Other Works', *The D.H. Lawrence Review* 21.3 (Fall 1989): 275–90.

Williams, Linda Ruth, *Sex in the Head: Visions of Feminity and Film in D.H. Lawrence*, Hemel Hempstead: Harvester-Wheatsheaf, 1993.

Williams, Raymond, *The English Novel from Dickens to Lawrence*, London: The Hogarth Press, 1984.

Worthen, John, *D.H. Lawrence and the Idea of the Novel*, London: Macmillan, 1979.

—— *D.H. Lawrence*. Modern Fiction Series, gen. ed. Robin Gilmour, London, New York, Melbourne, Auckland: Edward Arnold, 1991.

Wright, Anne, *Literature of Crisis 1910–22: 'Howards End', 'Heartbreak House', 'Women in Love' and 'The Waste Land'*, Macmillan Studies in Twentieth-Century Literature, London: Macmillan, 1984.

Wright, Terence, 'Rhythm in the Novel', *Modern Language Review* 80.1 (January 1985): 1–15.

Yetman, Michael G., 'The Failure of the Un-Romantic Imagination in *Women in Love*', *Mosaic* 9.3 (Spring 1976): 83–96.

Zytaruk, George, 'The Doctrine of Individuality: D.H. Lawrence's "Metaphysic"', *D.H. Lawrence: A Centenary Consideration*, ed. Peter Balbert and Phillip L. Marcus, Ithaca and London: Cornell University Press, 1985, 237–53.

228   *Bibliography*

General Works

Abercrombie, Lascelles, *Thomas Hardy: A Critical Study*, London: Martin Secker, 1912.

Aristotle, *The Complete Works of Aristotle*, the revised Oxford translation, ed. Jonathan Barnes. Bolingen Series LXXI, 2 vols, Princeton, NJ: Princeton University Press, 1984.

Barlow, Wilfred, *The Alexander Principle*, London: Victor Gollancz, 1990.

Barthes, Roland, *Writing Degree Zero*, trans. Annette Lavers and Colin Smith, Cape Editions 3, gen. ed. Nathaniel Tarn, London: Jonathan Cape, 1967.

Beardsley, Monroe C., *Aesthetics: Problems in the Philosophy of Criticism*, 2nd edn, Indianapolis: Hackett, 1981.

Beauvoir, Simone de, *The Second Sex*, trans. H.M. Parshley, Harmondsworth: Penguin Books, 1972; rpt. 1975.

Bell, Michael, ed., *The Context of English Literature 1900–1930*, London: Methuen, 1980.

―――― *F.R. Leavis*, Critics of the Twentieth Century, gen. ed. Christopher Norris, London and New York: Routledge, 1988.

Bernard, Harrison, 'The Truth about Metaphor', *Philosophy and Literature* 10.1 (April 1986): 38–55.

Black, Max, *Models and Metaphors, Studies in Language and Philosophy*, Ithaca, New York: Cornell University Press, 1962.

―――― 'How Metaphors Work: A Reply to Donald Davidson', *On Metaphor*, ed. Sheldon Sacks. Chicago and London: University of Chicago Press, 1979, 181–92.

Bowie, Malcolm, 'A Message from Kakania: Freud, Music, Criticism', *Modernism and the European Unconscious*, ed. Peter Collier and Judy Davies, Cambridge: Polity Press; Oxford: Basil Blackwell, 1990, 3–17.

―――― *Lacan*, Fontana Modern Masters, ed. Frank Kermode, London: Fontana, 1991.

Brooke-Rose, Christine, *A Grammar of Metaphor*, Mercury Books 65, gen. eds Alan Hill and Freddie Warburg, London: Mercury Books, 1965.

Bruns, Gerald L., *Heidegger's Estrangements: Language, Truth, and Poetry in the Later Writings*, New Haven and London: Yale University Press, 1989.

Carlin, Gerald, 'Art and Authority: A Comparative Study of the Modernist Aesthetics of Ezra Pound', Diss. University of Warwick, 1994.

Cassirer, Ernst, *Language and Myth*, trans. Susanne K. Langer, New York: Dover Publications, 1946.

―――― *The Philosophy of Symbolic Forms*, trans. Ralph Manheim, 3 vols, New Haven and London: Yale University Press, Vol. 1 'Language', 1953.

Cioffi, Frank, ed., *Freud*, Modern Judgements Series, gen. ed. P.N. Furbank, London: Macmillan, 1973.

Cixous, Hélène, and Catherine Clément, *The Newly Born Woman*, trans. Betsy Wing, Theory and History of Literature 24, ed. Wlad Godzich and Jochen Schulte-Sasse, Manchester: Manchester University Press, 1987.

Collier, Peter and Judy Davies, eds., *Modernism and the European Unconscious*, Cambridge: Polity Press; Oxford: Basil Blackwell, 1990.

Culler, Jonathan, 'Commentary', *New Literary History* 6.1 (Autumn 1974): 219–29.

—— *Structuralist Poetics: Structuralism, Linguistics and the Study of Literature*, London, Melbourne and Henley: Routledge and Kegan Paul, 1975.

Deese, James, 'Mind and Metaphor: A Commentary', *New Literary History* 6.1 (Autumn 1974): 212–17.

Deleuze, Gilles, 'He Stuttered', *Gilles Deleuze and the Theater of Philosophy*, ed. Constantin V. Boundas and Dorothea Olkowski, New York and London: Routledge, 1994.

Deleuze, Gilles and Félix Guattari, *Anti-Oedipus: Capitalism and Schizophrenia*, trans. Robert Hurley, Mark Seem and Helen R. Lane, London: The Athlone Press, 1984; rpt. 1990.

—— *A Thousand Plateaus: Capitalism and Schizophrenia*, trans. Brian Massumi, London: The Athlone Press, 1988; rpt. 1992.

Derrida, Jacques, *Writing and Difference*, trans. Alan Bass, London: Routledge and Kegan Paul, 1978.

—— *Margins of Philosophy*, trans. Alan Bass, Brighton: The Harvester Press, 1982.

—— 'White Mythology: Metaphor in the Text of Philosophy', trans. F.C.T. Moore, *New Literary History* 6.1 (Autumn 1974): 5–74.

Eagleton, Terry, *Exiles and Emigrés: Studies in Modern Literature*, London: Chatto & Windus, 1970.

Edge, David, 'Technological Metaphor and Social Control', *New Literary History* 6.1 (Autumn 1974): 135–47.

Eysteinsson, Astradur, *The Concept of Modernism*, Ithaca and London: Cornell University Press, 1990.

Fanon, Frantz, *The Wretched of the Earth*, trans. Constance Farrington, Harmondsworth: Penguin Books, 1967; rpt. 1990.

Foster, John Burt, Jr, *Heirs to Dionysus: A Nietzschean Current in Literary Modernism*, Princeton, NJ: Princeton University Press, 1981.

Freud, Sigmund, *The Standard Edition of the Complete Psychological Works*, trans. James Strachey, in collaboration with Anna Freud, assisted by Alix Strachey and Alan Tyson, 24 vols, London: The Hogarth Press and the Institute of Psycho-Analysis, 1953–74.

Goodman, Nelson, *Languages of Art: An Approach to a Theory of Symbols*, London: Oxford University Press, 1969.

—— 'Metaphor as Moonlighting', *On Metaphor*, ed. Sheldon Sacks, Chicago and London: University of Chicago Press, 1979, 175–80.

Haley, Michael Cabot, *The Semiosis of Poetic Metaphor*, Peirce Studies 4, gen. ed. Kenneth Laine Ketner, Bloomington and Indianapolis: Indiana University Press, 1988.

Haste, Helen, *The Sexual Metaphor*, Hemel Hempstead: Harvester Wheatsheaf, 1993.

Heidegger, Martin, *Poetry, Language, Thought*, Martin Heidegger Works, gen. ed. J. Glenn Gray, trans. Albert Hofstadter, New York: Harper & Row, 1971.

—— *On the Way to Language*, trans. Peter D. Hertz, New York: Harper & Row, 1971.

——— *Being and Time*, trans. John Macquarrie and Edward Robinson, Oxford: Blackwell, 1962; rpt. 1973.

Huxley, Aldous, *Ends and Means: An Enquiry into the Nature of Ideals and into the Methods employed for their Realization*, London: Chatto & Windus, 1937.

Jakobson, Roman, and Morris Halle, *Fundamentals of Language*, Janua Linguarum. Studia Memoriae Nicolai Van Wijk Dedicata 1, ed. Cornelis H. Van Schooneveld, 'S Gravenhage: Mouton, 1956.

Jung, C.G., *Jung: Selected Writings*, London: Fontana, 1986.

Kristeva, Julia, *Desire in Language: A Semiotic Approach to Literature and Art*, trans. Thomas Gora, Alice Jardine and Leon S. Roudiez, Oxford: Basil Blackwell, 1982.

Lakoff, George and Mark Johnson, *Metaphors We Live By*, Chicago and London: University of Chicago Press, 1980.

Laplanche, J. and J.-B. Pontalis, *The Language of Psycho-Analysis*, trans. Donald Nicholson-Smith, The International Psycho-Analytical Library, ed. M. Masud R. Khan, London: The Hogarth Press and the Institute of Psycho-Analysis, 1973.

Lecercle, Jean-Jacques, *The Violence of Language*, Routledge: London and New York, 1990.

——— *Philosophy of Nonsense: The Intuitions of Victorian Nonsense Literature*, London and New York: Routledge, 1994.

Leeuwen, Theodoor Marius van, *The Surplus of Meaning: Ontology and Eschatology in the Philosophy of Paul Ricoeur*, Amsterdam Studies in Theology, Amsterdam: Rodopi, 1981.

Lewis, C.S., *The Allegory of Love: A Study in Medieval Tradition*, Oxford: Oxford University Press, 1936; rpt. 1979.

Lodge, David, 'The Language of Modernist Fiction: Metaphor and Metonymy', *Modernism 1890–1930*, ed. Malcolm Bradbury and James McFarlane, Harmondsworth: Penguin Books, 1976; rpt. 1986, 481–96.

——— *The Modes of Modern Writing: Metaphor, Metonymy, and the Typology of Modern Literature*, London: Edward Arnold, 1977.

Magnus, Bernd, Stanley Stewart and Jean-Pierre Mileur, *Nietzsche's Case: Philosophy as/and Literature*, London and New York: Routledge, 1993.

Millett, Kate, *Sexual Politics*, London: Virago, 1977; rpt. 1985.

Murry, John Middleton, 'Metaphor', *John Clare and Other Studies*, London and New York: Peter Nevill, 1950, 85–97.

Myers, F.W.H., *Human Personality and its Survival of Bodily Death*, ed. Susy Smith, Foreword Aldous Huxley, New York: University Books, 1961.

Nietzsche, Friedrich, *Philosophy and Truth: Selections from Nietzsche's Notebooks of the Early 1870s*, ed. and trans. Daniel Breazeale, New Jersey and London: The Humanities Press, 1979.

——— *Friedrich Nietzsche on Rhetoric and Language*, ed. and trans. Sander L. Gilman, Carole Blair and David J. Parent, New York and Oxford: Oxford University Press, 1989.

——— *Untimely Meditations*, trans. R.B. Hollingdale, Texts in German Philosophy, gen. ed. Charles Taylor, Cambridge: Cambridge University Press, 1983.

——— *Human, All Too Human: A Book for Free Spirits*, trans. R.J.

Hollingdale, Texts in German Philosophy, gen. ed. Charles Taylor, Cambridge: Cambridge University Press, 1986.

―― *The Gay Science*, trans. Walter Kaufmann, New York: Vintage Books, 1974.

―― *Ecce Homo: How One Becomes What One Is*, trans. R.J. Hollingdale, Harmondsworth: Penguin Books, 1979.

―― *The Will to Power*, trans. Walter Kaufmann and R.J. Hollingdale, New York: Vintage Books, 1968.

Owen, Stephen, and Walter L. Reed, 'A Motive for Metaphor', *Criticism* 21.4 (Fall 1979): 287–306.

Richards, I.A., *Practical Criticism: A Study of Literary Judgement*, London: Routledge & Kegan Paul, 1960.

Ricoeur, Paul, 'Metaphor and the Main Problem of Hermeneutics', *New Literary History* 6.1 (Autumn 1974): 95–110.

―― 'Metaphor and the Central Problem of Hermeneutics', *Hermeneutics and the Human Sciences: Essays on Language, Action and Interpretation*, ed. and trans. John B. Thompson, Cambridge: Cambridge University Press; Paris: Editions de la Maison des Sciences de l'Homme, 1981; rpt. 1988, 165–81.

―― *Interpretation Theory: Discourse and the Surplus of Meaning*, Fort Worth, Texas: Texas Christian University Press, 1976.

―― *The Rule of Metaphor: Multi-disciplinary Studies of the Creation of Meaning in Language*, trans. Robert Czerny, Kathleen McLaughlin and John Costello SJ, London: Routledge & Kegan Paul, 1986.

―― *Hermeneutics and the Human Sciences: Essays on Language, Action and Interpretation*, ed. and trans. John B. Thompson, Paris: Maison des Sciences de l'Homme; Cambridge: Cambridge University Press, 1981; rpt. 1988.

―― *Time and Narrative*, trans. Kathleen McLaughlin and David Pellauer, 3 vols, Chicago and London: University of Chicago Press, 1984.

―― 'Word, Polysemy, Metaphor: Creativity in Language', trans. David Pellauer, *A Ricoeur Reader: Reflection and Imagination*, ed. Mario J. Valdés, Hemel Hempstead: Harvester-Wheatsheaf, 1991, 65–85.

Russell, Bertrand, *The Problems of Philosophy*, Opus Series, gen. eds. Christopher Butler, Robert Evans, John Skorupski, Oxford: Oxford University Press, 1980.

―― *An Outline of Philosophy*, London: Routledge, 1993.

Sacks, Sheldon, ed., *On Metaphor*, Chicago and London: University of Chicago Press, 1979. [Most of the essays in this volume appeared in *Critical Inquiry* 5.1 (Autumn 1978).]

Shibles, Warren A., *An Analysis of Metaphor in the Light of W. M. Urban's Theories*, The Hague: Mouton, 1971.

―― *Rational Love*, Whitewater, Wisconsin: The Language Press, 1978.

Sparshott, F.E., '"As," or The Limits of Metaphor', *New Literary History* 6.1 (Autumn 1974): 75–94.

Sulloway, Frank J., *Freud, Biologist of the Mind: Beyond the Psychoanalytic Legend*, New York: Basic Books, 1979.

Sully, James, *The Human Mind. A Textbook of Psychology*, 2 vols, New York: Appleton, 1892.

Todorov, Tzvetan, 'On Linguistic Symbolism', *New Literary History* 6.1 (Autumn 1974): 111–34.

Williams, Raymond, *Culture and Society*, London: The Hogarth Press, 1990.

Wittgenstein, Ludwig, *Tractatus Logico-Philosophicus*, trans. D.F. Pears and B.F. McGuinness, London: Routledge & Kegan Paul; New York: The Humanities Press, 1961.

Wood, David, ed., *On Paul Ricoeur: Narrative and Interpretation*, London and New York: Routledge, 1991.

Wood, David and Robert Bernasconi, eds., *Derrida and Différance*, Warwick Studies in Continental Philosophy, Coventry: Parousia Press, 1985.

Woolf, Virginia, *The Common Reader*, ed. Andrew McNeillie, London: The Hogarth Press, 1984.

Wright, Elizabeth, *Psychoanalytic Criticism: Theory in Practice*, New Accents, gen. ed. Terence Hawkes, London and New York: Routledge, 1989.

Index